THE DEAN OF DIS

STRAPPING

STUDENTS

By

Dee Vee Curzon

CONTENTS

CHAPTER 1

WHEN JAMIE MET THE PROFESSOR

Jamie and Professor Stones had met in unusual circumstances even when you considered their joint interest in spanking; Jamie had been bent over a very robust and rather intimidating woman's knees whilst completely naked at the time!

Jamie's interest and yearning for some wholehearted spanking action had finally led him, via internet searching, to a national group of likeminded gatherings spread throughout the country but linked by a national site that allowed communication by web-based chats that ensured a certain level of privacy. He had come across BADS, Bondage and Disciplinary Society, and after a bit of thought, Jamie had made contact and exchanged views and been politely questioned online as to his intentions in contacting the group. After a few weeks Jamie was invited to choose from three meetings in adjoining counties (apparently only the most confident and nonchalant members participated in gatherings close to home) and had plumped for a one-hour drive at a location just across the county border. Jamie received clear instructions concerning attending his first meeting, known as a Munch, in a pub, and was also informed that to ensure the protection of members' identities and privacy he should only refer to himself by his BADS name, which he selected as Porter for ease, and was required to pledge to respect everyone else's wishes regarding anonymity.

It was with a fair degree of trepidation that Jamie accepted his invitation to attend a first meeting, particularly as Cain, who had introduced himself online as the Regional Facilitator, had stressed that Jamie would have to undergo further assessment as to his suitability for group membership before he would be introduced fully to other group members. His final words had almost put Jamie off of his chosen course of action.

"Just come prepared for anything! Normally first nights are just a chance for us to feel each other out, so to speak, but sometimes, if things look like they are going smoothly, it can progress quite quickly."

It had been delivered as what seemed like a friendly enough piece of advice but had still sent a shiver of wariness and apprehension through Jamie, although he had to admit to a certain thrill as well. So, freshly showered, shaved and dressed carefully to try and hit the smart, but casual and confident mark, he had followed instructions and driven to the designated public house in the market town, just across the county border. Less than an hour later and arriving just before the agreed time, he had taken a deep breath and pushed through the doors at the rear entrance to the pub that, as promised, was clearly marked as 'PRIVATE PARKING – INVITATION ONLY'. A chap about Jamie's age, and to Jamie's relief dressed in similar garb to his own choice, was sitting on a stool in the small foyer sipping a class of red wine.

"Evening, are you here for the BADS meeting?" he queried politely as Jamie approached.

"Yes," said Jamie. "The name is Porter," he related as per Cain's online instructions.

"Ah, thought so. You're a new prospective member, aren't you? One of two being given the once-over tonight, so you're not on your own, as the young lady is already here and is with our president and chairman just having a private chat, so to speak. It's just committee and long-term members tonight as we are finalising our first social of the year which is in a fortnight's time. Let me introduce you to a couple of the committee and they'll get you a drink and settle you in until our pres is ready for you. Name's Joseph, by the way, as in the cloak of many colours. Pleased to meet you."

So far so good, thought Jamie. *He seems friendly enough.* He followed Joseph into the bar where there were just eight other people divided into two tables pouring over drawings, plans and lists.

"Heads up, gang," called Joseph. "Here's our other guest tonight… gang, this is Porter, Porter this is the gang. Names as we go along; we won't overload you yet."

Which Jamie surmised was the polite and diplomatic way of getting round not letting Jamie know too much information before he had passed muster.

"Thanks, Joseph," said a tall, rather striking man in his fifties. "Hi Porter, I'm Tom, as in the Piper's son who stole a pig and away he ran," he chuckled. "Come and sit with me at the bar for a while. I'll get you a drink and you can relax with me until her highness, El Presidente, is ready to see you! What's your poison?"

Jamie opted for a small draft cider due to his driving situation. His host slipped round the other side of the bar and skilfully poured, so Jamie surmised he was likely to be either very well connected to the landlord or indeed was the landlord himself. The following conversation was both quite bizarre, yet strangely normal and every day, as the subjects meandered through the weather, sport, parking and then seamlessly onto the reason why Jamie was actually there.

"So I am a submissive, as are most of us here. We have a shortage of dominants so your contact was quite timely and to be honest quite a relief for a few of the subs. El Presidente, or more formally and to her face The President, but she'll ask you to call her Pres, is, as you have now surmised, a woman, and, as I am sure you will find out, quite a formidable woman. She is also a dom, which is just as well for all of us subs who like being mastered by the fairer sex. However, we have three other females at this little meeting tonight, Jezebel, Isobel and Sloth. Wave ladies, although as you'll probably find out, 'ladies' isn't really an appropriate term!"

The three women seated all smiled and waved.

"All three of them are subs and frankly we are all rather hoping that you cut the mustard old chap, as they have all become a little bored of the few doms we have and having to wait in turn to be serviced, especially as their appetites are quite veracious and hard to satisfy. A certain amount of variety being the spice of life, of course, no disrespect to established doms intended. Furthermore, they are all ready to move onto a higher level of submission and disciplinary measures and we really need new blood and an experienced hand to carry that through. What's your speciality?"

Jamie had prepared himself well for this question.

"Role-play, discipline-based of course, is my area of expertise, generally working on scenarios such as teacher-pupil, doctor-nurse, manager-employee, master-servant and countless other varieties along those lines. I am happy with bondage, chains, bandages, rope, and have a selection of my own correctors to punish appropriately for crimes and rule-breaking. I generally only apply punishment to bare bottoms and I expect and demand obedience, acceptance and appreciation from any rascal I have to deal with," he stated firmly and confidently.

Joseph reappeared at that moment. "The President will see you now, Jamie," he said.

Escorted up a flight of stairs off the main room, Jamie was shown into a fairly bare, poorly lit room in which a large formidable-looking woman sat at a table in the centre, although Jamie sensed a further presence in a dark alcove at the far end of the floor. Joseph left them alone as the woman beckoned him to her.

"Welcome to our little group," she announced. "As you have been told," and she motioned towards a device on the table indicating that she had listened to his earlier conversations below, "I am the president of our little society and you should refer to me by that name or the accepted shortening of 'Pres', nothing else. You are Porter and that is the only name you can henceforth be referred to if you are invited to participate in our gatherings. I see from the record of your online conversations that you have stated that you have read and understood our rules and that you are willing to undertake any little initiation rites proposed to fully reassure us of your purpose for being here. My friend over there in the dark shadows has done due diligence on your application and has given me his nod of approval and now I just have to amuse myself at your expense to fully satisfy us." She stated this with a look that contained a fair degree of menace to Jamie.

"Yes indeed, President," he replied as a sharp slapping sound was heard from across the room followed swiftly by a snapped command.

"Get your tongue right up between the toes, you snivelling wretch!" A deep and severe voice barked before the servile response came.

"So sorry Master, I will, I will."

As his eyes adjusted to the dim lighting, Jamie could now make out the form of a seated and substantial looking man. He guessed him to be about sixty, with a young lady naked at his feet, crouched down, in collar and chain, clearly sucking his uncovered toes.

"Ignore the Professor," President said. "He's just putting our other new member through her paces. She's a submissive and a potential new slave if she behaves herself. It's always good to have a new piece of meat for the members to enjoy. Anyway, you can get your rags off and let me have a look at what you've got to offer. Come on now, look lively. You'll soon find that I am completely intolerant of slovenly behaviour and slackers!"

Gulping and feeling very apprehensive, and fighting an impulse to flee, Jamie took a deep breath and stripped quickly to his briefs before hesitating.

"For heaven's sake, don't stop there, this is the interesting bit. Off with the knickers now, get a move on."

Red-faced and feeling totally self-conscious, Jamie now stood totally naked before her.

"Hands on your head, now come along. Oh dear, this is neither complimentary nor promising, is it Professor?" She smirked and bent to lift his flaccid penis with the tip of a finger. The older man had appeared beside her.

"Give him a chance, Pres. There are signs that he may have something worth seeing purely judging by the limp version."

Pres strolled around Jamie, admiring his physique. "Certainly not bad shape for a man who's seen his thirties off," she opined. "Oh, and hold the front page!" were her next words in exclamation. "An arse to die for, I do believe! Well this has just improved my day considerably. Yummy!"

She stroked his buttocks lightly, nonchalantly running a finger up the crack of his bottom and Jamie felt the first signs of interest stirring.

"Lean forward, hands on the table, stick your cute little butt right out, spread your legs," she instructed in a barking tone. Jamie immediately complied.

"I noted that you put in your earlier commentary that you liked the occasional 'switch' so now we shall put that little claim to the test."

Pres was referring to Jamie's admission when completing the online questionnaire that every now and then he and Angie had changed roles and he had been on the recipient's end of a harsh thrashing or two and had played the submissive role in being well-abused by Angie wearing a strap-on cock to ream and peg his arse. Pres bent down and settled on her haunches behind him; Jamie could feel her breath on his cheeks that were now rather quivering in anticipation. One hand was reaching round to firmly grasp his building erection.

"Hello!" she cooed approvingly. "Definite competition here, Professor. He feels as long and as thick as you, and he's clearly got a yearning to have his bottom in play as his cock is now really throbbing in excitement." She continued as she slapped his bottom playfully.

"Get Wretch over here to suck your cock, Professor, and we can have a little comparison. But first of all I think I'll have a little taster of the new meat." Jamie had succumbed to the expert hand rolling his foreskin and tweaking his sensitive penis tip. *She can do what she wants*, he thought, as she parted his bottom cheeks and took a deep sniff between them.

"Ah good, a lovely nice rustic scent, good and manly."

These were the last words he heard from her before her tongue and lips sealed around his anus as she began to suck and lick alternatively on his opening. Soon his hole was relaxed enough to allow her long full tongue to inch its way up his rear tunnel, before it was suddenly replaced by a probing finger. Jamie's legs started to buckle as his whole body trembled with sexual ecstasy and he knew that she was taking him towards a climax. Suddenly her finger was pulled out unceremoniously and the large woman shuffled around in front of him, pushing him upright and dipped her head to engulf his total length into her mouth and, after taking one long, lingering suck, she allowed his cock to spring out. Using him to support her substantial weight, she pulled herself up in front of him.

"Enjoyable though this all is, I have the order of the day to be getting on with," she said and handed him a blindfold.

"Put that on and hands back to your head. It's time this naughty little boy had his bottom thrashed." The last thing Jamie saw as he covered his eyes was the Professor with his trousers and underwear around his ankles while Wretch (Jamie presumed that this was her society given name) knelt naked before him with his huge cock sliding in and out of her mouth. As the darkness took over and his sight went, Jamie conceded in his mind that not only had the Professor probably got at least a similar length, if not fractionally longer, cock to his, it might well be thicker!

Jamie stood for a moment and heard the scrape of a moving chair before he was snapped out of his contemplation as Pres pulled him by the arms and he found himself head down, arse up across her lap.

"A spanking to warm us both up for a few minutes and then I am going to let you have the honour of feeling my favourite switch. Now is the moment you say, "Yes please, Pres, thank you." There was no hesitation from Jamie as he meekly repeated her words and tensed for the first slap. The switch he was less sure about; while he had seen that it did not look as substantial as a cane, he had also seen that it looked quite whippy and was double-pronged to increase the effect. Jamie's muscles tightened automatically as he imagined the feel of it cracking against his backside.

"Excuse me, Mister. Unclench, legs wider apart, relax those

gorgeous cheeks and let me see you pointing your jam roll at me."

Jamie knew enough cockney rhyming slang to know what rhymed with 'jam roll' and quickly opened his body up, unclenched his cheeks and raised himself to expose his arsehole completely.

"That's better," said Pres, clamping his cock between her huge thighs. "And now it begins."

The first blow was a real shock. Pres's huge hand was hard and her arm powerful and within seconds his arse cheeks were burning. *Wow*, thought Jamie, *she can certainly spank*. He was struggling not to cry out as her large hand continued to fall punishingly on his rear cheeks. Much as he enjoyed a spanking, and in particular the afterglow sensation, he was verging on begging for mercy as his eyes filled with tears. Previous spankings he had received had been delivered by his late wife Angie, and an earlier girlfriend, but neither women had possessed the power, intent and stamina of the assault his poor scarlet bottom was currently undergoing. They had also been delivered by a loving partner with an element of fun involved and no malice or real intent to hurt. This was most definitely not the case here. The blows were delivered in a methodical, consistent manner, the constant slaps often hitting the same spot over and over again. He gritted his teeth and tried to concentrate his mind on counting, but painfully aware that his erection was subsiding and that the sexually exciting element of this had somewhat gone astray!

"That's two hundred, my poor love. Well done, Porter. Most crack and start their pathetic pleas and whimpers for mercy before the end," Pres commented, to Jamie's relief.

"Now up you pop and we'll move things up a notch to finish this part off," she continued, ominously pulling his blindfold off.

Up stood Jamie, trying not to look too ungainly and self-conscious as his half-erection swung free and his eyes blinked rapidly as he adjusted to the light. He tried to avoid staring as he saw Wretch still slurping rather noisily and with pure pleasure on the other man's cock. Grabbing her hair, the Professor, as Jamie assumed his moniker here was, detached the young girl nonchalantly and virtually shoved her to the floor.

"Eyes down and follow me on all fours. Be close by me on my right-hand side. Otherwise, I'll be fetching a whip to your skinny little baby backside," he threatened.

Jamie was snapped back to full attention by his own assailant.

"Don't relax too much, Porter. I'm quite loving your ass. Get over here and present in the correct manner over the table. Grip the edges, legs wide apart, pointing that jam roll up at me."

Jamie prostrated himself over the table and raised his buttocks, relaxing his arse cheeks to show his arsehole (jam roll), inviting her approval.

"Good boy," she said and moved forward and tickled the welcoming dark hole. Jamie sighed; he had little resistance to anal massage of any sort and his body immediately betrayed this as his arsehole opened beckoning her finger on and in.

"Oh, you do like a bit of anal don't you, new boy?"

Jamie relaxed as he wallowed in the expert fingering so it was a bit of a shock when the switch she had picked up without him noticing swung wickedly through the air before smacking across his raised bottom cheeks as her finger was snatched away.

"Aaaaarghhh!" he let loose inadvertently, caught unaware, as the shocking pain spread across his unready arse. Pres showed little interest in his discomfort as she wielded the switch with great accuracy, a fearful force and no sympathy. WHOP! WHOP! WHOP! The switch cracked down hard as Jamie tried desperately to retain some sense of composure and dignity. Red weals were rising on his thrashed cheeks, and the punishment continued without relent as Jamie slumped over the table, feeling defeated and truly mastered by this awesome woman, clearly illustrating why she was such an in-demand dominatrix. At last she threw the switch down and to Jamie's delight she dropped to her knees behind him and began to stroke, lick and kiss his beaten bottom.

"Yes. Make it nice and wet, my dear, and then I think I'll have a little bit of fun to finish him off."

The Professor's voice sent a tremble through his body but Jamie held it together as Pres treated him to a long, lingering anal kiss before moving aside. Jamie heard the swish of the switch a heartbeat before it landed. Gritting his teeth, Jamie was determined not to let this old man best him; no way was he going to cry out. Twelve times the switch slashed down on his unprotected buttocks. Jamie's eyes were closed shut as he focused on absorbing the pain and trying desperately to think of what this sacrifice could lead to. Then it was over, and again he felt the hands and lips of Pres on his poor throbbing bottom. His erection which had subsided considerably as the thrashing intensified now twitched back to full length. Pres reached round and began to toss him, causing Jamie to immediately react, forcing his bottom back into Pres' face, his arsehole clearly welcoming her probing tongue which she dutifully forced deeper into him in response.

"That's enough," barked the Professor, who clearly had the authority to call the shots. "It's your turn now to show us what you can do, Porter. Get those clothes off, Pres. Jamie, you may put your clothes back on."

Jamie was happy to comply and watched in awe as this formidable woman submissively obeyed the instruction and quickly unshipped her clothing to stand naked before them.

"Right Porter, she's all yours. Forget her standing, for now she is a naughty girl that needs a bloody good sorting out. Don't hold back — let's see how you deal with this miserable piece of utter disrepute. Sort her out, man, sort her out, and make this reprobate sorry."

Jamie barely hesitated as his eyes soaked up the magnificent creature so exposed before him. Huge breasts with the longest and largest nipples and aureole that he had ever seen, let alone the veritable forest of pubic hair that presumably covered her pussy. Her body scent was pure sex. Jamie could honestly say they he had never smelt such a strong and erotic sexual aroma. *She oozes sex*, he thought.

"Hands on head, eyes to the floor, you disgusting piece of filth," Jamie ordered. He was not going to take this challenge lightly. "Turn around, let me see the target, bitch."

Pres turned as instructed, giving Jamie his first sight of her enormous bottom. Fantastically formed, far firmer than Jamie had expected, and indeed was nicely in proportion to the rest of her. Jamie couldn't help but lick his lips. He could see that this was a challenge and his mind whirled with what move to take next.

"Bend over, legs apart, hands on your ankles if you can reach them, slut," he commanded, and audibly sucked in his breath as she obeyed, presenting him with her gorgeous buttocks, now taut and parted, displaying a matching growth of black curly hairs with her pinky-brown arsehole just peeping out of the centre of her dark vale.

Jamie could feel his erection pressing hard against his trousers and he knew that he so wanted to fuck this amazing woman. He stepped forward and slapped her left cheek hard but there was no reaction as the sound echoed around the room. He then hit her right cheek as hard as he could but again there was no movement or response. Drawing his arm back as far as possible, be began to spank the proffered cheeks methodically with as much force as he could muster.

After a good sixty slaps or so had been delivered accurately and with maximum force, Jamie knew he had to change tack. He grabbed Pres by her hair and pulled her over to the table using all of his strength to illustrate his superiority throwing her across the surface.

"Assume the position and present yourself for your thrashing," he commanded.

Pres complied without a sound and, picking up the switch, Jamie considered his limited options with just the switch available, which he rather suspected may be something that she could take all day judging by his failure to draw any kind of response to his valiant spanking effort. Without any preamble, he brought the implement down hard and fast, rapidly hitting one buttock over and over again as close as he could on the same spot. Changing buttocks after six strikes, he lashed at her, desperate to generate a response to assert his supremacy and dominance. He paused, and was horrified and dismayed at her snide retort in answer to his efforts.

"Oh, do please feel free to start my punishment at any point, oh masterful one."

He heard the Professor snort in laughter, fuelling his anger as undoubtedly intended. *Right, you bitch*, Jamie thought.

"Up on the table, slut. Your arse is so big it's hiding your arsehole and your cunt, and what's the point of a flogging if you don't get to be exposed properly. Go on now, bend right over, head hanging in shame to the floor, grab the table legs, arse up, up, up!" he snarled.

Forcing her legs even further apart, her anus finally fully showing through the forest of hair, the pink lips of her gash now becoming clearly visible beneath, he noted that the lips were well moistened and he garnered a certain amount of satisfaction that he had at least managed to arouse her.

Picking up the switch once more, he hit her rapidly another forty times but there was still no real acknowledgement of the effort he was applying. In a moment of inspiration, he paused and slipped off his right shoe, a cross between a walking shoe and a trainer, firm, heavy and quite flexible. He slammed the shoe down across the centre of her bottom and, at last, was rewarded by a yelp of pain as he finally caused her lower half to begin twitching and moving from side to side. He slammed the shoe across her substantial backside again and again, the flesh wobbling and readjusting to Jamie's fascination, and was rewarded with small cries of pain coming from below. After ten savage spanks, a clearly whimpering Pres started to force her arms up the table legs, raising her head and shuffling her bottom around to try and avoid further punishment.

"Oh no you don't, young lady." The Professor had appeared at the other side of the table, Wretch crawled after him, grasped Pres' shoulders firmly, and with one raised foot on the back of her neck, forced her head back down towards the carpet.

"You've been asking for this for ages, my dear. Finally one of the newbies looks like besting you and you can bloody well keep that fat arse up in the air to take what's been coming for a long time. Thrash away Porter, make her scream, make her holler, let's see those tears rolling down her face."

Jamie fully obliged and over the next couple of minutes rained the shoe unmercifully down on her unprotected and unmissable arse cheeks. Pres was no longer the arrogant, superior, confident dominatrix of earlier as she howled and begged for mercy, tears flowing down her cheeks. Finally dropping the shoe, he picked up the switch once more and taking careful and deliberate aim he landed his coup de grâce vertically down her open crack, ensuring the main lash of the switch landed on her open anus. It was a reasonably gentle stroke to a most vulnerable area but it had the desired effect.

"Yaaaaarrrrr! Yeeeoooooew! Yoo, yoo, yoo." Pres almost flung herself off the table and the Professor released her arms as she writhed and rocked in pain, her hands grabbing at her arse cheeks.

Jamie knew not to relent now his superiority had been established.

"Your punishment is complete but you will return to the desired presentation position unless you would like a further demonstration of my techniques to bring about obedience and compliance."

Pres quickly recovered her poise and got into position, presenting her split arse raised high into the air in the required manner. Jamie moved on to stroke her battered red hot cheeks softly, tracing the contours and the raised welts lovingly. Jamie found her voluminous bottom totally stunning, he felt bewitched by the magnificence before him and bent to breathe in the earthy, sweaty scent of her glistening vagina and anal crack. Her cheeks opened wider, surely anticipating and welcoming further intimate contact.

"In you go, Porter, in you go," she whispered sexily, impressively having recovered her composure and Jamie complied, his nose settling against the succulent arsehole, his mouth at the bottom of her wet pussy lips.

Jamie was in heaven, his nose nudging against the dark hole, her soft, almost luxurious, forest of damp anal hairs tickling his whole face, his tongue lapping at her pussy. He reached around to pinch her slimy, wet, hard cunny nub and started to work her rhythmically. Her sweaty bottom crack self-lubricated enough to allow his nose to slip into her arsehole easily without resistance, and he began to slurp noisily at the virtual river of her juices flowing from her soaking fanny. He became aware of the murmur of the Professor's voice and realised that Wretch was now covering Pres's face with fluttering little kisses while her tiny hands were locked onto the large erect nipples of Pres's heavy breasts. Jamie struggled to hold his position as this

15

sexual beast of a woman started to buck and shudder as she searched for her climax.

"Fuck, fuck, fuck, I'm fucking coming." She was screaming until her cries were stifled as the Professor grabbed her hair and swiftly filled her open mouth with his large cock and Wretch clamped her mouth, biting and sucking hard at one breast while both hands clawed and pinched at the other. Jamie almost choked at the sudden increase in her love juices and his nose was virtually flattened as she squeezed her arse cheeks together, her body surrendering to a mighty orgasm. Her groans were deep, long and animalistic as finally her sated body collapsed onto the table, dislodging her pleasurers. The dishevelled woman with her huge body lay across the table in an undignified pile. Jamie could see the Professor's semen hanging from her lips as he had clearly unloaded with expert timing as she reached her own paradise. Wretch meanwhile was laying prostrate, having been knocked clean to the floor by a flailing arm. Jamie watched with delight as before his eyes, his face resting on her lower bottom cheeks, Pres's arsehole opened and closed rapidly while her pussy lips vibrated and spluttered, releasing trapped air. *I am not sure about the morals of what we are doing here,* he thought, *but that was just amazing!*

After a quick wash and comfort break, the four gathered together, now fully dressed apart from Wretch who was back on the floor on all fours, naked and on her leash.

"Well, I have to say that you have passed with flying colours, Porter. Welcome to our little club. Just seems a bit remiss of us to leave you unrelieved, so to speak. Would you like our little slave here to give you her very best blow job?" Jamie hesitated; much as his erection had still not subsided fully, he could not help thinking that the moment had gone, particularly with the three of them now fully clothed. Wretch's response to the words of Pres had been to move immediately towards him with a discreet smile playing on her lips.

"Or maybe it wasn't Wretch you wanted?" teased Pres as she looked deep into his eyes and he knew that she could sense the longing in them. "Maybe another day, Porter. I have never allowed one of the members to fuck me yet. As the senior dominant and the president, I am not sure it would befit my position."

Jamie caught the sly look aside to the Professor and guessed that maybe there was one exception to that statement.

"However," she continued. "You were responsible for one of the harshest and the best thrashings I've ever received as well as one of the best orgasms I've ever had, so I could consider that you earned your reward. You have also introduced me to the beauty of taking a nose in my jam roll; that's a new one on me and most pleasant and sexy it was too. Think I prefer that to the usual fingers and their often poorly cut nails scratching my insides. Yes, that was most pleasant, maybe we will have to meet privately at some point." Her words were teasingly spoken, instantly bringing Jamie's cock up to full mast. Pres noticed and straight away moved quickly forward to grasp it through his trousers.

"I'm off downstairs to have a drink, I think. I'll leave you three to it for a few minutes," said the Professor as he departed the room and headed downstairs to the bar. "Tie Wretch to a post when you have finished with her. I'll sort her out later. There's a bowl of water in the dog's dish over there if she's thirsty; you might need to top it up," was his parting shot.

"Well maybe I'd just like to have your cock in my mouth and suck you off, Porter. I'm quite partial to swallowing sperm as it happens. Let's get the trousers and pants back down, in fact, take off all your clothes." Pres was now giving the orders again, retaking some sort of control, smacking her lips and eyeing Jamie as though he was a succulent meal. Jamie found himself almost hypnotically obedient to this formidable woman's words and quickly divested himself of his clothes and stood erect and naked before her.

"Now, let's see what we can offer you, Porter, as a final treat to put the seal on your membership," said Pres, stressing the word *membership*, in that husky, oh so seductive, voice.

"How about if I lay down on the floor?" Pres lay on her back and gestured Jamie to climb astride her, facing her and her waiting mouth. "Now shuffle yourself up here with that gorgeous dick and lean forward on all fours."

Jamie set his legs either side of her head, his knees under her shoulders in her armpits, and bent forward presenting his throbbing erection over her face.

"Now, Wretch," she instructed. "You come around in front of Porter on all fours and present your arse and fanny for him. Head down to the floor, bum up in the air up, legs wide open. Let him see what's on the menu. Aha, I can see you are clearly nicely lubricated already. In fact I think we are all well ready for this, aren't we? Now Porter I think that you can take it from here…"

Jamie bent forward to allow her to take his cock and slip it between her lips and leaned to grab Wretch's arse, each hand able to engulf her cheeks completely. Holding them wide apart, he stared in amazement at the smallest arsehole he had ever seen. Completely hairless and flawless, her anus was a tiny opening between very narrow cheeks and as smooth a crevice as you could imagine with no spider-web wrinkling or swollen rim, no puckering and no pitting. Dipping his head down he licked the neat little folds of her narrow and pretty pussy, relieved to find her soaking wet and very sweet tasting. So far her behaviour had perplexed Jamie as he truly failed to understand that anyone can have enjoyed the role she had been playing since he entered the room. However, it was indeed the case that, as Pres had pointed out, her pussy was liberally caked in her own juices and, along with the rock-hard clitoris his top lip had just discovered, certainly gave evidence to suggest that Wretch was enjoying at least part of the process very much.

"Haaaarrr," she moaned in undoubted pleasure as he licked and sucked noisily at her very juicy quim.

After initially hesitating at the thought of probing her arse, wondering if the rather available, but decidedly small arsehole, was just too tight to handle an exploring finger, he reminded himself that this was a potential slave girl, basically auditioning for a role as a sexual dogsbody for any of the dominants in the group. Dipping his thumb into her wet pussy he lubricated it thoroughly before presenting it to her anus and, wetting the tiny dark hole before him, he spat, aiming a mouthful of her juices mixed with his own saliva right into the centre of her crack and then forced his thumb slowly into the tightest, most discreet arsehole he had ever encountered. Whilst she did cry out quite sharply at the initial intrusion, there was no real resistance as he sunk his thick thumb to the knuckle deep into the beautiful textured, smooth interior of her anal canal. As Pres sucked expertly on his cock and added to his excitement by forcing two wet fingers into his own wantonly responsive arsehole, Jamie could sense himself already succumbing to an approaching orgasm. Feeling Wretch's frantically rubbing fingers against his face as her hand delved down to start driving herself to her own climax, Jamie dismissively flicked her hand away.

"None of that, no one gave you permission to frig yourself, you dirty little whore," he said, pulling his dripping mouth from her pussy before ramming his face back into the sopping wet folds.

With his nose and tongue working on her pussy and his thumb now pumping in and out of her tight arsehole, Jamie sensed her body tense and knew she too was about to climax. Instinctively, Pres pulled her fingers from his arse and treated him to a deep throat sensation, sealing her mouth around his cock and sucking him deeply and ferociously until he ejected his spunk into her throat just as Wretch's body started her convulsions of orgasm. As Wretch screamed out in ecstasy, Pres gargled and gulped, swallowing Jamie's cum down, as he spurted his creamy and copious load repeatedly into her.

"Warm, sour and a bit stingy but rather a tasty and decidedly thick offering, thanking you kindly, Porter," Pres declared as she let his sated cock slip from her mouth, wiping and smacking her lips with obvious satisfaction as all three bodies slumped in shared ecstasy and exhaustion to the floor.

After several minutes and with breathing returning to normal rates, Pres was first to rise.

"I'll just have a quick wash down and then I am off to have a drink and chat with my chums downstairs. When I am done, can you sort yourself out, give Wretch a quick once over, mainly give her arse and cunt a flush and clean so she's suitable if the Professor or indeed anyone else needs to use her tonight. Then attach her to the radiator using her lead and the chain that's fixed there, make sure her dog bowl is full of water and leave her the bucket from the toilet in case she needs to relieve herself. Wretch knows why she needs to be drinking a plentiful supply of water, don't you, my scraggy little one?"

Jamie looked mystified until Pres added, "Slaves are required to learn that peeing for and in front of their master, or mistress, is invariably considered a bit of a treat. Doesn't do it for me but hey, if it floats your boat, it floats your boat." She shrugged dismissively as Jamie processed this information.

With which Pres slapped Wretch's bottom in passing and

proceeded to the toilet-cum-bathroom for a quick wash and what was, it has to be said, a thunderously noisy and totally unladylike pee. No closed-door privacy for Pres; she had left the door wide open and squatted in full view. She then quickly washed herself down before leaving the two of them alone.

Minutes later, Jamie was alone with Wretch, wiping her all over with a flannel and then quickly soaping her lower parts before rinsing them down. It felt weird and odd to Jamie to be washing this young girl's most private parts but she was totally complicit in spreading her legs and turning her body to allow him full access to her intimate entrances. Jamie suspected correctly that it wouldn't do to engage in social conversation with her, as a prospective slave and clearly a confirmed subservient. Once in role it would be unfair and unhelpful to treat her as anything other than the submissive she was. Towelling her off, and noting her still aroused state, Jamie then led her to the radiator and attached her as instructed, passing her the dog bowl full of water and leaving a bucket by her side. Giving the top of her head a gentle stroke, Jamie left her as she settled down to await any further fate, or treat as maybe she thought of it. He pondered on what had passed. His eyes were certainly a bit more open to what went on behind closed doors of such gatherings, and with that in mind he returned to the main room of the pub.

Jamie left the pub an hour or so later with the Professor's email address in hand, as well as codes to allow full access to BADS' website and an invitation to Castle Hall, a stately mansion turned hotel in the countryside nearby, where the society was holding a social weekend in a fortnight's time. Jamie, his cock hard again at the thought of what could happen there, doubted that he would waste much time in considering whether or not to attend!

CHAPTER 2

A SECOND AUDITION FOR JAMIE

Jamie received his formal invitation to Castle Hall a couple of days later, offering him a two night stay in a small suite, fully inclusive at a very considerate rate for what was a former stately home. All costs of membership and activity through BADS were paid for, with the society operating as a non-profit making, private members club, everything legal and above board. Through his email exchanges with the Professor over the last two days, Jamie had been very reassured that there were no issues with the running of the society or the activities incorporated. It certainly helps when your national membership includes senior policemen, high ranking military personnel, top lawyers and business people from all sorts of backgrounds, with the odd ex-member of parliament and senior civil servant, ensuring that every aspect was legal and above board. All private functions involved accommodation sourced through contacts that ensured privacy was guaranteed and any non-member personnel staffing the residential properties used were totally sympathetic to the society's cause. That and the fact they very well paid served to ensure total discretion and respect of privacy as far as was possible.

It came as a shock initially that the Professor knew far more about Jamie than he had let on, but as he had explained during one long telephone call, he was entrusted with ensuring the region's activities and membership were secure, and protected from non-sympathetic or hostile outside influences. Jamie now knew that the Professor was the Dean of Discipline at the University City's most revered and influential female-only college, was a renowned academic worldwide in his field, and not only happened to be extremely wealthy but was also incredibly well connected. Furthermore, he had a reputation as a man not to be crossed which Jamie felt actually made him a tad nervous as well as feeling safe and protected.

Thanks to the Professor's input, Jamie was now aware that the big socials such as this one were often held in conjunction with other regional groups, giving members a chance to meet new contacts and arrange one-off liaisons, trysts and swaps for the duration of the weekend. Causing him slight apprehension, however, was the information that as a new member Jamie would be under the spotlight to a certain extent and, supposedly to help him integrate into the group, his first evening was to be the subject of one of the weekend's highlights. Jamie, the new potential slave Wretch, plus a married couple and a single younger man from the other region, were all to be the prizes in a sweepstake draw for any member interested in using their prime speciality for the rest of the night. This was part initiation ritual, part audition to ensure their suitability for membership, which the Professor had assured Jamie would be a breeze for him, although more challenging for potential submissives as this would be the real test of their claimed servile and deferential tendencies. Jamie had been invited to meet up with the Professor for a drink in a few days' time and presumed that he was going to be briefed in more detail. He had been impressed and encouraged by the attention he was receiving from the old hand, albeit worldly-wise enough that the thought that there might be more to this than met the eye had crossed his mind.

The evening spent with the Professor had reassured him that

everything was fine and had proved quite enlightening as he found himself let into the world of the Dean of Discipline at St. James' College with an invite back to the Professor's rooms for coffee. Jamie realised during the conversation that the Professor was sharing little-known facts about this highly thought of, female-only college. Certainly Jamie was now aware that corporal punishment was in use in this college and that it was the Professor who not only censured students for disciplinary rule breaking but clearly was the person who executed any physical punishment. His role at BADS made so much more sense now, Jamie thought, as he had now discovered that the Professor had been Dean of Discipline at the college for over thirty years and rather evidently was a man well-versed in dishing out chastisement. The two had got along extremely well considering the difference in age, upbringing and background and Jamie was happy to accept the offer of a lift to and from the hotel as well as getting a thorough briefing ahead of the stay.

The two set off together on the lunchtime of the Saturday, both attired casually but with formal wear packed, although not much else as the Professor had stressed that the hotel would be prepared for the event and that every eventuality, scenario or requirement would be catered for. One word of warning he had taken on board was the Professor giving him notice that the three senior submissives whom he had briefly met at the BADS meeting would likely be targeting him to service them in any way they could.

"Take heed, Porter, those three minxes will use every feminine wile and ploy they possess to be the first of the trio to sample your wares. Don't trust them an inch, young man, make sure that you call the shots and are not seduced into playing by their rules. You are the dom, make sure they know that; however, don't fall into the trap of playing one off against the others. Mark my words, they are three devious little hussies but they are firm friends and will cover each other's backs. My advice, and it's up to you whether you engage with them or not, is to have all three of them together if you get the opportunity and if the situation develops, as I expect it could, you should show them no mercy. They are very experienced subs and you will only win their respect if you master them completely and without mercy."

Jamie would have reason to remember that summing up and would appreciate the advice and the benefit of having the Professor's experience in his corner.

Booked in and unpacked, Jamie waited for the Professor's agreed knock to go down to the start of the evening's festivities. Showered and shaved, dressed conservatively as suggested by his mentor, Jamie was equally nervous and excited when Professor Stones tapped on his door. Although Jamie had been informed the suggested attire was formal for the reception and then the dinner, there were no hard and fast rules, so that Jamie was just about prepared for the sight that met them when they walked into the lounge reserved for pre-dinner drinks. Tethered to a post just inside the door, were two youngsters, a female dressed in a strange leather corset and a dog collar with a lead attached but naked from the waist down, and a young lad, wearing a dog collar and lead and a pair of tight leather shorts. The young lad's shorts, however, were designed with a diamond shape cut out at the back, exposing his buttock crack and a circle cut out at the front allowing his balls and cock to hang freely and highly visible. Both were playing their roles in totality and had dog biscuits at their feet and were sharing a large bowl of water. A quick glance round the room showed Jamie that of the congregation gathered of almost one hundred, most were dressed more formally; the men in shirts and jackets, some suited, the women in a variety of dresses with the occasional trouser-suited or skirt-top combos. The ones that stood out were clearly the group's most extrovert; there were several leather outfits and the occasional extremely tight trousers, short skirts or indeed, in the case of one woman, just a leather G-string on her lower half, her firm rounded buttocks nicely pronounced, Jamie thought, by her high sparkling diamante stilettos. The conversation was as any conference style gathering of delegates, with people catching up with old colleagues and being introduced to new ones, the weather, the news, details of the journey down and recent sporting occurrences being the most popular topics. The Professor got drinks and steered Jamie through the throng, nodding and hand-shaking as they worked the room, introducing Jamie as they did so. Jamie was aware of the scrutiny he was attracting but was relieved that it was well-mannered, polite and not over-inquisitive or intrusive. After a while, a large female arm hooked through his own and Jamie found himself being whisked away by Pres to meet other members of the local society. After greeting him with a forceful kiss on the lips, Pres rather held him in a manner that Jamie felt was her making a statement of possession but was happy, as the newcomer, to be under this powerful and formidable woman's wings. Pres led him outside to 'check on the dog' as she put it. The dog turned out to be Wench, the trainee slave, who was naked and tethered to a post outside the door.

"She's in disgrace, aren't you, Wench?" Her switch suddenly appeared in her hand and was pointed threateningly at the girl.

"Yes mistress, sorry mistress."

Pres smiled ominously. "Still not toilet trained are you? Tell Porter what you did then."

Wench looked down and responded quietly. "I couldn't hold myself through the night, sir, and I disgraced myself."

Pres sighed, "Turn around and present. I asked you to tell Porter what you did. I don't think I recall asking you to prevaricate, did I?"

A tiny sob escaped from Wench's lips but she dutifully turned round, dropped her head to the ground raising her bottom high and opening her legs. Jamie could see that she was already showing signs of being well beaten: lash marks were all over her back, buttocks and legs, but Pres didn't spare her and in no time at all had struck the girl a dozen times on her raised sore cheeks.

"Maybe you can remember now," suggested Pres, slipping the switch back into an inside pocket of the jacket she wore.

"Thank you, mistress, yes mistress, I am sorry, mistress. Sir, Wench couldn't hold herself throughout the night, sir, and Wench emptied her bowels and her bladder into her water dish sir. Wench is truly disgusting and is very sorry. I am really thankful to mistress for her beating and know mistress was very kind in not beating me too severely so I wouldn't be spoilt for anyone else who wishes to use me."

At that point a man who had been across the gravel path smoking whilst they had been talking came to them on his way inside.

"May I?" he said to Pres as he unzipped his trousers and pulled out his erect penis.

"Of course, feel free," said Pres. "She's yellow so help yourself."

Pres was referring to the dog collar Wench was wearing. The Society had its own colour-coded system for submissives and slaves. Yellow indicated an unowned trainee slave, no ownership rights established and therefore available for use to anyone with her trainer's consent. Black indicated an owned slave, the sole property of one person and not accessible to anyone else. Blue indicated an owned slave but accessible with the owner's consent to others, while red indicated a shared membership ownership, fully trained slave, freely available to anyone within that gathering. Green indicated an unowned, trained slave now available from the trainer and usually the subject of bartering, repaying favours or available on loan. As a yellow, Wench could expect to be well used and abused during any gathering and she was about to get her first taste of what her life could be like once fully trained. Without further words being spoken, Wench crawled into place at the man's feet and dutifully slipped his cock into her mouth and began slowly sucking and licking the length before her.

"Let's just see how she performs and then it is time to let the two that are inside out here for a toilet break," said Pres

Wench sucked enthusiastically, slurping loudly whilst surreptitiously watching the man's face to see his reaction as she tried different pressures and techniques to satisfy him. Clearly identifying that he was getting off on the less subtle and unrestrained moves, she sucked more noisily, harder and faster. His hands grabbed handfuls of her short hair as he finally deigned to touch her, and he forced his groin roughly into her face, his erect cock sliding in and out of her willing dripping wet mouth, saliva running down her chin, her eyes bulging as his length rammed into the back of her throat. With a loud groan, he unloaded into her mouth, pushing her face tight against his groin and holding her there as he jerked and spasmed to a conclusion.

"Nice one," he said. As he slipped out of her mouth, she pushed her tongue fully out to allow him to wipe his cock against it before he tidied himself away, patting Wench on the head and giving Pres a nod of appreciation.

"You're welcome," said Pres, turning back to Wench. "Good girl, very well done," causing Wench to beam with the pleasure of having pleased her mistress.

"It'd be rude not to reward you, wouldn't it? Excuse me a moment, Porter."

With which, Pres beckoned the girl forward and lifted the front of her skirt. "Come and have a little treat for being so good."

Wench's head ducked beneath the material of her skirt and Jamie could see her fingers pulling Pres's knickers aside, before clearly beginning to feast on her mistress's pussy. Jamie was happy to watch as the girl enthusiastically lapped away until Pres gently removed her head.

"Enough now, poppet. If you continue to behave, I might fuck you later. Or at least let you watch while I fuck someone else!"

Wench's expression quickly went from a contented smile with pussy-juice covered lips to a rather hurt looking scowl which earned her a sharp slap across the face.

"Uh, uh, bitch, remember your place and don't get sulky or you'll sleep outside the room tonight." Wench looked at Pres with such contrition that Jamie felt sorry for her, although his understanding of the slave mentality and desire was, he knew, pretty limited and he was sure that Pres was playing the girl to perfection.

"Right, let's go and bring those other dogs out to do their duty. Wench, don't forget, pee on the dirt where everyone can see you, the lead just stretches, and cover it up by kicking loose soil over your deposit."

A rather red-faced Wench nodded her assent. "Yes, mistress," she replied meekly.

Inside, Pres grabbed the male slave's dog lead, indicating to Jamie to take the girl's. Both, Jamie noted, were wearing green collars so he presumed they were up for grabs over the weekend.

"It's up to you how you address them. They are trained and unowned so they just damn well do what they're told, and with possession of her leash the bitch is under your control. She's called Meda, a good name for a slave girl, he's called Heron, which isn't so hot as Herons are noble birds and he is just a piece of property. I should imagine that, probably, we will find that his eventual owner will thrash the Heron out of him and call him something more lowly and appropriate. Heel, dog, come!"

Pres led off back through the doors and Jamie took her cue.

"Come on, bitch, outside, it's time for you to pee."

Meda's head went down submissively and she duly crawled alongside Jamie at the end of her lead.

"Right you two, I think you can come off your leads to do your business. They are afforded a bit more privacy than this pitiful specimen," said Pres, nudging Wretch out of the way as she unleashed Heron.

Jamie released Meda and the two slaves scuppered off into the borders both heading separately into the more densely planted areas, so were partially hidden by shrubs. Jamie was amused to note that Heron clearly had to stay in dog character to relieve himself as he could see him cocking his leg to pee. Pres winked at Jamie as the two returned.

"Watch and learn, just in case you ever fancy taking a slave. It's worth absorbing every bit of knowledge about the normal run-of-the-mill behavioural aspects of being involved in this lark. Knowledge is power and the whole Bondage & Discipline, Sadism & Masochism scene is ultimately a power play between individuals who want sexual favours and satisfaction for their own selfish needs."

Pres snapped her fingers at both slaves and they came to her feet.

"Right, Porter. Meda has come to me on my command as you can see."

Jamie noted the look of alarm and confusion on the girl's face.

She seemed to realise that she had done something wrong but was also giving the impression that she didn't know what to do to correct her error.

"What the bitch is struggling to get her head around is that I am her principal, in the sense that I am her lead trainer, and she has been under my control since she got here, albeit she didn't travel down with me. She's correct in that I have the power to give her orders, but what is now perplexing her is that as you are holding her leash, thereby I have ceded ownership and control to you. As the leash holder, you now in fact have total control of her, so in obeying a command from me she has totally disrespected you and your authority. Up to you now, Porter, but first what I was going to show you is more relevant to a bitch owner anyway. Shall I illustrate?"

Pres reached inside her pocket again and brought out a polythene pack and proceeded to take out two tissues, followed by two wet wipes. After giving Jamie one of each, she clicked her fingers at Heron causing him immediately to turn around, bow his head and present his raised rear end at her. Pres took the tissue, leaned down and put both hands between his legs, grabbed hold of his cock, shook it and then wiped the tip with the tissue.

Screwing up the tissue she then snapped, "Turn and clean!" Heron spun round and licked her fingers all over.

When he had done this to her satisfaction, she pushed him away and then wiped her hands herself with the wet wipe. Screwing the used tissues up she tossed it in the air for Heron to catch in his mouth and then he eagerly crawled across to the nearby bin and spat them in.

"Good boy," said Pres, and raised her eyebrows to Jamie as his cue to continue.

"Meda, here girl, turn and present yourself for a toilet wipe."

Jamie snarled and revelled in the total subservience of the girl as she whirled around at his feet, dropping her head to her hands and raising her bottom with legs apart to him.

Jamie knelt down behind her, and using his fingers only, felt the girl's arsehole and pussy.

"Just a bit damp," he said patting her dry with the tissue.

Following Pres' lead, he offered her his fingers which she sensually licked clean one by one. Jamie wiped himself dry and dropped the used tissues on the floor, clicking his fingers at Meda, who immediately picked them up in her mouth and crawled across to the bin to deposit the waste.

"Seems like they need a proper wash now anyhow," mused Pres aloud. "Let's take them around the back to the stables where there's an outside shower and toilet block for the hotel's occasional camping guests. I'll get someone else to come and get them scrubbed clean, I think."

The slaves were led to the stable area, where indeed there was, in keeping with the standards of the hotel, an impressive looking, aesthetically pleasing block of changing rooms, with full shower, bath and toilet facilities. However, Pres didn't lead them there but round the side where the actual stables were, along with a freshwater pump in the open. There were basic cleaning materials, large rough looking towels, scrubbing brushes, bottle of disinfectant and blocks of carbolic soap. Jamie heard Meda give a little sob as she realised that was where they were heading and not to the luxury of the amenities block.

"Sounds like someone might need to suck on the bar of soap to remind them to speak when spoken to," were the words from Pres that froze the expression of annoyance that had crossed the slave girl's features.

"Keep her in hand, Porter, don't let her develop any bad habits whilst she's under your care."

Jamie reacted quickly, dragging the girl into the nearby open stable. He sat down on a bail of straw, unhooked the lead from her collar and tugged her over his knees.

"How dare you try and show me up, you naughty girl. What do you have to say for yourself before I give you a taste of your own lead?"

"Sorry, Master, Meda is very sorry that she was bad sir, she won't do it again, sir. Meda hopes that Master punishes her well so that she will behave perfectly in future, sir."

As a fully trained slave, Meda was well aware of her role and that any deviation from the expected high standards of behaviour that her extensive training had instilled in her would nearly always lead to corporal punishment.

Tugging the back of the corset restraint she was wearing further up her back to fully expose her backside, Jamie folded the leather lead over double and took aim. Thwack, thwack, thwack, thwack, thwack, thwack went the strapping as Jamie went for quick and powerful lashes, concentrating on a thin strip of flesh across the centre of her buttocks. There was no sound or real movement from Meda as she took the punishment stoically and quietly. Realising that this was a resilient and strong woman, well-used to severe beatings and in most likelihood, someone who very much enjoyed them, Jamie decided to go high and low to the more sensitive areas with his next strikes. Six more, harshly delivered blows to the tops of her buttocks and legs did at least produce a whimpering, muffled moan from Meda, but she was clearly not a girl easily moved to the more theatrical screaming and screeching of many submissives.

Noting Pres watching him carefully and keen to ensure that he met with her approval, he rose, sending Meda sprawling at his feet.

Pushing her away from him with his foot, Jamie threw the leash down to the ground. "Fetch and hold it in your mouth, bitch," he snapped and walked across the barn where he had spotted a huge crate of carrots.

Jamie grinned as an idea formed in his head, and selecting the longest thickest carrot with a large leaf cluster at its head, he marched back to the waiting slave.

"Right, you can use the pump, soap and whatever you need to clean this properly. It's going right up your arsehole slave, so I'll leave you to decide how clean it needs to be. Oh and it'll need some lubrication to fit in, seeing as how long and thick it is, so once you've cleaned it, you had better make it nice and slippery to save reaming you too painfully, bitch. You have my permission to lubricate both the carrot and your arse with whatever you think will give you it the easiest passage – so to speak, ha ha!" Jamie taunted the slave girl whose expression was now looking decidedly perturbed and staring at the carrot with a certain amount of fear and trepidation. Jamie dropped the carrot and walked away, saying over his shoulder, "You have five minutes so don't hang about."

Pres settled herself down on a hay bale giving Jamie a smile and a definite look of appreciation. She flicked her shoes off.

"My feet are sweaty and tired, Heron; lick them clean and massage them."

Heron immediately set about his task, taking one of her big toes inside his mouth, clearly relishing the task and the taste.

Five minutes later, a frankly dishevelled Meda was at Jamie's feet, pulling the carrot from her pussy dripping with her love juices. It had been fascinating for Jamie to watch as she had quickly scrubbed the carrot with a brush under the pumped water. Then without any hesitation, she had squatted and inserted it inside her pussy and immediately began to thrust it in and out to its full extent. All the time she wanked herself with the carrot, her spare hand was scooping up her juices and quickly lubricating her arsehole with them, so by the end of the five minutes he noted that she had opened herself up enough to slide her complete thumb into her rear orifice and seemed to have done to good job of lubricating herself.

Jamie took the proffered carrot from her. "Lie on your back," he ordered.

Looking slightly confused and even more worried as to his intentions now, Meda duly obeyed.

"Lift your legs up, knees apart and spread, now bring them up towards your shoulders. Point your arsehole at me, come on, legs wide apart, arsehole gaping, bottom up, get on with it."

He snarled at Meda, who was distinctly ill at ease and apprehensive but took her position in the required manner with her head down and bottom up in the air.

Happy that she was arranged as he required, Jamie knelt down between her splayed thighs and without further ado started to slide the carrot into her back passage. Meda cried out and gasped as he pushed through the tight early resistance without allowing her time to relax her muscles naturally.

"Don't fight it bitch, it's going all the way."

Almost a foot long, the carrot was beyond the size of any penis or dildo that Meda had previously taken in her arse and her eyes bulged and her face screwed up in a tight grimace and she willed herself to relax and accept the intrusion. With one final push and a yelp of anguish from Meda, the carrot top suddenly sucked into her arsehole and her stretched opening started to close around it leaving the sprouting green bouquet flowering from her.

"Excellent, now go over and present to Pres," said Jamie, running his hands under the pump now to wash off the girl's slimy juices.

"This is a brilliant idea," said Pres. "Do let us have a matching set. Heron, go and fetch the biggest carrot you can find in there. Wash it and get it lubricated please. Hmmmmmm, I am not sure if I fancy shoving a carrot up my cunt for you. How shall we lubricate this one?" She looked enquiringly at Jamie.

"Oh no, Pres, please use the bitch's twat, we can see how wet and juicy she is. She looks to have enough slimy juice for everyone!"

Pres looked down at the girl who immediately presented herself for inspection. With no preamble, Pres thrust her fingers into the slave's pussy.

"Yes indeed, a very, very wet and horny little girl. Good idea, thanks for that, Porter. I'll fuck her with our carrot too."

Heron handed over the carrot, which unnoticed by Meda but observed with wry smiles by both Jamie and Pres, he had copiously coated with the carbolic soap.

"You evil little bastard," laughed Pres but with a grin as she patted his head. She had left Meda in the presenting position and leaned down, parted her vaginal folds and quickly pushed the soap-coated carrot right into the slave girl's fanny. There was a couple of seconds or so pause before Meda, who was clearly able to accommodate the long carrot easily within her quim, felt the sting of the soap.

"Aaaaeeeeeeoooooww! Yaaaaaaaah!" she cried and whipped the carrot out. The stinging was clearly intense and she writhed on the ground, her hands clasped between her legs, causing Jamie to take pity.

"Go to the pump and wash yourself out."

Meda ran across and pumped the water between her legs, spooning and scooping handfuls to her pussy.

Heron had turned and presented, his bottom raised high and his hands pulling his arse cheeks apart, exposing the soaped-up anal hole completely and displaying its deep red internal colouring. Pres knelt down and with one hand grasping his waving, throbbing cock, she positioned the carrot and then rammed it up his arsehole with no hesitation. The last two inches stayed poking out and Pres just lifted her knee and slammed it in, Heron bucking and gasping as she did so. Pres fluffed up the green leaves and looked admiringly at the sight.

"Better get the bitch back and return these two to the room as it'll soon be time for dinner and I need to quickly change, I think," said Pres, brushing down her legs.

"I'll take them, Pres, you get on," offered Jamie, and Pres handed over Heron's lead and indicated to Meda to dry herself off and return to him.

Jamie saw the venomous look Meda gave to Heron and decided that she had a fair point.

"We will return you to the reception in a moment but first I believe a little balancing of the books is required."

Meda looked at Jamie with a flash of respect and admiration but unfortunately made the mistake of verbalising her pleasure.

"Thank you, sir, that soap was…" Meda dried up quickly as she noticed the angry look Jamie was giving her. "Er…sorry, sir, Meda spoke out of turn, sir," she finished tamely.

Heron then made the mistake of smirking at her discomfort.

"Right, the two of you are now just royally pissing me off. As far as I am aware, slaves should barely acknowledge or communicate with each other in the company of their master, mistress or owner. Heron, wipe the stupid look off your face, I was already planning a little levelling up of the playing field because of your spitefulness and you have just added to that. On your knees, facing the other way,

37

head up, hands on top of your head, straight back, facing away from me."

Heron gulped but moved into the position straight away.

"As for you, you pathetic reprobate, you can start by taking one of those towels from the pump and going over to the brambles there and bringing me back a bunch of the stinging nettles. Mind you don't sting your hands, I'm sure you'll need them later."

Meda looked in horror at Jamie; the seconds ticked on as she hesitated.

"Oh, I can't believe this. Stand up. Pull your breasts out of the corset."

As she obeyed, Jamie grabbed her nipples hard and twisted them sharply causing the girl to cry out. He then spun her round, bent her over and harshly pulled the carrot from her arsehole causing a second scream, then turning her back round, he pushed it into her mouth.

"Stand still, bitch!"

Meda, eyes full of tears, trembled as she was quickly forced to reassess the thought process that had her thinking that Jamie might be a soft option now that the imposing and intimidating presence of Pres had departed. Things had gone in a new direction with their introduction to this "Porter"; normally a spell with a newbie signalled an easy time, but in this instance Meda was growing rather fearful, especially with the threat of the nettles which would be a new experience but not one that she felt was going to be much of a treat. Meda might welcome virtually all opportunities to behave subserviently, adore being mastered and humiliated, and love the after-pain and buzz she experienced from a thorough thrashing...but stinging nettles, Jamie could see, were a different kettle of fish!

"Fetch the fucking nettles, bitch!" Jamie broke into her reverie and with a quiet sob she scuttled off to obey. She may be hoping that this was a threat and not a promise but Jamie intended to install as much fear and respect in these two as he possibly could.

Jamie marched across to Heron.

"Bend over and stay there with your arse up and ready."

Unceremoniously, he tugged the carrot from his back passage, grabbed his hair and pushed it into his mouth. Heron's unwavering look of satisfaction and smugness was so annoying Jamie that he grabbed his lead once more, doubled it over and, holding him upright on his knees, lashed him twelve times across the shoulders, back and upper legs, avoiding his leather-protected bottom. The whimpering noise from Heron was enough to quell his rage at his impudence and, placing his foot into the small of his back, he pushed him firmly to the ground.

Meda was carefully laying down a bunch of nettles she had picked, wrapped in a towel and looking absolutely terrified at the thought of what might happen next.

"Right Meda, making sure the carrot is nice and lubricated, turn it around with the leaves carefully in your mouth. Heron you do the same and then you can put your hands on your arse cheeks and pull them wide apart."

Leading Meda over to Heron, he pushed her down behind the man's presented bottom, tugging the side poppers of his skin tight pants to release them and leave him naked apart from his collar.

"That's better, let the bitch see the bone, so to speak. On my word, push your carrot up Heron's arse as quickly as you can, all the way, using only your mouth while your hands wank his cock."

Meda knelt and positioned the carrot at the entrance to his inviting dark hole. She'd guessed what was coming next and her whole body trembled as she clearly heard Jamie carefully pick up the nettles.

"Now!" Jamie ordered as he brought the bunch of nettles down swiftly across her bottom. Meda pushed the carrot top firmly with her curled tongue and was rewarded with it sliding in smoothly to the hilt. As the first stinging sensation of the nettles struck her consciousness, she used her lips to seal the penetration and, as well as she could, fluff up the leaves. Shutting her mind to the swishing sting of the nettles, she concentrated on finishing her task as quickly and as effectively as she could. She drew back triumphantly as Jamie swiped her cheeks for the fifth time with the nettles, earning praise from her tormentor.

"Well done, good job. Now stop that snivelling and turn and present; the sooner it's over, the sooner you can get your sore, stinging arses under the cold water."

Meda resisted the urge to scratch and rub her bottom; she turned, ducked down and reached back to pull open her arsehole as wide as she could, but was hindered jointly by the irritation of the nettles and the inability to relax in the wake of the forced intrusion that was on its way. Heron was at her behind in a thrice, positioning the top of the carrot in her tightened entrance.

"I'd advise taking a breath and relaxing, Meda, or this is going to be hurt you both considerably. Heron, when you feel the nettles land, you can start pushing and I want to see your fingers twiddling her fanny properly."

Jamie laid a gentle swipe on the protuberance of his taut thin buttocks and Heron began forcing the vegetable into her reluctant rectum. The air became filled with the scream of Meda as her anal muscles failed to yield to the carrot's thick top and the groans of dismay from Heron as the stinging sensation hit home, with Jamie determined to ensure that the cocksure male received the more severe aftershocks of the nettles poisonous barbs. With a final thrust with his chin, Heron successfully breached the tight reluctant ring of Meda's arsehole as Jamie swiped the nettles continuously along his backside. He reared up to announce the completion of his task, grimacing at the thousand needles pain of the nettles.

"Ok, well done slaves. Now scuttle over to the border there where the dock leaves are and rub each other bottoms to soothe them, then you are to select new carrots to replace the mess you've made of these ones. You can select each other's, but ensure you have a good sprouting top, then you may stick your arses under the running water for a while and get yourselves and the two replacement carrots nicely washed and clean. Once that's done, lubricate the carrots with saliva or Meda's fanny juices and replace them in each other. Go!" Jamie ordered, and the two scuttled over to the garden.

Heron, Jamie was pleased to note, was clearly in more discomfort than Meda, as the two worked in harmony, picking dock leaves and presenting their backsides to each other in turn. Arses rubbed sufficiently, the bedraggled and wilted carrots out, replacement carrots selected, they pushed their behinds, touching together, under the flowing cold water. Jamie gave them time to treat themselves and recover completely, before telling them to lubricate and insert their new carrots into each other. He was pleased to see that Meda took both carrots in turn inside of her, allowing Heron's carrot to slide a bit easier with the benefit of her sex secretions rather than having to rely on saliva. She seemed to have forgiven him his earlier misdeed and Jamie felt that he had made his mark. He reattached their leads and returned them both to the house. Leading them back around to the front entrance and taking them back into the reception room, carrots sprouting in full leaf from their bottoms, he was greeted with backslaps and a smattering of applause that increased and spread as the gathering noticed the vegetation and the obvious signs of the nettle rash.

"Good show, Porter," said the Professor, materialising beside Jamie. "We were wondering where you'd got to but this is excellent entertainment, good show, good show. Nicely timed too as it's just about time for dinner. Tie those two here and leave them; they'll be taken care of shortly as they will be allowed to dress and join the dining throng. Excellent, I think they might remember you, young man!"

Dinner was good fun as Jamie sat between Pres and the Professor and was greeted wholeheartedly by the others on the table. There were no roles to keep to at dinner and Jamie felt that it would have been impossible for any neutral observer coming into the room then to have ascertained or predicted what the majority of them would be getting up to later! The conversation was light and generally good-humoured but there was certainly an air of expectation and Jamie noted a few whispered conversations and what, he assumed, was a bit of early manoeuvring going on in preparation for the action to follow. Jamie's slight nervousness was more around that he had been forewarned by the Professor that a lot of the post-dinner activity was a shared room experience and that he could expect some quite outlandish behaviour, a possible orgy and a lot of pairs and group activity being conducted in full view of a roving audience as people mingled for the night's entertainment. As a dominant, Jamie had been reassured to find that he had a powerful role and therefore any of the myriad rooms available off the main hall room, in the specifically prepared giant basement floor, would be available for him to determine any privacy settings he desired. He had yet to see the basement area but the Professor assured him that it was a treat to savour and not to fear.

As after dinner coffee was served, Jamie knew that he was to have a moment in the spotlight as his 'victim' for the evening would be drawn from those who had applied, and were still applying throughout the meal, explaining the blatant stares of lust and assessment that he kept noticing as the submissives sized him up. Pres had explained that within the larger group, there were far more subs than doms, so each dom from the regions present was a prize that the subs would be prepared to fight over, and especially a newbie available for the first time.

"Desperately running through things in my head to make sure you are well prepped, but as a first-timer, you are guaranteed help and advice on demand. Which reminds me, wristbands!" she announced theatrically. "They'll be distributed shortly. You will have two to wear at all times. Black denoting that you are a dom, and green as well to show you are a first-timer and as such should be free to ask anyone anything. The slaves will have their collars on so as we've already seen evidence of, subs wear red wristbands, and switches wear black and red but can configure them to show one colour more prominent than the other to indicate their preference at that time."

It was a strange situation for Jamie as he would have no say in the choice of his first partner under the auspices of the society. However, as the dom he knew he could control the situation and do whatever he needed to, to ensure that his passage into the wider activities of the society was opened up to him in the future. He was quite pleased when the meeting's host, a president of an adjoining area's group, rose to announce the sweepstake results for the new members' first assignations. When his name was called out, he rose to applause and waited as a slip of paper was picked from a bowl to select his partner.

"Our winner of the first session with our new dom, Porter, is...wait for it...I can see there are some hopeful faces out there," he teased his audience, "is...Fairy."

There were a lot of groans as a demure young lady in her thirties, raised her hand and then rose as the speaker beckoned her forward.

"Right, Fairy, come and stand behind Porter. You are officially his sub until he relinquishes his hold on you or the weekend ends, whichever is soonest."

Fairy duly walked around to stand behind Porter, her head bowed but there was no disguising the look of both triumph and anticipation on her eager face.

Jamie ignored her, going straight into role, and sat and chatted with other table members as after-dinner drinks were served. After a few minutes, Pres rose and announced that dinner was over and all present were free now to return to their rooms to prepare themselves for the evening's activities, finishing with the ominous words:

"The Basement of Baseness will open in thirty minutes. All in attendance to remember society rules of behaviour but primarily respect limits, and if you are deemed drunk and incapable or behave in an unfitting manner, you will be removed and suspended. Otherwise, everyone please have a good evening. Remember we have a second day tomorrow so don't overdo it straight away."

Most scurried away; there were costumes to don and preparations to make, equipment and bindings to put into place, and positions to adopt.

Jamie turned to Fairy. "My room is number 216. Be outside it appropriately dressed in thirty minutes. Now be off."

"Yes, sir, thank you, sir," said Fairy, obsequiously.

After a quick shower and shave, Jamie went for the black trousers and waistcoat, with a white shirt and tie, sleeves rolled. His aim was to look reasonably authoritative, slightly menacing and ready for action. He was just about ready for whatever action this night would bring when there came a polite knock on the door.

Fairy stood before him, head bowed. "Fairy is your servant, sir," she whispered in a respectful voice.

"Enter please, Fairy, let's have a chat before going downstairs, shall we?" Jamie invited her into the room.

She was dressed in a short black cocktail dress and back shoes; no other clothing was visible. She adopted a demure aspect, and a respectful and submissive manner.

"Right, Fairy, relax and please let us just have a quick chat. I am Porter and you are mine for tonight, but just for a moment I give you full permission to tell me anything you want, to assist us both in having an enjoyable and fulfilling night. You may also take this opportunity to tell me in particular what you don't like or object strongly to. You may also ask me questions. For my part, I thoroughly enjoy beating naughty bottoms, I love licking pussy, adore ladies' bottoms and am partial to analingus, both giving and taking, and I do appreciate a quality blow job."

Jamie managed to play his role perfectly and was thankful that Fairy stood before him with her head bowed. It didn't yet come naturally to Jamie to act the dominant partner; it was something he enjoyed rather than obsessed about but he was aware what would be expected of him and was keen to develop his opportunities through the BADS connections.

"Oh, thank you, sir. I wasn't expecting this at all, sir. Um, sir, I can really speak freely, sir?"

"Yes, Fairy, I am not trying to trick you, please speak freely. This is your one chance. Do take it, or don't, your choice, but the opportunity will not be repeated. Once we leave this room, you are nothing, you are whatever I want you to be, you are worthless. Do you understand?"

Fairy nodded, finally raising her head to look at him in the eyes.

"Thank you, sir. Please sir, I enjoy being mastered, I love being spanked and don't mind a caning. I like being tied down, blindfolded, fucked, sucked – pussy and asshole. I like being come on, I like nipple clamps, I love to be forced to do weird sexual things, sir. I adore being completely dominated and acting totally subservient, sir. And, sir, I love being made to come sir, and I can't stop masturbating, sir. I love coming, sir. I do come buckets!"

Fairy hesitated, causing Jamie to prompt her. "So, come on now, what don't you like? Come on, let's hear it."

"Porter, sir, I don't like rough anal, very harsh caning and being abused in front of others, sir. I don't like being shared with other members; I like to be mastered by just one person preferably, sir. I would very much like it, sir, if it was just the two of us up here and that it would be just you using and abusing me, sir."

Jamie smiled. "Some of that may happen but later, Fairy. For now, I want to see what's on offer in the basement. Right, I've noted your preferences and may bear them in mind. Follow me, just be two steps behind me, don't speak unless spoken to and obey my every command. Follow."

Jamie had no idea what to expect but both the Professor and Pres were both with the little entourage of senior BADS personnel and stepped forward to greet him.

"Pres will walk you round to start with, Porter, then you can do what you want. Fairy is yours and yours alone, so will wear a red collar, if I may." Pres fitted it around Fairy's neck before continuing. "You wear a black wristband with the capital D. The gold star means you are identified as a guest of honour and, as such, all subs and slaves are available to you unless they have a gold star on their collars, as I will give Fairy now to ensure that she is recognised as yours alone

46

until you discard her."

Fairy flinched at Pres' words and was almost knocked over by the manhandling she was given as the gold star was affixed to her collar. On entering the room, Jamie tried his best to adopt a nonchalant, 'been there, done that' attitude, and stride, but of course he hadn't and he felt quite nervous and apprehensive to what the room may have in store. However, there was no rampant orgy taking place, no gang-banging, no communal flogging, very few black leather masks on show and, as far as he could see, no actual copulation or sexual intercourse underway yet at all.

There were about seventy people already there, both sexes seemingly evenly represented and ages from twenties to seventies. A couple were just strapping down a female sub, still partially clothed, over a gymnasium horse, one of them clearly a dom whilst his partner appeared to be acting as his servant. There was some canoodling going on around the edge of the room and some slow dancing to the soul ballad being played in the centre of the floor but, Jamie mused, nothing outrageous at all.

The dom finished binding his sub over the horse and, spotting Jamie, beckoned him over.

"Hi, I am Swish, you must be Porter. I saw what you did with the two slaves earlier. Rich, man, very rich. This piece of worthlessness is Doormat. She's due a good beating for being tardy. Would you like to be my guest and give her a taste of your own particular form of punishment? It would be an honour for her, and a pleasure for me, to see one of our Gold members give her some treatment."

Well, thought Jamie, it would seem rude not to, as he walked around the horse to look at the offered victim. Doormat was about thirty years old, with long blonde hair and an attractive face, he noted, having grabbed her head up by her hair, her hands fastened to the legs of the horse, her legs still free.

"My pleasure and thank you," seemed the only response to Jamie, keeping reasonably taciturn while he figured out his role in this company.

Still in her bra and panties but not for long, as Jamie unfastened the bra and leant around her to massage her breasts, feeling the nipples harden instantly on his touch.

Doormat pushed back with her bottom when she felt Jamie hardening as he leant in against her. Not the greatest of moves as Jamie immediately pulled away and applied a couple of sharp stings with his flat hand to the backs of her legs.

"Let's have these down and off," he said, yanking her panties off her legs in one movement and discarding them. "Fairy, buckle her legs please, nice and wide apart. We will have her opened up to everyone."

Fairy leapt to obey. Jamie had noted her rather petulant expression whilst he was playing with Doormat's breasts and was just biding his time before he took action. For now, he watched as she rather roughly strapped and buckled up the compliant submissive's legs. Looking at the result, Jamie could certainly admire the firm jutting buttocks facing him but was slightly disappointed that her muscular cheeks were so defined that they were still touching over her crack and her arsehole was not exposed nor her pussy lips barely on show.

"Well, this won't do, far too discreet and prudent. I want those cheeks relaxed and apart. Right, Fairy, loosen both leg restraints a notch, please." As she did so, Jamie pulled Doormat's flanks away from contact with the horse slightly, mystifying the growing audience as people drifted over to watch the spectacle.

"Fairy, sit between her legs facing me. Now lean back and push your head up into the gap and place your mouth on her pussy."

It certainly had the desired effect as it forced Doormat's bottom out at an angle that made her cheeks protrude and open up to reveal a full display of her arsehole, a mass of wrinkled miniature dark pink folds surrounded by fine blonde hairs, her lower pussy lips now visible. Jamie had noted Fairy's body language and the little stamp of her feet as she reluctantly settled with the girl's wet lips against her mouth. He decided that he needed to act now to establish his control over the sub and also firmly establish his credentials with the watching audience.

"Fairy, come out from there, you naughty hussy. I do not approve of your petulance, your silliness or your reluctance to obey any polite command. Strip off now!' His tone brooked no argument and much as Fairy displayed a rather listless expression, she remembered her training and her chosen role well enough to begin discarding her clothing. Jamie looked around, as the literature had stated there were several clearly labelled assistants in the room, there to run tasks, and he beckoned over a scantily dressed young woman wearing a 'Helper' sash and asked her to collect up Fairy's clothes and take them back to his room.

Jamie looked at the rather forlorn-looking Fairy as she removed her knickers to stand naked before him. A cracking body, he thought, sizeable breasts with large aureole and long nipples, a flat stomach and a dark bushy-haired fanny.

"Now young lady, you appear to consider it your right to question my decisions and actions with your haughty and sulky little expressions. So to show you how wrong you are and teach you a quick lesson, you will remain naked for the rest of the time you are in this room and you will present on your knees for a thrashing to remind you where the authority is held. Move!"

Her eyes welling up, the naked woman quickly dropped to her

haunches. "Yes master, sorry master, sir," she said, presenting her fleshy buttocks with a dark crack housing a dark centre with a flourishing crop of black tight curly hairs hiding a small, very discreet arsehole.

Jamie went over to one of the three double-sided units in the room, holding a myriad instruments and implements for restraint, castigation, correction and punishment. Each display was attended by a helper who logged your selected item against your room number and helped you select from straps, buckles, cuffs and headgear, as well as canes, paddles, straps, switches, tawses, whips and birches of all shapes, lengths and thicknesses.

Jamie selected a straightforward cat-of-nine-tails and walked back to Fairy, her rounded arse cheeks pointing up at him as she held the submissive position with head resting on her crossed arms. Without pausing to break stride, Jamie raised his arm and brought the cat flashing down diagonally across the target area. Not allowing any recovery time, he swiped hard again and again, streaking Fairy's lower back, upper thighs and prominent buttocks with vivid red groups of stripes. Fairy audibly groaned as the lashes started to land on top of previous strokes but was otherwise restrained and fully compliant in taking her punishment. Jamie paused and moved to stand above her head, locking it between his calves, and with a final swipe brought the cat down between her cheeks, the ends of the strands whipping under her open bottom crack to land flush on the lower lips of her pussy, the middle tighter mass of the lashes firmly slapping against her open anus.

"Yaaaaaaaaaaaay! Yaaar, yar, yar!" Fairy's control on her reaction disappeared as the stinging on her sensitive private parts sent a ferocious pain throughout her body, and she shook and squirmed without constraint.

Jamie allowed the response; it was intended to cause her distress and he had achieved his aim.

"Painful, isn't it, Fairy? Maybe you will now re-think your poor attitude and remember your place. If you give me reason to chastise you again while we are in this room, not only will I bring the cat to you once more but I will give you six lashes between your legs and invite our audience to beat you as well. Do you understand?" he queried as he bent down close to her tear-streaked, snivelling face.

"Oh sir, yes, master, I understand and am so sorry to have earned your displeasure, sir. I am so sorry, sir, and am truly your servant, oh masterful one."

Fairy had quickly recovered her composure and, although still sobbing, dropped back into role with admirable forbearance.

Jamie was quite impressed and began to think that they might have an enjoyable end to the evening when they returned to his bedroom. He was quite looking forward to testing her fortitude further but meanwhile he had unfinished business with Doormat. He could see from Fairy's expression that she was waiting for him to give her the order to return to her earlier position between Doormat's legs and at Jamie's nod she scampered across to do so.

"Good girl," Jamie encouraged her, and noted with approval that she had knelt, head back, knees apart, displaying her own reddened pussy lips as her mouth closed around Doormat's waiting lips. "Keep her nicely lubricated and don't waste any of her juices. Lap it up, please," Jamie ordered, receiving a slurping acknowledgment which he assumed was in acceptance of his instruction as Fairy definitely appeared to have her mouth full!

Jamie went over to the implements selection and chose a medium-thick, quite long strap, booking it out.

Returning to the fastened Doormat, he announced, "Six hard

stokes with this strap, then I'll have a taste of that lovely bottom. After that I will give you six more straps on top of the first ones. What do you say, Doormat?"

The woman was experienced enough to know exactly what was required.

"Thank you, sir, Doormat would be very honoured to receive such a just and fair punishment from you, sir."

Jamie flexed the strap between his hands and then raised it high, pausing to wait for Doormat to naturally relax her buttocks. As she did so, he swung his arm down powerfully and with speed to hit the centre of her bottom with tremendous force and a loud splat. There was a moment of relative quiet as the audience watched in a reverent silence, and the strains of the final lilting bars of the soul ballad faded away, before Doormat let loose a low, strangled groan as the thick vivid and livid red line clearly displayed the impact mark across both cheeks. With barely a pause, Jamie applied the second strike to land barely the width of a hair above the first. His victim mewed and struggled in her bindings as Jamie wasted no time in striking for the third time just above the first two, before following it immediately with a fourth just below so the centre of her buttocks were now almost glowing in a bright red mass. The fifth stroke landed on the lowest parts of her suffering buttocks before Jamie paused and watch as the stricken girl clenched and unclenched, vainly trying to dissipate the stinging sensation. With a real flourish, Jamie applied the final stroke to the sensitive, tighter skin of her upper cheeks, finally being rewarded with a shriek from Doormat as the pain hit home. Jamie dropped the strap to admire his work before some of the watchers moved in for a close up of Doormat's twitching arse cheeks.

"Good job, old chap," said Swish admiringly. "There's some fair force in your arms as well as cold blood in your heart, I suspect."

"Thanks. The second six should be fun on top of those, but first I am going to have a taste." Jamie moved towards the blazing cheeks of Doormat and leaned in to speak to Fairy.

"You will lick and suck her to orgasm while I enjoy her arsehole. The quicker she comes, the sooner you'll be out from under there. Now, put your arms around her and hold open her arse cheeks for me. I want a wide-open crack please."

There was a slurped grunt of acknowledgement from Fairy, her face jammed into Doormat's pussy, her nose wedged against the woman's already rock-hard clitoris. Jamie helped her place her hands where he wanted them and watched as she dug in her fingers, probably using more force than strictly necessary, to fully expose the bound and beaten woman's arsehole. Two can play at that game, he thought, stretching under Doormat to place his own hands in Fairy's hair and forcing her face even harder into the other's groin, causing a spluttering gasp as Fairy suddenly found her breathing options even more curtailed.

Jamie lingered close to the centre of his attention now, enjoying the anticipatory moments as he studied the puckered rose before him, kneeling in to draw in the earthy, sweaty aroma from the dark hole with its pinkish centre. Gently he nudged the enticing entrance with the tip of his nose, the scent of her love juices and Fairy's saliva mixing with the more sour smell of the anal opening. Drawing back, he flicked with his tongue at the tiny cushions of skin making up the wall of the entrance, and then leaned right in to French kiss the offering fully, relishing the bitter acrid taste and the differing oral experience that each woman gave from her nether regions.

As Jamie started to lick and probe Doormat anally, made easier as she relaxed and opened to accept his tongue, he could sense that Fairy had increased the speed and force of her lapping and rubbing of Doormat's clearly dripping wet sex lips, indicating that a climax was not far away. Jamie dipped his tongue to join Fairy's as they lapped at the pussy folds together and Jamie eased his nose into Doormat's well lubricated arsehole as the frantic movement of the penetrated woman was joined by a building moan.

The moan soon turned into a triumphant yell of ecstasy as Doormat came, her thrusting almost suffocating Fairy as she mashed her groin hard into the trapped girl's face. Jamie pulled away and then thrust his thumb hard into the gaping anus and fucked her rapidly as she bucked again as a second wave of climatic euphoria flooded throughout her body. Withdrawing his thumb with an audible sucking plop, he stood up and quickly picked up the strap pulling Fairy out from under her, gasping for breath with her face glistening wet from the cunnilingus.

Before Doormat had time to realise what was happening, Jamie started to lay the strap hard on her gyrating bottom, matching the thick stripes of the earlier punishment perfectly. Doormat's ecstatic throes of orgasm were now replaced by piercing screams as the third, fourth and fifth strokes landed. Jamie paused to gather himself and then laid on the sixth stroke across the top of her buttocks with real force, giving the sensitive skin a purple hue, and causing Doormat's scream to falter for a moment as all the breath seemed to leave her body. A choking groan of real pain followed as, without Fairy's presence, she was able to rotate her hips in a desperate attempt to ease the agony, her arse cheeks opening and closing as she twitched and twisted.

Jamie nodded to Swish, clicked his fingers at Fairy, and strode back to return the strap. There was a smattering of applause from the lingering watching audience before they parted, as it became apparent that the show was over. Jamie kept up the air of nonchalance he had adopted as he wandered around the room with Fairy's uncovered feet pitter-pattering behind him. Aware of eyes on him, Jamie turned to see the two of them virtually being stalked by the three submissives from the local group, Jezebel, Isabel and Sloth.

Glancing around the room, he espied Pres who was just attaching nipple clamps and a chain to a blindfolded male sub, dressed solely in a pair of white lacy ladies briefs.

"Ah, Porter, looking for more entertainment?"

"A word of advice, if you could spare me a moment, please, Pres."

Out of earshot of Fairy, Jamie explained the behaviour of the trio of minxes who followed him around the room, and ran through a proposal of what he would like to do to distract and dissuade them from continuing to do so. Pres laughed.

"You evil man, but it will teach them a lesson. Give me a minute to set it up. I've got a little job that Fairy could do in the meantime if you could repay the favour."

She outlined her task and told him how to go about it.

"I'll see you back here in fifteen minutes."

Pres left Jamie holding the chain hanging from her playmate and departed.

"Come on you two, we're off to the bathroom. Apparently, our friend Silo here needs a good scrubbing from you, Fairy."

Seeing a fleeting scowl of anger and disapproval cross Fairy's face, Jamie pushed her down to the floor.

"Right, you will now crawl everywhere behind me until I get a sense of compliance and obedience from you, you bad girl."

He slapped her buttocks hard three times to emphasise his annoyance.

"Sorry, sir, ow, ow, sorry, sorry."

Fairy looked most unhappy now tasked with remembering her

place and the need to curb her emotional displays. She seemed worried that Porter might be tiring of her and he suspected that she would be fearsome of him giving her away, being passed on or just discarded, as was his right. Jamie thought that the worry was her own fault and was happy to allow her to fret.

Jamie led them to the huge and luxurious bathroom suite set into the entrance of the basement. This housed several shower cubicles, changing rooms and individual toilet closets.

"Panties off, Silo, and get yourself a locker. Then we will lock your hands to the nipple clamp chain so Fairy won't have any trouble with you. Fairy, grab a brush, flannel and some shower gel and get this cock and balls scrubbed up nice and clean for Pres. I want this conducted in silence, do not communicate with each other at all. Expect to be eating a bar of soap each before you get a whipping if I hear as much as a word. Do get stuck in, Fairy. I want to see soapy fingers sunk deep in his arsehole and a cock so clean you could use it to stir tea and serve dinner with!"

Fairy set to her task with diligence but with a certain amount of care not to cause Silo too much unnecessary suffering. As Jamie watched, she bent Silo over in the large shower cubicle and soaped his whole body before she worked a frothy lather up and with her left hand stroked his cock to full erect mode as she worked on opening up his arsehole with the other. A grunt from Silo indicated a finger had breached his entrance, a more high-pitched squeal was evidence that a second finger had joined the first. Silo's increased breathing rate was evidence that she had gone deep and he could see that she had begun to piston her digits.

"If he comes, you will be licking it up from the floor of the stall, Fairy, soap suds and all!" Jamie warned, as Silo's fists clenched and his body began to thrust between Fairy's hands. She immediately ceased her activity, gently removed her fingers from his now gaping arsehole while she tightened her grip on his cock to force him to stop his attempts to climax. As Silo's breathing returned to normal and his twitching arsehole relaxed and closed, she showered him down before she wrapped them both in a giant bathrobe and dried them off.

"Good job both of you. Now let's get you back to Pres."

Jamie knotted Silo's briefs to the nipple chain and led them both back, Fairy dropping to her knees to crawl submissively behind her master, into the main room. From the quick movement outside the door, Jamie was sure that the three subs had just watched the proceedings and had now slipped back to prepare their next move, which Jamie surmised may not be the one they would have expected presuming that Pres had fulfilled her part of the bargain.

Pres was ready for their return and greeted them with a big grin on her face.

"All sorted, Porter. Room number seven is set up for you. It's one of the rooms off this main room, set as a private room but with foldaway front walls to open it up if, and when, required. Let's have a look, shall we?"

As Silo and Fairy followed behind, Pres took Jamie across the main dance floor to a small room that now housed three pieces of apparatus similar to pommel horses but without the central handles. Straps underneath the main body and on the legs gave a fair indication as to how a discipline subject could be strapped lengthways along the top with head supported and arms and legs buckled down. The horse legs were splayed in such a way that would spread participants' legs well and there was a height adjuster and a moveable wedge that fitted between the partaker's legs, forcing them further apart and raising the midriff to slightly higher than the prone torso.

"Spot on, Pres, absolutely perfect, and I see I have a selection of gags, hoods and sex toys to have my fun with."

Jamie was delighted that his plan to play hardball with the rather imperious threesome might come nicely to fruition.

"Oh yes, and the additional items you requested are on their way from the garden, just being washed and cleaned first," Pres smiled. "Got a thing about carrots, have you Porter?"

"Ha ha. No, Pres, just that they are a perfect toy in that they come in all shapes and sizes and therefore fit into certain parts of the body that can accommodate the variety they offer. Not 'one size fits all'! Parsnips will do the job too, but cucumbers and courgettes just don't have the heads to hold on to or the firmness required!"

Jamie could see that Fairy listened intently to the conversation and he could tell that she had picked up on the fact that things might not be going so well for the annoying threesome who Jamie was certain she felt might have been a threat to what she saw as her just and rightful desserts later. No doubt she suspected that they might have met their match and that if they were to be humiliated, she would be keen to witness it.

"Would you be up for participation in a little bit of comeuppance, Fairy?" Jamie found her amusingly easy to read and knew she was very wary of the threesome having occupied some of Jamie's thoughts whilst with her.

"Oh yes, sir, Fairy would love to do the master's bidding, sir."

At that moment Jamie spotted that Isabel was trying to sneak a look inside the room from the almost closed door.

"Do come in, Isabel, you seem desperate to join us. Why not come and have some fun with us?" Jamie ushered her into the room, closing it behind her.

Pres then left the room saying, "I'll perhaps give you a moment, then I'll pop back with the rest of the pack."

Suddenly Isabel, who had entered quite haughtily, almost with a sneer of triumph towards Fairy, didn't quite look so confident. Her mouth certainly dropped open when one of the assistants entered the room with a tray full of carrots!

"Ah, thank you. They look perfect, all shapes and sizes. I am sure we can find some nice fits amongst them." Jamie took the tray and fingered the carrots, particularly paying attention to the longer, fatter ones.

"Right Isabel, a real treat for you as you're here first: put your arms out and my little helper Fairy here is going to slip your clothes off. A bit unfair her being naked and you being fully clothed even if it is in a tart's uniform," said Jamie, deliberately trying to wind Isabel up as Fairy pulled her dress over her head to reveal her skimpy underwear beneath.

Isabel didn't resist. Although she resented Fairy's involvement, she allowed the other sub to unhook her bra, freeing her small breasts and stood motionless when her G-string was unceremoniously pulled down and off her legs.

Jamie looked at the nude girl before him: neat small breasts and trimmed pubic hair around a discreet pussy slit. He walked round to have a look at the tight little backside with its cute rounded cheeks. He was attracted to her and was already thinking ahead to the opportunity that could be presented at some point with this girl and her two mates.

"Get over the horse and assume the position, Isabel. I take it you know how to present?"

Isabel nodded her compliance. A submissive for several years, she automatically obeyed a dominant's instructions, especially someone like Porter who the three chums had quite lusted after ever since they had laid eyes on him. She had originally looked chuffed to be the first one in a situation with him but Jamie could see that she was now looking rather apprehensive about the direction things had taken. As Porter and Fairy arranged her over the pommel horse, they could see that her vulnerability was making her aroused and she was showing signs of wetness between her legs.

"Oh, look here, Fairy, she's dripping already. Perhaps she won't need much lubrication, eh?"

Fairy smiled; he could see her pleasure in being included in his plans had made her happier by the minute. He also spied a sparkle in her eyes that suggested that she had perhaps herself become quite horny.

"Let's have her hooded and gagged for now."

Jamie chose a leather, full mask, with no eye holes and with a built-in ball gag and slipped it over Isabel's head. Isabel's worried expression was the last they saw of her full face with just her nose and fully plugged mouth now visible. Jamie then selected a large dildo and with a quick swipe along her wet slit to aid entry, slipped it in brusquely with no fuss, deep into Isabel's rather gaping and eager wet entrance. There was a garbled response as the totally constricted and restrained recalcitrant reacted to the less than sensual intrusion.

Jamie paused as, at his nod, Fairy opened up a tube of lubricant.

"You go ahead Fairy, be my guest, anoint her lovely arsehole first then choose a carrot. You can stretch her open with your fingers first if that takes your fancy but then forget the niceties and ram it in her to the root. Take care not to crush the flower. I definitely want to see her flower sprout." Jamie stroked Isabel cheeks as he talked and then moved in to sniff at her rear opening.

"Ah, reminiscent of corn fields after rain, with a touch of lavender scent body lotion, I believe. Very nice. OK, Fairy, in with those fingers now, get her nice and ready for her treat."

Jamie gave each cheek a kiss of appreciation as Isabel started to contract her arsehole in fear of what she could hear was about to happen.

"No, no, sweetheart, relax now, it'll be so much easier if she's invited in rather than having to force the back door open."

He teased his victim as Fairy moved in, fingers covered in lube.

Isabel's body slumped in defeat, knowing full well that any intrusion into her back tunnel was going to be far more acceptable if she didn't resist the invasion. Fairy gentle teased her anus open before sliding in her middle finger to the knuckle, working around inside to smooth the way for the far larger item to follow shortly. One by one, Fairy slipped her fingers in and out, working inside Isabel to prepare her, then, with her thumb firmly inside, she quickly started a thrusting motion before jerking it out, leaving Isabel's most private hole momentarily gaping open. Picking up the carrot, she deftly added additional lube and presented it to the target. Taking note of her master's instruction, she pushed hard, and wedged the carrot part-way into the dark passage before she paused to allow the muscle to relax and accept the intrusion, and then rammed it all the way home, causing a stifled groan of complaint and discomfort from the recipient. At that instance, the door opened and Pres arrived with a headful of hair in each hand as she dragged Jezebel and Sloth into the room to see their friend bucking on the pommel horse, hooded and naked with a large dildo protruding from her fanny and a carrot top apparently blooming from her arsehole.

"Oh shit!" and "What the fuck?" were the less than eloquent responses from the young women, both looking in horror at their friend's disposition.

"Now don't be jealous, ladies, you are going to get your turns.

Right, Fairy, help our new entrants divest themselves of their clothes and then we can get them prepared properly."

Jamie smiled at Jezebel and Sloth who were desperately trying to maintain some kind of air of indifference and composure but their eyes betrayed them.

"Come along, ladies, don't be shy. You've been seeking my attention since I arrived so let's not pretend that you haven't. Arms up, let's have those slut dresses off and you can join in the fun with young Isabel here."

With the presence of Pres and her decidedly icy glare fixed on them, both women allowed Fairy to lift their short dresses up and over their heads. Jamie removed the hooded restraint and gag from Isabel, who greedily sucked in air, blinking rapidly as her eyes adjusted to the light.

"It stays off if you behave. Understand, Isabel?"

"Yes, sir, thank you, my master."

"I don't wish to hear anything further from your mouth, unless I ask you a direct question. Just nod in response."

Isabel nodded in acquiescence as she tried to sneak a look at her two friends before Jamie used her hair to twist her head back round to the front with a warning look that caused her to dip her head in contrition.

"Ok, let's have a look at you two," Jamie said, moving to unfasten both women's bras.

Jezebel's large breasts hung loose now, full and soft, the white freed orbs contrasting starkly to the tanned skin surrounding them. Her nipples were dark and jutted out, set amongst large, lighter pink aureole, and her pride in them was obvious in her stance. Jamie went around behind her and whipped her tiny panties down, kicking off her shoes and leaving her naked before seemingly dismissing her. He had noted, however, the forest of dark pubic hair framing her thick vaginal lips, extending under and up into her bottom crack. Clearly not one to spend time on shaving her pubes, noted Jamie, who moved away from her quickly as he felt a stirring in his loins that her rather entrancing body had clearly affected.

Moving over to Sloth, he gave her breasts a quick glance, much smaller than Jezebel's, with discreet, almost shy-looking, petite nipples, then reached around pulling her panties down and flicking her shoes off. A smaller, slimmer girl, she still boasted well-rounded prominent buttocks that Jamie thought would be a pleasure to spank. Obviously more inclined towards pruning her lady garden, Sloth had a very neat Brazilian landing strip consisting of small curls, her tight cheeks concealing any view of her anal region. Not for long, Jamie smiled to himself.

"Climb on the pommel horses both of you, quickly now, don't dawdle."

The women gave each other a questioning look, Sloth clearly showing that she was looking to Jezebel to give her a lead. Pres put a hand in each of their backs and pushed them forward.

"I don't think that was a request. Move yourselves immediately," she snapped.

"Reap what you sow, reap what you sow," were the words from Jamie that accompanied the two as they advanced. Jezebel stepped forward with a degree of resolution, Sloth a bit more reluctantly dragging her heels behind. Jezebel climbed on, quite blatantly and proudly giving a full display of her pussy and arse cracks, her legs forced apart by the design. She compliantly fell forward and reached her arms and legs down to be harnessed.

"Your servant, sir," Jezebel declared.

Jamie was trying very hard to make sure he looked detached and unaffected by the sight that was now on show but he was truly mesmerised by the luscious-looking pussy lips showing amidst the forest of silky black hair. His eyes couldn't avoid noting the dark valley effect the hairs produced with their bush-like cloistering around her arsehole, an arsehole too enticing to resist as he leaned in to breathe in its aroma.

"A scent of sweat mixed with wet soil," he murmured as he struggled to keep his tongue sneaking out to taste her and his hands from caressing the beautiful symmetrical globes of her full bottom. Jamie realised that the twitching of her arsehole was deliberate and showed that Jezebel was well aware of his enraptured gaze and he immediately regained his self-control.

Switching his attention to the other woman, Jamie could see that she was far more reticent to put herself in such an unprotected position. Partly straddling the pommel horse, she had yet to allow her body to settle completely and was holding her abdomen high. With a quick jerk of one ankle, Jamie caused Sloth to sprawl in an indignant and rather indecent heap on top the horse. He tugged her legs down and pushed her flat with force as Fairy dived underneath to fasten her. Unceremoniously, Jamie put a hand under her groin and positioned her on the lip of the apparatus to part her upper legs and force her bottom into the air.

"Not impressed with your attitude so far, Sloth. You may well be heading towards earning yourself a little extra treat."

Sensing that she was the weak link of the three, Jamie decided to push the point home and test her a bit more publicly.

"I will just have a nose about in your cute looking little slit of an arsehole, I think."

Jamie made sure his nose touched her anal entrance causing the girl to immediately tighten her cheeks, her arsehole sealing right up. A little bit of chiding now might be something she remembered later as an encouragement not to be so slow on the uptake, was Jamie's thinking.

"Oh, don't be shy, soon you'll be welcoming a nice juicy carrot up here. Just checking out that it's a good planting spot. Hmmmmm yes, smells a bit earthy already with a touch of white musk lotion rubbed in there, I do believe. Lovely little arsehole though, Sloth, lovely downy fair hairs and a nice slit of an entrance."

His words were having the desired effect and Sloth had gone bright red in the face but her body had slumped in defeat, her resistance draining away. Her bottom though was tensed all over again as Jamie turned to Fairy saying:

"So, my dear, let's have these two nicely lubricated ready for their dildos and carrots then. Up to you with their fannies; if you want to juice them up naturally yourself, please be my guest. I suspect you can do both at the same time if you so wish."

A very much happier Fairy almost skipped into position between the two raised torsos facing her, and while her left hand dipped straight into the wetness of the already-aroused pussy of Jezebel, her right fingers were gently going to work on the apprehensive Sloth's drier, unaroused lips and clitoris. Within seconds, with some excellent application from Fairy, both women were clearly wet enough without need of artificial lubrication and Jamie stepped forward with the huge dildos and slid them up and down the two sets of labial lips.

"Nip round to the front and get them to lick your fingers nice and clean, Fairy."

A big beam appeared on her face as Jamie continued. "And don't cross your arms to ensure that they are each licking clean the fingers that have been in the other one's juices."

Sloth was now getting into the swing of things as she happily performed the task as requested and sucked Jezebel's internal nectar from the slippery wet fingers of the triumphant-looking Fairy. Both women suddenly baulked and jerked as Jamie pushed the dildos deep into them. Jezebel's pussy made a very wanton sucking slurp noise as she took the sex toy to the hilt, while Sloth, with a smaller channel than Jezebel, had the additional indignity of the dildo being worked in and out, before, with a clear slurping plop, it disappeared leaving only the ring pull showing.

"Nice. Now for the main course and tonight it's carrot pie!" said Jamie with a certain amount of glee as Fairy handed him the first carrot well-lubricated, and moved to Jezebel with her fingers coated and started to open up her arsehole for the vegetable.

"That's it," encouraged Jamie. "Fingers first and then your thumb, pump it in and out to get her nicely prepared. Excellent, well done, that looks about right, nice and slick inside so should make it a smooth entrance for our friend here. In with the carrot, then please."

As Jamie instructed, Fairy slid the carrot fairly effortlessly into Jezebel bottom, meeting little resistance, and in an instance all that remained to be seen of the large carrot was the sprouting green head rudely protruding from the woman's backside. Jamie nodded and Fairy moved to Sloth who was unable to offer the relaxed bottom that her friend had, causing Fairy to exert a fair deal of pressure in working her fingers in the much tighter arsehole.

"Give her your thumb and a good thrusting. We haven't got all day, Sloth, so relax your muscles and help Fairy or this is going to hurt far more than it needs to."

Jamie's threat brooked no argument and Sloth took a deep breath as she clearly willed herself to let her rectum fully relax. As she did so successfully, Fairy's thumb slid straight in and she immediately started to give Sloth's arsehole a pummelling, causing the woman to buck and moan.

"That'll do. Time for her carrot."

As Fairy withdrew her sticky thumb, Jamie slipped the carrot straight in, forcing it past her tight sphincter until it rammed home to the hilt, leaving only the green foliage showing as her anal opening closed up around the carrot top.

"Yuuuuurrrrr!" was Sloth's acknowledgment that the vegetable had breached her resistance and now sat snugly up her back passage.

Jamie noted Sloth's earlier reticence appeared to be leaving her now as she rocked on the horse, seeming to embrace the sensations from the forced intrusions, and certainly did not look to be the shier, reluctant creature of minutes before.

"Right, all secured comfortably? Now, listen up, ladies."

Their attention attracted, Jamie delivered news that they were probably not expecting nor hoping for.

"I am leaving you here for others to deal with while I enjoy taking in the sights and sounds of this wonderful evening."

Pres interrupted. "Pardon me, Porter, but just to let you know that Blaze has arrived and is looking for new blood to use his 'blazer' on."

Jamie had no idea who Blaze was but he could see the fear and unease in all three women's eyes. Meanwhile, Pres had begun laughing at the view facing her. Three attractive but rather ridiculous looking bottoms offered an interesting view. Their owners, with carrot tops protruding and their back tunnels being full of the vegetable, were finding themselves unable to control their arseholes from tightening right up in fear at her words, which had caused the green shoots to wobble absurdly.

Pres explained to Jamie that Blaze was a Dominant Supreme, the ultimate level in their world, which meant most members, let alone submissives, were pretty much in awe of him. She informed him that

Blaze was a powerfully built, six foot six man who dealt only with the Super Subs, at the very top-end of the scale. Blaze was reputed to deliver the fiercest and most ferocious thrashing of any dom known amongst their membership and it was considered the ultimate goal of most subs to take a beating from him. It was fully appreciated that many of his victims had used their safe words during a session with Blaze, which for a Super Sub meant immediate reclassification and loss of their title. To be considered to have failed and been defeated was not, perversely, a badge of honour for a sub. None of Pres's group were Super Subs although Jezebel was close to being considered and Isabel not far off being at the level required.

"Well girls, best behave, because tonight is an open night and Blaze is our guest of honour. He is available, on request from any dominant, to give a "blazing" to basic subs. And guess what, my little sweethearts? As your President and lead dom, I have proprietary rights on you scoundrels on open nights according to our rule book. So any nonsense and Blaze will be asked to give you a no-nonsense fifty-stroke thrashing. Please be advised that I am not sure that any of you little minxes would be able to survive that. Of course, you would always have the opportunity to speak your safe words but we all know that you would then be sent home in disgrace. So, think on, you sluts!"

To her delight, the man of the moment had appeared and Pres made clear her glee as Blaze walked around the three strapped-down women, chuckling.

"Actually, Blaze, since Sloth was asking so politely for a punishment perhaps you could let her taste one stroke, if that's ok with you, Porter?" Pres gave Jamie a questioning look.

"Be my guest, Pres, Blaze."

Blaze shook Jamie's hand in passing and ignored the frantic

babbling of Sloth, desperate in an attempt to retract her earlier words. He wasted no time in drawing back a huge muscular arm and then bringing his crop down ferociously on Sloth's bottom, almost decapitating the carrot top as it landed.

There was a moment of relative quiet, a respectful pause as the room filled with onlookers, now numbering almost thirty. Other guests discreetly joined the throng as word spread as to what was going on, and looked on in something approaching awe at the impact of the fearsome blow which was now apparent. Then Sloth split the air with an agonising and piercing scream.

"Yooooooooowwweeeee! Yaaaaaaaar!" was the approximate noise breaking force from the stricken woman.

There was no simple red stripe forming on her buttocks but an instantaneous fully raised, brutal-looking purple welt, the skin remaining unbroken, but a grisly blister appearing which disfigured the beauty of the young woman's bottom.

Sloth bawled, incoherent and desperately trying to wriggle her rear end to quell the vicious aftermath of the burn.

"If you don't want another one, my dear, then you better pull yourself together."

Jamie showed no compassion as he ignored the tear-stricken woman's beseeching eyes and turned his back on her. Isabel, meanwhile, was stretching her bindings in an attempt to track the movements of the phenomenon that was the legend Blaze standing just a few feet away.

"Oh, if you are trying to attract Blaze's attention then I'll assume that's because you're jealous of the attention he's paying to Sloth, shall I?" Jamie taunted her.

"No sir, please no. I am sorry, sir." She quickly resumed her submissive position, her tightened buttocks rather signalling that she was aware of the danger that she had now attracted.

"Is she nicely secured, Porter?" queried Pres. "Because I think she does need to have a taste. That look was rather wanton and naughty and I bet she really would not want her and Jezebel to miss out. What do you think? In fact I think they should have a proper taste, three each and two more for Sloth. Let's not waste the opportunity to impress this trio. Mercy is not a word I want attached to my reputation going forward."

Jamie glanced at Blaze who raised both eyebrows back as all three sealed their fates by starting a cacophony of objections.

"Ah, they seem to be illustrating a need to remind them how to behave."

A grin from Jamie and the words stuck in their throats as, within the space of seconds, Blaze had stepped forward and brought his crop down hard and harsh on the three sets of rounded buttocks with the expected result. As virtually everyone gathered around grimaced, Blaze attracting a throng of followers, the air was again rent with banshee-like howls as Isabel and Jezebel joined Sloth in her agony. It was only three strokes each but the effect was as if they had been on the end of a long and serious flogging. Once more, the roomful of watchers crowded close to watch as the white skins of their proudly protruding buttocks were split asunder with long ridges of ferocious looking, purple mottled welts. Sloth and Isabel's screeching reactions lasted way beyond Jezebel's, who had controlled herself down to just whimpering, before eventually calming to a more monotonous keening.

"Pull the door right back now. Let's share their shame with anyone who wants to see," Jamie suggested, and eager hands pulled the concertina-style doors open.

The main room was now packed as the night had reached full

swing, and immediately the doors opened, the audience numbers swelled. The lights had gone low although there were many spotlighted areas where various scenarios were being played out, the occasional scream of joy or anguish filling the air alongside the sounds of an assortment of implements meeting flesh mixed with the unmistakeable sounds of sexual congress as some of the doms were openly claiming their spoils from their subs and slaves.

"My work here is done for the time being," Jamie teased the three stricken subs. "Be good girls and I'll be back later to check on you." He ran his fingers along their blazing welts, all three women flinching at his touch.

Jamie went round to the heads of the apparatus and, to a scowl from Fairy following in his footsteps, gave each woman a kiss on the lips.

"Not tonight ladies, but maybe one day," were his parting words as he led Fairy from the room to nods and winks of appreciation from the gathering.

"They are to be touched, probed and fingered by anyone who wishes but not to be fucked or beaten," Jamie instructed clearly and loudly to further looks of dismay from the three women. "Any dissent from the three of them to be noted please. It will be dealt with later." A nod to Pres and he walked away.

"Please don't for one moment think that I did not clock your sulky little face just then, Fairy. Do you remember what I said would happen if you showed such contemptable and disobedient behaviour again?"

Fairy stiffened; she remembered his earlier words of warning only too well.

"Oh sorry, master, Fairy didn't mean to show any such thing sir and is really sorry if master thinks she was showing disrespect. Fairy is only keen to have her chance to show master what a good girl she can be."

"Did I not just ask you a simple and straightforward question?" Jamie faked a very angry tone, trying to hide his actual amusement at the panic that was showing on Fairy's face as she tried desperately, and rather incompetently, to get herself out of the hole she had dug.

"Oh, sir, master, yes sir, sorry sir." Fairy was starting to burble now, sensing that her fate was sealed but still not taking the bait.

"You will now be quiet until I ask you further questions. Over there to the wall where Switch is chatting to the Professor." Jamie directed her across the room.

"Gentlemen," he announced to the two men who quickly acknowledged that Jamie's demeanour might mean that an opportunity had arisen for them!

"Despite previous warnings, this wilful child continues to repeat the same error over and over again. The punishment promised for continuing with this behaviour is a six-stroke cat whipping from me and a thrashing of choice from another member. I am just going to book out the cat. Could I interest you gentlemen in selecting an item to assist me in dealing with her? I think we can expand the punishment to both of you being given the pleasure."

Fairy was now trembling all over. He had indeed promised and threatened what he proposed and knowing full well that Fairy had a bit of an aversion to public beatings, he was aware that she was truly terrified. She could not argue that her transgression was not deserving of such harsh treatment as that right of contest was not available to a submissive. Jamie could see that she was very cross with herself for letting this happen but there was an acceptance that she had basically caused her own downfall and he appreciated that she was trying to gird her loins for the undoubted thrashings that were going to come shortly.

"The paddle for me, please, Porter. Just a leather one as it is still quite early in the night and I am sure you have a lot more fun lined up for this bottom. Don't want her too bruised for you later, eh?" said the Professor, now moving Fairy over to an alcove of the room with vacant seats and sofas. "I'll have a moment to inspect her lovely bottom while you fetch the equipment. I've not had the pleasure of this one before. Come with me, girl. You don't mind if I have a minute, Porter?"

The Professor's huge fist wrapped around her arm and Jamie nodded his agreement, as he rather propelled her towards an armchair. Stopping by the wall he flicked a switch and the cosy area became bathed in light.

Swish followed, pondering aloud. "Yes, fair enough, let's not ruin her for later. I'll give her a slippering; it's been a while since I've done the naughty girl across my knees routine. Think yourself lucky, girl, I am called Swish for a reason and so you are getting off lightly by the looks of things."

Fairy distinctly did not feel lucky in the slightest, as her 'owner' Jamie went across to book out the three weapons of torture that she was now going to have to endure after having her legs spread wide by the infamous Professor. He was now unceremoniously pulling her bum cheeks apart and sniffing at her arsehole and pussy!

"Oh lovely, lovely. A nice scent of grimy sweat with a smoky pungency, quite alluring. Pussy lips a tad moist so not too worked up about getting paddled, slippered and whipped then, my dear?"

Fairy made a small murmur, desperate not to offend this large old man groping her private parts, and was fortunate that the Professor decided that this was an acceptable response in the circumstances. Fairy would be well aware of the importance of the Professor in the organisation and knew of his reputation for merciless beatings and intolerance of any misbehaviour. Her ability to relax and stay silent was tested as his large fingers slid over her arsehole and down to her pussy lips, then back up again. The display was now no longer in any way discreet as an audience gathered, attracted by the increased lighting, a known code that something was about to take place for the members' perusal and pleasure.

Jamie returned and handed the paddle over to the Professor, who slapped it against his hand then swiped it through the air a couple of times before laying it on her back.

"On second thoughts, open up, my dear, I have had a rethink. You can hold this in your mouth while I warm up your lovely buttocks and my arm with a little old-fashioned hand-spanking."

Fairy looked happy to accept the leather weapon in her mouth just to put off the moment it would begin to land on her backside. Her longing to be thrashed by Jamie and be alone with him to do whatever he wished was going to be sorely tested by being beaten in front of a leering group of co-members. The disquiet on her face as she peeked up at Jamie, giving away unhappiness at her current situation, was quickly replaced by a look of shock and pain as the Professor landed an almighty spank flush on her right buttock before following up likewise on her left.

Jamie grinned at Fairy's reaction and suspected that she was in a long line of females who had not taken seriously the threat that this pompous and proper old gentleman carried. If Fairy had ever felt a hand spank that had caused her more pain, he would be surprised. The realisation that she had severely underestimated the strength and power of her tormentor was so apparent to the watching, enthralled crowd. Within seconds, Stones had landed a dozen spanks on her now brightly glowing bottom and she was unreservedly keening loudly in anguish. She barely noticed the Professor slip the paddle from her lips but she certainly became aware when it was lashed down on her right cheek for six fast, consecutive slaps! The Professor paused to study the result of his work, gently stroking her buttocks as the audience, which had grown to be around fifty in number, watched on with awe at the man's power, timing and accuracy. The next six strokes landed on top of each other on her left cheek as he held her gyrating body with his left arm to still the target. With one motion as the sixth stroke landed, he flipped her body so that her arm and head were now on the floor and her legs straddled his waist, her bottom laid in perfect position on his lap as he began to mould the blazing cheeks with both hands.

"There, there, my dear, all done. That's my part over; I'll just rub away the first waves of pain for you and then I'll pass you on for you to enjoy the slipper from my friend here."

His fingers were everywhere he was sure that she would rather they not be, as he combined his massage with fingers flicking down to stroke her pussy and tickle her arsehole, his fingertip rubbing lightly round and round, threatening to probe into her dark entrance.

"I do love a nice hairy anus, I must say. All those lovely black tight curls. Lovely, lovely."

His fingers twisting and pulling at her intimately and then suddenly wrenching her buttocks wide apart.

"Do look closely, my friends. Fairy has an anus to be proud of. Please come closer to have a good look, one and all."

The professor lived up to his reputation as Fairy put her face in her hands in horror as about thirty or so people moved in close and peered at her opened cleft and fully exposed arsehole. Stones held her a moment then pushed her off onto the floor at his feet and prodded her throbbing bottom with his foot, pushing her towards Swish.

A ripple of applause broke out as the gathering appreciated the humiliation of Fairy as much as the sound beating.

"Well, well," said Swish. "I am not sure if I should have gone second. What can I do to match that I wonder? Right, well never say die. I'll give it a go. Bend over and touch your toes, Little Miss Prissy. Let's see if you can take a proper gym shoe walloping."

A thoroughly chastened Fairy did as instructed. The gym shoe beating was once a popular role play scenario, based around misbehaving students being punished by their gym master in front of the rest of the class. Interestingly, it was one of those punishments much favoured by male submissives rather than females but it certainly was a situation that suited a punishment in front of an audience so Fairy at least understood his call, even if she was dreading the reality of what was to follow.

"Usual rules, keep your hands wrapped around your ankles, knees straight for each stroke, five seconds recovery time. Then you will count the stroke, thank me for it and ask for the next one. Do you understand?"

"Oh, Mr Swish, sir, please sir, I fully understand and ask that you please give me my deserved slippering on my naughty, naughty bottom, sir."

Jamie could see that Fairy was looking through her legs and had spotted Swish's obvious erection bulging in his tight shorts and the smile on her lips at her small victory.

As the slipper flew through the air, Fairy took a deep breath and then exhaled with a *whoosh* in a manner that suggested a much-practised strategy for handling a beating. A small cry escaped her lips, but she stayed in place and clearly announced, "One sir, thank you. May I have another one now please, sir."

There was a murmur of approval amongst the watching ranks.

Whilst everyone appreciated a good spanker and deliverer, there was no greater accolade reserved than that for the spankee who took a beating uncomplaining and with dignity and honour.

The second swipe landed lower and caused Fairy to suck her breath straight back in to stifle the screams that she knew would come but she fully displayed the importance for her as a sub to illustrate that she could take punishment without going all 'drama queen' about it.

"Two, sir, thank you, sir. May I have another one now please, sir?"

The third blow landing above centre and solidly on her right cheek caught her more unawares but she leaned rather than stumbled and was able to absorb the sting without fuss.

"Three, sir, thank you, sir. May I please have another one, sir?"

The fourth one landed as she would have expected, high on her left buttock, and she took it without complaint as she did with the next two when Swish went right, then left, either side of her crack. The seventh landed on her upper right leg, causing Fairy to produce a small squeal as the stinging burnt badly on that sensitive area, but managed to voice her thanks and request another, which predictably landed on the upper left leg. Fairy struggled to stay composed and for the first time her voice faltered and lacked its earlier confidence.

"Oh sir, eight, sir. Thank you, sir, oh sir. Um, can I have another one, please sir, thank you sir."

The next two were 'up and unders' as Swish aimed down and then up to catch her lower arse cheeks, both times raising Fairy onto her tiptoes, but she held firm and carried on with the count mantra. Desperately wanting to show his prowess with the gym shoe, it was obvious to the audience that Swish put a lot of effort into his next blow as he slammed the shoe down high across the centre of her bottom. He got his reward as Fairy stumbled forward crying out,

"Yaaaaar! Ooooh! Fuck it! Oooh shit!" But she gathered herself in seconds and, resuming her deferential position, she called out far louder than previously. "Eleven, sir. Thank you, sir. Fairy apologises for her foul language and weakness in taking punishment, sir, and requests that she receives another very hard smack, sir, to teach her a lesson please, sir."

This earned her a smattering of applause and a smile from both Swish and the Professor. Jamie was surprised at how proud of her he felt in that moment and the thought of enjoying that body was becoming quite something he was eager to get on with.

Swish repeated the blow, accurately hitting the same spot, and Fairy wailed loudly, her legs trembling as she struggled to keep some composure.

"Ooooh, sir. Fairy says thank you very much sir, for that punishment stroke, sir. I am ready for my final stroke now, sir, please."

Splat! The final blow was aimed at the same spot once more as Swish sadistically went for the most painful blow he could muster. Fairy's knees buckled and she went halfway down to her knees before putting out her hands. The scream was contained although the tears could not be held back any longer and she wept copiously as she strived to return to position and retain some composure. Taking a deep breath, she was able to get the waited-for words out.

"Twelve, sir. Thank you, sir, thank you so much for my punishment, sir, and Fairy would like to offer herself still, sir, if you wish to beat her further, sir."

"Good girl, Fairy. That will suffice. Thank you for taking your punishment in the correct and approved manner." Swish withdrew, thanking Jamie for the opportunity and acknowledging the stoicism of the beaten sub.

"Well, young lady," said Jamie, the dreaded knotted cat-o-nine-tails dangling from his hand. "I think I'll leave this for later as you have behaved so well for Swish and the Professor. I've got things to do down here for an hour or so but I think you can go back to the room and take a nice bath to prepare yourself and recover fully. Let's book out what we need now and you can take them back and lay them on the bed ready and waiting for me."

He walked Fairy over to the selection of implements. "We're keeping the cat. I'll have a nice thick strap and a medium cane, please. Along with some leg and ankle cuffs, a gag, a blindfold and a double-headed vibrator. Anything specific you would like, my dear?" Jamie placed his order and allowed Fairy her chance to show preference for the activities ahead.

"Oh no, Master, unless Fairy can get something for the master's pleasure. She touched the selection of cock rings and butt plugs, and smiled rather demurely at Jamie.

"Well, thank you, Fairy. Choose a cock ring and a butt plug. I'm sure there's condoms and lube in the room, so I think we have what we need."

Jamie pulled Fairy towards him and for the first time kissed her directly on the lips, his hands sliding down and round to stroke her very hot bottom. Fairy found herself reacting automatically and slipped her tongue without hesitation into his mouth with quite a fiery passion, shocking herself with her own sudden lust. She pulled back quickly.

"Sorry master, Fairy was perhaps acting like the disrespectful harlot she is. I beg the master's forgiveness if I was far too forward, sir."

"No Fairy, I enjoyed that little display of passion," Jamie responded, his erection now hard as he ran his finger in the smooth skin at the top of her bottom crack, tantalisingly stopping short of her arsehole as he ran his fingertip up and down the silky skinned valley. Fairy squirmed; that she wanted him alone and that she was fighting the urge to cling on to him and rub her naked body up against his obvious hardness was not to be doubted.

"Take these back and have your bath, then prepare me one and I'll be joining you in an hour or so," he said, as he gently slapped her bottom and sent her on her way.

CHAPTER 3

FAIRY GETS HER PRIZE (AT LAST!)

Jamie spent the next thirty minutes or so exploring the room, chatting with the Professor and Pres, and watching some of the activity taking place. The atmosphere was now positively steamy and those dancing were now into smooch mode whilst the alcoves and private rooms were mostly full, with the sounds of punishment rituals and sexual exertion very apparent. Jamie was quite entertained standing and watching as Silo the slave was caned, straddled over a pommel horse, and then fucked hard and fast up his butt by a feisty dominatrix wearing a two-person strap-on, the dom clearly a master of the vaginal muscle control required to perform her task in the expert manner she was achieving. Both of them had what he estimated to be thick nine inch rods, that made Jamie wonder at the stretching ability of the body's orifice to take such giant intrusions. Just before Silo came, his mistress bent down and twisted around him in an impressive feat of contortion to encompass his straining cock into her mouth in time to slurp down his ejaculation. With his come dribbling down her chin, she swung back again in triumph to a round of applause that made Jamie realise that this was a well-practised exhibition from an expert at her art. With a sudden increase in her violent thrusting, and with her body now rammed hard up against his backside, she strived for her own climax, clearly without thought for the now yelling Silo, as, being spent, his libido satisfied and his cock visibly wilting, the force of her thrusting, in his sensitive portal, had become hard to bear. Luckily for him, his vicious reaming was soon over as she clawed at his back, causing deep scratches and bit down hard on his shoulder, teeth marks clearly visible, before coming dramatically and noisily. As her excitement subsided, she slipped off the strap-on and just walked away, leaving him straddled with the rubber cock stuck fast in his backside. Jamie could see him straining his rectal muscles as he tried to work it back out of the depths, unable to use his handcuffed hands, to jeering and catcalls from the watchers. Eventually, to a loud cheer, the huge rubber cock dropped out of his arsehole and fell to the floor beneath him, leaving the audience to witness the spasms of his anal opening as it recovered from its ordeal.

A turntable flogging, a spit-roasting and a gang-bang of a slave by a group of six of mixed genders were the next three scenarios that he stopped to watch, fascinated at this pure abandon and freedom of sexuality that had been opened up to him. His final port of call in the main room that night was to return to the room where he hoped to see Jezebel, Isobel and Sloth still suffering and maybe just learning a lesson. Jamie had enjoyment their fascination with him since joining the club and was grateful for the tutoring by the Professor and Pres that had meant that he had been well able to deal with their little games and play acts, but it also made him determined to best them and teach them a lesson. They were subs after all, and any evaluation he made should take that into account. He mulled over the situation as he ambled up to where they were still strapped down rather ungallantly to the pommel horses. Yes, he determined, they were indeed subs and therefore out of order in their little game of pursuit with him. He had toyed with the idea of entertaining them the next day but now felt that would be too much like a reward and decided he would continue to play tough and out-of-reach.

"Evening ladies, although that's a bit of a misnomer isn't it? I see that you've all been good girls and done wee wees."

Looking down, Jamie could see that all three had at least half-filled the containers beneath them, and moving round to face them was delighted to see all three with dropped heads looking quite subdued and chastened. As reasonably experienced attendees at these functions, all three would have been well-versed in the fascination by the BDMS members in watching the degradation of submissives in this manner. Rarely allowed to use the toilet facilities without permission, usually denied, the women would have been well aware of the sexual gratification achieved by many of the more dominant members by the reluctant but unavoidable emptying of their bladders. He was glad to have missed it: the sight of the three urinating was not something that he yearned to witness but was happy to accept its appeal to others. He reached underneath and one by one pulled the dildos from their pussies, each girl undergoing their own reaction, Isabel's pussy belching in a very unladylike manner, Jezebel's slurping as it closed quickly and Sloth's dribbling body fluids and gaping quite open for several seconds after the removal.

"Charming, I'm sure. Now what's next? Do you each want to drink your own piss or would you prefer to swap?"

Jamie kept his face totally serious as he teased the women and was rewarded with absolute gasps of horror, and poor Sloth looking as though she was about to throw up her earlier dinner.

"Please, no, sir, that would be horrid sir, can we please not do that, sir?" Jezebel being the most street-wise was probably first to realise that it was in all probability a wind-up but was bright enough to know the best way to respond.

"Just my little joke, bit like the threat of the nettles…or *was* I joking? Maybe, ladies, there is a lesson to be learnt here about how far you push your luck, don't you think?"

Jezebel's look of resignation clearly showed that she did; Isabel just looked thoroughly fed-up and quite defeated, whilst Sloth looked confused, scared and desperate to escape any further punishment or humiliation.

"We'll have these carrots out of your arseholes now, shall we? Let me see if I can get them out with my teeth." Jamie winked at them and moved around to their protruding rears.

He smiled to see their ridiculous-looking bottoms; the carrot heads had wilted badly and clearly had not suffered from minor dips into the potties.

"Oh dear, I think the carrots have got a bit wee-stained so I won't be going near them with my mouth. Let's have you unbuckled first and then we can have a think about whose mouth is going to go where."

With the three unbound and standing uncomfortably in front of him, Jamie decided their fate.

"Sloth, turn around and bend over." As Sloth reluctantly obeyed, Jamie gestured to Jezebel to come round behind her. "Bend over and place your mouth over her arsehole. Isabel! You come and do the same to Jezebel."

While the women arranged themselves as instructed, Jamie went behind Isabel and grabbed her carrot head.

"Right, you two, seal your mouths around the carrot heads and one, two, three pull!"

Sloth had it easy with just the carrot being yanked out of her bottom. For Isabel and Jezebel, trying to concentrate on the task in hand whilst feeling either a mouth or, in Isabel's case, Jamie's fingers, pulling intimately at their own backsides, it was a tougher call which they both managed successfully to a smattering of applause from their onlookers; Jamie had attracted a sizeable following due to his fresh approach which added a high degree of interest. Discarding the carrots, Jamie pointed at the potties.

"Now ladies, your march of shame to empty the potties, if you please. I will expect them washed out, dried and returned to the assistants in quick time. You must clean up your own filth, you dirty little scallywags."

Jamie watched as the threesome took on board what he had said, aware that the watching crowd was spreading the word and a guard of honour was starting to form. Jezebel was the first to react, and knowing that there was no alternative she bent gracefully and carefully lifted her potty.

"Come on girls, follow me, heads high. Good submissives proud to do their master's bidding."

The other two automatically followed suit and, with a nod of assent from Jamie, Jezebel led the trio in single file slowly and with a certain amount of dignity and nods of approval from those nearest. Holding their potties, they proceeded out of the smaller room and went into the main body of the room as the ever-growing crowd of watchers began to rhythmically clap their parade through the gangway created.

The Professor moved across to speak to Jamie.

"Excellent Porter, another job well done. I think we may have some interesting and entertaining times ahead, young man."

Jamie smiled to himself. None of this had come without quite a lot of thought and effort to keep his wits about him, but quite a lot had come instinctively and he was pretty self-satisfied with his performance. Now, he thought, it's time to escape from the spotlight and have a bit of private time with his prize for the rest of the night.

So he bade his farewells to those around and made his way back to his room and to the company of Fairy.

On entering his room, he was greeted by the site of Fairy, standing naked, hands on head in the corner of the room facing the wall. He picked up the telephone and rang down to room service. Ordering a bottle of New Zealand Sauvignon Blanc and two glasses, he requested that the drinks be brought directly into the room as he would be indisposed and unable to answer. He saw Fairy stiffen as she overheard the request, but she remained silent.

"I'll be in the bath which I see you have run for me as requested, thank you Fairy. When room service has left, you may bring me a glass of wine, and yourself one, and then you can give me a thorough wash. I presume you know how to wash a man properly?"

"Yes sir, of course, sir. It will be Fairy's honour and duty to do so sir, to your satisfaction."

Jamie stripped his clothes off, and leaving the door ajar, relieved himself noisily.

"Oh Fairy, I've got a drip left on the end of my cock. Please come and wipe it off."

Fairy immediately obeyed, and carefully using a tissue, dabbed very gently at Jamie's cock, and then flushed the toilet for him, before returning to her former position against the wall. Jamie stepped into the bath and settled himself and a few minutes later he heard a knock on the main door before it was clearly unlocked from outside and then followed the sound of a tray of drinks being delivered. As the door closed, he could hear Fairy scuttle over to serve the drinks and a few seconds later she came into the bathroom with two glasses in her hand. While Jamie sipped his wine, Fairy lifted his feet from the bath one by one and soaped them. Jamie leaned back and raised his legs allowing Fairy to soap all the way up to his thighs before washing them down with a sponge and flannel. As Jamie shuffled himself forward she began to soap his shoulders back, chest and stomach before rinsing him off.

"Fairy hopes she is satisfying Master and would like Master to choose whatever position he would prefer so that Fairy could have the honour of washing his private areas please, sir."

Jamie moved onto his hands and knees, bringing his groin and bottom clear of the water. Fairy immediately leaned into the bathe to begin delicately soaping his cock and balls, licking her lips quite provocatively as she finally laid her hands on his thick throbbing erection.

"You're a little while off having any further contact with that, so don't start getting carried away with your dirty thoughts and sluttish behaviour," he warned her, whilst the evidence of his hardness rather belied the state of indifference that his words portrayed.

"No sir, sorry sir, Fairy is a very naughty girl, sir, and knows that the Master will do what he can to make her behave less like a strumpet and a harlot in the future, sir."

Jamie reared up to allow her better access to his balls and she lovingly soaped and rinsed them off. "If Master could now lean right forward and push his beautiful bottom back and up, then Fairy will do her extra special best to give Master a special Fairy bottom bath, sir."

Jamie followed her request, dropping his elbows down to the bath floor and raising his flanks and parting his legs to allow her full access within the limitations of the reasonably spacious bath.

"Oh sir, it is an honour for Fairy to see and feel your beautiful bottom, sir."

Then Fairy seemed to lose herself in the moment as no further words were spoken for a while as she soaped and massaged his cheeks, delving with her fingers into his crack and caressing his anus. Again and again her hands expertly swept round, lightly touching and massaging him. He sighed in total pleasure as she began tentatively to probe a soapy finger at the entrance to his arse, circling a finger round and round, causing Jamie to fully relax, at which point she slid a finger fully into him. Using no noticeable pressure, she allowed her digit to stay almost motionless inside of him as he automatically used his muscles to try to pull her finger deeper. Fairy then started to twist and rotate her finger simultaneously, cleaning and caressing to drive his state of desire higher. Then, choosing the moment to perfection, she commenced a solicitous pumping, her finger slightly pulling out before driving deeper and deeper into his arsehole. As her other hand wrapped around his twitching cock, Jamie started to worry that he would be taken to orgasm far earlier than he wished.

"I think that's about as much of that as I need, thank you, Fairy."

She slipped her finger out and released his cock causing Jamie to groan involuntary.

"If Master would like to lie back now, Fairy will just swill him out a bit more to finish off."

Jamie felt almost beguiled by her voice as he relaxed and laid down in the water. Her undoubted expertise with her fingers had illustrated a woman with well-honed skills and Jamie, very prone to anal pleasure, now felt at her disposal. Fairy's fingers fluttered once more around his anal ring, before sliding her fingers and palm of her hand under his bottom and inserting the tip of her forefinger just inside his arsehole. Creating a vacuum with her cupped fingers, she started to piston water into his back passage in a plunging motion. Her fingers gripped and nipped into his buttocks to hold him, as, with her administrations, Jamie could feel his arsehole involuntarily opening and closing and was aware that water was being pumped into his rectum, then draining out as she cleared the soap residue created earlier from his dark tunnel. His eyes closed and he found himself swooning under her administrations as her fingers played like magic wands around his willing arsehole, his erection twitching constantly in his arousal.

"Fairy is finished cleaning Master now, sir. May Fairy give Master a kiss now please?"

Jamie looked into this little magician's eyes with total longing and admiration, his role as dominant being lost and forgotten in the moment as he took the gorgeous woman's head in his hands and kissed her lovingly and with such longing.

"Fairy will dry the master down now." She pulled away from the clinch and picked up a bath towel as Jamie snapped out of his reverie and stood up, his cock rampant and throbbing proudly.

She was very gentle as she towelled him down, stroking his cock lightly before bending him over and parting his cheeks to dab at his wet arse.

"Fairy is hoping Master will let Fairy show him how she uses her tongue and lips to give pleasure, sir."

"Fairy needs to remember that she is due a damn good beating and she better take herself over to the wall and get into the position for waiting for punishment." Jamie rebuked her as he snapped himself out of his sexual daze and remembered their positions in this role play.

Fairy bowed her head with a smile that barely touched her lips and immediately returned to her sub position against the wall, hands on head. Jamie took the glasses of wine through and placed them by the bed, topping up his own glass before settling himself in a sitting position, pillows bunched up behind him, duvet pushed clear off the bed.

"Fairy, bring me the cat, the cane and the strap and then lay down over my knees." Jamie decided that if they were going to have sex it would be when her arse had experienced what she had been surely been expecting when she had entered the raffle to win this evening's little meeting.

Fairy came across with the implements in her hand which she laid down on the bed, before prostrating herself as Jamie directed, her cheeks presented in place for a beating.

"Open your legs please, my dear. I do love to see an arsehole working away while I am spanking."

He slid a fingertip over her anal slit, her arsehole opening for him in response. Slipping his fingers down to the hairy pussy beneath he was delighted to feel the slickness of her lips.

"You've been a very naughty girl, Fairy. I have been left with no alternative but to beat you thoroughly."

Fairy's bottom had been perfectly unmarked when he had first seen her naked and his eyes feasted on it while carefully checking to see if there were any signs of old bruising. There were no tell-tale signs amongst the pink flush still present from earlier, and he surmised that she hadn't had a thorough thrashing for a while. She stilled herself before him and Jamie became sensed that she was desperate for the beating to begin. He did not make her wait long and began to spank her, from left to right in a fast rhythm, her cheeks soon turning from pink to red under his hard and fast assault. She began to breathe harder and faster, and was clearly struggling to remain in place, as she fought the stinging of the hand he was ferociously laying on her behind.

Jamie sensed the moment she became torn between wanting him to stop to give her respite and her desire to be totally mastered by him. She grabbed the bed sheet as hard as she could and then bit down on a knuckle. Jamie could feel her wriggling and rocking herself against his cock beneath her and he allowed her to position her mound to rub against it, the hardness of his cock matching the hardness of her clitoral bud. Jamie continued to rain blows down on her scarlet cheeks, determined to raise a verbal reaction before he changed tack. He was confident that he had both the stamina and the strength to make her yield and lose control, and he fully intended to persist with the spanking until she was begging him to cease. He subtly altered position, his cock now nesting amongst her wet pussy folds and exposing her sensitive upper legs and lower buttock cheeks to a new avalanche of smacks. Fairy whimpered, but it sounded half in passion and half in pain, over two hundred blows had landed and Jamie continued pummelling the bright red cheeks as he sought his triumph and conquest of her. Eventually with a rapid cascade of blows on the very top of her buttocks, her control went.

"Yuuuur! Ooooooo! Yuuuuur! Yaaaaar! Oooowwww, ow, ow!"

At last she began to cry and protest, her writhing body giving evidence of her effort to avoid the blows. Which, Jamie thought, was just as well as his hand was stinging ferociously so he could not imagine how much her bottom must be burning. He fired off another ten smacks on each cheek alternatively, which, he was glad to see, made her start to buck and twist quite violently as well as drawing small squeals from her reluctant mouth.

Jamie couldn't resist stroking the gorgeous arse cheeks as she rotated them to ease her suffering. One hand slipped down and she immediately lifted up to accommodate his fingers as they slipped along her juice-laden pussy. His middle finger searched out her clitoris and he began to rub it lightly whilst his forefinger was almost sucked inside of her as he probed through the wet folds.

"Nnnnnggggggah!" was the approximate response from Fairy as

91

she began to almost hump his hand.

"Yes, yes, fucking yes, yes, yes! Yowseeeeeeee!"

Jamie held her firmly as she began to buck in orgasm. He was enjoying her pleasure but knew that he needed now to reassert his authority and bring her down from her sexual high.

"Oh dear, Fairy, how naughty. I don't recall you asking permission to come all over my hand!"

"Oh, sir, no sir, but thank you sir, it was wonderful, oh sir, I am sorry, Master."

"You don't really sound sorry enough to me, you disobedient and impudent little hussy. Now lick my fingers clean and then I want you lying face down on the bed while I give you a bloody good strapping. Having a grubby little climax without your Master's permission is outrageous. I will not stand for such a thing!"

Fairy finally sensed the change of atmosphere and quickly spun round to suck his fingers, desperately trying to clean her own juices off as quickly as possible.

Jamie pushed her off him and slipped into the bathroom to wash his hands. In truth, he didn't mind but during the role play he was determined to stay completely in character and ensure that this sub would report back that she had met the person that could truly dominate her completely without brooking argument or distraction.

He returned to the bed and, grabbing some of the pillows, hoisted her with one hand and squeezed them under her torso, raising her flanks and exposing her pussy as well as presenting her rounded bottom to meet his needs.

"Master, Fairy is sorry to have earned your displeasure so and Fairy is ready to be beaten to teach her a lesson sir. Please strap me hard, sir, to cure my wilful and naughty behaviour." Fairy reacted submissively, having seen Jamie pick up the strap, and bowed her head to the mattress in submission.

"Certainly I will accept your request and apology. Hold still now while I beat the naughtiness from you." Jamie matched her tone as they played to perfection their respective roles and raised the strap high before bringing the first lash down across her shoulders, catching her unawares as her buttocks visibly clenched in expectation of the strap landing there. The next two strokes landed on her upper back, followed by powerful lashes to the backs of her calves, behind her knees and her upper legs. By now Fairy was wailing into the mattress and her hands had a vice-like grip on the headboard as she struggled to stay in place and not turn away from the wicked burn and torment of the strap.

Finally to Fairy's relief, albeit a painful experience, the strap landed flush across the top of her buttocks. Thwack! Thwack! Thwack! Three further harsh and quickly delivered strokes jolted Fairy's bottom, making her jerk and kick, as she continued to mew and bawl into the bed.

Jamie aimed the next four strokes to land on top of the others as her buttocks turned from red through scarlet to purple. As the final stroke landed, the thrashed girl rendered an almighty scream, causing Jamie to appreciate the need to have such a discreet location for this absolutely frenzied night of sex and passion of such a sado-masochistic nature.

Allowing her a few moments to collect herself, Jamie rummaged through the bedside drawer until he found what he was looking for: cuffs, nipple clamps and a small lipstick-shaped vibrator. Tossing the sobbing and subdued woman over onto her back, he sucked hard on each nipple in turn, pinched them erect and nipped each one with the clamps, causing Fairy to buck her body and screw her eyes tight shut. Jamie reached up and stretched her arms to cuff her wrists to the headboard. Sliding down her body, he dropped his head to her welcoming wet pussy and licked the length of her sex.

Fairy moaned and pushed her mound up to meet his mouth and he greedily slurped at her soaking wet quim. Opening the vibrator, he switched it on and ran the powerful little juddering point along her lips to nestle against her pulsating, erect little clitoris. He slipped his thumb into her soaking pussy and felt her vaginal muscles tighten around it, almost sucking it further inside of her. As he wedged the vibrator hard against her clit, he felt her brace herself as he used the juices dribbling out of her pussy to moisten a finger, which he ran around her anal ring, her arsehole opening eagerly, offering little resistance to the suggested intrusion.

Fairy continued to moan and writhe under his manipulation, rattling the headboard as she pulled on the cuffs, her head shaking from side to side as he increased the friction with his thumb inside of her. He slipped the finger into her unresisting arsehole and fluttered his fingertip deftly inside the dark orifice where he could feel her rectal muscles squeezing his finger and then relaxing so that it lodged ever deeper in her arse.

"Shit, fuck, bullocks, I'm coming, I'm coming. Fuck! Fuck! Fuck! Oh yes, Oh yes. Here we go, fuck! Fuck! Aaaaarrrrggggghhhhhhhhhh! Yes please, Master, yes. Yes! Yes! Fucking Yes! Fucking, fuck!" Jamie allowed her climax to begin then slipped his thumb out of her pussy and eased his finger out of the tighter rear hole.

"Oh dear, yet again you have come without asking permission. This is not acceptable behaviour for a sub and I will not put up with such a shoddy performance and clear lack of respect for my authority. You are just a selfish, greedy little slut, wilfully disobeying instructions and patently in need of a most severe thrashing to try and bring you up to the standards I require from my submissives. I obviously have not beaten you anywhere near hard enough to earn obedience from you and I will put that right."

Fairy gulped and even in the blissful after-throes of a sensational orgasm she recognised that she had transgressed after being given fair warning. She took a breath.

"Master, Fairy has indeed been a thoroughly disobedient servant and apologises deeply to sir, especially as she was given a warning and a beating to warn me of acting without permission. Master, Fairy's only excuse is that Master is such a good lover to Fairy that she finds it very difficult not to be so sexually aroused by such wonderful and skilful attention, sir. But Fairy knows she is bad, sir, so Fairy will be very happy for Master to punish her severely to help make her a better servant, sir. Oh, I am so sorry, Master, please forgive Fairy."

Her voice trembled as she spoke and Jamie could see the doubt and fear in her eyes as he unbuckled her and pulled her grovelling to her feet.

"Nice try, fine words. Won't do you any good though, Fairy, as I've heard it all before. Actions speak louder than words and now you will learn what the word repercussion means. Bend over, legs wide apart, hands on ankles, do not move!"

Jamie now had the cane in one hand and the knotted cat-o-nine-tails in the other. Her beaten flanks were clearly marked from earlier and he knew further harsh strokes were not only going to cause her a high level of pain but the longer term soreness and bruising would also serve to remind her of this moment for many days to come.

Thwack! He whipped the cane down hard and true, landing low on her cheeks and forcing her up on her toes and a sharp intake of breath.

"Good girl, take your punishment properly and you will be rewarded with the honour of taking my cock in your very lucky mouth and then your ravenous cunt. But you will not be having any more orgasms until you have paid your dues and requested permission. Do…" Thwack! "You…" Thwack! "Understand?" Thwack! Thwack! Thwack! Thwack! Thwack! Thwack! Thwack! Thwack!

Ten vicious strokes had landed now, covering Fairy's bottom with additional fierce red angry lines. Fairy was openly wailing, tears running down her face, the speed and strength of the blows delivered breaking any constraints. Her hands kept coming off her ankles but she stoically and wisely resisted grabbing her buttocks to alleviate her suffering and hinder her beating.

"Oh thank you, Master. Yes. Yes." She spluttered the words out, her blistered cheeks tensing and relaxing as her buttocks danced the dance of many a thrashed behind.

"Oh, I've not finished yet, I'm just taking a breather," Jamie taunted her.

"Now lie on the bed and bring your knees up towards your shoulders, legs wide apart and fanny and arse crack all nicely laid open, hands behind your head."

Fairy did what she was told, enduring the belittling treatment in a sniffling attempt at silence and compliance, and presented herself in the most unladylike and subservient sexual pose possible.

Jamie teased her by stroking her wet folds and tickling her open arsehole, still wet and wanton. Fairy could not stifle a sigh of yearning.

"Hmmm. So incorrigible, so lustful. Up on your knees with those buttocks stretched tight. Let's see if a further ten on top of the last strokes gives you something else to think about other than your shameless and lewd lust for being used and abused."

Fairy's body visibly tensed and Jamie hoped that he taken her close to her limits. He looked down at the naked, beaten woman laid completely open before him, her bottom thrusting out and covered in a sea of raised welts, some turning purple before his eyes. He feasted on her captivating arsehole with its jungle of small black silky curly hairs and her decidedly luscious and sodden pussy lips with its matching black pubic carpet. He could see that her nipples, still clamped, were standing proud of her full breasts, firm and erect, the skin around them pinched so tightly that they had turned a blueish white. He so wanted to make love to this feisty and highly sexed woman but wanted her completely defeated and under his control before he allowed himself to return her the power that comes from draining a man's cock. His penis was throbbing and jerking in anticipation, the blood surging through him as his excitement reached fever pitch, and he knew that he would have to have her soon. He yanked her upper body up and roughly pulled the nipple clamps from her, making her scream out. This was soon followed by a further primal howl as he followed up by whipping the cat across her breasts, catching her upper arms. She spread her arms out in her anguish, thrusting her breasts forward.

"Oh, giving me room to do that again? My pleasure then – it would be rude not to," Jamie taunted.

The cat slashed down onto her unprotected breasts. Fairy screeched and tried to turn away but Jamie used his strength to force her back up and then whipped her breasts again. The braided knots seared into the soft flesh, marking her pale skin with further red lines, and clearly blotching where the knots hit home. Jamie pushed her down and, grabbing her legs, forced them up over her head with one forearm and, with her most tender areas exposed, brought the whip down as quick as a flash and landed three true strokes down the two cracks within a couple of seconds. Regardless of the fact that Jamie had applied little force in respect to the sensitivity of the target areas, the response was dramatic. Earlier screams and screeches had nothing on the long banshee wail of agony that Fairy now let forth. The scorching pain of the braided leather whipping into her anus and love lips was so intense that Fairy looked shocked beyond anything she had ever experienced or imagined. Then the cat was slicing into her bottom cheeks as Jamie changed angles and gave her six quick lashes before he dropped the cat and reacquainted Fairy with the differing but still agonising and torturous effect of a further application of the cane. As the promised ten more strokes were applied with no sympathy or regret, Fairy began to scream the word 'approaching' twice in quick succession as, for the first time she allowed herself to issue the society's given safe word to indicate that the recipient was approaching her pain and punishment threshold.

All members sign up to the code that uses the same safe word, 'approaching', which is to be said twice quickly in succession as a warning that the submissive is close to her breaking point. If this is repeated three times, then it is accepted to be an undisputable clear indicator of a limit being attained, at which point the session has to stop immediately and the contact between the participants is over, must not be resumed and the event is concluded. To bring an episode to an immediate end without warning, there is no use of the indicating word 'approaching'; instead, the word 'finish' must be said clearly three times, and again all activity must cease and the event is over for good. Any episodes whereby a safe word has been used to bring a session to an end, has to be reported by all parties and, in most scenarios, the recipient would then be asked to take an absence from society activities of several months. As all members would be terrified of the consequences of not adhering to this rule, expulsion from the club being the obvious result, there is rarely any deviation.

The codes were rarely used to end a session as no true sub wishes to be suspended from future activities. Fairy's use of the warning words once was a private signal that she was under duress, close to her endurance levels, and in itself was merely a flag rather than an instruction of any sort.

Jamie finished the ten strokes without hesitating. He had no intention of delivering more and was confident that the last few strokes wouldn't produce the second and penultimate cry for real mercy. He was correct, as scream Fairy did while the blows landed on top of the previous ones; her bottom was now close to laceration, but no further warning plea was made.

Jamie dropped her legs and went into the bathroom to pour a cold water bath and after a couple of minutes returned to pick up the quietly weeping form of Fairy, as she lay curled-up on the bed.

"Good girl, all done. Into the cold water and just lie back and let the cold water cover all your sore points."

Fairy tried to jump from his arms as the shock of the cold water hit but Jamie held her tightly until just her shoulders and head showed, the rest of her shivering body submerged.

"Master, I'm absolute frozen, please can I get out?" Fairy's teeth were indeed chattering and her body was trembling quite noticeably, but Jamie held her firmly by the shoulders as her body gradually got used to the temperature and she began to calm down.

"Hush, hush. Just let the cold water do its work for a few minutes, then we can get you towelled down."

Fairy shut her eyes and let her mind wander. Her body was thrashed to an extreme like never before and for once she felt her desire had been beaten out of her. She knew that she had been bested, completely defeated and conquered, but perversely she recognised that she had also lost her heart to this cold, callous man who could deliver pain beyond anything that she had ever dreamed of. Master indeed, Fairy thought.

Jamie released her and left her alone for a moment and looked down at his now less than erect manhood. He knew that he had gone past his comfort zone for enjoying inflicting punishment and pain and was not comfortable with the level he had inflicted on Fairy. He was concerned that the role play had gone beyond the pale and wasn't sure that he felt good about himself after causing her so much distress and damage. However, his self-recriminations were interrupted by the soft voice of Fairy:

"Master, Fairy would like permission to get out of the bath now, please," her plaintive voice called from the bathroom.

Jamie returned to the room and gestured to Fairy to get up and he enveloped her in a huge bath sheet.

"Fairy would just like to thank Master for such a well-deserved and beautiful beating and apologise again for her dreadful behaviour. Fairy is so thankful to master and would love to show master how thankful she is, please."

Jamie was stunned at her words of contrition and the obsequious manner. Her eyes looked at him from under her lashes with clear adoration and devotion and Jamie cast aside his doubts as he felt a stirring below and his sexual interest in the woman definitely reawakening. He towelled her down very softly and as he reached her pussy, he let a finger slide down her vagina, feeling the moist juice within. She closed her eyes and Jamie swept her up in his arms and carried her through to lay her gently on the bed.

Looking down at the naked form below him, he dropped his head and began to kiss and lick the long red lines with the vivid impact points from the knots of the cat. Her bruised breasts responded to his ministrations and he took a nipple gently between his lips as she moaned and squirmed beneath him.

He stared into her eyes as he slipped a finger into her eager pussy and began to work her up.

"Oh God, Master, you make Fairy feel so good but Master it is time for Fairy to make Master feel good." She smiled sexily and lustfully at him and raised herself up and gently put her hands on his shoulders encouraging him to lie back.

"If Master has any wishes, Fairy will do anything, sir, anything to please her Master."

Jamie's erection, now fully hard, twitched in response as Fairy leaned to whisper in his ear, her fingers wrapping around his cock.

"My fingers are yours, my mouth is yours, my pussy is yours, my bottom is yours, and Master may have anything he wants, anything, dear Master, anything. Fairy just wants to give her Master pleasure."

From so feminine and submissive, Fairy had now become a sexual and sensual temptress and Jamie certainly had the need and the will to allow her complete freedom to perform in any way she wished. He looked deep into her eyes and their gazes locked; she blushed under his penetrating state, first her face then her whole torso flushed pink. Jamie smiled at this little success as he knew that, for all her front and bravado, her body and emotions had given her away. She might like to assume an element of control but they both recognised where all the power was held.

While it was accepted that within their society, if not in the world at large, the submissive had a sole role which was to please and obey whoever was their dom, it was also every dominant's duty to ensure their submissive received what they craved for.

"Sixty-nine me now Fairy, you on top, and when you feel that I am ready you can move down and take me reverse cowgirl for a while. Then you will come back to my mouth to allow me to lick you some more and you can suck my cock clean of your pussy slime. Then you can get on your knees, head down while I fuck you doggy style. One hole or the other, I haven't decided yet whether to come in your mouth, your arsehole or your cunt."

Fairy lowered her head in deference and then swung her legs over Jamie's face and presented her pussy and battered bottom to him as she dropped her head to gently lick at the tip of his pulsating erection. Jamie breathed her in, the musky acrid pungency of her still-smarting and reddened anus exposed as her bottom cheeks separated, mixing sensually with the bittersweet malty aroma of her clean but unscented vagina. He ran the top of his tongue in a light circle over her hard little clit and then nipped the nubbin gently between his teeth, feeling it throbbing as if it had a life of its own. His lips slipped off and he gasped as her pursed lips slid down the length of his cock, sucking him hard into the warmth and wetness of her heavily salivating mouth. They both began to work their lips and tongue on each other in tandem, and the only sounds you could hear in the room for a while was a combination of slurping, sucking and little moans and gasps as they devoured each other's most sensitive places.

Fairy, feeling his growing passion and excitement, released his cock from her mouth and shuffled quickly down the bed to position herself, ready to take him into her dripping pussy. She looked coquettishly over her shoulder as she positioned his cock at her entrance and, at his signal, plunged down on him. Jamie soaked up the sight of her gorgeous bottom slamming up and down on his cock, her lips wrapped around him, her arsehole wide open with her cheeks parted.

"Yaaaaaaaaaarrrrrrr!"

"Aaaaiiiiiiiyyyyeeee!"

The sounds of their pleasure filled the air and Jamie had to exert tremendous self-control not to immediately drive for his climax whilst Fairy felt all the air squeezed from her as she was filled internally as never before.

"Fuck! Fuck! Fuck, you are so fucking big, oh my God. Yes, fuck it, fuck it, fuck it, right up there, baby." Fairy spoke injudiciously, forgetting where she was and who she was with for a moment, and there was a pause before she gathered her senses.

"Oh Master, Fairy is so sorry to have spoken to you like a common tart. Fairy meant no disrespect and understands if Master needs to beat her further for her naughtiness."

Not being one who liked to disappoint a lady, Jamie slapped her sore buttocks hard with his hand, Fairy holding herself perfectly still as he rained several harsh blows down on her until his hand became sore.

"Thank you very much, Master, I hope you forgive Fairy now for her impudence," she quietly whimpered.

Jamie didn't bother to reply, just grasped her hips and slammed his cock into her as before. Fairy dropped her head and began to suck on his toes. With her bottom crack so open, Jamie felt he had denied himself for long enough and, wetting a finger from her dribbling fanny, he began to gradually work his forefinger inside her arsehole. He paused as she tightened and then her whole bottom relaxed and his finger slipped easily in to that most secret place, causing Jamie to sigh in satisfaction. He gently twitched his fingertip which, to his joy, caused her to buck and moan in approval, to the point whereby his finger was sucked into its maximum access. He slowly began to finger-fuck her arse in tandem with his cock, sliding in and out of her pussy.

"Oh sir, Master, please sir, Fairy is going to come again soon, sir. With your permission of course, Master. Oh yes, oh yes, soon sir, oh yes, here we go, here we go, here we fucking go!"

Jamie whipped his finger perfunctorily out of her arsehole, causing her to squeal with discomfort as the lack of ample lubrication burned her inside, and lifted her bodily off his cock. Adopting a very frosty tone, he instructed her:

"Fairy, stay still and control yourself. You are not to come yet. If you do come, then our lovemaking is over and I will thrash your open pussy with the cat for ten solid minutes. After that I will take you down to the basement and have you tied down, gagged, bottom-up to be caned, whipped, flogged and fucked up your arse by anyone who wishes. I will leave you there all night so you would be a public facility and a public spectacle in your disgrace. You will have a large potty wedged between your legs so you would only be able to relieve yourself by peeing in front of everyone. I hope this is getting through to you. Do you understand me, Fairy?"

Fairy swallowed again and again, squeezing her vaginal muscles tightly, and willed the orgasm that was building to die away. She had no reason to distrust his promise as she knew that he was aware that this would be the most supreme punishment, and he had made it perfectly clear during the evening that he was a man of his word. Sighing with relief, she was finally able to respond with confidence.

"Master, thank you, Fairy did understand and was a good girl, sir. Does sir want me to wash his penis clean in my mouth now, sir? It would be an honour and my duty to do so, sir. Fairy would also like to give Master a little treat then, sir, if Master would allow?"

Jamie was intrigued.

"Certainly, Fairy, you may give me your pussy now and cover my face with that gorgeous bottom. From now on, Fairy, you are free to climax when you wish and free to make me come in an orifice of your own choosing."

Fairy moved into place and lowered her cleft over his nose and her slick pussy to his open mouth.

"Oh sir, Master does me such an honour. Fairy will do her best to make sure she earns this honour and satisfies you. Fairy is so excited about having the Master's love juice offered to her. Thank you, Master, thank you so very much."

Jamie began lapping at her dripping pussy and soon his lower face and the underneath of his chin were coated with her juices, despite the fact that he felt that he was swallowing pints of the nectar she produced in such copious quantity. His nose was nuzzling into the tight opening of her arsehole and he was in heaven even before she began to deep-throat his cock! He reached out for the butt plug from the bedside table and slid it into her only mildly protesting arsehole, stretching her to her limits and almost causing her to bite down on his cock. She contained herself as a spasm of pain passed, allowing her rectum to accept the implement, and as she allowed her muscles to relax around it, she began to moan as she encompassed the intrusion wholeheartedly.

Heaven was about to turn into paradise on earth for Jamie as, after sucking him like he had never been sucked before, she dropped her elbows under his upper legs and, lifting his bottom up, she slid her tongue between his buttocks and licked his anus. As Jamie shuddered from the shock and ecstasy of the feel of Fairy's wet tongue circling his ring, she probed him open and forced her tongue inside of his dank tunnel. Grasping his cock in one hand, she began to wank him while forcing her tongue deeper up his arsehole. Jamie, feeling his climax approaching, decided to match her actions and slipping his fingers around her and into her pussy whilst rubbing the heel of his hand against her clitoris, he moved his mouth from her pussy to her arsehole. Pulling the butt plug out with his teeth, he slid his tongue into her gaping dark pink-ringed hole, delving into her secret chasm. In tune with each other, their fingers worked simultaneously with their tongues probing in and out of each other's arseholes. Fairy climaxed first and she replaced her tongue with her thumb so she could release a scream of ecstasy and total abandonment, her orgasm rocking and shaking her whole body. Still shuddering, she plunged her head down to suck hard on Jamie's cock as he forced his body up, spluttering into her dark back passage, kissing and sucking her open anus as by now most of his hand was thrust into her pussy as she came and came. Swallowing his salty offering, she spun round on him and kissed him deeply as they mixed saliva, spunk and anal sweat and secretions with a wanton lack of inhibition and with total licentiousness.

Eventually they lay back together, exhausted, before eventually sharing a shower without speaking, washing each other down before retiring to the bed to cuddle together until sleep took them both.

The next morning, the unspoken agreement, which they both clearly understood, not to speak of or discuss what had occurred, continued. They both seem to know naturally that the spell would then be broken. Again they showered together and Fairy slipped to her knees to suck him to the point of orgasm before quickly turning and presenting her soap lathered arsehole and gently guiding him partly in. With Jamie standing virtually motionless, she slowly worked herself onto him with a soft rocking motion backwards and forwards until he came with a quiet groan, ejaculating his spunk deep into her bottom. She smiled, gave him a lingering and loving kiss before slipping from the shower, wrapping herself in a towel, leaving him leaning back against the shower wall, sated and weak at the knees. When he eventually towelled himself down and went back into the main room, she was gone as he'd expected. Their assignment was completed and over.

After breakfast, Jamie spent the rest of the day amusing himself with Pres and the Professor until it was time to take their leave. They enjoyed a non-participatory couple of public punishment beatings, watched some recorded highlights of the evening's events and enjoyed a good quality school class role play put on by a professional group specialising in entertaining one-act spanking scenario dramas on stage.

An especially pleasurable weekend, decided Jamie, which he suspected, and very much hoped, would lead to interesting times ahead.

CHAPTER 4

IN WHICH SARA GETS HER FIRST

COMEUPPANCE

Having finally invited him to stay overnight at her home for the first time, Sara hoped that Jamie recognised that this was a significant step in the development of their blossoming relationship. The obvious implied suggestion, that her first proper spanking as an adult should be carried out at her home, had surely not been misread by Jamie as anything other than an outright invitation? When he had playfully slapped Sara's bottom the other evening, as she had ridden him furiously cowgirl style, she had leaned in and huskily whispered for him to wait until the right moment to do it properly. As she had followed that up with an invitation to come over to her house and stay overnight in the pretty, little village a few miles away, she remembered how her nerve had almost failed her. She had had to turn away, blushing, from his gaze when she had hinted that she felt that she was probably long overdue for a bit of correction if Jamie thought that he was man enough to be the one to deliver it. When he had tried to prolong the conversation, to ascertain that she was asking for a spanking, she had become so embarrassed and had begged him to talk about something, anything else. He had dropped the subject as she requested but he had definitely noted the lack of resistance from her, as they cuddled before parting, when he had slipped his hand down the back of her trousers and squeezed and pinched her bare bottom cheeks, his fingers digging in hard enough to cause Sara to yelp. She had met his querying look with a demure and submissive expression, though, and, so encouraged, he had repeated the action. This time, Sara managed not to react at all. The nod of acknowledgement from Jamie suggested that the message and been received and understood. Sara's mind drifted back to her memories of her teenage years and the last time that she had received a serious thrashing.

In their household, it was their mother who had handled the disciplinary stuff, but it was not until Sara and her younger sister by two years, Carrie, had hit their teenage years that punishments had taken a turn for the worse. An occasional clip around the ear and a quick slap on the backs of their legs had been enough previously to keep them both on the straight and narrow. However, Carrie's minor shoplifting incident was to bring about a new dawn and the introduction of over the knee spankings and the first appearance of the dreaded wooden salad fork. Sara had originally been happy with her mother's instruction that Sara was to witness Carrie's retribution. They were close as sisters but continually fell out, and Sara was feeling very holier-than-thou about Carrie's little act of criminality and therefore quite content that she should pay the price and receive the oft threatened, but never delivered, damn good spanking their mother deemed appropriate for the crime. Sara remembered the shock, and, if she was to be honest, the thrill she felt when her mother had ordered Carrie to strip down to just her knickers. Carrie had been sobbing almost continuously ever since she had been caught and exposed earlier that morning, but this revelation caused an increase in her distress and her wails had filled the room. The scorn and fearsome look of disdain from her mother sent a shiver through Sara's spine and at that moment she had started to feel some empathy and no little sympathy towards her younger sibling. When their mother had sneered that the knickers wouldn't be on for much longer anyway and for Carrie to place herself over her knees, the reality of what was about to happen sank in. Sara was soon transfixed as her sister's pert bottom was lifted by her mother and her little panties virtually ripped from her legs. Not a small woman, their mother, and her vice-like grip on Carrie's waist suggested that resistance was futile and escape impossible. The barrage of hard slaps on Carrie's bare butt, accompanied by high-pitched screams from the recipient, had been methodically and consistently delivered, and soon the pale white skin was a different colour entirely. Fifty painful smacks fell before Sara's mum had asked her to go down to the kitchen and bring up the wooden salad fork and spoon. Sara hadn't even thought about what this might mean, so keen was she not to rile her mother any further. She was already having serious second thoughts about this new development in the girls' lives and what exactly it might mean to her. It certainly did not seem quite so exciting when she considered the possibility of being on the end of this treatment herself. She was generally a well-behaved sixteen- year-old, but was only too aware that she had escaped censure for certain misdeeds in the past.

Carrie was still in the ungainly position over her mother's knees, her mother actually now stroking the red cheeks and talking to Carrie in a soothing tone, somewhat leading Sara into a feeling of danger being passed. She was soon to be disabused, although thankful that she was the audience and not the recipient, as their mother calmly explained that in future a hand spanking would just be the hors d'oeuvres and that the main course would involve either of the long-handled thick wooden implements she was slapping against her palm. Carrie, she announced, would receive six strikes with each server so as she could assess the most appropriate of the two to use on their backsides in future. Carrie's cascade of begging entreaties fell on deaf ears as their mother tightened her grip on the naked girl once more and then laid into Carrie's cheeks one by one, six strokes with the spoon on her left cheek and then the same again with the fork on her right. The ragged intakes of breath, the strangled, choking screams gave clear evidence that the pain was equal to the loud impact of the implement on her cheeks. There was no doubt that the fork had produced the most discomfort, the prongs having left stark raised welts that Sara imagined must be causing her distraught sister so much pain. Little did she realise at that moment that it would not be that long before she too would feel the wrath of her mother and the sting of the salad utensil. Carrie's ordeal turned out to be not quite over as she was ordered to stand naked, her bottom glowing and her hands on her head, in the corner of the room to await the arrival home from work of their father. Their parents worked well in tandem, Sara had to admit; the disappointment in their beloved father's voice as he questioned their behaviour was like a knife to the heart of the girls. As Sara had comforted Carrie afterwards, with soothing moisturiser on her battered buttocks and soothing words in her ear, she listened to the younger girl's distress as she recounted the final part of her punishment. Called by her father to join her parents in the dining room, Carrie had to endure their father's close inspection of her thrashed bottom, whilst they openly discussed and touched the most serious marks. Then to Carrie's total chagrin, she had had to turn and face her parents in all her full-frontal naked glory and apologise at length for her behaviour and then thank her mother for punishing her. Just how humiliating that was as an experience,

Sara was to discover first-hand.

Well, thought Sara, that was then, this was now. Maybe she would live to regret opening up this avenue but the excitement that being involved in student punishments had aroused in her was rather hard to deny and she knew that she had been heading in this direction for a long time. Her on-off sexual activities with Jenny had opened her mind entirely to the idea of intimate behaviour that she previously would never have countenanced. Sara was now beginning to question as to whether she had been quite the malleable, docile and inoffensive little submissive that she often liked to think of herself as in that relationship.

Later that week, probably realising that he needed to take some sort of control, Sara had received a text from Jamie laying down specific instructions on how he expected dinner to be almost ready and her to waiting at the door with a glass of wine when he arrived. Sara smiled as she considered the thought that he was gambling on his assessment of her willingness to commit to what they had discussed, but nevertheless felt that he needed to be the driver and possibly thought that Sara would be complicit but needed leading. He had broadened the story to say that as a maid he had found her service poor and was seriously considering dispensing with her services as he didn't feel that she was earning the high salary she was being paid and this was her last chance to put things right. The text Sara had sent back, in a moment of bravado, had just consisted of the one word "whatever", and she hoped he had had taken that as confirmation that the game was truly on!

It was not until the third ring on the doorbell of the pretty little house that Sara deigned to open the door, but Jamie was not in the least bothered as, when the door was finally opened, it revealed a dishevelled looking Sara sipping a glass of red wine.

"Oh, if it isn't the great Master back from his travels," she sarcastically greeted him and took a gulp of the wine. "This was supposed to be for you but fuck it, I'm having it," she added cockily, knocking back the remainder of the alcohol. "You can get your bloody own."

She then proceeded to belch into his face. In truth, it was the second glass of the evening for Sara as she had looked to bolster her confidence in playing the role she had fantasised about but was finding the reality much more daunting!

She had no idea what Jamie thought as he took in the choreographed look, the badly buttoned blouse showing off her breasts, housed in a tiny black push up bra; the short black skirt barely covering her behind and the panti-hose and half-stilettos giving her the appearance of a second-rate, drunk French maid. Jamie moved her aside and went into the kitchen, poured himself a glass of wine and then made his way around the house ignoring her questioning looks. He obviously knew that she was waiting for him to make the next move and his nonchalant attitude succeeded in disarming her of most the sureness she had earlier possessed.

"What time is dinner then?" he enquired as he stared at her with a look that, to Sara anyway, felt devoid of feeling or passion.

"Well, sir, I have made it, I just may have forgotten to turn the bloody oven on...so it'll take as long as it takes after you pull your finger out and switch the sodding thing on." Sara could feel the shakiness in her voice now and was starting to appreciate that he might be the better role-player than she was.

Jamie was checking the recipe displayed on the kitchen table and would have been able to see that the dish required one hour in a pre-heated oven. Switching the oven on to the required temperature, he turned to Sara.

"I'd guess fifteen minutes to heat up and then an hour's cooking time, so we have plenty of time before you'll need to lay the table. Prior to that I think I need to lay you, but before that…"

He left a long pause and Sara found herself holding her breath before he spoke again, his voice rising ominously.

"Before that, I think that I need to flay you! Upstairs now, young lady, I have had just about enough of your disgraceful behaviour, you are going to get a damn good hiding."

He grabbed Sara by the neck and marched her upstairs to the bedroom that was clearly hers. Pushing her down onto the bed, he flicked her heels off and took both of her hands in one of his. Before Sara could really think about what was happening or had chance to reconsider her situation, she found herself lifted and twisted over his lap on the edge of the bed, scrabbling for balance. In an instance, Jamie had whipped the little skirt over her back and sat looking down on her beautiful bottom sheathed in sexy lace knickers.

"Hmmmm, pretty as they are, they have got to come down," and without ceremony Sara found herself naked bottom up, face down, and perfectly placed to receive her first spanking by a man in adulthood. Jamie started spanking her quite softly and was rewarded in seeing her cheeks relax as she accepted the spanks without resistance. As he reached double figures with the cheeks hardly pink, he decided to test the waters properly. His hand started to crack down and the response was immediate as Sara tried to reach back with her hands to protect herself and started to resist.

Grabbing her straying arm, Jamie slapped the backs of her legs high and hard.

"Yeeeeoooww!" squealed Sara.

"In position and still, open your legs, touch your toes to the floor or you'll be getting a lot more like those and a lot harder."

Sara continued to struggle but Jamie showed no mercy. Slap, slap, slap went his hand on her red rosy cheeks as his lover started to mew and grizzle.

"Naughty girls get their naughty bottoms walloped, you know that, my girl, and that's what you are getting."

Jamie's strikes on her rear got harder and harder as Sara's whimpers turned to full on sobbing. She had no doubt that he was determined to give her the full experience of a punishment spanking and she was hardly in a position to claim that she had not truly wanted or earned this treatment. She was relieved to hear him announce that the last six smacks were going to bring her up to the round one hundred, albeit the increased strength of those soon wiped most thought processes from her mind! Sara soon found herself in full-throttle screaming mode before finally an extra harsh slap announced the end of the spanking.

The pointless struggling finally stopped and he relaxed his grip, as though anticipating a bid for freedom but none came. Sara stayed where she was, her face pressed to the duvet, her arms now seemingly lifeless beside her. Her legs had ceased their kicking and her bright red bottom was now still before him. Approaching forty years old, Sara now lay placidly across his lap, having finally succumbed to her first spanking by a male lover. As she absorbed the stinging pain, she began to appreciate that afterglow and sexual stirring that a spanking brought forth as Jamie stroked her smarting buttocks. His touch was one of love and tenderness, causing Sara to open her legs wider inviting his fingers to her moist pussy below. She responded immediately to his delving fingers, her sex juices flowing and her breath quickening as he expertly manipulated her wet folds. Ahh! She turned to look back at him with loving eyes; she saw the knowing smile and she sensed his satisfaction in receiving the confirmation proved that he had been correct and that she had really wanted the hard spanking that he had delivered.

"If a student had been so naughty, would they have only got a spanking?" she asked rather coyly. Jamie considered before answering:

"Possibly a paddling as well, but don't forget it's the Professor who determines the students' punishments."

Sara giggled. "Oh well, perhaps you ought to ring him then and ask his opinion on whether or not I should be paddled. Maybe I need to address the engine driver and not his oily rag then," she provocatively taunted him as she raised herself on her knees, his fingers still between her thighs.

Ok, thought Sara, *now we should surely both understand the serious game we are playing.*

Jamie's cock twitched rather obviously in his trousers and Sara had to refrain from reaching out to touch the hard bulge deforming his trouser front. She could tell that he was pondering his next move and suspected that in his wildest dreams he had not anticipated this scenario going so well.

Sara had adapted to the idea of her new lover having access to the naked bodies of many young and attractive female students, and had been fully ready and prepared to accept that their relationship would involve including her in his punishment of other female bottoms rather than her being the only recipient. As long as she did nothing to curb his activity, she hoped he would be content with that arrangement, but she had decided not to leave it to chance. He would have now realised that he had unleashed the hidden subservient in her and hoped that it was perceived as a bonus that he hadn't really even considered. She was quite shocked as how deep her feelings had become for him in a short space of time and knew that there was little she would not do to keep their partnership together. As well as things had gone thus far, she decided that she wanted to offer him so much more. Just how subservient she could be he was likely about to find out.

"If you are just going to sit there like a lemon with that thing sticking up, then I'm off," Sara broke into his reverie as he slipped his fingers in and out of her wet and rather gaping pussy and moved to get up.

"The only place you are going is into the kitchen to put our dinner in the oven and to choose a wooden spoon for your paddling, young lady. Now off you pop," he sternly pronounced, accompanying his words with a sound slap across the full meat of her crimson bottom. Sara slipped off his lap, the French maid's skirt falling back over her perfectly rounded buttocks. She looked around for the lacy black knickers.

"You don't need panties on to go to the kitchen, young lady," said Jamie. "For the sake of clarity I can tell you that you certainly won't be requiring them when you return." Jamie scooped up the briefs and slipped them into his pocket and, as Sara skipped off into the kitchen, the last thing she saw was Jamie moving her large hairbrush to be close at hand. Sara's face turned red, out of sight, as she remembered how she had used the hairbrush on her own bottom a couple of times as a precursor to a masturbation session. A little tremor also passed through her body at the thought of the strength of Jamie using that rather effective and solid implement on her already sore buttocks.

Sara deliberately took her time. She felt brazen and in control; the spanking had stung and hurt just as she remembered from her early teenage years when her mother had had just cause in delivering good hidings to her bare backside similar to what she had just endured.

The big difference was of course that they had been exactly that: a punishing thrashing from an angry and understandably disappointed parent whom she had let down yet again. Plenty of love, of course, but no joy and no fun element and certainly no sexual desire, no juices flowing through her sex, no blood rushing through her body in excitement, no hardened nipples and no lust to be well and truly fucked. She wanted more. She had thought so often and for so long about this possibility, and remembered the shame and shock she had felt when just occasionally she had met the Professor's eyes during one of the sessions where she had played that role of miscreant's support and comforter. He had on two occasions intimated that he was willing to assist if she wanted him to thrash her. She knew that he had recognised the intrigue and probably the desire she had shown, but she had protested her lack of interest and tried to convince him that she most certainly did not, thank you very much. But she knew that they both knew she was bluffing. Sighing, she bravely picked the heaviest serving spoon and sauntered back to where Jamie was still sitting on the edge of the bed. She was pleased to see an impatient expression on his face.

"Oh, we look rather proud of ourselves, don't we? Maybe a little lesson in manners is called for," said Jamie as she cheekily and rather nonchalantly juggled the wooden spoon from one hand to another. Grabbing the padded chair from the dressing table, he motioned to Sara to approach.

"On your knees on the chair, legs spread to the edge, over the back you go and hold on tight when you've correctly presented. That's it, good girl, nice and round, open enough to be displaying the quality of the goods available." Jamie's taunting words accompanied a finger tickling her arsehole before he ran it down her still moist pussy lips.

"Oh listen to you, aren't you the expert," Sara taunted him.

"Far too much lip for a naughty girl. Clearly a lot to learn, let's get on with teaching you manners, shall we?" With that, Jamie brought the heavy wooden spoon down hard and central with a vicious blow that landed perfectly in the middle of her cheeks.

There was a strangled guttural sound from Sara, followed by a deep intake of breath. Jamie didn't hesitate though, and placed two quick and equally hard blows in the middle of each buttock. Now the screams began.

"Yaaaaaaaaaaaaaaaar! No, no, no. It hurts, it's too much." Sara attempted to shield her bottom with one hand, using the other to help her as she began to get up from the chair.

Jamie easily forced her down.

"How dare you move, young lady. Remain in position or I will be forced to strap you down, in which case I would double your punishment. At the moment you're only having a novice's dozen but that can easily be doubled or maybe tripled if you don't damn well behave yourself."

"Sorry Jamie," came the contrite response, the previous cockiness having drained from her.

"It's sir to you, you disrespectful little scoundrel. Maybe these extras will teach you some respect."

The wooden spoon smacked down hard on the tops of each leg, eliciting a high-pitched screech from Sara.

"No, no, no, ah, oooh, sir ,sorry sir, please sir, no more!"

Jamie's chuckling response was not exactly how Sara wanted him to respond but her mind was soon focused on coping with the stinging pain of her buttocks as the spoon landed on her unprotected cheeks. Sara grabbed the table legs as hard as she could, making a real effort not to lose it completely as she became a mess of yells, pleas for mercy and spluttering sobs. It took a moment for her to realise that the blows had stopped, her bottom felt so on fire, but Jamie had reluctantly kept to his word and the twelfth smack had been the last.

"On my God, oh my arse, oh that stings, it stings, oh my, oh my," Sara babbled. "Thank the Lord that's over. That was too much." She pulled herself to her feet and rubbed frantically at her bright red cheeks, and then heard the ominous words of a stern-faced Jamie.

"Oh you don't get to decide when it's over, my dear. We've got another little session to go through yet, so come here." Jamie had sat himself down on the chair and grasped one of Sara's wrists, pulling her to him.

"No, no more please. I'm so sore already, please Jamie...er, I mean sir." Sara changed tack seeing Jamie expression of annoyance, without realising that she had sealed her fate by reconnecting with the role play scenario, this giving Jamie the confidence to go ahead.

"Over my knee now," easily positioning her legs akimbo head down. "Legs apart, come on show off your goods."

Sara obeyed just as Jamie's hand began slapping hard against the rose red cheeks. After a thirty- slap spanking, Jamie paused, and unknown to Sara had picked up the hairbrush with its wide flat reverse side. Sara started to rise, believing that her ordeal was finally over, only to buck dramatically before screeching in agony once more as Jamie brought the brush down hard on her left cheek. Sara jiggled her bottom cheeks furiously as if trying to shake off the stinging pain. Jamie watched in fascination as her cheeks danced before Sara slumped, howling, the redness darkening.

"Oh fuck, that hurt, what the fuck was that?" Twisting round, Sara knew that she would see that the offending item was the dreaded hairbrush, setting her off again with a crude response. "My fucking hairbrush, you absolute bastard, no fucking more, you dick.

Yeeeeeoooooeeerrghhhh!" Her angry response came to an end as she felt the full force on her right cheek as the hairbrush landed with a resounding slap.

"I'll be deciding when I'm done with you, and it certainly won't be while you are using such foul language and being so offensive. You are a naughty little potty-mouthed girl and a sore bottom is the only remedy. I certainly will not be stopping until that nasty little temper has gone away."

Sara should have realised that by now Jamie was proficient at this punishing business. Sara had been present many times when Professor Stones had worked through the disciplinary victims' emotions. The resistance and denial, the contrition, the anguish and then the anger, before the agony of the harsher period of beating brought forth true remorse and eventual correction.

The next four blows left her virtually speechless as she tried to process the incredibly stinging sensation, her mouth hung open her eyes wide and wild.

"No Jamie, no, please, I'm sorry, Jamie…I mean sir, pleaaaaaaaassssssee!"

The next crack of the brush cut her garbled plea off as it landed squarely and with full force across the centre of her buttocks. She tried to imagine Jamie's view as she could feel the force, first flattening her cheeks completely, before they sprung back into place. She wriggled and struggled, no thought given to the view of her gaping buttocks and open arsehole as any sense of coyness or discretion was driven from her. Jamie's experience with punishment and disciplinary beatings, whether for fun and on demand as in the BADS contingent or assigned by the Dean of Discipline at St. James' College, was turning him into somewhat of an aficionado and connoisseur of the art. He might be nowhere close to Professor

Stones' level of expertise but he had learned more and more from each beating he delivered and he was using that knowledge to build Sara towards her breaking point. Sara had only one thing on her mind now, though, and that was to endure the phenomenal pain coming from her burning backside and get through this torment with some shred of dignity left. Her breathing was now quite ragged and desperate, her tears flooding down her face, her cries frantic and despairing. It would be much later before she would appreciate that she had been well and truly thrashed by an expert at his craft and that he had delivered what she had sought and what he had wanted to. At that point she would accept that, like Stones, when he was delivering his punishments, Jamie was mastering her completely and the beating contained no element of mercy, because no mercy was deserved or warranted. Then she would think back and appreciate the perfection of what she had undergone. Now she was just a blubbing, wailing mess with a bottom that was being given the most sensational and painful beating. Three final extra hard blows landed, one on top of the other over the central part of her buttocks, before Jamie dropped the brush. Even after the blows had stopped, Sara found herself unable to contain her writhing and squirming as she searched for anything that would ease the burning that seemed to penetrate into her inner being.

"I'll pour you a shallow cold bath now, which you will sit in until I deem otherwise," Jamie informed the sobbing Sara as he left the room, leaving her gyrating over the chair back.

Sitting in the cold water gave Sara time to reflect on what had happened. So she was clearly not averse to being treated like a naughty child and even found the act of being lowered by her lover into the freezing cold water strangely sensual. The door was left open, with Jamie gone from view, and she missed his presence already and was shocked at how much she longed for him to return. However, she did realise that she might have discovered her limits, much as she loved the sexual elements of being spanked. She had found the wooden spoon challenging and the hairbrush far too painful for her liking. True, she thought, the stinging, once it was over, was actually quite erotic with its burning sensation, and being mastered and subdued was a role she found a huge turn on, but she certainly didn't think there was much chance that she would be encouraging Jamie to be bringing a strap or cane home for personal use! Her dilemma, of course, was where did this leave both her and Jamie as far as his activity with his other little interest group, the fetish society, that she had to admit intrigued her? There was undoubtedly a spark of jealous possession entering her head and her heart and she was not sure she wanted to share Jamie with any of his club members. However, she pondered, maybe there was a possible role that she could play similar to her role with the professor. *Master's Little Helper* had an appeal; watching Jamie beat other women wasn't something that bothered her particularly, since that was how they had met, making Sara wonder if her true sexual role was actually as a voyeur.

When Jamie walked back into the room with a glass of wine for both of them and turned on the hot tap and added some bath oil, Sara almost cried with joy. This, she thought, is definitely going to mean an end to my little lesbian trysts with Jenny.

Unfortunately for Sara, Jenny was not to take this news well…

CHAPTER 5

IN WHICH JENNY BECOMES AN ISSUE

Having decided that her relationship with Jamie Adams, a part-time porter at another college and nowadays a close ally of the college's Dean of Discipline, Professor Stones, was something that had a future, Sara Morgan realised that she had to make a clean breast of things with her casual lover Jenny Goldman. Their on-off relationship had lasted far longer than either of them had expected after the initial spark that Jenny's punishment session had generated. Sara well remembered visiting Jenny in her room a couple of days after her thrashing and the intimate moment that had luckily earned her only a stern warning from the Professor. Admittedly, Sara had lived in fear of being caught out since, which probably added to the excitement of the illicit encounters, and having been party to the horrific beating handed out to the Senior Tutor for a similar offence, she would be relieved to no longer have that threat hanging over her. The fact that Jenny had left the college did mean that the relationship was beyond the Professor's jurisdiction now, which was a saving grace, but Sara was well aware that if he ever found out that the relationship had been of a sexual nature when Jenny was still an undergraduate at St. James', she could easily be dismissed in disgrace. The rules regarding relationships with undergraduate students were perfectly clear: there was no room for misunderstanding and every new member of staff was verbally told to their face that the consequences would be grave. Sara knew that Celia, the Senior Tutor, had probably only held onto her position at the college, despite the episode when an undergraduate, a first year called Emily Govan, was punished, was because she had been at the college for over thirty years, student and academic, and that it was well-known that she and Professor Stones were lovers. Sara knew that Emily had also assured the Professor that she had no complaints about the incident and indeed had been allowed to repay the Senior Tutor with a reciprocal act during that punishment session. Sara blushed now thinking back, as she had watched, stunned, as the student, encouraged by the Professor to lessen Celia's traumatic ordeal by doing so, had licked and frigged the Senior Tutor to orgasm whilst Sara herself had sucked on one breast and grasped her other nipple firmly between her fingers.

Sara loved her job as Chief Academic Administrator, reporting directly to Celia Ford, the Senior Tutor, a good boss but one that Sara was keeping more than one major secret from. Let alone the fact that Celia seemed unaware that Sara had partially witnessed her thorough beating and humiliation at the hands of the Dean of Discipline, and that she had been active in the sexual exploitation of her during it and yet was guilty of the far more grievous misdemeanour in having conducted a sexual relationship with an undergraduate. At least Celia's crime had been very much a moment of indiscretion, a slip of the tongue you might say. Sara chuckled to herself, remembering her shock as the Senior Tutor had leaned forward to kiss and lick a bound Emily Govan's pussy. Sara herself had entered a relationship knowing full well that it was a clear breech of college rules and had developed and continued that relationship on college property. Her saving grace she felt was, that although the relationship had continued, albeit at a distance after Jenny had graduated, as far as Sara could see no one could ever prove that she had misbehaved during Jenny's undergraduate time at college now. It's in the past, thought Sara, and now I am bringing that relationship to an end it will be confined to history and can go in the box marked 'the one that I got away with', she thought confidently.

Thinking back on the relationship, Sara tended to think it was just destiny and found it hard to regret that she had allowed things to develop with Jenny. Virtually ordered by Professor Stones to check in on Jenny in the aftermath of the young student's thrashing, Sara felt that she had no option but to comply. A tentative email had set into motion an exchange of communication that resulted, after about a week, with a fulsome invitation to visit after the working day had ended, and Sara had duly arrived early evening at the student's single room, one of the college's prized single en-suites indicating quite clearly an ability to pay the rather exorbitant fees such accommodation attracted. An indication of the direction the evening might head in was rather highlighted by the fact that Jenny opened the door, dripping wet, fresh from the bathroom.

"Whoops, running a bit late, but come in please, Sara." Jenny leant in to kiss the Chief Academic Administrator on the cheek, ushering her into the rather lavish room.

"I've got a bottle of red and a bottle of white on hand, so I hope you aren't in a rush. I've taken the liberty of cooking a pasta dish that's now in the oven in case you'd like to stay and have something to eat. I realise that you've been working all day so might be hungry. Save you a job later, huh?"

Sara realised that the young woman was burbling on nervously and her eyes were betraying her lack of confidence and uneasiness at what her proposal might be interpreted as and was keen to relax her.

"Well, that's a very nice offer. I'd be delighted. I've nothing planned and am all yours."

Sara's response was less than innocent. She was aware that the thought of Jenny's nakedness beneath the towel was stirring her loins. Sara couldn't pretend that she had not spent a long time contemplating the events of a few days previously and the frisson of excitement that had run through her body when she thought about massaging the soothing cream into Jenny's beaten buttocks. The student had a superb bottom, Sara had to admit, and Sara knew that she would struggle to resist the opportunity to see and touch it again if Jenny granted her that option. There was a bit of a struggle going on in her head as she tried to determine what the attraction to Jenny really meant. Sara didn't have any issue with lesbianism or bisexuality but it hadn't really occurred to her before that she possessed these inclinations. She had tended to dismiss it as something that the circumstances had developed, the empathy and sympathy that had come to the fore when she had realised Jenny's predicament was combined with natural caring instincts. What she couldn't argue with were the emotions that she could barely disguise, and that was that the thought of laying her hands on Jenny's naked body again was bringing forth lust!

"Well, as I remember, I was virtually all yours the other day so it would be only fair if you were all mine," Jenny giggled nervously in response, and Sara sensed that the point of no return was rapidly approaching.

Sara couldn't pretend that she hadn't fantasised that something like this may happen but now she faced the reality of the situation it was difficult not to keep hearing the voice of the Professor warning her against such conduct. The next decision she took would decide whether or not she was prepared to put her dream job in her chosen career at risk. Lovely location, excellent colleagues, perfect if sometimes antiquated working conditions and a very high salary that she knew she wouldn't match elsewhere. In addition to that, the Professor had granted her a special role to play as far as disciplinary action in the college went. He had certainly wetted her appetite but probably hadn't foreseen exactly how prone Sara was to the temptation that he had instigated in placing before her. Sara knew that Jenny was 21 years old, and evidently not exactly the sweet, naive young woman that she had perfected in the Dean's rooms. The students at St James' were not permitted to enter college until the age of 19, after having completed a year in the workplace to give them a grounding in the realities of an adult working life before they began their degree studies. Not a common practice but a principle that the college had adhered to for many years and, with a much-envied academic record, it was a difficult policy to challenge. It did mean that their undergraduate students were often a bit more streetwise than those at the city's other colleges and Sara was confident that Jenny knew exactly what she was doing with her supposedly accidental appearance.

"If you don't mind, I had only just popped into the bath when you rang. My fault entirely for losing sense of time, but I'd like to quickly finish off if that is ok with you?" Jenny threw the words nonchalantly over her shoulder as she headed off through an adjoining door and Sara doubted that it was by pure chance that she began to drop the towel as she walked, exposing the tops of her buttocks. Sara suspected that she was being led by the nervous but clearly determined young lady, who was showing signs of wanting to be the dominant one in this meeting. Sara was conflicted, not recognising herself as either an obvious dominant or submissive. She had always seemingly preferred consensual sharing sex, although ultimately in her heterosexual relationships she knew that she had always ceded, in part at least, to the man. In fact, as her mind went into overdrive, she came to the conclusion that in reality she certainly did allow myself to be dominated but more by it being the easy option than a preferred choice. *Not this time, Sara, not this time*, she chided herself.

She took the decision to follow Jenny into the room which was a spacious bedroom containing an enormous king-sized bed and some exquisite furnishings. An open door across the room obviously led to the en-suite bathroom and as Jenny approached it, she allowed the towel to slip off her body completely before moving into the steamy room. Sara saw again the beautiful bottom that had fed her fantasies since the student's beating; she noted the still visible but receding, blackish-blue marks illustrating the bruising caused by the Professor's harsh punishment days before.

"Come and talk to me in here," called Jenny. "Let's not even pretend there isn't a part of my body that you haven't seen very close up already. You've looked at bits of me I haven't even seen! It's all rather unfair and unbalanced really, isn't it?"

Sara licked her lips. Jenny was playing the coquettish madam very well, and she felt any resistance begin to drain away. Opportunity was being handed to her on a plate; there was going to be no innocent explanation or claims of a terrible misunderstanding to fall back on this time. Sara accepted that she was not going to miss this moment or resist the temptation. She was kidding herself that it was even an option; she was aroused and sensible thinking was being discarded! She moved into the bathroom, kicking her sandals off.

"I suppose you'd like your back scrubbing, then?" She wanted to take back some control and tried very hard to put some authority into her voice. Sara felt that it was important that she made it clear that she was the alpha in whatever was to happen now, however much it was a role she was not practised at, used to or completely comfortable with. However, she suspected that Jenny was putting on a brave act to draw Sara into the situation and her assessment was that Jenny could soon turn pliable and submissive. *You are the Chief Academic Administrator,* she chastised herself, *damn well act like you are and remember your job is all about handling students.*

"Well, I don't want to get my work clothes wet and I suppose after a day's work I could do with washing down the result of a hard graft and toil in our stuffy offices," she said, staring straight into Jenny's eyes as she began to remove her clothing and was pleased to see a responding blush. It was not to stop the younger girl widening her eyes with rather obvious desire as Sara freed her breasts and then unhooked her skirt. With no hesitation, she pulled her flimsy knickers down and smiled as Jenny's eyes feasted on her exposed bush and pussy lips.

"Maybe you're the one that needs scrubbing, then." Jenny's voice was slightly strangled now. "I think I had better clean you now, please, Sara. Come and stand in the bath." Jenny was on her bent knees in the spacious bath and had begun to cover her hands with soapy, creamy suds. Sara stepped into the bath facing her, and parted her legs to the extent that she could, trying hard to keep an air of composure about herself. She was conscious that it was almost twelve hours since she'd showered and was torn between the horror of having a day's worth of natural body smells exposed to this lascivious young woman's appraisal and an overwhelming lust to be submitted to the shame of having the day's musty aromas washed off her by this pretty, naked nymph. Lust won as Jenny's slick hands moved up her stomach to her breasts, tweaking her hardening nipples and then sweeping under her arms.

"Let's get those sweaty pits sorted first, shall we," said Jenny who, with a real glint in her eye, made Sara realise that she had allowed the student to regain the upper hand as the two females wrestled for control of the situation.

Sara cringed but showed no resistance as Jenny rinsed her armpits and then re-soaped them, her head now perfectly placed to allow her lips to move from one nipple to another as she gently ran her hands under Sara's arms and over her shoulders. However much the realisation that pure lust and longing was guiding her into a more submissive role than she would have liked, Sara still felt powerless to resist the force of the younger, supposedly less experienced woman. Suddenly Jenny changed track and as one hand glided down to encircle a breast, the other slid straight down to Sara's pussy and began to soap the fine hairs, the fingertip of her little finger tentatively brushing her vaginal folds. Sara gasped, giving in to the feelings that were being generated by the deft fingers, her hands gripping Jenny's head and twisting in her hair as she sucked hard on one of her nipples. The finger in her pussy became more pronounced, her wet lips parted and as Jenny probed inside her moist pussy, Sara could feel her juices readily flowing.

"Your front's clean," said a rather breathless Jenny, pulling back from the trembling and incredibly aroused older woman. "Turn around, let's not neglect your back and I do so want to see that bottom."

Sara found herself obeying even as her mind was frantically backtracked through the day, trying to remember whether or not she was clean enough for visitors there. Jenny dispelled any hope she had that this was not going to be a most intimate of washes.

"Come along and open your legs; we all need a good wash here after a day's hard toil," teased Jenny, clearly having sensed Sara's reluctance, as a soapy hand landed straight onto Sara's bottom crack.

"Come on, open up the poop desk." A second soapy hard landed on her cheeks, this time with some force and threat.

"Um. Jenny, please, can I do it myself?" ventured Sara, totally aware that Jenny had now taken over complete control.

"Ha ha, no you bloody well cannot. I think you might be forgetting how utterly exposed I was in front of you the other day. How bloody humiliated I felt, how demeaned, how ashamed and how belittled. So no, you cannot wash your own sweaty, smelly arsehole, bitch, you can damn well feel some of the shame that I felt. Put your hands on the wall and push your bottom out, legs wide open, let's see how you like having your crinkle exposed so crudely."

Sara was shocked, and somewhat ashamed, at her own capitulation as she totally complied, and seconds later was forced face first into the tiled wall in shock as a soapy finger thrust straight into her arsehole. Gasping, Sara tried to decide what she should do to stop herself falling further into this submissive role and, just as importantly, did she really want it to stop? Jenny's other hand meanwhile had scratched long and hard down her back, slipped under her bottom, between her legs and two fingers were slid straight into her pussy. Jenny twisted the finger, embedded in Sara's protesting arsehole, brutally around several times before pulling out and then inserting a different, soap covered, digit. Sara steeled herself to maintain her position and keep her anal muscles as slack as possible to curtail the discomfort of this rectal invasion. She gritted her teeth as that finger then popped out and she felt the width of Jenny's much thicker thumb now make its way into her arsehole.

"Now sit down in the bathwater, legs pulled back, knees to your shoulders, legs apart and I'll swish you out," commanded Jenny, her tone brooking no argument from Sara, as the thumb was removed in a perfunctory manner.

Her mouth opened and closed but no words would form as Sara found herself now taking a position exactly as commanded, tugging her legs, by pulling under her knees, towards her shoulders. Sara was rather lost in shame while an inner battle developed in her head as she displayed herself in such an intimate and personal manner for the most invasive and debasing process. Feeling spellbound, she meekly obeyed Jenny and accepted that she must be getting what she wanted otherwise why would she even be here, let alone in this position?

Kneeling between her legs, Jenny lifted Sara's buttocks onto her own knees causing Sara's back to slide down until her head was almost in the water and her bottom raised out. Sara was once more treated to a soapy finger sliding intrusively, and not particularly with gentleness, up her back passage. Jenny then dropped her bottom slightly and as she snatched the one finger out, two others began swishing water into the rapidly closing tunnel of Sara's arsehole. Sara closed her eyes and gave in to the debasement of her body as Jenny started a piston and suction motion that swilled bathwater inside of her.

"How's this feel then, my little bitch?" taunted Jenny. "What's it feel like having your dirty arsehole washed and flushed out by someone half your age, eh? Pretty bloody humiliating, isn't it?" With that, Jenny pushed Sara down into the water almost submerging her and stepped out of the bath.

"I need drying now, bitch, come on, get out and grab a towel." Jenny hung out a hand and virtually hauled Sara from the tub. A second helping hand from Jenny came in the form of her taking a handful of her hair and Sara stumbled onto her feet and out of the bathwater, dripping wet.

"The quicker I am dry, the quicker you can have the towel wrapped around you to dry yourself off and warm yourself up. So, chop-chop, you tardy woman, get on with it and make sure you do a good job."

Sara briskly and effectively obeyed her tormentor, her mind racing as to how to turn the tables and get some sort of control back. But having clearly seized the initiative, Jenny wasn't about to give it back easily and stepped away from Sara.

"Get yourself dry quickly and then come through and I'll get us some wine," she said as Sara wrapped the towel around herself and soon followed Jenny from the bathroom.

As Jenny returned with the glasses of wine, Sara sensed her opportunity and tightened the full length towel around herself. Steeling herself, she adopted her most severe and authoritative voice.

"Take your wine and get onto the bed please, Jenny. If we are going to fuck, let's do it in comfort, shall we?"

As Sara had expected, Jenny's composure was suddenly no longer so self-assured. No longer as confident in her nakedness in front of the completely covered Sara, she faltered and her eyes betrayed her loss of control. Sara was so aware that both of them were acting out of character as they manoeuvred in this early stage of their sexual relationship. At the moment it seemed as if a battle for control was taking place, with neither of them really knowing whether they wanted to be the victor or the conquered.

"Yes, you've had your fun. I have allowed you a certain amount of leeway and a little bit of petulant revenge that you seemed to think was your right. Now, however, we will do things my way." The glint in Sara's eye added to Jenny's sudden supposed unease but she didn't fight the seamless turnover of power and, head bowed, walked ahead of Sara into the spacious bedroom.

Keen to press her advantage home, Sara grasped her upper arms from behind and forced the younger woman down on to the bed facing them as they entered the room.

"Now it is my turn to have some fun, my impetuous and arrogant little friend. I think you need taking down a peg on two and I know exactly the way to do that."

Before Jenny had a chance to consider any resistance to this turn of events, she found herself being dragged across Sara's knees, her bottom now clearly the target of Sara's revenge.

"Yarrr! Yarr! No! No! No!" were the first sounds from Jenny's mouth in protest as Sara's arm rose and fell rapidly, the fully fledged spanks landing less than a second apart. Holding the struggling naked figure firmly, Sara began to exact her revenge in earnest, and in not much more than a minute she had landed 100 blows across the girl's buttocks and the tops of her legs. The crimson colouring clearly indicated telling evidence, combined with the mewing and heartfelt sobbing from her victim, that this was no play-spanking but a good old-fashioned bottom walloping.

"Right, up you get, stand in the corner, legs apart, hands on your head. I am not done with you yet, my pretty, that's just for starters. There's the main course to come yet. Although if you are a good girl, you might find the dessert I have planned somewhat more of a treat."

A quick slap of the girl's bottom to hurry her into position and Sara stood back in satisfaction at her success in completely cowing this haughty female. She wasn't to see the sly smile that played around the edges of Jenny's mouth slightly belying the body language of a beaten and subdued young girl!

Sara went over to the girl's wardrobe and began flicking through the clothes hanging there until she espied a thick leather belt looped through a pair of trousers.

"This should do the trick. Onto the bed Jenny, on your knees, face down and we will have that peachy bum up in the air, legs well apart."

135

The acquiescence now seemed complete as Jenny meekly complied, positioning herself in the middle of the bed. Sara laid the thick belt across her upper haunches and knelt beside her, fingers straying to the exposed vulva and gently tickling the engorged damp lips displayed. The sigh from Jenny was all the encouragement that Sara required, as one finger found the hard slippery clitoris while the others tickled and eased apart the moist folds. Leaning in, Sara began first to kiss and then to nibble the bottom cheeks above, before dipping her head further and sliding her tongue along the sensitive rougher skin between the arsehole and fanny of her now completely willing partner. Sighing rather dramatically, Sara ceased her activity and picked up the belt.

"I suppose a job worth doing is a job that is worth doing well," she said obliquely, as she slashed the leather down hard across Jenny's raised cheeks.

Jenny drew in a breath noisily but otherwise did not respond or react, her raised buttocks holding position, inviting Sara on. The belt rained down as crack after crack resounded in the room until her resistance was broken and her knees twisted down, her body shying away from the belt.

"No more, no more, please. I've had enough."

Sara smiled triumphantly and acted quickly to loop the belt around the beaten girl's wrists, securing her hands behind her back.

"Oh no, my sweet, not done yet, not done at all," Sara taunted Jenny, happy that she had now completely turned the tables and held the upper hand.

"Someone needs to remember who is in charge here and who is just a play object, a distraction, an inconsequence. Do you understand me, bitch?"

A tearful Jenny, her head now held firmly by Sara, could only mumble into the pillow.

"Yes I do Sara, sorry Sara. You are in complete charge, Sara, but no more spanking please Sara, my bottom is so sore."

Sara's response was to march into the kitchen area, flick through the utensils, and return to Jenny's side with an oval-ended thick wooden stirring spoon. Smirking at the stricken girl whose eyes now bulged in her head, Sara twisted her back flat, face down.

"Do not speak again until I ask you a question. You are allowed to scream, you are allowed to howl, you are allowed to sob. You are not allowed to speak. How simple to understand is that? Now shut the fuck up and take your dues. If you are a good girl then maybe nice Sara will give you a damn good seeing to afterwards."

The lack of fight in Jenny belied her reluctance for the delivery of further punishment and Sara was definitely going to take full advantage. The salad spoon slapped down hard on Jenny's right buttock, which turned firstly white then rapidly red. A slight squeal from Jenny but little resistance as Sara raised the spoon high and then slapped down with maximum force. Another stifled scream and a sharp intake of breath were all the encouragement that Sara needed and she began a rhythmic spanking from one cheek to the other, turning the surfaces an even brighter shade of red. Each stroke brought a jolting movement and a sob from the pliant Jenny, defeated and submissive, her fight long gone. Sara paused for a moment then unleashed a six stroke torrent rapidly on the crack between the matching, well-thrashed cheeks, before throwing the spoon aside and dropping her mouth down to rain kisses on the glowing flesh.

Minutes later the two were in the classic lesbian lovemaking position, legs scissoring each other, clitorises rubbing hard against the other's, both women panting frantically and sweating profusely in the warm room as they had their first orgasm together. Soon Sara was astride Jenny in the sixty-nine position, both females lapping at their lover's pussies, bottoms firmly grasped and tongues working furiously up and down slits before sucking noisily on their hard clitoral nubs. Jenny was the first to reach her climax this time, her mouth clamping on Sara's sex, her fingers scrabbling at the bottom above her face, one digit seeking the opening of Sara's arsehole and penetrating as her body gave into its abandon, her fluids unleashed and one orgasm merged into another. Slumping beneath Sara, releasing her hold, Jenny's super-charged body started to come down from its orgasmic peak. Her sexual energy began to subside as with a last lingering shudder down the full length of her body she lay sated and fulfilled. Sara's eyes feasted on the intimate details of Jenny's pussy and arsehole; she watched fascinated as Jenny's body flopped like a rag beneath her own. Conscious that she needed to remain in control of the relationship, she turned and re-adjusted so that she was now facing her lover and kneeling above her face. Taking hold of Jenny's head, she thrust her own pussy into Jenny's mouth.

"My turn, bitch. Start licking, I am going to come all over your pretty little face." Jenny's eyes snapped open at the order and she looked up the length of Sara's upper body, the expectant face of a triumphant looking Sara above her. She worked her lips and tongue into the wetness pressing into her and reached her hands up to Sara to grasp her breasts firmly and pinching the erect nipples.

"Good girl," sighed Sara. "That's it, work your tongue up my pussy, rub your nose on my clit. I am so going to come all over you and you're going to drink every last single drop of my juices, my sweet."

The only sounds in the room from then on where animalistic and very basic as the two women concentrated on their personal objectives. Sara reached down behind her to deftly shuffle her fingers in rhythm amongst Jenny's labial lips whilst Jenny sucked and licked for all she was worth under Sara's grinding, thrusting body. Eventually Sara twisted fully around and slumped forward to return the cunnilingus favour. She reached under Jenny to slide a wet finger deep into her arsehole, whilst Jenny's fingers latched onto Sara's erect nipples, pinching and twisting them, her tongue sliding up and down the dripping pussy, her wet nose poking at her anal hole. Within seconds, the two were writhing and groaning in ecstasy as they reached their goals and their shuddering bodies embraced the climactic surges that waved over them both.

That episode led to repeat visits by Sara to Jenny's room on several occasions over the following months, carefully plotting and planning their treasured moments while the two journeyed on that voyage of sexual discovery as only practised and wholeheartedly committed lovers can. They experimented with complete trust in each other, both confident that they were the dominant character in an almost equal relationship. However much they switched from dominant to submissive, it usually ended up with Jenny being on the top and Sara the bottom. True that Jenny's bottom received the majority of the spankings, paddlings and whippings but that was as much Jenny's doing as Sara's, and it was true that Sara got the pleasure of receiving far more of the appendages, strap-ons and paraphernalia inserted in various orifices that the two of them bought. What Sara took a while to realise was that the scenario suited Jenny as much as, if not more than, her and when she looked back on their relationship, it was generally Jenny who had the ideas and inventive thoughts that directed their sexual activity. Some of their more unusual practices were not what Sara herself would have chosen and she recognised that Jenny had led her into a more depraved sexual lifestyle. There were certainly some fruit and vegetable episodes, as well as copious amounts of yoghurt and double cream that Sara had meekly obeyed instructions to purchase. Earlier experiences with Jenny meant that she definitely knew that they were intended for use in the bedroom rather than the kitchen, but she very much assumed that their private lives would remain exactly that!

Any repercussions of their actions were not dwelled upon; caution and secrecy seemed to serve them well, and their good luck held. Sara did not allow herself to spend time considering the fact that Jenny's role in their partnership would never be considered a breach of college rules and regulations in the way that Sara's participation would. Jenny's time at the college passed, but the two stayed in touch, in every sense of the word, and the relationship continued and developed, albeit on a more occasional basis as Jenny began her career in one of London's leading legal and financial institutions. It seemed a perfect relationship, one that they had both embraced wholeheartedly, as it suited both their needs. However, that depended somewhat on their relationship remaining a jointly beneficial one. Sara's flourishing partnership with Jamie was not something beneficial to Jenny, however, and that was to prove more of an issue than Sara had ever considered.

CHAPTER 6

EMILY SETS THE BALL ROLLING

Emily Govan was not surprised when her mobile phone pinged to alert her to an email from one of the Seven Sisters, an elite group of privileged and affluent third year students at the college. The seven beautiful, arrogant and confident young ladies were equally feared and envied by their fellow students and, in truth, by some of the academics and staff at St. James'. Emily's heart skipped as she read the message which basically summoned her to Hilary Brook-Boyde's room after lectures on the following day. She had been waiting, since a major incident towards the end of the previous academic year, for Hilary to make her move and inadvertently put into action the loose plan that Emily had discussed with the Dean of Discipline, Professor Stones, their intention being to trick the Seven Sisters into a major transgression so that they would fall foul of the college's strict disciplinary code. Emily's treatment at the hands of the gang meant that she would have no compunction or reluctance in assisting the Professor in taking them down. Her dream was to be present in Professor Stones' rooms as he thrashed the naked backsides of seven distraught and shamed young ladies. Hopefully, she fantasised, over a period of several hours and with much sobbing, howling and begging as the group were reduced to pitiful, begging wrecks by the harshest of punishments! Meanwhile, Emily couldn't help but feel a frisson of anticipatory lust and desire when she considered what Hilary's order to attend her room promised. The whole episode earlier in the year had left her somewhat confused as to her sexual inclinations as she had found herself masturbating while spanking her own bottom, offering herself to the elderly but incredibly imposing Dean of Discipline, as well as licking the pussies of Seven Sisters' member Chloe and her flatmate Georgina. Having not considered herself to be a fan of sado-masochistic behaviour nor having a penchant for older men or indeed a leaning towards lesbianism, her behaviour had left her mind a whirl as far as her sexual leanings went. Although she had been in Professor Stones' company on a couple of occasions since those days, she still felt her cheeks blush bright red in front of him when the memory of how she had presented her beaten backside to him and invited him to take her anal virginity flashed through her mind. She had no understanding of her connection to him but knew that his thrashing and total humiliation of her had created an amazing loyalty, love and devotion to him that was beyond any emotion and attachment that any other person had ever generated in her.

Emily prepared herself early the next evening; she was under no illusion that Hilary was planning a sexual encounter and was happy to entertain the idea of a lesbian relationship, particularly if it could lead to a reckoning for the loathed Secret Seven. Not altogether happy with her lack of morals and her rather pronounced, in her mind at least, sexual drive and thirst for adventures of an erotic nature. She wondered if her rather open and experimental behaviour indicated a true bisexual outlook but was reasonably content to follow her instincts and see where they took her. An appreciation of the perceived security of university life was, she suspected, part of the answer. It certainly felt like a safe environment and seemed like the ideal time and place to make the most of what was on offer. *Or maybe I am just a bit of a lusty tart,* she pondered, a rather sly and self-satisfied smile playing on her lips. Hilary was certainly an attractive young woman, although she came across as a bit conflicted, and Emily supposed that the risk involved with such a contrary personality was part of the fun. There was no way of anticipating the direction that this relationship, if that is what it was, would take and Emily was fully aware that she was likely to find herself used rather than the user. She had to admit that she felt very little fear and quite a lot of excitement, so she could hardly complain if things did not turn out well, and was relatively sanguine about that thought.

Dressed demurely in a summer dress and a matching, pretty rather than sexy, set of underwear, she tapped on Hilary's door.

"Enter!" came the snapped response from within which Emily sensed did not necessarily bode well for Hilary's mood.

"Oh, don't you look the pretty little virgin then?" Hilary was standing centrally in the lounge area of her single occupancy, high grade room, hands on hips, dressed in skinny top and tracksuit bottoms. Emily took a breath and with a fixed smile trying to evoke anticipation and excitement at being in her presence, went straight to her and planted a kiss directly on Hilary's lips. Hilary jolted and immediately responded, grabbing Emily's neck and kissing her passionately back, long and hard. Emily's hands purposely slipped around her to caress the firm track-suited buttocks of her adversary and nemesis. A hand circled her breast through the dress and Emily could feel her nipples harden as her mixed feelings towards Hilary again came to the fore and any reluctance to engage faded away in her sexual wantonness. As their breasts came together, Emily became instantly aware that the other girl was not wearing a bra, nor was there a sign of panties to be felt through her fondling. If Emily had previously had any doubts about why she had been summoned they were being very quickly dispelled. Hilary was clearly prepared and ready for sex to take place. Emily found herself being manipulated to the couch and opted to take the compliant route to see where things would lead. Pushed face down onto the cushioned surface, she laid still as hands quickly unbuttoned her dress, slipping it over her head before fingers deftly unhooked her bra and went straight to her nipples, squeezing and pinching them fully erect. Hilary began to kiss her back and neck, switching to much gentler mode as she sighed and positioned her groin against Emily's bottom, very casually rolling her hips as she pressed against her.

"Hilary's going to fuck her little slave girl. Hilary's little slave girl is going to lick Hilary's lovely juicy pussy. Hilary's little slave girl is so going to have her cute little arse spanked. What does Hilary's little slave girl have to say to that?"

Emily didn't have to work too hard to go along with this little role play; she was already aroused and nothing Hilary had said so far had caused her any concern – in fact very much to the contrary!

"Oh thank you, Mistress Hilary, your little slave girl would be honoured to do as you say," Emily purred demurely.

Hilary dropped to her knees behind her and deftly slipped Emily's knickers down before beginning to plant delicate kisses on her exposed buttocks, her knees edging Emily's legs wider apart. Emily gasped as a hand snaked around her thighs and fingers fluttered amongst her already moistened vaginal lips. As Hilary's mouth dipped underneath her bottom, Emily lifted her hips and spread her legs further to allow a flicking tongue to make contact with the lower reaches of her eager pussy. With one rock hard nipple held firmly between the fingers of Hilary's left hand, an equally erect clitoris being massaged firmly with her right, a probing tongue tantalising her pussy and her arsehole bring nuzzled with a nose tip, Emily was well on the way to an early climax. This, however, was apparently not to Hilary's liking as all contact was suddenly broken and she grabbed a handful of Emily's blonde locks.

"Enough of this, you're having all the fun, slave girl. My turn now, get your head down there and drink my sweet nectar, bitch!" Hilary had quickly slipped her top and bottoms off, as Emily had surmised she was indeed naked beneath, and thrown herself onto the couch at Emily's head and, with her open her legs, encased Emily's face and pulled her into her crotch. Emily allowed her to assume control; she had no doubt that she was the fitter and stronger woman but could see no advantage in making that clear to Hilary. Playing her part to perfection, she looked up at Hilary with fake love and admiration all over her face saying, "Oh mistress, your slave girl is so honoured and will worship your beautiful sex and drink your golden nectar." Her thoughts might not have quite matched her words but as she lent in to breathe the sweet scent of Hilary's arousal, she couldn't deny to herself her lust and excitement as she kissed the wet lips gently, enjoying the velvet feel of her moist swollen folds. Her hands reached up to close around the pert breasts above her, her fingernails flicking at the dark nipples. Emily found herself audibly slurping as she lapped the secretions dribbling liberally from Hilary's quim, her face soon becoming smeared. Hilary's hands once more grabbed Emily's hair as she began to thrust herself into her face. Emily reacted by circling her clit with her tongue, causing the other girl to moan loudly. Pushing inside of her and applying pressure with the bridge of her nose to Hilary's erect clitoris, Emily massaged the inside of her pussy with her long probing tongue.

"Yes, yes, my beauty, fuck me, fuck me." Approaching her climax,

Hilary began to ride Emily's face harder and harder. Emily responded by forcing her tongue deeper inside, mimicking a plunging penis as she did all she could to bring on Hilary's zenith.

She devoured the dripping pussy, sliding two fingers in to join her tongue, her thumb now flicking the hard clitoral nub. Another digit searched out Hilary's arsehole and forced its way inside her tight tunnel, using her oozing liquid to smooth the passage. Hilary's back arched, her whole body writhing as she reached for the pinnacle of her sexual desire.

"Aaaaargggghhhhhhh!" she groaned as she submitted to a shuddering climax, her flanks slamming down onto Emily's face, covering her with glistening juice. Hilary face contorted in ecstasy, her cheeks flushing bright red as she slumped over Emily, her breath coming in long trembling gasps as she recovered slowly from her draining frenzy.

"That was excellent, and now it's time for a little spanking fun," Hilary jeered at Emily as she pulled her arms to turn her over. "Get that luscious booty over the arm of the couch, bitch, mamma's gonna break your sweet ass!"

Emily sighed as she allowed Hilary to enjoy her seemingly controlling position. She was still very aroused and she doubted that her paramour possessed the wherewithal to cause her too much discomfort with her hand. On the contrary, Emily thought, a good spanking was maybe the missing ingredient of recent weeks and could actually be a real treat!

Her round and perfectly formed bottom received the first spank without any reaction save a slight quiet sigh. Hilary began to smack her bottom with strong, sharp slaps using the flat palm of her hand causing a satisfying loud reverberation and a stinging sensation rather than much in the way of actual pain. However, she yelled out theatrically, surmising that Hilary would get off on her apparent distress. Each time Hilary's hand landed on her butt, she edged closer and closer to her own orgasm as she slipped a hand under and began to frig herself.

"You can pack that in. I well remember that you have a penchant for spanking and wanking. I'll decide if and when you get to come. Up you get and into the bedroom, face down, head on your arms, arse up in the air, legs apart." Hilary barked her instructions as she took a handful of Emily's hair and dragged her into the adjoining bedroom. Again Emily obeyed without hesitation while trying not to look too keen as she very much suspected that a little too much eagerness to comply might threaten Hilary's little power trip.

The slam of the flat-backed hairbrush on her lower left buttock cheek drew a yelp of both pain and surprise, and Emily realised immediately that the game had moved up a notch or two.

"Not feeling so smug now, are you? I am going to make you beg for mercy, slave girl. Take that!"

The brush landed, flattening Emily's cheeks with the power of the blows; her knees buckled and her body collapsed down to the bed.

The onslaught that followed was relentless and Emily found tears flowing from her eyes as she battled to hold back the screams of pain she felt. She recognised eventually that it was just pointless pride and stubbornness that caused her to refrain from begging for her tormentor to cease.

"Stop! Oh please, stop. Please, please, please. Aaaaargh! No more please."

The barrage halted and Emily heard the sound of the discarded brush dropping to the floor with relief. She tried to contain her weeping as she realised that she had been reduced to a blubbering wreck by someone that she held in little respect and now had a diminishing amount of desire for. The idea that this episode might be a big step towards the downfall of the nasty little gang, that had become such an established order in the college, gave her renewed vigour and the courage she knew she would need if the idea that was brewing in her mind was to come to anything.

"So, was that your best shot then? Because I've had better and had worse, whichever way you look at it." She taunted Hilary as she rolled herself off the bed and inspected her red battered cheeks in the mirror.

"Hmmmm. Bet this mirror has seen a few things. Mainly you wanking yourself off though, I suspect."

A silence hung in the room as Emily watched Hilary's stunned expression in the mirror, her mouth literally hanging open.

"Oh you really do want it, don't you bitch? Well then, you're fucking going to get it! Back on the bed, all fours, legs apart, back arched, put the goods on display, slut." Hilary almost barked at her before looking wildly around and then flouncing off, muttering and cursing, into the adjoining kitchen. Emily allowed herself a wry smile as she positioned herself as instructed, feeling a small amount of trepidation but more honestly quite aroused and decidedly wanton.

"Dear God, Em, what is wrong with you?" She mumbled to herself as she felt her vaginal lips moisten once more with lust and expectation.

Hilary marched back into the room and Emily suddenly found herself without vision as a large towel was wrapped around her head.

"Let's add an element of surprise to proceedings, shall we?" Hilary's voice was quite breathless and Emily realised that she was fairly agitated. "Not only can you not see me, I won't have to look at your blubbing face or have your pathetic tears and ghastly running nose dripping into my sheets. Because you, my little toy girl, are most certainly going to be weeping and begging for mercy when I have finished with you!" This promise was accompanied by a hard slap from what Emily could only guess to be a wooden serving implement.

Emily knew that her quickly formulated plan might require some flexibility as the second blow slammed against her cheeks causing her to yelp. The third blow brought tears to her eyes and Emily realised that her tormentor's prediction of her distress may not be so far off kilter! The blows continued to rain down and soon Emily was sobbing freely, the stinging approaching a level that she recognised was wherein the sexual excitement of the ritual became outweighed by the sheer pain. At that moment, Hilary chose to apply her vicious and wholehearted swipes to the backs of Emily's thighs, causing her knees to buckle and her body to slump to the bed. Hilary laughed in triumph and cockily sneered the words that would seal her fate:

"Not so fucking tough now, are you, bitch? Let's see how you like having your bum fucked by a wooden spoon shall we?"

As Hilary attempted to part Emily's arse cheeks with one hand whilst positioning the spoon with the other, a furious Emily bucked her off. Ripping the towel off her head and twisting quickly, her hands grabbed Hilary's head and she threw her off the bed with considerable force. Delighted to see that Hilary was still naked, she moved her hands to her breasts and squeezed hard.

"Right, you nasty little cow, let's see how you like it."

Hilary's resistance was futile, as Emily forced her face down into the bed and, grabbing the wooden spoon, began to thrash the other girl's buttocks with extreme force. From sputtered indignation to subdued and conquered victim in seconds, Hilary was soon wailing and begging for mercy.

"Aaaaargh! No please Emily, stop, I'm sorry. Yaaaaar! Yaaaaar!

Yaaaaar! Noooo! Ooooh yaaar!"

Emily was in no mood to show mercy and, still swiping at the scarlet cheeks, she tugged Hilary to her feet and frog-marched her into the bathroom. Kicking at the backs of her knees to bring her down, she soon had Hilary bent, kneeling over the lavatory bowl.

"What? What? What?" were the only words she managed before her head was unceremoniously pushed into the toilet as Emily pulled the handle to flush it.

Hilary had barely come to terms with the indignation and discomfort of that, when Emily forced a shower gel bottle to her arsehole and squeezed a quarter of its contents into Hilary's back passage.

"Noooooo! No, no, no. Uuuurggghhh!"

Hilary's entreaties fell on deaf ears as the handle of the wooden spoon slid effortlessly into the well-oiled channel which Emily forced to the hilt. Down went Hilary's head again as the toilet flushed once more.

"Not thinking you're such the big boss now, then?" Emily said as she picked up a bath brush and slammed it down with all her might onto Hilary's bottom.

Again and again the flat side of the brush landed on Hilary's rosy cheek as Emily got into a rhythm. The bottom beneath her turned bright red, then a mottled scarlet, as the blows rained down. Hilary had succumbed, the fight had gone, the screams now rather guttural with a quieter anguish evident. Emily discarded the brush, forced Hilary's head back down into the bowl and repeated the flushing process. Emily stood and looked down at the defeated young woman before her, her bottom cheeks ablaze and the wooden spoon still embedded between her cheeks.

"So fuck you and your silly little gang. How do you like them apples?" a triumphant Emily taunted, adding, "You can stay right where you are while I get dressed and if that spoon isn't still proudly sticking out of your arse when I come back, then I will push it up there bristle-end first."

She left minutes later, leaving Hilary still bent over the toilet and struggling to hold the wooden spoon inside of her, fighting against her body's natural inclination to eject from her arsehole. Emily realised it had not been her finest hour but she dismissed thoughts of the repercussions of her act and vowed to enjoy her moment of triumph while she could. Hours later, when the cock of a local youth she'd bumped into at a city centre nightspot was slamming in and out of her pussy, it was thoughts of her conquest of Hilary that drove her to climax rather than the manipulations of the sweating, groaning body fucking her.

It was over a week later when she was suddenly caught unawares walking through the college that she knew it was time to talk to Professor Stones. The Seven Sisters swarmed around her, Chloe and Zoe manhandling her into an alcove in the cloisters. Threats and promises were made, reprisals outlined and a warning issued that she would soon find out what happened to those who crossed the gang. Emily had no doubt that they meant every word and knew that she needed to speak to Professor Stones as soon as possible.

She was so relieved when she spilled out her story to Professor Stones that he found the situation both funny and ideal. She got a lecture about her temper but otherwise he seemed to think that it was a pretty good opportunity to set up the gang for a big fall. Emily was not quite as happy as she sat listening to him outlining her next role in the developing saga but had to admit that it all made sense and that she had made her bed, and now she would probably have to do a bit more than lie in it!

CHAPTER 7

EMILY IS FLUSHED OUT (ALMOST)

Several weeks passed, often with Emily ducking and diving to avoid bumping into the group again, before she found herself face-to-face with no escape route available. Surrounded by the eager young ladies, Chloe moved into the middle of the gathering as the others closed in around them, shielding them from the sight of anyone passing. Chloe placed her hands gently on Emily's cheeks and spoke quietly and menacingly.

"So my brave little warrior, we meet again at last. It honestly feels like you have been avoiding us. Now let me see, why could that be?" The teasing Chloe stroked her face and moved in closer so that their lips almost touched.

"Oh yes, I remember. You decided to pick on my friend here when she spurned your perverted lesbian advances. You presumably have been hiding since hoping that time would heal, wounds would repair and memories would fade. Surely not? Well, time is up, loser. You had your fun and now you have to pay your dues. I'll be getting a message to you soon when I've finally prepared your payback, and believe me, bitch, it is going to be some payback! But the time is coming. I promised you that we would have our revenge and now we are just about ready. You will do as you are told because I am going to give you an example of what could happen if you don't."

Emily blanched; Chloe had an air of threat and chilling intensity that sliced deep inside and Emily was so grateful that she had the Professor in her corner to, hopefully, cover her back. Chloe surreptitiously moved her fingers down to the crotch of Emily's jeans as the mob closed tightly around them. As her fingers forced themselves between her legs, Chloe edged forward so that their lips brushed against each other's once more. Emily stood frozen in the encased centre of the circle as simultaneously Chloe's tongue slipped into her mouth which automatically opened as she fiercely and painfully dug her fingers into her crotch.

"Like I said, your time is up, bitch. You are now going to face the full force of the vengeance of the Seven Sisters." Chloe released her with a theatrical flourish and the group departed leaving Emily shaking and breathing deeply. She hated that she had been so intimidated by the gang but knew now that the play was on and, pulling herself together, she text Professor Stones to update him.

The following day Emily returned to her rooms to find her flat mate Georgina naked, bound and gagged in her room with a small flag waving from the stem planted in her arsehole. Her bottom was bright red, clearly recently beaten, and her terrified face was wet with tears. Emily quickly released her and stepped back as her furious friend unleashed. "You stupid fucking cow, Em! What have you gone and bloody well done now? Those bitches were here and said that this was all down to you, they fucking spanked me and played with my cooze. That fucking cow Chloe kept shoving her fingers up my bum and cooze and telling me how she was going to put milk bottles up there if you didn't do as you are told. Why the fuck have you pissed them off, Em? They are fucking evil and that bloody Chloe is terrifying!"

Emily did her best to soothe Georgina, stroking her hair and whispering calming words before venturing:

"Report them to the Dean, Georgie. Don't let them get away with it. I'll come with you, sweetheart, and we can make a joint complaint."

Georgina shot out of her arms, her nakedness in front of Emily now having become incidental since they had both been beaten and humiliated in Professor Stones room before being subject to further abuse at the hands of the Secret Seven.

"Are you fucking out of your crazy fucking little mind? Do you really not realise how those bitches will destroy us if you take them on, Em? Do you know what that bitch Zoe said before they left? She told me that if I breathed a word of complaint or they got to hear anyone else talking about it they would come back, all use the bog and then stick my head in it and flush it to give me a piss shampoo! Please just do what they want, for chrissakes, Emily, they fucking terrify me!"

Emily knew when to let an argument go. Certainly one thing that she was happy to credit Professor Stones with.

Emily had decided it would be prudent to keep her rather special relationship with the Dean private. Certainly, the strange attraction that the man of over forty years her senior held for her was not something she was content to share with anyone else. The frankly quite ridiculous crush she had on him was something beyond her comprehension anyway, but none of her sexual activity since she had been across his knee had given her anything close to the longing and desire he had unleashed within her when she was in his company.

"I'll sort it Georgie, please don't worry my sweet."

Minutes later Emily received a text informing her that she was expected to attend HGR1, the Honoured Guest Room 1, a luxurious suite that was available for overnight stays for major dignitaries visiting the college. Rarely used, it was a fascinating destination for the Seven Sisters to have access to, set in the college's visitors' hub, which housed a small theatre, a special-occasions dining room and various meeting and conference rooms. Run by the college's Catering, Conferences and Events team, it was normally access controlled to such a degree that mere students like Emily had had no occasion to enter. Somehow, the notorious gang must have got hold of keys to the top accommodation suite and Emily could not help but be impressed at discovering the set scene for her planned denouement. However, the text cited the session was to take place in two days' time and Emily's heart fluttered in panic as she frantically text the Professor to see if he would be in a position to prepare whatever it was he intended in order to entrap the group.

Stones' response was quick but not welcome as he told Emily that two days was insufficient notice and that she was to do her part in ensuring that the Friday rather than the planned Tuesday was the first acceptable day for what he had planned to take place. Her growing panic subsided when she read that he would place obstacles in the way to manipulate the thinking and planning of the Seven Sisters to ensure that the date would get postponed to suit his needs. As it happened, the Professor's stalling tactics worked perfectly as notices appeared on the block housing HGR1 that some plumbing remedial work was necessary and the building would not reopen until 9 a.m. on the Friday. Later that day, walking through the town window-shopping, she received a text from Zoe telling her that she had to be at HGR1 at 7 p.m. on the Friday, not the Tuesday, and that if she failed to turn up, the consequences would be off the scale. Her heart skipped a beat as the next text told her that eyes were on her and not to spend too much money shopping. She spun round but could see no one she recognised. She took a calming breath and replied, stating that she had no thought of failing to keep to the instruction and just wanted to get this over and done with. When she returned to college she was delighted to see a request from Professor Stones for a briefing to discuss how things would go.

Friday took an age to come as Emily went through a range of emotions. Trepidation, fear, horror and, yes, she had to admit just a tad of excitement were feelings that surfaced as the hours dragged by. She ate and drank little; after what she had done to Hilary, she was expecting certain aspects of her punishment to be more toilet based than others! She showered, shaved and washed herself very intimately several times; she dressed, undressed and then dressed again, aware of the irony that she was taking so long on deciding what to wear when in all likelihood her clothes would be removed fairly soon after she entered the room! She was conscious that the Professor had told her that virtually every inch of the rooms in HGR1 were now covered by hidden cameras, hence his insistence on delaying the event until his technical people had the time they needed to carry out his wishes.

The message from Zoe, as the deadline approached, was simple: "Be dressed like a virgin, no trousers. Make your way towards HGR1 and you will be met and brought up to the room. Make sure you leave any attitude behind, do as you are told and with any luck you'll still be able to walk afterwards!" *Great*, thought Emily, deciding that she needed yet another change of clothes. She quickly slipped a reasonably new matching white bra and knickers and an off-white shirt-style dress, adding little white socks to top off the look of purity she was aiming for. She was quite proud of her general calmness and acceptance of what was to come but in her mind she likened it to a painful dental visit – it would be fine until it hurt and then it wouldn't be so fine, but hopefully it wouldn't last long! She was well aware that she was partially excited about what the seven would do to her and had found herself having to distract herself to resist masturbating on several occasions over the last few days. Her faith in the Professor's plan was absolute but she knew that her pride, her bottom and probably her pussy were all going to have to take a fair pummelling before she was rescued. However, her lust for revenge was total and the thought that the Secret Seven were maybe only hours away from destruction gave her the necessary bravado to believe that she could pull this off. Of course, pleasing Professor Stones was a big part of this and she accepted that she was desperate to earn his favour, his gratitude and his respect.

Her rooms being a few minutes walk from the central block that housed the guest room where she was to meet her tormentors, Emily set off in good time and left her staircase to walk the walk of the condemned. Immediately, Zoe appeared beside her.

"Just coming to fetch you bitch, now link arms, smile and walk along with me. I'm especially looking forward to feeling your tongue in my fanny tonight so I hope you've cleaned your teeth, slag."

As an opening gambit, Emily thought she'd heard better! However she kept her thoughts to herself and stayed mute.

"Cat got your tongue, has it bitch? Or are you too terrified to speak? Don't fucking ignore me, you stuck up cow, or I'll take you in a doorway and kick your arse!"

Emily took a moment and decided to play the passive, subdued role rather than antagonise Zoe further.

"I am really sorry, Zoe but I am just so scared about what's going to happen to me. Please can you give me a chance to make things OK. I'll apologise to Hilary and do anything for her to make things right. Anything Zoe, anything she wants or perhaps anything you want?" She leaned into Zoe and put her most doe-eyed, submissive expression on. The way the evening was going to go was made clear in an instance as Zoe's hand fastened on her chin and she stared deep into Emily's eyes saying, "Don't try that shit on with me, slag. You are full of it, and you are going to find out how we deal with that shortly." She pushed her away as they reached the back staircase that would take them up to the guest room and, opening the door with a key, pushed Emily ahead of her.

"Up the stairs, you piece of trash, now this shit is about to get real." With that, Zoe pushed her forward with one hand on her back and the other slipping under her skirt to grab her crotch. "We are going to fucking wear you out. You'll need a new fanny and arsehole when we've finished with you, you blonde slapper."

Emily stumbled into the room where Chloe, Charlotte, Hilary, Helen, Saffron and Miranda were sprawled around the large, exquisitely furnished lounge. They had clearly been drinking as several bottles of wine were open and a cheer went up as Emily tumbled into the room.

"Lamb to the slaughter, lamb to the slaughter!" shouted Saffron.

"Pigs to the trough," Emily snapped back without thinking. A silence descended. Chloe was the first to break it.

"So, no pleas for mercy, no sobbing heart-rending apology, no pathetic tears of repentance. Just straight in with your smartarse quips and smug comebacks. Well, fuck you then Emily Govan, let's get straight to it then." With that, Chloe stood up and slapped Emily hard across the face, grabbed a handful of her hair and dragged her to the sofa where Hilary was sitting.

"Right bitch, you can start by apologising first for the unprovoked attack on my friend here."

Emily knew that her mouth had yet again worked faster than her brain and her first thought was that the watching Professor, who had promised her that every moment in the college set would be filmed, would already be disappointed in her performance. But now she had chosen that path, Emily decided to continue.

"Yeah right, like little miss two-faced sadomasochistic lesbian has done nothing wrong then? Oh, Hilary haven't you shared the details? Don't your friends here know about your surreptitious activities, your love of pussy, well my pussy, really. Oh Hilary, didn't you share with your friends the way you beat me and fucked me? Oh sorry, was it a secret?"

Hilary's bright red face and wild eyes full of panic rather gave her away and Emily knew that her supposition that Hilary had kept her actions in her room from the others was spot on.

There was a long pause as eyes turned towards Chloe.

"Not saying anything, Hilary? Not disputing Emily's version? Not got more lies to tell us? Not going to let us know what you two minge munchers have really been up to behind our backs?"

Emily watched fascinated, and enjoyed the respite, as all attention turned to a shaking and panicking Hilary who started to talk pure gibberish.

"No! Yes, but so did she. I didn't, please Chloe, it was nothing, I just said, I'm sorry, she's such a bitch...oh, Chloe, sorry."

Zoe and Saffron had risen, their eyes flicking between coldly furious Chloe and the stricken, trembling Hilary.

"I fucking told you what would happen if you lied to us again. We are as one. We are together. We are the Seven Sisters. What are the simple five words that make up our code, dipshit?"

"I know, I know. *Loyalty, Trust and Honesty Always*. I'm sorry Chloe, she just makes me feel...oh I don't know. She's evil, Chloe, let's beat her, let's make the bitch squeal. Come on everyone, remember why we are here, let's get started on this fucking cow. Remember what she fucking well did to me. Let's tear her a new arsehole, let's beat the shit out of the smug cow!"

Emily watched in a detached state; She could read the atmosphere and the power-play going on in the room even if Hilary couldn't. For the moment she knew she was just secondary business. For the present Hilary was the one seriously in the shit and Emily was happy to quietly watch this develop. Chloe, on the ball as always, caught her eye.

"This changes nothing, sweetheart. This just delays the inevitable, so watch and sweat. This is just a minor holdup that will make the worst night of your life last longer. Helen, fetch one of the bamboo canes from the bedroom. Hilary are we doing this the easy way or the hard way?"

As Helen slipped into the next room, giving Emily a fleeting view of a large bedroom containing a huge bed and, more disconcerting for Emily, a table covered in what looked like a vast assortment of sex toys and strap-on dildos, as well as a black cloth-covered, odd-shaped piece of equipment of some sort.

Chloe nodded at Zoe and Saffron. *Clearly the two lieutenants to Commander Chloe,* thought a philosophical Emily, feeling oddly calm as the focus passed briefly to Hilary's predicament. Hilary was blubbing now, begging for mercy and frantically grabbing at Miranda and Charlotte as she desperately looked for support.

The next words from Chloe were cold and unemotional and Emily realised that Hilary had been on borrowed time with the other gang members.

"I told you last time that one mistake was acceptable and just made a fool of you. A repeat is deliberate and means you chose to make fools of us. We agreed the punishment, when we joined forces, that any major breech of the code that constituted betrayal was punishable by five strokes of the cane from each of the other members. To be taken with remorse and gratitude, to seek forgiveness and to be allowed to continue within the society. Am I correct, ladies?"

Helen joined Saffron, Zoe, Charlotte and Miranda as they stood over the cowering Hilary and they all voiced their assent.

"Please Chloe, no." Tears ran down Hilary's cheeks as she searched the faces of her supposed friends for any dig of support.

"I asked if everyone agreed, Hilary. Do you agree that you have broken our rule? Five words is all you had to remember and each stroke of the cane from each one of us will be spoken to signify compliance with the code. You have no time to consider options Hilary; either you agree and accept your fate or you leave this room and our group now. So I repeat for your little brain one more time: am I correct?"

Emily was impressed when Hilary broke the hanging silence in the room.

"Yes, Chloe, you are correct. The code was agreed and I broke it and must be punished accordingly. I am sorry ladies, your friendship is my priority and I love you all. I transgressed because of the spell this witch cast on me. Beat the evil from me and then we must destroy the witch!"

Whoops, thought Emily, still relaxed and calm. Much as the pain of a serious beating was something she knew she'd dread and hate while it was happening, the before-and-after she found exciting and intensely sexual even in such intimidating circumstances.

"Stand up, Hilary, your witch friend is going to undress you now, aren't you bitch?" Chloe snarled at Emily.

"Of course, Chloe, my pleasure. In fact, can I beat her too?" Emily smiled serenely at Chloe, aware that her internal radar was sensing a mutual attraction between her and Chloe that was disconcerting but adding to Emily's thrill factor.

Chloe raised her eyebrows as Emily lifted Hilary's dress over her raised arms, ignoring and disregarding the look of total hatred that Hilary was trying to direct at her.

"Fucking butch cow," Hilary hissed at Emily as she reached around her to unhook her bra straps, releasing her breasts.

"Tut, tut, now Hilary, your time for talking has long gone. In fact, yes Emily, you may start the ball rolling and enjoy a moment being on the winner's side of the cane."

Emily kissed Hilary lightly on her lips before she slid down her body to put her face at the level of Hilary's groin. She slipped her knickers down breathing in the sweet pungency of the sweating, fearful student.

Emily looked at Chloe, showing demure respect as she waited for the gang leader to issue instructions.

"You know the position, Hilary. Turn and present, knees on the sofa, head and arms over the back, find something to grab onto, legs apart, bottom up proudly, please."

Chloe took the long bamboo cane from Helen.

"Bitch first, then Charlotte, Miranda, Helen, Saffron, Zoe, and then I'll finish off and also apply any additional punishment strokes she earns." This caused a long sobbing intake of breath from Hilary, whose fortitude Emily was definitely questioning.

"Emily, the mantra is loyalty, truth and honesty always. One word, one stroke, then pass the bamboo to Charlotte. Let's get started and thrash the treachery from our friend, forgive her and move on. Apply the rod please, Emily."

Silence descended. Emily raised the bamboo high then brought it down sharply across the centre of Hilary's bottom.

Hilary grunted, let out a sob, then clearly said, "Loyalty. Thank you, Emily."

The second stroke went inches lower, two red lines stark against the whiteness of the displayed buttocks.

"Oh, oh, oh. Truth. Thank you, Emily."

Emily sent the third stroke even lower to the sensitive spot where the legs joined the buttocks with little protection.

"Grrrrrr. The fuck! Fuck! Fuuuuck!!!!!" was the reception and response from Hilary, followed by, "And. And. And. And. Please. Thank you, Emily. Oh my. Oh my. Oh my."

Emily adjusted her position and aimed just above the centre of the writhing and smarting cheeks. The cane flashed down and the slap resounded throughout the room as it bit harshly into the fleshier part of Hilary's bottom.

"Oh fuck! Fucking fuck, that fucking hurts, you bitch!" Hilary raised up, her eyes alight with pain and anger. Chloe was on her immediately and a hand clamped her neck as she forced her back over the sofa back, her backside raised high off the ground.

"You have not said the word and you have left your position so that's three punishment strokes you've earned from me. Now say the word, apologise to our guest and ask her to repeat the stroke. It would be best then it you could just shut the fuck up and take your punishment."

A tearfully contrite Hilary sobbed out the demanded words.

"Honesty. It's honesty. So sorry, Chloe, and I am very sorry that I was so rude, Emily. Please beat me again."

With Hilary's bottom raised high, as Chloe continued to hold her head down, Emily went to the obvious spot where the thighs met the lower buttocks. The cane flashed through the air before landing forcefully on the targeted strip of flesh with a slapping thud. The screech from Hilary was her reward and, although only a small victory in the terms of what was ahead, it was a reward that gave her great satisfaction and some much needed bravado that she was certain to need shortly.

"What do you say, Hilary?" Chloe said in that quiet, sadistic tone that sent a little frisson of fear down Emily's spine.

"Oh, sorry, Chloe. Always. I'm so sorry and thank you for having me punished," whimpered the mewling and defeated body hanging limply over the sofa back.

"Yes, that's all very well, Hilary, but surely I don't need to remind you of punishment responses or maybe this is your way of asking for some extra strokes from me?"

"No, no, no. Sorry, Chloe. Please, no more. Emily, Emily, I am so sorry and I would like to thank you for my beating, yes, thank you Emily, thank you so much."

At Chloe's nod, Emily leaned forward and stroked Hilary's hair, brushing her neck with her lips as she whispered in her ear.

"It was all my pleasure, Hilary, my absolute pleasure to beat your naughty little bottom hard. I hope you enjoy the rest." She patted the red cheeks and stood aside as Charlotte took the cane, immediately raised it and swiped across the centre of the striped bottom before completely catching Hilary out.

"Yaaaaaar! Fuck. Oh no. One. I mean *Loyalty*, thank you Charlotte."

As the cane fell again Chloe brought Emily right back to earth.

"You, my little bitch girl, are looking far too comfortable. Get your clothes off now," she ordered.

Emily disrobed, carefully placing her clothes in a neat little pile on a bookshelf. She wasn't sure at all how this would go and at what point the Professor and whoever the 'little team' he had mentioned to her would consist of. But if the scenario involved the room being flooded with people that she didn't know particularly well, she would want to grab something to cover any remaining dignity this sisterhood left her with.

As Hilary's beating continued, she stood between Chloe and Zoe as demurely and innocently as she could. Emily was sure that they were already pissed off enough with her to be considering doing serious damage to her in one way or another, and rather doubted that she needed to do anything much to egg them on.

The last of the second set of five strokes landed across the backs of Hilary's legs and although Emily was certain that her own strokes had been delivered much harder, Hilary was now sobbing and gasping rather dramatically as she struggled to get out the words of contrition and thanks to Charlotte.

"Hmmmm. That'll do, I suppose. Miranda can take over now."

The cane was again passed on and Miranda stepped forward. With no other sound in the room, Emily felt oddly detached from this weird authority power-play that she was certain was all down to Chloe and her desire to inflict suffering on those who crossed her. The others seemed only too happy to turn on one of their own and Emily suspected that partly it was relief that it was Hilary rather than any one of them who had earned what she was categorising in her mind as "The Wrath of Chloe". As Zoe's hand slipped down to stroke her bottom, Emily smiled sweetly at her and steeled herself not to flinch or move away whatever happened.

Miranda's final stroke landed, strokes which Emily were sure were all in the energetic sweep of the arm but lacking potency at the point of contact. *She does not really have the spirit for this,* mused Emily. *God knows why she ever got mixed up with this bunch.* As Miranda passed the cane to Helen, Zoe spoke words that boded rather badly for Emily:

"What I really hate you for is your fucking gorgeous body; your superb tits, the perfect fanny and an arse to eat supper off of. Let alone that you're slim, blonde and oh so fucking beautiful. I really despise you, bitch! It's important that you understand that. Especially when I ram a foot long plastic cock deep in your arse. I am going to ruin you bitch and that will be after I've flayed the skin off those oh so perfect orbs. You won't feel like such a queen when we've finished with you. No more lording it over the rest of us with your fucking smartarse remarks and those cocky little looks that I see you handing out. I hate you Emily Govan, just so as you know!"

"Hey ho, Zoe. Why don't you just tell me how you really feel, my darling." *It was probably unwise,* thought Emily, *but, sometimes, what the fuck!* That Zoe did not really know her hardly seemed the point as Zoe had clearly formed a picture of her that was giving Emily much food for thought. *Not the best time for some introspection,* she decided, but Zoe's words had caught her by surprise in their pure malice and clear envy.

A vice-like grip on a nipple and a wicked fingernail based pinch on a buttock were her answers, and tears were springing to Emily's eyes before Chloe's voice cut through the air, silencing Hilary's screams and Helen's arm as she had continued to rain blows down onto the scarlet and severely marked buttocks before her.

"Wait Zoe, her time will come, but let's first enjoy her before we spoil her, my friend."

The hands fell from her body and Emily felt that her execution had been stayed and promised herself that she would try a little bit harder to keep her smart mouth closed.

Hilary spluttered over her supplicant's words as the cane was passed wordlessly to Saffron as her nightmare continued. Each one of Saffron's strikes was targeted accurately at the centre of Hilary's cheeks, the savage blows causing the skin to blister up before the transfixed women's eyes. The beaten student was barely coherent now, lost in the babbling mantra of apologies and gratitude that she spouted automatically.

"Right, Zo. Time for a bit of fun. Shall we let our gorgeous chum Emily join in again? Ladies, help our guest get up and over Hilary. Come on put her right over as though she is just climbing off after taking Hilary doggie style."

Chloe's words caused much mirth in the room, the gang looking eager to start taking their revenge on Emily. Emily resisted sharing with Chloe now that her remarks brought to mind a group of naughty little boys practising swearwords as the gang began to man handle her. She allowed herself to be positioned on top of Hilary, her head hanging down beside the distraught, sobbing student.

"How is it working out for you then, Hilary?" she whispered huskily and tauntingly into her ear, enclosing Hilary's smaller hands in hers. She gave her cheek a kiss and, as the blood rushed to her head, she prepared herself for the assault that she knew Zoe would relish giving her.

Emily felt hands on her ankles as two of the gang took a leg apiece and stretched her wide apart. She took a moment to imagine the picture presented, her bottom rudely displayed, her arse crack spread, perched on top of Hilary's battered backside. That image left her as she sensed the movement of Zoe's body, in the act of swinging the bamboo, before the blow landed and the fearsome burn registered.

Partly, Emily felt relief that her ordeal was finally underway and that this essential part of the plan to bring down the despicable septet had begun at last. *On the other hand*, she ruminated, *it hurts like fuck!*

She managed to still her reaction before letting her breath out slowly as she heard the air swish and the cane land on Hilary's bottom. What she hadn't expected was the impact from the tip of the cane on her inner calf and this provoked a wholehearted scream as it bit in deeply to an area hitherto untouched by human malice.

Miranda appeared at her head, grabbing her roughly, exclaiming, "Keep still bitch!" but under her breath so that only Emily could hear. "Play up all you can, scream and cry for all your worth or they'll bloody well flay you alive." Underneath her Hilary was calling out her motto word, tears dropping to the carpet. The cane fell on Emily's backside again, causing her to thrust her pubic mound into the top of Hilary's arse crack. She screamed out, heeding Miranda's words, although the strike had caused her enough pain that not much acting was required. Hilary hollered again as Emily managed to pull herself up high enough that she didn't get caught by the cane stroke. Zoe drew back the cane again and applied the next strokes in quick succession so that both girls screamed out in unison. When the fifth stroke sliced into their tender behinds, both girls were crying loudly and begging Zoe for mercy. At Chloe's command, Emily thanked Zoe for the punishment and was dragged off Hilary and sent to the corner to stand with hands on head. Hilary was being readied for the big finale from Chloe, who was reading her the riot act about her breech of the Seven Sisters code.

"So, final warning my dear, one more lie, one more piece of deceitful behaviour, one more backstabbing piece of crap, and we are done. Now pull yourself together and I am going to give you ten quick hard strokes of this cane. No words, don't even speak, just feel these fuckers and don't ever fucking cross me again."

Emily cringed as Chloe delivered the vicious cuts of the cane with force. A quick glance and she could see the strokes landing virtually one on top of the other, over and over again. Hilary's screams filled the room as her punishment came to its painful conclusion and, despite Chloe's command, she blubbered out apologies and contrite words.

"Quiet, Hilary, for goodness sake! Right, get Emily bitch over here and let's really get this show started, shall we? Helen and Miranda are now going to spank your arse, my little vixen, then Saffron, Charlotte and this pathetic excuse," she indicated the noisily sobbing Hilary now struggling to dress, "are going to paddle you. Zoe will bring the strap to the party and finally it will be my fair and delicate hand, or more exactly a special little whip I've got bought especially for the job, that will beat the living daylights out of you!"

Emily allowed herself to be draped over Helen's lap and she readied herself for what sounded as though it would be a long and painful experience. *Oh well,* she thought, *whatever they come up with surely would not match her nightmare in the Professor's room and that awful couch of horror that she had been chained onto?* The pain of that day was etched into her mind but still, she considered ruefully, she had fingered herself to a climax reliving it alone within weeks of it happening. She had accepted that she had masochistic tendencies along with the obvious bisexual signs and had decided that she'd go with the flow and see where it took her. She was determined not to feel guilty about her lusts and fantasies; rather than waste energy and time in angst over her sexuality, she would just embrace her desires for now.

Helen began to spank her bottom but even with the foundation of the bamboo strokes to inflame, Emily found herself distinctly unimpressed at the impact of the student's admittedly small hands and her mind drifted as the slaps went into the thirties. Then Miranda was beside her, a handful of Emily's hair in her hand, saying, "not quite so cocky now are you, slag?"

However, her eyes were telling a different story and Emily heeded her earlier words and responded to her prompting. "Oooooh! It really stings. Yikes! Ouch! That one hurt. Oh dear! Oh my!"

A wink from Miranda indicated that this was the correct response and a sideways glance with her head hung down was enough to see that the others' attentions had been roused and they were crowding around to watch the blows land.

There was a sudden flurry of slaps from Helen, and Emily upped her volume with her over-dramatic performance as Helen's turn came to an end and was greeted by a smattering of applause.

"Well done, Helen. One hundred spanks successfully delivered to the cow's rear end. Tip her off, Miranda's turn next."

With help from pulling hands grabbing any body part available, Emily found herself dumped unceremoniously onto the carpet.

The spanking from Miranda was quick and whole-hearted but Emily was well aware that Miranda had recognised that however hard a hand spanking was delivered it was unlikely to cause her that much grief. However, she acted her role to perfection, writhing and crying out as though in great distress. The fact that it was Miranda's hand that was smacking her bare behind was ensuring that Emily was enjoying the experience rather enduring it!

Saffron took over and patted her lap. "Look what I've picked up from our favourite sex shop in the city." She waved a flexible black hand-shaped leather paddle at Emily.

"Over you go my lovely, I do find these cheeks rather sexy. I hope I get a chance to feast on them later."

The spanking was almost pleasurable, the lusty slapping sound of the leather hitting flesh was deceptive as Emily remembered Miranda's words and wriggled and struggled with little squeals to try and suggest that it was causing her pain rather than turning her on. All too soon, this particular session was over and Saffron was pushing her off her knees and to the floor, leaving space for Charlotte to take her place. Emily obediently settled herself over Charlotte's lap and sighed as fingers ran along her arse crack. Charlotte stroked her cheeks, and Emily had to stop herself moaning in pleasure as inquisitive fingers slid down her arse crack to the damp folds below. However, Charlotte's words soon reminded her of the reality of the situation.

"Oh Helen, Miranda and Saffron, I've got sticky fingers. I think she might have rather enjoyed the spankings you gave. What do you say girls, should I maybe increase the amount we had decided on from 25 to 50 with my nice thick wooden paddle?"

Shut the front door and slam the lock across! thought Emily. That is not in the plan. She made the decision to lose just a little bit more of her pride as she could sense the others' approval to Charlotte's proposal.

"Oh no, no, no. Please ladies, please no. I'll never get through this, the paddle will hurt so much," she whimpered.

"Whatever. But my fingers still smell of your fanny so you can lick them clean, butch bitch."

Emily complied, taking as long as she could to give her some recovery time, waiting with a heightened fear level. Things were getting serious now, the paddle looked quite thick and formidable; she moaned and sucked each finger slowly and sensuously but

Charlotte was not fooled and snatched her hand away.

"Charlotte, give the 25 we earlier agreed but let's allow Hilary some revenge and she can give as many as she chooses to her little girlfriend," Chloe's voice cut through the others' discussion and the room went quiet once more as Charlotte raised the paddle and Emily steeled herself for the attack.

As she had expected, the change from the cupped hands of Miranda and lighter touch of Helen was a contrast not in her favour. No winks or nudges were needed from Miranda now as Charlotte went for the fast fully-fledged approach and, five hard and rapidly delivered slaps in, Emily was gasping and grunting. Halfway through with no let up on the speed, Emily was reduced to shrieking and writhing on Charlotte's lap, with hands having moved in to hold her legs and shoulders down. Within a minute it was over but Emily wailed on for several seconds, her bottom ablaze, as the paddle was handed on to Hilary.

"Good job, well done," said Chloe. "Hils, are you recovered enough to give her another treat?"

There was no let up as she lifted herself off Charlotte's lap and laid herself obediently, albeit reluctantly, over a suddenly more cheerful Hilary's knees. There was a sniggering from her erstwhile lover as she took the paddle from Charlotte with her right hand, her left hand fondling Emily's smarting buttocks.

"Oh, I have been so looking forward to this, Emily. For days after your attack I could taste toilet water in my mouth and smell it in my hair. Since then I have done nothing but dream and yearn for this day. We are going to roast your behind then we are going to spit-roast you, ho ho. Your arse is going to be on fire both inside and out by the time we have finished with you and your poor pussy isn't going to want as much as a fingertip going anywhere near it for months. You utter fucking bitch, now you are going to get yours!"

With those words hanging in the air, the second painful paddling began as Hilary raised her arm high and brought it down with real force on the upper thighs of Emily, targeting the white, previously unblemished, silky thighs where they joined her lower buttocks. She had recovered from the vicious cane strokes delivered by Zoe remarkably well, and Charlotte and Saffron's paddlings had been borderline but bearable retrospectively, if bloody painful in the moment of delivery, but she had expected that Hilary, with clearly more evil and personal intent, would be a different kettle of fish. There was no need to pretend now and Emily began to wish she had asked the Professor to make his planned entrance, and her rescue, much earlier than they'd agreed. She totally understood his wish that the gang be caught on film, having been seen to abuse her in a manner that brooked no argument, plea of misunderstanding, no ambiguity and no option of claiming consent was given. However, as another stroke of the thick wooden paddle stung Hilary's new target of the thinly protected and tighter skin at the very top of her bottom, she wondered how much more of this flogging she could actually bear. She ruefully remembered her ridiculous show of bravado when the Professor had suggested that it wouldn't be a bad idea for her to be seen and heard, on the filmed evidence, begging for mercy. She had loftily replied that she really did not wish to demean herself by grovelling to this bunch of sadists and that the Professor should allow her to retain some dignity and degree of self-respect. Of course, all-knowing as he was, he had said nothing but his eyes had spoken volumes with clear doubt as to her ability to show such resilience once on the end of seven angry young ladies with a thirst for revenge and little concept of what consisted of abusive and excessive behaviour. As Hilary went beyond the promised 50 strikes with the paddle, Emily found her thoughts concentrated on surviving each individual stroke as Hilary brandished the weapon with real ferocity on her lower cheeks.

The battering continued, on and on. Emily's arse was now stinging and burning with such intensity that her writhing was causing Hilary to struggle to contain her over her lap. But the paddle still fell down on any part of Emily's threshing upper legs that Hilary could reach. Emily was now screaming continuously, her fingers scrabbling at the cushions, throws and the carpet in turn as she pointlessly struggled and searched for any form of release from the torment. Her backside had developed a life of its own and was twitching and jerking uncontrollably even though Chloe had moved to stop Hilary with a firm hand on her wrist. To her disgust, she was blurting out absurd pleas for mercy, and howled in horror when she heard Chloe agree that Hilary could deliver another ten strokes. There was a pause that became excruciating long for Emily as Hilary waited for Chloe's permission to continue and Emily became conscious of other hands lifting her back to the traditional over-the-knee position for Hilary to resume.

"I think that before you finish Hilary, Emily should thank you for applying such a lenient punishment and ask you to give her an especially hard final set. On the other hand, she could choose not to, in which case I would suggest that she is enjoying this little bottom patting so much that she wants you to continue ad infinitum!" Chloe's voice contained the level of malice that had always made Emily so much more fearful of her than the other gang members.

Emily also became aware that Hilary had allowed the fingers of her hand, which was resting on her lower cheeks, to have dropped between her legs and a digit was gently working on the lower lips of her vagina. Emily, to her horror and annoyance, could feel the wetness there and even in this perilous situation was unable to control her sexual wantonness. *Yup*, she thought, *I am such a ruddy tart.* She snapped out of her reverie though, the pain of the constant beating paused for now, and she realised that she needed to respond, reluctant though she was to cause the resumption of the thrashing, but she knew the script she needed to bring to this party!

"Oh, of course, Chloe. Thank you so much, Hilary, for my much deserved punishment but I think I ought to have a few more really hard smacks to make sure that I remember what a naughty girl I have been and how I have really earned a very sore bottom, please. I am so sorry for the way I treated you and want to thank you for being so lenient."

Hilary's fingers lingered far longer than was necessary and it took a rather pointed throat clearing from Chloe before Emily's mind was snapped back to reality as the pleasuring stopped and she heard the paddle being raised high. What little respite the pause in the beating, followed by what was, she had to admit, a rather nice few moments with her pussy being played with, counted for nothing as the paddle slammed down across the curve of her buttocks. Emily's head jerked up and she unleashed an unadulterated screech of pain into the room. Hilary's dalliance gained her nothing as the paddle continued its battering of her swollen cheeks, now deep red and igniting the intense pain and heat once more. The final five blows were concentrated on the most tender lower buttocks, the searing pain taking Emily to what felt like the edge of consciousness. She knew that there were two sessions with the horrendous looking bamboo cane to follow and, for once in her life, she doubted her ability to finish a challenge that she had set out on. She hoped that the Professor really was watching and that everything was being caught on record, but knew that as far as the beating went she would receive no respite. Their agreement was that the Professor wanted her to have been severely thrashed and then specifically sexually assaulted so that the seven would have no leg to stand on to explain away their actions when challenged. As the wooden paddle was dropped to the bed, and Hilary pushed her to the floor off her knees, Emily just curled up into a ball, weeping and snorting as tears covered her face.

"Not got anything cocky or clever to say then, cuntface?" said Chloe as she gave Emily a sly kick in the ribs. "It's me and Zoe with the bamboo canes to come yet, bitch, and by fuck are we going to make you holler! If that does not work then I have a nice bunch of roses in the vase on the windowsill and I would really love to see how you cope with those lovely thorny stems being whipped across your sweet cheeks!"

As Emily wiped her face on the overhanging sheet, she risked a look up at Chloe, who with the most evil of grins continued ominously: "After that, it is a real treat for you which we're all looking forward to delivering." Chloe's head nodded towards the nearby table at the covered item that Emily had noticed when she first came into the rooms. There was some piece of apparatus hidden beneath the cloth and Emily felt a sickness in her stomach as she tried to imagine what this twisted woman had lined up for her later. Over Chloe's shoulder, Emily could see that Zoe had picked up one of the two bamboo canes leaning against the wall and was taking practice swings with the long formidable looking cane through the air. The laughter of the other girls took her attention then and she could see that Saffron was affixing a double-headed strap on to her midriff. Chloe followed Emily's eyes as they opened and she inadvertently let loose a rather large gulping swallow.

"Now, now Saffron. Look, Emily's getting all excited at seeing your cocks." Stroking Emily's hair she said, "You can see it's not all bad, you are going to get well and truly shafted after your caning and your special treat. Guess what? We have one each that we've picked out and bought especially for you. We are so going to ruin your pussy and your arsehole little girl. This is a gang- bang that you'll never forget. You won't mess with us again."

Dragging her by the hair, Chloe threw her onto the bed. Emily decided that compliance was the only option she had; rousing her any further did not appeal as a choice as Emily found her switch from cold anger to spiteful laughter very disconcerting!

"Sit on her head, Miranda. Helen and Saffron, grab a leg each, pull them apart and hold tight. I am going to bamboo her arse until it catches fire!"

Emily had seen that all the gang were fixing strap-ons of a variety of colours, sizes and number of appendages and hoped that the moment Professor Stones would come to her rescue was not too far off. Those thoughts weren't her priority a second later when Zoe appeared at a run and slammed the bamboo cane across her bottom. Emily screamed, her flayed flesh so sore, and surviving the next few minutes became the only aim in her life for the moment as her fingers scrabbled at the fine cotton sheets beneath her. *Focus, Em*, she thought, *focus.* She heard the air moving and realised that Zoe had passed the cane over the bed to Chloe. The cane slammed down on her lower cheeks and again she screamed and almost bucked Miranda off of her head. Clamping her head between her thighs, Miranda bent down placing her head close to Emily's and whispered in her ear.

"Think of something nice, block it out, Emily. Shit!"

Emily's head jerked up into Miranda's forehead as the cane landed again. At Miranda's yelp of pain and surprise, Chloe snarled,

"If she does that again Miranda, I'd turn her over and shit in her mouth." Her comment, vile as it was, caused much merriment amongst the others, and Emily hoped that this didn't portent badly for anything else they had planned.

There was no respite as the two women switched the cane between them, lashing it down to bite deep into her inflamed cheeks. Miranda held her tightly but didn't attempt any more words of comfort as Emily writhed, screamed and cried copious tears under this latest onslaught. Finally, Chloe's voice cut through the air as the cane was discarded.

"Right ladies, time for her flushing out before the big treat with our cocks! Get the small table into the bathroom. We are going to have some water fun with her now, ladies. She'll need holding down. Perhaps someone else can hold her head this time, Miranda, save you getting head-butted again!"

Chloe's laugh sent a chill shuddering throughout Emily's body as the gang unceremoniously picked her up and carried her into the bathroom, where they deposited her onto the small kitchen table Zoe had placed there. She was still weeping and trying to blank out the throbbing and stinging of her very sore behind and could feel individual blistered stripes taking turns to signal searing pain in her head. The fact that she had been taken into the bathroom permeated in Emily's brain and she looked around desperately to see if she could see any indication of what the next torturous punishment was going to be. She did not need to speculate for long as Chloe reappeared, wheeling in the covered equipment she had spotted. It took her a minute to work it out as the large container and the spout and tubing came into view. With Helen and Saffron holding her knees up and bent back towards her shoulders, and Charlotte with both hands on her head, Emily's view between her legs was enough for the fear and dread to hit her.

"Oh no. I don't fucking believe this, you are not going to give me a fucking enema. Oh Chloe, Zoe, please no. Oh my God. No. No. No!" Every time Emily thought that she had shed enough tears during this evening of torment, there was another challenge planned and waiting around the corner, it seemed. By now, all the women were naked and all had fixed the strapped appendages around their waists and groins. Fake penises appeared whichever way she looked. Hilary, the last to arrive in the bathroom, was sporting a massive black plastic cock and wearing the most evil of facial expressions. Chloe had a double prong attachment as did most of the young women. Zoe, clearly with strong vaginal muscles, was wearing a three pronged dildo with one shaft already held inside her own pussy.

"Poor sweetie, doesn't know which way to look but don't worry little girl you will see all of them close up soon, because after every fuck you are going to lick the cocks clean. However, we first have the little matter of flushing your dirty cock-hungry arsehole out so you are all pristine and clean for our cocks to pay a visit. If you are a very good girl you will only get my friend's cock here up your fanny."

Chloe began masturbating the huge cock sticking obscenely out from Hilary's groin.

"However, if you misbehave at all, imagine the damage this twelve incher will do up your bum." She waggled the cock in Emily's face, leaving her praying silently that Professor Stones was set to pounce and that this nightmare was not going to be allowed to play out any further.

Zoe meanwhile had filled the container with warm water and was apparently sending the liquid through into a large rubber pump.

"I imagine she can take half a gallon up that fine arse, can't she?" queried a very eager Zoe, now holding a nozzle primed and ready.

Emily was quietly weeping now; she knew there was no way out and that she was set to undergo a horrendous indignity, though thankful for heeding the Professor's words of warning about attending this session with a completely empty bladder and bowels.

"If you are a nice well-mannered and polite girl and ask Hilary nicely, she will lube up Zoe's nozzle, oooo-er, before it's slid right up you. So here's your chance, do your best and we'll see if we think you've done enough." Chloe knelt so that her taunting face was centimetres from Emily's pussy as Saffron and Helen forced Emily's legs to their widest and lifted her knees up further to present her arsehole open and accessible to welcome the nozzle and the rubber tubing. Chloe knelt further and licked her long tongue all the way up Emily's vagina, teasing into her upper folds and then swirling around her clitoris.

"It doesn't matter what we do to you, does it? You are still always juicy and ready, aren't you? Now ask the question."

Emily had given up on pride and dignity a long while back; it was survival of the fittest now.

"Oh Hilary, I am so sorry for what happened earlier. You know that I didn't want to cane you really and I am sorry if I caused you trouble. I have been so ungrateful and rotten to you. I do love you and still would love to spend some special time alone with you. Please forgive me and give the tube lots of lube so that it slides up easily. I would really love it if you push lube in my arse with your fingers as well, please, Hilary my love."

Not my finest hour, thought Emily ruefully, but was hopeful that she had appeased Hilary.

"Not bad, dear," said Chloe. "I think she's done quite well, Hils. I bet you cannot wait to get your sticky fingers up her arse anyway. Go on then, go for it. Let's get this fountain show on the road."

With a grin that mixed pure lust and a certain amount of evil vengeance, Hilary pushed a lubricant-covered single finger into her rear entrance. With a smile and a blown kiss, a second finger followed, causing Emily to grimace as her anal muscles adapted to the invasion. She squealed as a third finger followed and opened her right up. Miranda had managed to get the tube nozzle between Hilary's fingers, and between the two of them they worked it up her tunnel. Zoe awaited a signal as she held the pump switch and, at a nod from Miranda in warning, Emily took a deep breath and tried to relax as Miranda gave Zoe the go-ahead. *Fuck it*, she thought, *I am not doing this!* With an almighty backward kick, Emily sent the equipment crashing to the floor, the tube whipping painfully from her arsehole. But that was immaterial to her as she heard the smashing sound that pre-empted the spray of liquid as the contraption fell noisily apart.

As the gang split apart to avoid being soaked, the ever-practical Zoe turned off the water supply and began to throw bath towels over the wet floor. As Emily pushed herself off the table and tried to escape from the bathroom, Chloe grabbed her by the hair, pulled her fist back and aimed a punch at her. Emily, seeing her intentions, managed to sway and ride the blow, however, it had enough force and anger behind it to knock Emily down. Chloe, still with a firm grip, dragged her into the bedroom and flung her face down onto the bed.

"You fucking bitch, you are so going to pay for that."

The threat from Chloe sounded ominous as she reached under Emily, grabbed a breast and squeezed hard. The next few minutes passed in a whirl as Chloe picked up the paddle and began to rain hefty blows down onto her so tender buttocks and legs.

"Well, I hope that you think your little display of temper was worth it then, Emily?" taunted Chloe as she threw down the paddle.

"Oh dear, spoiled your fun, did I, pervert?" Ignoring the tears streaming down her face and her throbbing lower body, Emily was determined that she would feed off her small victory. Whatever Chloe did now, she figured it could not be worse than getting a public enema.

"Shut your fucking mouth, bitch. Now you can clean the bathroom up and then the girls here are going to give you a very intimate wash so you are clean enough to take our cocks. Then we are going to take turn in splitting your holes apart. You'll be lucky to be able to walk after the gang bang you are going to get, bitch! Added to that, you have just earned yourself a whipping with the rose stems!"

Emily's face dropped but she knew that she just had to have faith in Professor Stones' plan and the protection he had promised. Albeit the raging soreness of her blistered backside did give some doubt as to how much pain she would have to endure before he made his assured rescue! Not allowed time to linger, Helen and Zoe had her roughly by the arms and she soon found herself in the bathroom with a mop, buckets and plentiful cleaning cloths and sprays flung at her. Thankfully, Emily could see that all the glass had been picked up and the broken equipment stood rather forlornly to the side. The anger in the eyes of all the girls boded badly but Emily could not resist pushing her chin out and putting up a show of defiance.

"Oh dear, it is a bit broken, isn't it?" she taunted them.

"Get cleaning, bitch!" spat a furious looking Zoe. "Then we are going to give you a bloody good scrubbing before we fuck you stupid, you smug cow!"

Emily had little choice but to clear up the sodden mess and contemplate whether Chloe was really considering applying a thorny branch to her extremely sore arse! Minutes later, Charlotte, Saffron and Hilary were rubbing harshly at her body, orifices roughly invaded by fingers once more as they went through the process of giving her the most vigorous scrubbing of her life. The appendages bobbed up and down rather ludicrously as the women worked on her, and even though she knew that she could be facing at least some intrusion into her body with one or two of the dildos and probes before, fingers crossed, the Professor brought the farce to an end, she could not help but smile.

"I am assuming that that is a nervous smile, Emily," whispered Miranda as she wrapped her in a huge bath sheet. "Otherwise, I really advise you to stop looking as though you're actually enjoying some of this or Chloe is going to bloody well whip the skin off your back before you get out of here."

"Yes I know, Miranda, but even now you are prodding me in my bottom with your strap-on. You've got to see how preposterous you all look."

Luckily no one overheard the exchange as Chloe was calling them all through to the bedroom.

"Right, what order shall we do this in, ladies? I think we should start with a proper spit-roast to get her used to what's coming. Positions, ladies, as we practised the other night."

As Zoe and Miranda held Emily still by her arms, Saffron lay on the bed face up, Helen knelt at her head and Hilary stood at the end. At Chloe's signal, Zoe and Miranda encouraged a pliable Emily to kneel on top of Saffron, her head facing Helen whose swinging phallus was pointing at her mouth, while beneath her Saffron was positioning her strap-on against Emily's pussy. As Emily felt the bed move, she realised that Hilary was behind her as Charlotte moved beside her with a tube of lube, and Emily felt her fingers at her arsehole once more as the gel was spread around the outer rim before fingers pushed inside of her.

Chloe's voice rang out as she directed operations.

"Go for it Charl, lots of lovely lube up her arse, she'll need it to take Hilary's big cock. What's her fanny like, Saffron, need any lube, or is she dripping wet as usual, the nasty lustful little slut?"

Within seconds, Emily's mouth was full of the hard rubber protuberance that Helen was starting to thrust in and out, her cheek bulging obscenely as she struggled with the girth and length. Saffron had worked her thick cock into her pussy, large but bearable and it did cross Emily's mind that she would have been happy with this if she and Saffron had been alone! However, any pleasure derived from her pussy being fucked was soon dispelled as Hilary rather forced her appendage into Emily's bottom with no sign of tenderness or care. Tears welled up in Emily's eyes as Hilary pushed her way into the tight tunnel, not allowing Emily a chance to prepare or relax muscles to accommodate the sheer size of it. The lubricant allowed her to be breeched before she was in a state to receive such a size and the pain was fearsome. Not that Emily could do anything other than issue a strangled gurgling sound as her mouth was inconveniently full of pounding rubber cock. To compound her misery, Chloe and Zoe had moved either side of her and taken hold of a hanging breast each and although Zoe's rubbing of her breast, against Saffron beneath her, was not without pleasure, Chloe was digging her fingernails in and twisting a nipple rather painfully.

Charlotte and Miranda, the spare parts in this endeavour so far, had started a chant that the gang had clearly been practising as they all joined in.

"Gang bang! Gang bang! It's a gang bang. She likes it in her pussy and she likes it up the bum." This repeated over and over to the tune of 'Sex Bomb' by Tom Jones.

The fourth repetition was not completed as suddenly the room was full of people and all hell broke loose!

Emily's ordeal was over.

CHAPTER 8

THE PROFESSOR TO THE RESCUE

(EVENTUALLY)

The college's CCTV network was of the highest quality as dictated by Professor Stones himself. He had no problem in persuading an extremely wealthy member of the college's alumni that this was a worthwhile and important funding operation and she had willingly handed over a cheque, of an amount that had reached six figures by the time he had achieved the total coverage, within legal guidelines, of the college and its environs. Of course, these things were much easier to achieve when your 40-year-old ex-student is standing in the corner with a bright red bottom after receiving a thorough spanking. Mrs Fenella Harding, CBE, tended to book a visit every couple of years for a regular hand-spanking, occasionally something a bit stronger if Stones determined, based on a list she kept of her 'little astrays', her pet name for the not so innocuous sexual adventures she enjoyed outside of her marriage. She was a wealthy woman and rather keen to please him, so had been ridiculously happy to fund any worthwhile project that her mentor, and tormentor, proposed. Stones was, as always, willing to oblige if called upon for "assistance and improvement" by college alumni, supposedly purging her of guilt and sending her out presumably with the freedom to err again. His was not to reason why, he thought, his was just to thoroughly enjoy the experience of bouncing his hand off the bent-over cheeks of another, rather delicious, bottom!

Following the text alert from Emily, Stones was monitoring the routes to the guest room that the Secret Seven gang had gained access through devious commandeering and copying of the keys for the intention of their occasional nefarious activities. Emily had been easy to spot coming, with her long blonde hair and sporting her near virginal-looking and pristine outfit. He saw Zoe slip out of the stairwell where she had obviously been concealed, and glide alongside Emily. Even from a distance, Stones was aware of the disdainful manner in which Zoe was speaking to her and knew that this did not bode well for Emily. He lost them on part of the staircase but his system, now having placed Emily with its sophisticated facial identity recognition system, immediately switched to the guest room as Emily fairly fell into the room.

Chloe, Charlotte, Hilary, Helen, Saffron and Miranda were waiting in the room, lounging on the beautiful furniture that had been sourced for the top guest accommodation in the college. A small cheer went up as Emily appeared with Zoe behind her from the group, and Stones noted the detritus that suggested that a fair amount of alcohol had already been partaken.

"Lamb to the slaughter, lamb to the slaughter," shouted Saffron.

"Pigs to the trough," Emily snapped back without thinking.

Stones grimaced but acknowledged her pluck, albeit she was once again showing the imprudence and impudence that usually ended up with her in trouble. He realised that he had quite a long way to go in his venture to turn his young protégé into the perfect college graduate.

Chloe's ominous words broke a long silence.

"So, no pleas for mercy, no sobbing heart-rending apology, no pathetic tears of repentance. Just straight in with your smartarse quips and smug comebacks. Well, fuck you then, Emily Govan, let's get straight to it then. You know why you are here. Let me introduce you to my friend, Vengeance!"

A further grimace from Stones as Emily took a full force slap across the face from Chloe, before she was dragged over to the sofa and to the feet of the cause of her forced attendance, Hilary. The next words from Emily were provocative enough that Stones burst out laughing

"Yeah right, like little miss two-faced, sadomasochistic, lesbian has done nothing wrong then? Oh, Hilary haven't you shared the details? Don't your friends here know about your surreptitious activities, your love of pussy, well, my pussy, really? Oh Hilary, didn't you share with your friends the way you beat me and fucked me? Oh sorry, my lover, was it a secret?"

Stones' buzzer went and he was joined by Philippa Stanford, the Graduates Manager, who was standing in for the Mistress who was unavoidably detained, and Celia, the senior tutor.

"Join me, my friends, we are just getting underway. Sara, our Chief Academic Administrator, Sonya, our Pastoral Care Tutor, Ronald, our Head Porter, and Elizabeth, our Head Nurse are all on call and available for the duration. Ronald has senior porters posted and free if we need. The Mistress is keeping up to date with things, by her own feed that has been set up, and will possibly join us later. You have only missed young Emily showing probably unwise, but very entertaining, pluck and spunk so the main event is about to start I suspect. Everything is in place for later so, with a bit of luck, and expert planning obviously, all should go well. I think that we are just about to have a side show as Emily has rather dropped Hilary in it with her mates – a little matter of duplicity and a fair amount of latitude with the truth is not appearing to go well for her, hoorah!"

Hilary was now beseeching Chloe to concentrate on Emily but her face as Chloe spoke next was an absolute picture and Stones could not help but laugh out loud at the quandary the duplicitous young woman had gotten herself into.

"Helen, fetch one of the bamboo canes for the bedroom. Hilary are we doing this the easy way or the hard way?"

Stones could see Emily crane forward, attempting to see what Stones had noticed when he had watched the gang set up earlier. There was quite an assortment that, although it did not match his own collection of sex pleasure aids in number, was certainly impressive as far as the intent to subject Emily to the use of strap-ons went. Unlike Emily, Stones had seen what lay under the black cloth, which had angered him, as it was clear that Emily was likely to be receiving a rather unpleasant liquid invasion in the form of a colonic irrigation via a sophisticated enema. However, his early view had given him the opportunity to do some research of his own as regards his aim to treat like-for-like when it came to the young women's recriminations.

Stones found it entertaining as Hilary blustered, then confessed, and finally submitted to Chloe's will. Emily was outstanding, he thought, as he watched her play her part superbly, whilst knowing that she was soon going to be experiencing all sorts of hell at the hands of these reprobates.

It intrigued Stones to watch Chloe manipulate Hilary in a way that he himself was so proficient. *She is most decidedly a prospective total dominant*, he mused, as the audience in his room watched the gang leader reduce Hilary down to a malleable submissive jellyfish. When Hilary realised that she had no option other than to accept the punishment as dictated by Chloe, Stones could see the joy flicker across Emily's face which she then struggled to conceal as. Chloe determined that Emily herself was to increase Hillary's discomfort and shame by being given the opportunity to undress and cane her. The enjoyment on Emily's face was undisguised as she brought the bamboo cane down wickedly on Hillary's reluctantly offered buttocks. Stones could not fail to admire her fortitude, surely knowing that what she had to come was undoubtedly going to be far more severe than anything Hilary received.

He found himself objectively judging Emily's caning technique, and was self-satisfyingly impressed with the evidence displayed, that showed that she had learnt fast at his hands. Her execution was exemplary and his chest swelled with pride.

He found, disconcertingly, his penis swelling considerably as Emily was told to strip and he feasted his eyes on her naked body. At least, in this instance, he could feel secure that there would be no chance of her being aware of the lust that she stirred up in him whenever he viewed her stunning, naked body. Celia was quick to notice this as he adjusted his clothing which to her plain annoyance he disregarded; he would use his desire for Emily and turn it into a weapon against her if she spoke out of place. He returned his gaze to the screen as the other gang members beat the legs and backsides of their disloyal comrade in turn.

Zoe's nasty little diatribe of hate, aimed at Emily, he found quite disturbing. Her voice carried a level of threat and malice that seemed unnecessary and he was sure its foundation was in pure jealousy. Emily to her credit seemed amazingly unperturbed, her off-hand remark in response once more making the watching audience laugh.

"Hey ho, Zoe. Why don't you just tell me how you really feel, my darling."

As Hilary's backside started to blister, Stones hoped the group would realise that this was the point whereby the cane would start to draw blood if they continued much longer in this manner.

As Emily was manipulated and positioned over Hilary, Stones spotted her whispering into the other's ear and knew that she was still taking every chance to belittle and undermine Hilary. The secret cameras were perfectly placed to capture the stunning picture of Emily's splendid golden bottom spread wide and, in perfect contrast, over Hilary's battered and red raw cheeks. With Celia watching him intensely from the corner of her eyes, Stones managed to refrain from his subconscious habit of licking his lips when viewing a bottom that really turned him on. He did not want Celia distracted from her duty here. It was important to him that his team were all on the side of Emily, the less-than-angelic Emily admittedly, but definitely nearer to the side of good than this shower of seven was!

Stones was able to switch off his emotions easily as Emily began to suffer. They had both accepted that it would be for the greater good. They had talked at length as to how she would best handle this. Emily had never wavered from her determination to bring the evil gang down and Stones was content that her pain could be handled and that it would bring her the ultimate reward.

Stones concentrated hard as he saw Miranda talking to Emily. She had highlighted to him her suspicions that Miranda was a reluctant member of the cabal and Stones was eager to see if this would be apparent during this session. As Emily was sent to the corner while the punishment of Hilary was completed, Philippa finally voiced her concern at the cruelty and severity being displayed.

"My God, Edward, if this is what they will do to one of their friends! I hope you are ready to jump in quickly if they look like causing your girl serious harm?"

Stones shrugged. "Your concerns are noted, Philippa, now just let me watch please."

They all cringed along with Emily as Chloe delivered the vicious cuts of the cane with force; a quick glance and she could see the strokes landing virtually on top of each other again and again. Hilary's screams filled the room as her punishment came to its painful conclusion and despite Chloe's command she blubbered out her apologies and contrite words.

Then Emily was draped over Helen's lap and made ready to accept the proposed punishment. They watched intently, Celia and the Professor with decidedly more enthusiasm than Philippa, as Helen launched a sudden attack of slaps on Emily's bottom before she was passed onto Miranda. Her spanking looked hard but Stones could see that it was not as painful as it sounded, and Emily played her part by yelling throughout. Miranda kept her hands cupped, deliberately he presumed, to avoid causing Emily much discomfort. He pointed this out to his companions as her spanking finished and they were able to spot the look of gratitude from Emily to Miranda as she was pushed off the young woman's lap.

Saffron then took her turn, proudly showing off a flexible black hand-shaped leather paddle before the only sound heard was the sharp slapping impact of the leather meeting flesh. Stones watched Emily carefully and was confident that this was a fine acting performance of someone feeling pain rather than any sign that she was in too much discomfort. Charlotte then took Saffron's place, bringing a wooden paddle which she was slapping threateningly into her hand, a look of evil intent on her face. As Emily obediently settled herself over Charlotte's lap, the three watchers all leaned in together as they saw Charlotte's fingers deliberately run down between the cheeks of Emily's bottom to the labial lips below. Any thoughts that they were entertaining that Charlotte was about to take some sexual advantage of Emily's position, though by now Stones was pretty sure that all three were of the same thought that Emily would not necessarily mind, were soon dispelled as Charlotte spoke:

"Oh, Miranda and Saffron, I've got sticky fingers. I think she might have rather enjoyed the spankings you gave. What do you say girls, should I maybe increase the amount we had decided on from 25 to 50 with the paddle?"

"Whoops," said Stones. "I think Emily's been outplayed here. Hold tight, ladies. I think young Emily's ride is going to get rougher."

They could see that Emily played for time as she diligently sucked and licked at Charlotte's fingers to clean her of her vaginal secretions before Charlotte cottoned on and snatched her fingers away.

"Charlotte, give the 25 we earlier agreed but let's allow Hilary some revenge and she can give as many as she chooses to her little girlfriend." Chloe's voice then, more or less, commanded that Charlotte just give Emily the agreed 25 strokes with the paddle but then gave Hilary carte blanche to give her hell once Charlotte had finished. Again, Stones took heed of the fact that Chloe seemed in sole command of the show and his heart hardened further against the young woman.

The paddle was applied, quick and hard, causing Stones to grimace in sympathy. Philippa yelped and covered her mouth as she struggled to comprehend the level of punishment that was being dispensed.

Celia was stone-faced as Emily began shrieking and writhing on Charlotte's lap and others moved in to hold her legs and shoulders down. Emily wailed for several seconds after Charlotte had ceased and passed the paddle over to Hilary, and the three shifted uneasily in their seats.

The diatribe from Hilary hung in the air before they saw Emily wince in pain as Hilary thrust a finger into her back passage, while detailing exactly what she would like to forcibly insert in its place.

"Take a breath, ladies, this is going to hurt her a lot but it has to be endured." Stones warned while checking his monitor that all was in place as far as his intended raid on the room went.

Emily's second paddling began as Hilary raised her arm high and brought it down with real force on her upper thighs. Emily shrieked in utter despair and pain as Hilary targeted her white, previously unblemished skin, where her thighs joined her lower buttocks. It was a terrifyingly fierce onslaught, a solid thrashing with no respite and there could be no doubt of the agony that Emily was experiencing.

"That's enough, that's 60. Save us a bit of skin for the cane and strap. Stop, Hilary!"

Chloe's voice was a relief to Philippa, especially as Stones and Celia took a joint, unspoken decision not to mention the tears rolling down her face. Stones' attention (he was so good at spotting the minor details) was drawn to Hilary's passive hand that had discreetly slipped between Emily's legs and he espied a digit working on her lower labial lips.

"She's enjoying that," said Celia who had followed Stones' eye line and had also seen the discreet activity.

Not that anyone was expecting Emily to have the fortitude to give voice to the next few words in response to prompting from

Chloe. Stones smiled, as Philippa's face was a picture of confusion at Emily's pronouncement. Stones, and indeed Celia, had far more understanding of Emily's capacity for receiving punishment and the sexual stimulation that she revelled in when the after-burn of a thrashing seared into her consciousness.

"Oh, of course, Chloe. Thank you so much, Hilary, for my much-deserved punishment but I think I ought to have a few more really hard smacks to make sure that I remember what a naughty girl I have been and how I have really earned a very sore bottom, please. I am so sorry for the way I treated you and want to thank you for being so lenient."

Hilary was clearly lost in the moment as silence descended in both rooms and the only activity was Hilary's hand moving between Emily's legs. The pointed throat clearing from Chloe stopped all that and once more the paddle was raised high, before Emily's bright scarlet cheeks received a thunderous slap from the paddle. Again and again the paddle slammed down across the curve of Emily's buttocks as her body rocked and twisted within the limits that she could. Her screams restarted and seemed to double as Hilary went for five colossal final hits on her most tender, lower buttocks.

Stones reminded his two companions that Emily had most definitely agreed that she would have to undertake a severe thrashing and accept some form of sexual assault so that the seven would have no leg to stand on to explain away their actions when challenged. However, watching Emily as she laid on the floor curled up into a ball keening in pain, it was hard for him not to feel that she was maybe going beyond the call of duty.

With Emily looking rather scared and in considerable discomfort by now, Stones' face hardened considerably as he heard Chloe threatening Emily with a beating from the rose stems. Celia turned to him saying, "This one is in serious need of work, wouldn't you say? Professor? Very nasty young lady with a real attitude problem and a penchant for violence. Oh, I see, that's the game then, how far are you going to let this go, Professor?"

The look on the Dean of Discipline's face at that point boded ill for Chloe Tang, as she continued to goad and threaten Emily. The picture had switched and they watched in fascination as they had a perfect close-up view of the double-headed pegging kit that Saffron was fixing around her body, the two hard rubber penis extensions swinging rather ludicrously from her hips as she manoeuvred the straps into position.

"I shall call a halt when I think they are crossing the boundary of what Emily is willing to suffer for the greater cause. The girl is incredibly resilient, ladies, believe me. I will stop it when I think she wants me to."

With Emily being thrown across the bed, following Chloe's instructions, Miranda climbed and sat on the back of her neck while Helen and Saffron pulled her legs wide apart. All three cringed as Zoe ran across the room and swung the long bamboo cane against her buttocks. The crack of the impact was loud, the scream from Emily louder, and Philippa visibly cringed as the flayed bottom had a scarlet stripe added to the damage. They saw Miranda lean down and whisper in her ear, coinciding with Chloe taking the cane and slamming down straight away. Emily's jerking head smashed back into Miranda's causing her to join Emily in yelping in pain.

"If she does that again Miranda, I'd turn her over and shit in her mouth." Those words from Chloe stilled the room for a moment.

"Oh no, I can't believe it, surely she would not do so a disgusting thing?" Philippa's piousness about the language of students was beginning to grate on Stones and he flashed her a look of annoyance that carried a palpable warning.

"No Philippa, she is just trying to wind her up. It's a childish threat, no one's shitting in anyone's mouth, now just be quiet, watch and listen, please!"

All there was to listen to for the next couple of minutes was the swish of the bamboo, the loud crack of its landing and the long anguished scream in response from a beleaguered Emily as the two women took turns to deliver harsh strikes. Stones was concerned about the state of her buttocks as he could see countless abrasions on her seriously blighted skin. He very much hoped they would not draw blood as the risk of scarring was something that he didn't find acceptable. He suspected that Emily was getting beyond caring by the time the group picked her up, carried her into the bathroom, and deposited her onto the kitchen table that was beside the bath.

As Chloe reappeared wheeling the covered equipment in, Celia and Stones exchanged glances, knowing full well what was to be revealed. Philippa gave a cry of horror, and threw a guilty look towards Stones, as the cover was removed and the large container with its spout and tubing came into full view. As Emily was forcibly moved into position, and they watched in horror as she panicked and started to beg for mercy, Stones quietly spoke into his radio and was assured that the numbers for the planned intervention were in place. All seven of the protagonists had now donned strap-ons and appendages of various shapes, sizes and colours and were proudly comparing them.

"Good grief, where on earth did they get those disgusting things from? They are truly obscene." Philippa's mouth hung open. Celia and Stones passed knowing furtive glances at each other, their eyes twinkling at Philippa's outrage.

"I am sure we can ask them, if you are interested, Philippa. Was there any particular protuberance or attachment that has caught your eye?" Stones could not let the opportunity to wind up his rather prim colleague and got the expected response.

"Oh, good heavens, Professor Stones, I most certainly do not! That's disgusting. You couldn't possibly think I would be interested in such deviant equipment. Oh no, no, no, most certainly not." Philippa had turned bright red and was decidedly flustered by the remark. Celia meanwhile was trying desperately not to laugh; exposing any weakness like this to the Professor was never advisable!

"Philippa, if you have nothing constructive to offer, you do need to hold your tongue, please. I surely don't need to remind you what your role is here and how we intend to deal with this situation?"

Philippa gulped. She had been at the college long enough to realise that Stones was not a man to get on the wrong side of and that, like all academic staff members, she had pledged strong support and belief in the stance that the college took in disciplinary matters. St James' ideals and principles were not universally popular and certainly not considered very politically correct but the staff, scholarly and otherwise, and students were all enshrined in its philosophy and ethics concerning the use of strict discipline. They were expected to have embraced the notion that students graduated not only with high qualifications but also as fully rounded, worldly-wise individuals who understood their standing in society and their responsibility as a St. James' scholar and alumni. Sometimes the students needed assistance and improvement along the way and although St James' philosophy concerning the manner in which the help was applied might not meet with other institutions' ideals, there was certainly very little dissent that their methods produced results. Philippa was well aware that her senior position at the college depended on her embracing and committing to the cause as far as disciplinary action went and was astute enough to realise that she had overstepped the mark.

"No, Professor Stones, my apologies. I will try to keep a focus and an objective mind in future. I do beg your forgiveness and bow to your superior understanding of these matters. Oh my word, oh heavens. Sorry Professor, but that poor girl. Yes, I know, I will keep quiet, apologies again."

She had just seen Zoe's preparations with the large rubber pump, and then heard and processed her threat to fill Emily's colon with half a gallon of warm water. Stones and Celia however, were engrossed with what was happening and ignored her comment completely. Stones was particularly interested in Chloe's attention with her tongue and lips to Emily's pussy and pondered exactly what this indicated. He had sensed throughout the conflict with the gang that this might be a bit of an individual battle between Chloe and Emily and suspected that Chloe somehow felt threatened by Emily's sense of assurance, confidence and nonchalance when dealing with her protagonists.

Stones' face hardened as he saw the grimace appear on Emily's face when Hilary's fingers invaded her anal chamber as she was lubricated for the nozzle that Hilary and Miranda then slid inside of her. He was not at all surprised though to see the look of steely resolve on Emily's face and then her mouth set as she suddenly kicked back against her tormentors, sending the water container crashing to the floor, smashing instantly.

He felt for his young protégée as the nozzle and tube slipped out of her back entrance and she was assaulted by Chloe, then dragged back into the bedroom to receive another battering with the paddle as the rest of the gang picked up the detritus of the broken equipment.

The ridiculous sight of the six young woman, with fake penises waving around, all picking up glass and mopping up spilt water with bath towels caused Stones to chuckle aloud, much to Philippa's consternation. Stones got to his feet as Emily was sent back to the bathroom to complete the cleaning.

"Right ladies, coats on, looks about time for us to make our way there. I'll take my tablet so we can see what is happening and intervene at the appropriate time."

When the three of them left the room, the picture showed Zoe and Miranda holding Emily's arms as they guided her over to the bed, her body blotched with red, sore marks all over now from the scrubbing she had received, and assisted her as she knelt over the prone body of Saffron. Stones was pleased, but again not at all surprised, to see that Emily was now totally compliant as she knelt facing Saffron whose protuberance was grazing her pussy while Helen was obscenely swinging and aiming her phallus at Emily's mouth. Hilary moved behind Emily, with Charlotte producing a handful of lubricant that she set about working into Emily's rear portal, causing Stones to urge the others to quicken their pace as he could see that Emily was about to face a three-way penetration. As they approached the room, the support team of Chief Academic Administrator, Sara, Pastoral Care Tutor, Sonya, Head Nurse, Elizabeth and Head Porter, Ronald, appeared from the shadows. From Stones' tablet they all heard Chloe's voice, clear and full of menace:

"Go for it, Charl, lots of lovely lube up her arse, she'll need it to take Hilary's big cock. What's her fanny like Saffron, need any lube, or is she dripping wet as usual, the lusty little slut?"

The Professor urged them forward now, content that he had seen and recorded all the evidence he required to bring the group to heel.

"Right everyone, follow my lead. Elizabeth, as agreed, get Emily and her clothes up and out of there and to the Health Centre immediately. The rest of you just keep the others apart from each other and listen to my instructions."

Stones and the group headed quietly up the stairway to the room as Stones' screen showed Emily being triple breeched and the picture was full of naked writhing bodies. They reached the door with perfect timing as the women started their "Gang bang" chant and, at Stones' signal and whispered initial instructions, they burst into the room.

Stones lifted Hilary clean off her feet, the strap-on's sudden removal causing Emily to buck dramatically in pain as Celia and Elizabeth threw a blanket over her and lifted her up and off Saffron. Sara took hold of Saffron's shoulders, pinning her to the bed, while Philippa had hold of Miranda, Stones being fairly sure that she would be the most compliant one. Roland had a fair grip on Chloe's arms and Sonya had hold of Zoe. As Elizabeth gathered Emily's clothes up and quickly drew her from the room, Celia took one arm each of the remaining two, Helen and Charlotte, who had frozen at their entrance.

"Everyone, keep your mouths firmly shut!" shouted Chloe as the panic induced by the sudden realisation of their situation showed on all of their faces.

"Everyone please be on notice that there are a multitude of concealed cameras recording every moment that is happening and has happened in this room. You are much too late and in far too deep to play any 'no comment' or 'taking the fifth amendment' line. Please be advised that the only policy you have left is total honesty and full co-operation. All other avenues are firmly closed." Stones' voice was considerably quieter than Chloe's but the menace in his tone seemed to freeze the air.

"Let's get one thing clear, you bunch of despicable reprobates.

Chloe Tang is not in control of you and she is certainly not in control of this situation. There are grounds for arrest and prosecution galore in what we have witnessed this evening, so if you prefer for there to be no police involvement then I suggest that you look to me for your instructions and not Miss Tang. Who will not bloody well speak any more! Shut your mouth, young lady, and keep it shut! You are so close to being driven straight to the police station to see my good friend the Chief Superintendent. Now stand in front of me, hands on heads. Hopefully you are aware of how ridiculous you all look with those disgusting things on!"

Chloe's mouth hung open. Finally the arrogance and cockiness had drained from her face and for the first time he saw a scared and vulnerable girl. The young women dutifully lined up and faced the professor.

"Now, hands up if you would like to be marched over to my rooms naked with your disgusting appendages on show for anyone passing to see?"

It got the perfect reaction he had hoped for. Tears welled up in the eyes of all of them now. The possibility of exposure to their peers and fellow students, let alone any staff, visitors or Fellows around was a thought that reduced the whole gang to looking far more like terrified and guilty little children than bulletproof and untouchable as they purported to be.

"I thought not," said Stones, who had no intention of carrying out the threat. He was well aware that the instant they were spotted, camera phones would be on the go and footage would be going viral across social media platforms in minutes. The damage to the college would be inestimable and he himself would find that he had questions to answer! The sordid group was not to know that, so he knew that his next question would receive unanimous support.

"Who would rather be given an initial good hiding up here and then be allowed to wear a sheet over their embarrassment for the walk?"

Zoe and Chloe hesitated for a few seconds, but Miranda's hand went straight up, quickly followed by Helen, Saffron and Charlotte. Hilary's was half-hearted and so very reluctant but up it went, and Zoe took a long quizzical look at Chloe before making it six. Chloe joined them but Stones could see her mind ticking over as she desperately tried to formulate a plan of escape from this.

"Miranda, your hand went up first, so you get the first whopping. Ten for you for being first, 12 each for the others, apart from Chloe who will receive 20 for being so slow and so reticent in realising the trouble she's in." The petulant look on Chloe's face didn't endear her to Stones and he found himself relishing the future path he had planned out for her.

"Celia, please stand here, you know how this goes. Miranda, please bend down in front of the Senior Tutor. You can all leave your accessories on, I think it will add to the humiliation of having your bare bottom beaten in front of an audience. Not forgetting, of course, that this is all on film. Celia, tuck her head between your knees, hands on the side of her hips. Miranda spread your legs wide, I need to make sure I don't beat the Senior Tutor's hands now, don't I?" Stones was enjoying himself, the task of prepping a victim for punishment was one of his favourite hobbies.

He slipped his thick leather belt from his trousers and looped it around his hand.

"Now girls, as you can see, Miranda is now in the perfect pose, if we can just forget about the ridiculous plastic penis! Nice rounded buttocks, legs parted to open up her bottom crevice so we can see her anus nicely as the bullseye for lining up my belt, and the additional shame of knowing that her still rather disgustingly moist, lower vagina is peeking out. This is a pose of chagrin, of disgrace, for the ultimate chastisement of a bare bottom beating that you all undoubtedly deserve. I do hope you all agree, but we will soon find out. Miranda, do you wish to receive this beating?"

Miranda swallowed, but had clearly resigned herself to what was coming.

"Yes sir, please sir. I would like you to beat me now, sir. I am so sorry, sir."

"Not me who you should be apologising to really, but that will do for starters. The word starters being most apposite as this is a mere forerunner of what is to come for you all."

His ominous words preceded the whip of his belt and harsh strokes across Miranda's taut buttocks, which soon brought screams of pain from the student as he beat her quickly and methodically to a background of sniffles, gentle weeping and mewing from most of the others.

Charlotte, Helen and Saffron quickly followed without resistance. Each of them beaten hard and reduced to squeals, screams and racking sobs, but held firmly in place between Celia's legs. Each sent to stand facing the wall with bright red bottoms and now in no doubt that they were in serious trouble. Hilary was the first to resist, and Stones needed to adopt a much firmer tone and take action to get her to comply.

"Two additional strokes for disobedience," Stones snapped, yet still Hilary stood stock still in front of him and made no move to yield to his entreaty to bend and allow her head to be held between Celia's thighs. Eventually his patience snapped and he took a fistful of hair and plunged her forcefully down while Celia assisted by restraining her wriggling body as she twisted and turned to try to avoid being positioned.

"You've already earned yourself six further strokes now, Hilary. If you do not cease your ridiculous and childish resistance, I will take you outside and we will do this in the centre of the courtyard for all to see!" His thunderous voice cowed the struggling student and she was finally held in place.

"Lock your hands behind the Senior Tutor please, Hilary, and do not release your grip until your thrashing is completed. I will not give you any further warnings."

The 18 strokes fell hard and fast, with Stones taking care to ensure that the most sensitive upper legs and tops of her buttocks were particularly favoured areas of impact. Her screeches were long and high-pitched, and Celia had to work hard to keep her in place, but at last her ordeal was over and Stones fairly flung the distraught student away and into place with the others.

"Stand up straight, you pathetic urchin and desist with the over dramatic noise." Accompanied by his huge hand slapping her sore, and very red, tram-lined cheeks, Stones was taking no nonsense and Hilary wisely took a couple of deep stuttering breaths to calm herself.

"Zoe, in place, over you go. Hold her tightly, Senior Tutor please."

The splatting sound of the belt hitting Zoe's tight, bent-over bottom became the latest sound effects to fill the otherwise silent room. As Stones paused for a moment and glanced at the beaten rather shell-shocked young women, he fervently hoped that they were experiencing turmoil in their minds as they faced up to what they must have surely realised was a potentially disastrous and life-changing scenario. Zoe was now weeping openly and each stroke of the belt was greeted with a small, strangled yelp, her bottom now a fearsome shade of red as Stones landed the final strike across the tightest skin on the top of her bottom causing Zoe's legs to buckle as

Celia held her firmly to keep her from dropping to the floor.

"Just young Chloe left for now. You girls can sob away to your heart's content but take notice that this is not your punishment. Let's call this a little admonishment for misuse and misappropriation of college property. These rooms will need to be stripped and deep cleaned now and this is your price for that. For the heinous acts you have conducted this evening, and in certain other episodes I have documented, you will be facing the most severe punishment of a level that this college has rarely had to dispense. Be warned, you scurrilous band of misfits, this college does not take lightly to being placed in danger of disrepute. You are facing the full might of this institution being brought down on your filthy, nasty little heads!" Stones was determined that the group should be subject to the mental pressure of facing up to their position, and from the tremors and sobs his words induced he was happy that he was instilling a high level of fear and anxiety, albeit that Chloe appeared to have recovered her poise. He intended to break through that calmness now, despite a grudging respect for her forbearance.

"Chloe Tang, step forward and bend over. Head down and between the Senior Tutor's legs, hands locked together behind her please. Twenty strokes of my finest for you. Legs apart, point that backside up at me. Come on, you know the drill, show the room that anus please, let us all see the bullseye!"

He was steadfastly resolved to break through this young woman's stoicism but admired her immediate compliance and lack of shame or reluctance in exposing herself to the riveted gaze of her audience of Philippa, Sara, Sonya and Ronald. Sara seemed the most composed, Sonya looked slightly flustered, Philippa's bewildered expression rather illustrated that she had strayed into a situation beyond her understanding, whilst Ronald was wide-eyed, open-mouthed and clearly enjoying every moment of these pretty young females' shame. Celia, he knew, would find none of this in the slightest bit unusual and unsettling; her sexual antics with Stones over the years meant that he had little in his repository of punishments that she had not personally experienced. She had made no secret of the fact that she was also a voyeur at heart and thoroughly enjoyed watching others being put through their paces. She smiled at him now, her eyes full of desire, as he took back his arm ready to begin the cascade of swipes of his thick belt to Chloe's waiting buttocks.

It was eight hefty strokes in before Chloe let loose a long, low guttural moan but Stones could tell from Celia's expression that Chloe's grip around her upper legs was tightening and the slight swaying of Chloe's body gave away her attempt to withstand the pain without a fuss. Her resilience did her no favours as Stones was determined that any resolve not to cry out was just a challenge that he would not lose. His next strike swept low under the bottom cheeks at the point where the legs met the buttocks, an area renowned for its sensitivity. As the slap of the belt echoed around the room, there was a moment's pause before Chloe released a high shrill scream of agony. Stones did not hesitate and hit the same spot again with a savage stroke. The scream became fully fledged and as he hit that sweet spot for the third time, Celia had to adjust her feet as she struggled to hold a writhing, screeching Chloe. The final strikes were across the fullness of her cheeks just under the centre line. The student's scream changed to a higher pitch as she suffered, any reserve blown apart, her legs trembling uncontrollably, her buttocks ablaze, her pride dismantled. Job done for now, mused Stones, with some satisfaction.

"Up and over there with the rest of the rabble, pull yourself together child, have some dignity please."

Stones slid his jibes in, as always turning the screw and adding to his miscreant's suffering.

Minutes later, the sheet-covered students who had been escorted, without incident, across to Stones' quarters, awaited the next stage in their ill-fated evening. The first thing the seven noticed as they entered the Professor's rooms was the large screen suspended in the air which showed pictures of a couple of porters who were clearly collecting up odd items and taking photographs of various angles of the room. Their defeated looks as they saw their clothes being bundled up and thrown into black plastic rubbish collection sacks gave Stones satisfaction. The wide-eyed students all blanched and grimaced to varying degrees as they then noticed the figure of the Mistress of the college, Professor Dorothy Winslow-Bellingham, seated in a corner of the room with a furious look on her face.

"Ah. You are here, Professor Winslow-Bellingham. Welcome. Not an evening that brings a great deal of credit to the college I am afraid. Line up, ladies, give me the sheets and face the Mistress."

Stones, as always, had chosen his words carefully, prompting the desired response from the college Mistress.

Her face was thunderous and her voice dripped with cold fury.

"Look at you and your ridiculous and preposterous attachments. Take them off now and put them on the table there. They are your belongings and you can take them with you when you leave. Rest assured that you will all be leaving the college tomorrow and we may well never see you again on these premises. Yes, I can confirm what you are undoubtedly most worried about. Your parents and guardians have all been informed of your nefarious activities and I have personally assured them that I am satisfied that the evidence we have complied against you could result in criminal charges and arrest if the college and the relevant injured parties wish to pursue that course. I will not pretend that this fine institution would not suffer if this became publicly exposed. However, if that is where this episode leads us, then so be it. We will deal with it. Notwithstanding that, you women are a disgrace to humanity and society. Bullying is one thing but this form of vicious and violent sexual assault is nothing short of abominable. We have an excellent record of examination and qualification success, so we accept that failure reflects as badly on us as it does our students and therefore we strive to guide you to a point and level that exceeds expectation. You are an embarrassment to the college, and you will be receiving your just desserts. However, you are our disgrace and our embarrassment and as such I will do my utmost to ensure that the appropriate punishment is dispensed by the college. I will expect you to accept whatever punishment is deemed fit by the college council and in the future will attempt to bring an element of deportment, grace and dignity to proceedings. Those proceedings will be of the highest level of severity possible, mark my words, but the intention is to deal with you under college regulations if possible. Rest assured our main aim is to correct and improve your behaviour."

As the doorbell buzzer sounded, Stones turned to Chloe.

"Now once you have put your clothes on you can get out of my sight. Chloe, you may go to the door and collect the black bags that should now be on the doorstep. If you are lucky, there will be no one passing to see you in your disgraced state of undress. You will dress quickly. You will then be escorted back to your rooms where you will be isolated until you take your leave from these premises that you have misused so badly. Mistress, have you anything further to add?"

Professor Winslow-Bellingham peered at the seven miscreants, all in various states of distress.

"You have all let yourselves down very badly. I have no idea on the thought processes you all employed that would lead you to believe that your actions have been anything but reprehensible. I am deeply ashamed that young ladies under my leadership would act this way and I am so very angry with all of you. You will be punished and, as Professor Stones says, that will be punishment of the highest level of severity that we can bring to bear. I hope that you will embrace this chastisement as part of your learning process and that there is to be redemption, contrition and improvement. There is certainly a lot of room for it. Now get dressed and get out of my sight!"

As Chloe scampered back into the room with the black bags, the seven hastened into their clothes contained within, and were soon escorted out. Stones asked his remaining colleagues to stay to review the day's events and begin the work that would now take place to progress the situation. It would be a while before he would have his day, but he was a patient man and quite content to bide his time knowing that there was only one obvious conclusion to this sordid episode and he was damn sure he would be the main player in the endgame!

CHAPTER 9

SARA'S FEARS ARE REALISED   (THE

COMEUPPANCE PART 2!)

Stones ruminated as he read through once again the recently received letter, from ex-student Jenny Goldman, addressed to the Mistress, Professor Dorothy Winslow-Bellingham, and himself, complaining in detail about Sara Morgan, the Chief Academic Administrator, citing an illicit sexual relationship with her during her time at college. A scornful Jenny claimed that Sara took advantage of her while she was in a vulnerable state and had manipulated her since to continue the relationship purely on a sexual nature until, in Jenny's words, she had come to her senses. Stating that now she had worked in a more adult environment she had come to realise that she had been victim of a serious breach of college rules. Jenny quoted the college handbook that forbade staff in forming and developing relationships with undergraduate students and she therefore asked that Sara be called to account, and punished accordingly. Jenny had written that she would be happy to come into college to discuss the matter further and would provide written and text evidence to support her accusation. Stones, being well-versed in the wily ways of human nature, was very much aware that Jenny's nose had probably been put out of joint by the appearance of Jamie Adams as a new attraction in Sara's life and was confident that this was behind Jenny's newly discovered sense of moral outrage.

Stones had a brief discussion with Dorothy, in which, as expected, she declared that she would expect him to resolve the issue quickly and that, of course, he had her complete backing as to how he carried that out. Her disapproval of what had clearly taken place originally on college property was obvious and Stones harboured concerns, particularly on Sara's behalf, as to how this would pan out.

The meeting with Jenny had gone pretty much as he expected. She had laid out her evidence, claimed that she had been abused, sobbed heartily and then demanded that Sara be sacked after being thrashed by the Professor in front of her. A threat to tell her tale to the media, if her demands were not met, seemed to be played as the ace up her sleeve. Stones had allowed her to have her say and agreed that she should return to his quarters in in two weeks' time when decisions would have been taken. Within days he had been in touch with several old girls, ex-colleagues and friends of the college. Favours had been called in and any risk of media exposure had been summarily removed. The college's support circle and reach was a very wide and encompassing one and contained leading figures in many fields across the globe. Satisfied that all threat to the college's welfare and reputation had been removed, he now had safer ground to work on. His back door bell chimed to herald the arrival of Dorothy, the Mistress, and Celia, the Senior Tutor. It was time to outline his plans before they were joined by Sara and Jamie.

Sara's face when she and Jamie arrived in response to the Professor's request to attend a disciplinary meeting rather betrayed that she was a woman who had been waiting with dread for such a summons for a long time. As they both acknowledged the presence of the two senior college figures seated on either side of the Dean of

Discipline, Sara's expression of guilt and fear rather betrayed her thinking. Within minutes, she was admitting the relationship and detailing the rendezvous between her and Jenny, a single tear running slowly down her cheek as she haltingly spelled out her shame.

"So," said the Professor in his most grave voice. "You admit that you took advantage of a vulnerable young lady in a calculated and persistent manner, and you continued to do so throughout a part of her college life here. You thereby breeched college rules in the most severe way, tantamount to sexually abusing a young lady given to us to keep safe, be protected, be educated and delivered back to her parents and the wider world as a wiser, improved and stronger form. You clearly were aware of the position you placed yourself and the college in, particularly as you were witness to a similar breach by a senior member of staff."

Celia reddened and squirmed at this reference to her misdemeanour of a similar nature, but kept her eyes fixed on the wilting, now gently sobbing, miscreant senior member of her staff. Stones knew full well that Dorothy would have noted the remark and that would have intensified Celia's shame. There was a seriousness behind his words as the threat of full exposure of the college's stance on corporal punishment was real. It would be a great story for the scandal sheets and although he was confident that damage could be controlled and limited due to the college alumni's extensive reach and high-level connections, he would much prefer not to be fighting that fire. The punishments were recorded, evidenced, accepted and, in theory at least, requested by the recipients. They were deemed to be appropriate and conducted as pure chastisements with documentation on file to support and substantiate. They were also legal and arguably moral, however, any sexual element in reference to the treatment of undergraduates was the stalling point. The college was not a supporter of corporal punishment for any reason of sexual gratification, fetish, kink, perversion or otherwise. There was a commitment that the disciplinary action of the college be shown to be proven as above board and beyond legal reproach. Stones recorded everything, with the exception of private trysts with the likes of Celia, and also collated clear documentation of the students' acceptance of their castigations. Dorothy had a live stream to virtually every session that Stones conducted and could watch live or scroll back to see what had occurred on any day.

Stones had stood outside of the college's sub-committee which had written the policy around acceptable disciplinary action. He had, however, fed into the documentation and had approved the policy wherein it stated that any chastisement must avoid the effect of unreasonably interfering with an individual's work performance or creating an intimidating, hostile, or offensive studying or working environment. The college had taken into account that their traditional methods of punishment laid them open to the legal clauses that covered sexual harassment in the workplace and beyond, and there had been long conversations around acceptable behaviour leading to and during the thrashing of the students. An unwise student had once taken steps to prosecute the college for 'quid pro quo harassment' after being reluctant to sign the release. Each student and her parents or guardians were encouraged, but not forced, to sign before they accepted their final place. This signed and binding agreement gave the college full power and permission to use corporal punishment when it was deemed as warranted and considered apposite. The student had made a statement that accused the college of requiring sexual favours and sexual contact from a student as a condition of their acceptance into college. Of course, Stones had been tipped the wink by a contact, the sister of an alumna, within the legal profession, and the student's parents had been alerted to their daughter's activity. Her mother, a graduate of the college and a one-time visitor to Stones' room for disciplining over a minor infringement, had stepped in spectacularly, immediately driving to the college. This mother had escaped with toilet cleaning as a punishment for her misdemeanour but a lecture from Stones and the mere threat of a bare-bottomed spanking had ensured exemplary behaviour for the rest of her time at college. Stones fondly remembered the student's howls as her mother took her over her knees and, with the Professor's eagerly given permission, proceeded to pull down her knickers and give her daughter a thorough bare bottom spanking in front of him. Stones being invited to inspect the result of her handiwork had possibly caused the daughter as much anguish as the spanking, and he had milked the moment fully as he prodded and admired the beaten buttocks. A single swing of his favourite thick strap on her bottom as a parting shot, whilst her mother held her firmly down, seemed to put the seal on the quelling of her rebellious nature, and a vanquished and defeated young woman had left his room wiser after the event! The college had certainly kept a firm watch on how situations developed after that episode and Stones was confident that he had most scenarios covered. He was therefore not at all pleased at Celia's earlier misdemeanour, albeit she had paid a high price, and now this incident with Sara and Jenny that had seriously breeched the rules caused him further concerns.

The college had taken steps to check and clarify how much they could use humiliation as a form of, or a constituent of, punishment. The independent findings were that shaming was considered an integral part of chastisement and as long as maliciousness, spite and a thirst for revenge were excluded in the reason for discipline, then they were on safe ground. *Which was a damn good job*, thought Stones, as he was totally convinced that there was indeed a humiliation aspect in the disciplinary process that stood outside of harassment, bullying and misconduct, by the beating of fully displayed, naked flesh. The students' voluntary acceptance of a beating rather than their parents being informed, or suspension possibly leading to expulsion by being 'sent down' in the most serious cases, meant the incidents were always viewed as 'punishment by their own violation' in law.

Sara's transgression bothered him; he accepted that he had put temptation in her way, but felt extremely disappointed that such a previously exemplary member of staff had fallen foul of the rules so easily. Her lack of discipline and willpower concerned him as much as her apparent casual approach to college rules and regulations. He felt heartened by her acceptance of blame and willingness to atone but there would be a long path to forgiveness in his view. He waited as he saw her draw breath and he raised his eyebrows expectantly at her.

"Yes sir, I am so sorry, sir. I didn't know how to stop once I started, and we did develop very strong feelings towards each other. I am absolutely horrified to hear you discuss our relationship in the terms you have and ashamed to have let you all down so much. I can only say that I did become ridiculously in thrall to Jenny and believe that my worshipping of her made me blind to the other offences I had committed. I can only beg for your mercy and will of course immediately write my resignation if you would allow me to do so." Sara's breathing had become disjointed as she struggled through her little speech of contrition and Stones could see the outright terror in her eyes at the situation she was now faced with.

"Of course, you are sorry, you stupid, stupid, selfish, lustful woman! Why do you think we have these rules in place? Many of these girls come to us in a half-formed state and it is our duty to transform them into fully fledged, capable young women. For well over 100 of them, mostly undergraduates, some post-graduates who are not protected by the same severity of restrictions on them due to being so much older and wiser supposedly, that has meant being bent over naked with a sore bottom and their bodies as well as their shame put on display. They are humiliated, they have their spirits broken, they lose their inhibitions, some in a very carnal manner, but we do not take advantage of them and we do not bloody well fuck them!" Stones' voice had now risen and his anger was clear to all in the room.

"Jamie, please take a seat." Stones and Jamie had agreed that within college he would now be referred to as Jamie, keeping the title Porter as his moniker just for their nefarious activities in the fetish club, BADs, that they both belonged to.

"Sara, you can bloody well take your clothes off and stand facing the corner. I don't want to see your face at the moment. However, I certainly don't think you should be standing there to be treated like a respectable adult. You are a very naughty, naughty girl and the best place for you now is in the corner of the room with your hands on your head and your bottom exposed. I do not know how we are going to get through this situation with you retaining your senior position at this college but I suppose that you have given us some years of quality, dutiful work. The truth is that I really have appreciated your support and commitment in the past. Nothing, however, excuses your arrogance, wilful disobedience, lack of respect and this disgraceful abuse of your position. I am fully cognisant of the fact that you were aware of my suspicions concerning your intent with young Jenny, yet despite that you ventured into an unwise sexual relationship, taking full advantage of your position of power in this college. You are a disgrace, young lady, and your future career is now hanging by a thread. Virtually unforgivable. I am so disappointed in you."

Sara's clothes were off in a thrice and she complied immediately with his words, her cheeks burning as she wept quietly and walked to stand in the corner. Stones acknowledged that she was wise enough to hold off the expected begging for mercy, delivery of pathetic excuses and hand-wringing regret but for now, at least, he wanted her to think of the consequences of her actions and a future outside of the college. There was no need, for the moment, for Sara to know that he had oiled those wheels and was confident that there would be no external repercussions for her actions. Jenny had yet to be dealt with but he had certainly fried bigger fish than her and was in no doubt that she would succumb to his power and intent. He deliberately averted his eyes as Sara undressed and then took her shameful position facing the wall in the corner of the room. With Jamie present, he felt the need to temper his natural reaction to make an assessment of her body and comment on his findings as he would normally, to aid in stripping away his target's remaining dignity as well as their clothes!

"Tricky times for you, Jamie, I'm afraid. Jenny has requested satisfaction in the form of a 500 stroke caning for Sara, for which she would be an observer and this caning to be administered by you, and then she should be subject to summary dismissal. Tricky indeed, my friend."

Jamie took a deep breath and looked at the three senior college staff members before he spoke clearly and with confidence. They all appreciated his difficult position with his lover in so much trouble, standing buck naked whilst her shame was discussed as though she wasn't there.

"I would be perfectly happy to carry out my part of the punishment, Professor. I have to admit that Sara had made me aware of her actions and although has expressed much regret to me concerning her behaviour, I have always felt that it wasn't the breaking of the rules that concerned her but just the fear of getting caught. She can have no complaints that it has come to this, the rules are clear to us all concerning our attitudes and relationship with undergraduates. Indeed, as mentors and pastoral carers, our duty of care towards them is paramount and written in stone. Sara had transgressed out of initially a silly infatuation and her heart getting the better of her, but then progressively out of straightforward lust and passion. If she was a man, we would be saying that she had been thinking with her cock! In her defence, I am convinced totally that she regrets her action and is truly sorry. Sara values her job and her relationship with you all enormously and I believe that she is a good and diligent member of your team, so I would ask you to consider with your hearts that she is a good person who has made a mistake and done a bad thing. Please consider giving her a final warning rather than dismissal; in return I think you will find that she will repay you with endeavour and loyalty of the highest degree. As to her physical punishment, this is entirely up to you, of course. I have no quibble with the proposal that she receives the most extreme thrashing possible, regardless of who carries this out. I also have no doubt that Sara herself would accept and welcome any such physical chastisement as the just comeuppance for her actions."

The Professor considered Jamie's words for several moments, the silence being broken by the unpleasant background noise of Sara snivelling and sniffing quite loudly. He jumped up and, brandishing a tissue, he marched towards her.

"Oh for goodness sake, stop that disgusting racket!" With that, he wiped around her face before putting the tissue to her nose. "Blow!" he barked.

Folding the dirty tissue and dabbing at her nose, he continued:

"Please pull yourself together now, woman, it's time to be a big girl. Now come and stand in front of us and let's see if we can make a decision."

A terrified and trembling Sara stood naked in front of the four of them, Jamie sitting slightly to the side and Sara obviously avoiding meeting his eyes.

"Jamie has delivered an articulate speech in support of you continuing in your post and I can tell you that I have no intention of being blackmailed and coerced by a young scrap of a girl. To that end, I can reassure you that we do not intend to dismiss you from your position here."

"Oh my goodness, thank heavens and thank you, sir. Oh God, I am so sorry that I have been so unbelievably stupid. My behaviour was reprehensible and I am afraid that I got involved in something that started off as a bit of fun and then I sort of got a bit obsessed with Jenny, sir. She was my first female partner and it was…"

"Yes, blah, blah, blah. I'm sure. Lust and obsession with a little penchant for rule-breaking and chancing your arm. Now, get your hands back on top of your head and stand up straight. Come on, thrust those perky breasts out and stand tall, young lady. We do understand that you have had a bit of a disconnect between this and that, eh?" The Professor rose and stood directly in front of her, Sara jolting as Stones' finger flicked her head and then her pubic mound to illustrate his words.

"Jamie, I believe that it would be improper for you to stay further, my friend. This is an internal disciplinary matter and however much young Jenny would like to add to Sara's humiliation, but mainly, I suspect to the amount of pain you could cause her, it would not be appropriate for you to be involved in her chastisement any further. I will be dealing with Jenny and believe that we will come to an agreement that she finds acceptable as far as Sara's sentence goes, so I would be grateful if you could somehow detach yourself from this matter and leave it in our hands. Your relationship seems to be flourishing and I have no wish to put anything in the way of the pairing of two associates that I have high regards for. Yes Sara, indeed I do, otherwise you may well have already left the building in disgrace. But Sara realises that she has put us all in a very delicate position and, I sense, is happy to pay the price, albeit the severity of the price is going to have to be substantial. However, you clearly have a penchant for experimental sexual activity and I think I know where that could be put to good use. That is perhaps for another day and will involve you and Jamie discussing things further. I think Jamie has a good idea of what I am talking about and my feeling is that this could be an appropriate time for you two to have the discussion. Jamie, I can see, is on my wavelength. Sara, you will just need to allow your mind to develop what I suspect is already lurking there. Anyway, thank you for your input, Jamie. We are going to have a chat with Sara about the workings of the college and what we expect from its senior staff before she regales us with the plan she has formulated to help us see our way through the turmoil and near disaster she has led us to."

Stones spotted the look that Jamie directed at Sara that managed to portray sensitivity and love but carried also the unmistakeable message of an expectation of duty to be carried out and penance to be accepted. Sara's return look betrayed her rising panic and sense of isolation at his leaving and Stones knew that his decision was the correct one if he was going to successfully apply his usual systematic manipulations to inflict mental as well as physical pressure on his errant staff member. Stones waved Sara off to the corner of his room and stroked his chin as he looked at her naked back view.

"I certainly see the attraction you hold for Jamie and Jenny, young lady. You do have a lovely body, a beautiful back, I may say, the back being much underrated in terms of sexual stimulation and arousal I always think." He sauntered over and knelt down behind her, his hands roaming around her bottom.

"Good girl, you see you have learned not to react and to hold onto some degree of dignity in your demeanour. Obviously we will break that apart when it comes to the nitty-gritty, but it is admirable that you are seemingly accepting your fate. Now open your legs up a bit, I just want to apply the sniff test to ensure that you have been bright enough to prepare for any eventuality when being summoned to this room."

At that Sara did flinch and tense but steadfastly refused to buckle under what she would have clearly recognised as part of the psychological torment that Stones put his sufferers through. The Professor parted her cheeks but although he did have a look at the exposed anal hole he did not move his face towards her.

"Just checking for compliance, Sara, relax you are spared that particular indignity for now, although why we should treat you with any respect at all is open to question. However, it was a pleasure to see your rather neat anus with its pretty little flower garden of tight brown, curly hairs. I will look forward to having a closer encounter of your lovely delicate areas soon, my dear girl."

He was taken aback and well impressed when Sara spoke in a clear and self-assured tone.

"If it would suit you sir, I am happy that I am sufficiently clean and fresh not to offend you and would be happy to volunteer that I take my punishment as soon as you like and at your convenience. I do acknowledge that I have let Professor Winslow-Bellingham and Dr Ford down as well as you and the college in general, so believe that it would be most appropriate for them to witness my punishment for my disgraceful behaviour, sir."

The Professor looked towards his two colleagues and received facial expressions in response that suggested both had the time and the will, Celia looking particularly eager, he noted, to take up Sara's offer.

"Well, young lady, that may be most acceptable as I am considering an initial two-part process for you. This misdemeanour being so serious, I believe that the necessary chastisement would require two episodes to fully deliver the correct retribution deserved. Yes, so session one could be today and a follow-up, a more intense follow-up I should add, in a week's time. Excellent. We will discuss in more detail the other possibility I wish to pursue at a later date. Firstly you will put on these headphones, listen to a little Beethoven and sit here at the desk and write a concise note to me admitting your act of folly. I would like to hear how much you regret it and how you suggest that we go about bringing you to full contrition to help alleviate the shame and guilt your disgraceful misdeed has created. You are aware of the drill, so that I would expect you to be explicit and pertinent with your report. When you have finished put your hand up and do not move until I come over and take off the headphones. Understand?"

"Of course, sir. Yes sir, whatever you say, sir."

"Good girl," said Stones patronisingly, patting her head as she placed the headphones over her ears.

Dorothy, Celia and Stones then had a painful conversation around damage limitation, with Stones stressing that all was well and that their contacts network had fulfilled the criteria to dismantle any of the danger Jenny had posed. The Mistress was adamant that Jenny face the full wrath of the college for daring to break the unwritten code that forbade any disloyalty to the institution. Nonetheless, she did agree that Jenny's request for Sara to undergo serious chastisement was fair and she gave her full approval for the thrashing process that Stones proposed. They agreed that for the second part of her punishment they would allow Jenny to attend, although the plan by then would be that the tables would have been turned and she would be joining Sara in punishment rather than just watching! Jamie would not be invited to attend or take part as this was an internal staff and alumni incident and should be handled entirely internally. The Dean informed his colleagues that he was confident that his plan to make Jenny pay, for what they saw as a betrayal of the college ethos, was achievable without repercussions. He had established the line of communication at her place of work that had led him to discover that it was very strongly suspected that she had recently had an affair with a married senior female partner. The information was that things had been hushed up, to save the partner's marriage, but that, if the affair were to be exposed, Jenny's career with the company would be well and truly over. Whilst his information was that the liaison was in the past and that the participants had swept the matter under the carpet, he knew that this would be useful knowledge to fall back on.

The three continued chatting for a few minutes about the situation that Sara's indiscretion had got them into and formally agreed on the steps that would be taken that day. As Sara's hand was raised to indicate that she had competed her work, Stones went to one of his cupboards and wheeled out his automatic spanking machine out of Sara's eye line. He then crossed over to Sara and removed her headphones, directed her back to the corner of the room and ordered her to place her hands back on her head.

Sara then had to suffer the indignity of Stones reading out her words of contrition. It was written in language as though she was a suppliant sinner seeking forgiveness and Stones was quite taken aback at her total humility and earnestness, coupled with the clear remorse and acknowledgement that she was fortunate and grateful that she still had her position in the college. He heard her quiet restrained sniffling from the corner and for a moment, just a moment, he did feel some sympathy for this errant member of staff. That moment passed though – his hardheartedness was renowned – and he quickly dismissed any thoughts that would allow his personal regard for someone who had a high reputation as a dedicated and very effective team member to temper his actions. As she stated quite clearly, she had let the college, her colleagues and herself down and no punishment would be severe enough to totally eliminate her misdeeds. She asked that she undertake corporal punishment of the highest level, 'supreme' was the word Sara had used, he noted. Sara had made it clear that she expected no grace or favour and that she would accept her chastisement as a privilege extended by a college in lieu of dismissal and would in fact be in debt to the institution and Professor Stones in particular for the offer of some form of absolution. Interestingly, she indicated that she would feel honoured if her punishment consisted of humiliation and belittling of a level commensurate with the physical chastisement as her behaviour was both disgraceful and unworthy. Stones had never read a more heartfelt and open plea for admonishment and was happy to tell Sara so.

"This is most impressive and very pleasing to hear, Sara. Please rest assured that we will do our very best to meet your request and do you proud. I also think we should get to this straight away. Come over here and meet my recently acquired little contraption, Sara. It saves my arm somewhat and does a very good job. Now you will be strapped over the chair for about an hour as, due to your request to suffer and embrace the most acute and harsh punitive treatment possible, I have decided to double your original decreed punishment from 250 to 500 strokes from my mechanical friend here. Must be music to your ears, I would have thought!" Stones tested her commitment to the script she had written.

Sara gulped. Her eyes widened and fixed unwaveringly on the machine before her.

"Of course, sir. Absolutely. It will be my honour to suffer this in front of you all. Thank you very much, sir."

Stones smiled; her voice betrayed her fear and apprehension even if the words she spoke did not.

"Oh, you can thank us all afterwards. Now I suggest you just go and perch on the lavatory for a couple of minutes to ensure that your bladder is empty. We don't want any accidents now, do we, my dear?"

Sara's head dropped, her cheeks blushing red. She took a deep breath in, and then complied, walked tentatively into the bathroom and positioned herself on the toilet seat aware that the chairs of the Mistress and the senior tutor were placed so that they had full view of her. Stones meandered in after her and took a position to her right, keeping the sightlines from the room unobstructed. He knew that Sara would fully realise that this was part of the process, to embarrass her, to break her spirit, to undermine her, to shame her, but he well knew this knowledge would not detract from the awful experience and he saw the utter chagrin and defeat in her eyes as she peed audibly into the bowl. She closed her eyes as he bent between her legs and dabbed in a very perfunctory manner at her damp vagina.

"There you go, all done and dusted. Let's get you back and flush your shame away, shall we? Ha ha!" Stones flushed the toilet and patted Sara's bottom as he ushered her to wash their hands together at the sink before leading her back into the main room towards the instrument of her coming torture.

Strapped down to the specially adapted chair, her open buttocks raised and pointing at her audience, Stones was rather confident that she would regret the day she undertook to begin a relationship with Jenny for a long while to come! He made some minor adjustments to the device as he positioned it ready to apply the whippy cane attached to the waiting target of Sara's cheeks. With only the warning of a slight whirring sound, the metal arm holding the cane whipped round and slashed Sara's bottom. The inadvertent scream from Sara's mouth certainly supported his feeling that he had put it on a high enough setting concerning the speed and strength of the action, albeit he was aware that he had caught her unprepared.

"That was just a tester so that one is not one of your 500, Sara. So, based on your reaction we might expect to be hearing rather more of you than we anticipated this afternoon. I will give you a couple of minutes recovery while I change over implements at every 100 strokes, but you may have to find a large dose of mettle and toughen up a bit to get through this. It has whipped round on your hip a bit further than I would like so I have just adjusted the aim to make sure we get a full moon landing. Ho, ho! I do not want any cuts so the meat of your cheeks will be getting the full length from now on. Let the punishment commence!" he cheerfully announced as he set the timer and returned to his chair to join Dorothy and Celia for the spectacle.

The mechanism was set to strike a cane stroke every six seconds, so ten strokes a minute and ten minutes for the full 100 strokes to be delivered. The workings of the device allowed it to be set to alter the height of the blow either as directed or at random, with the third option of every blow hitting the same spot. Stones had set it to strike randomly to ensure that Sara was kept alert and could not prepare, and from the screeches that started on the seventh stroke, he was feeling quite satisfied that he had made a good call. By the time the machine whirred to announce the completion of its task, Sara was sobbing hysterically and her buttocks were completely covered in thin red criss-crossing lines.

"Well, that appears and feels most satisfying," said the Professor as he rose to closely inspect the damage done, his hands feeling over the whipped cheeks.

"Celia, can I ask you to clean her face up of the disgusting mixture of snot and tears and then let her sip some water? Best use the straws beside the glass I think, otherwise she'll probably spill it everywhere with all the fuss and performance going on here. Please try to pull yourself together woman, you are embarrassing yourself with all this nonsense. That was just a little old whippy cane to warm you up; the serious business starts now."

"Sorry sir, yes sir, I will try sir, thank you," Sara spluttered in response, but the trembling in her voice increased as Stones waved a leather belt in her face to show her the next attachment to his contraption.

"Let us see how this one makes you feel, shall we? Just another 400 strokes to go," he chortled.

He set the belt up and the onslaught renewed. By six strokes in, Sara was wailing and rather pitifully begging for mercy. Her words soon dried up as screaming became the only sound she then found herself capable of producing. Her screaming soon became very primitive and base, her bottom ravaged with thick weals rising all over. Stones watched closely as it crossed his mind that this level and amount of punishment may actually be too excessive. The pain she was obviously feeling did not concern him, but he had no wish to break her skin and cause any long-term markings or blemishes. He was proud of his skill when thrashing his misfits, and his judgment on severity was supreme, but the machine was rather new and he was as of yet not totally cognisant of the damage it could do. He allowed it to complete the second hundred strokes before inspecting Sara's battered and severely marked buttocks in more detail.

"Celia, further duty at the nose and mouth end, please, while I consider how much further we can take this element of Sara's chastisement. Sara, please desist from making that awful noise, it is most unpleasant."

Stones studied Sara's bottom intensely, a prodding finger here and there as he assessed the damage caused. The fact that his administrations were causing Sara to tighten her cheeks and anus due to his close attention was an added bonus and, of course, all grist to the mill as far as Stones' forms of punishment went.

"Do try not to clench so much, Sara, it is slightly distracting and annoying when I am trying to determine how much more you can withstand today. You really do not want to be annoying me at this moment, I can assure you. Please keep those cheeks wide open now as I have noticed that the insides are untouched and therefore quite good fertile ground for a further spot of admonishment. Yes, we will test out my little device now and try for some downward horizontal strokes with a small lash I think."

Sara began weeping loudly again.

"Now listen to me, young lady. If you keep this persistent and childish blubbering up, I will be tempted to set the lash to fall on your anus and lower lips. At the moment I am doing you a favour and setting my toy here to give you a central band that will not be in the target area. Would you like to waive that? I can certainly do so if you continue to be such a cry baby. I doubt that your anus will thank me but it is your choice, my dear."

"Oh my, no, please don't sir, I am so sorry, sir, please do not let it whip me there, sir. I will be good, sir, I will try my hardest to behave, sir."

"Hmmm. If I were you, Sara, I would stay very still over the next few minutes." With that, he stood away from the machine, which now had a small thin lash attached ready to strike down at the bright red bottom in front of it.

There was the same whirring noise as the machine began to vibrate and then the lash whipped down fast, striping a fierce red strip from the top of her left cheek to the bottom. The shrieks started from Sara immediately and this time Stones had set the delay to five seconds with the aim moving fractionally from left to right as the blows sliced through the air and whipped into her bottom. He had set it to deliver five sets of 12. They watched transfixed as the lash drew back, paused, then flew through the air. All three leaned in as the lash sped through the sir and then hit two further perfect stripes evenly spaced inside the left cheek, the lighter coloured, untanned skin soon displaying bright red marks. Within the next 20 seconds, three further bright red stripes appeared on the formerly almost white skin. Sara's scream was continuous, just changing pitch levels as the after-sting of each stroke worked through to her consciousness. With a slight jerk, the machine readjusted as Stones had dictated and the next stripe appeared on the very inside of her right inner cheeks, very close to her arsehole, causing Sara's head to jerk up.

"Keep still, or you may move your anus right into the target area," Stones snapped a warning that Sara, even in her almost out of control distress, managed to take heed of as the next stroke landed almost on top of the last. The speedier strokes may have caused Sara more intense distress but, to Stones at least, the 60 strokes were over in no time at all and as the last stroke fell, he put his huge hands on the beleaguered cheeks and spread them wide to show the others the end result. The inside of Sara's bottom cleft was a mass of bright red, with much darker red spots everywhere as though she had a rash, with her central crack left as a thin white strip with the darkness of her arsehole starkly standing out, her dark pink coloured inner ring exposed by his manipulations. Her pussy was completely untouched and the rainbow of shades of red and pink provided compelling viewing for the most engaged audience.

"Well, that is an excellent job, if I say so myself. A beautiful aesthetic result that only a machine could produce and the suffering of our malefactor, I believe, is of the level that she deserves and which does the machine credit, don't you think, ladies?"

Stones was well aware that both of his companions were not of weak stomachs or challenged emotionally by the thrashing and humiliation of a miscreant. Much as Sara was someone they both, Celia in particular, admired and respected, they had no qualms that her punishment was warranted and totally justified due to her behaviour and breach of regulations. Stones could see from Celia's eyes and flushed cheeks that she was sexually aroused and plainly excited by what she had witnessed, while Dorothy looked on more dispassionately but totally captivated by the state of Sara's flaming buttocks. She turned to him saying,

"Dean, you have excelled yourself. I do not think I have ever seen such a well-thrashed, blistered and throbbing backside in all of my time here, and, trust me, I have watched a lot of them!"

The agreement between her and Stones to ensure that he had some form of insurance concerning his activity with the young college females that caused his ire was that Stones kept a live link open through his CCTV system that Dorothy alone had access to. This meant that she could view, in her own rooms and in her own time, any live or recorded coverage of his study and his garden, wherein all punishments were delivered. Stones had the power to turn this access off when he was entertaining guests for non-punishment or personal sessions, including his time spent with Celia privately, but Dorothy was well aware of these exclusions as his relationships over the years were always discussed with her, and she trusted him implicitly.

"Yes, I am inclined to leave it there for the time being. I have no wish to do permanent damage and I do believe that Sara is feeling a mite repentant and has received the message loud and clear. The remaining 240 strokes can, of course, be brought into play at any time and for any reason at a later time, Sara."

"Oh yes sir, thank you, sir. Thank you. Thank you. Thank you."

Stones felt that he could probably ask her to agree to anything in the moment and, reluctant as he normally was to cut a decreed punishment short, he was aware that the consistency of the strikes from the machine took some bearing. He stroked her ravaged cheeks affectionately and deliberately. The psychological impact of his intimate and rather nonchalant touching, prodding and stroking being to emphasise to his victims that he had a rite of ownership to their bodies. Over the years the acquiescence he had teased out of his miscreants meant that he was attuned to the vagaries of human nature and rarely surprised or blind-sided by any reaction.

"I think the bidet of ice for you, my dear. Celia, please take her to the bathroom and get her settled."

Much merriment was caused when they were treated to a final full volume scream from Sara as Celia forced her down into the iced water. Dorothy and Stones then talked through the options for completing Sara's punishment and although Dorothy had some reservations about his idea for some extra curriculum off-site specialist disciplinary activity, she bowed to his finer judgment and Sara's fate was sealed. Stones intended to instigate a meeting and double punishment with both Sara and her accuser and partner in her sexual exploits, Jenny Goldman, but then unveiled his plan for a further punishment session that would incorporate the external activity he and Jamie were involved with at their fetish society. Dorothy, he was confident, would now have no further reservations, but, from the expression on the on-looking Celia's face, as she returned to the room, Stones could well see that she did not approve of his plans. However, Stones knew that this was petulance rather than any regulatory disapproval, because it would exclude her involvement. He filed away her display of sulkiness for later; their relationship was such that they both understood that he brooked no argument or disrespect from her and that there would be repercussions if she displayed her disapproval in this manner. He had once offered her the opportunity to join him for a weekend away with his society members and her nerve had failed her. Stones had made it clear that it was a lifestyle choice and her reluctance was of no consequence to him but he knew that Celia had been very disappointed in herself that she had failed to attend. He had told her then that the offer would be available one more time in the future but that for now she was to accept that maybe it was not for her. He strongly suspected that her issue was her reluctance to share him as much as her fear of the unknown in a true fetish club environment, and that was a battle he left her to fight for herself. He loved her truly but was adamant that he had desires and needs that she could not possibly meet and while the BDMS lifestyle was available to him, he could not forego its attractions.

He stared her down until she dropped her eyes and he could see her make the effort to allow her anger to dissipate. He threw her a small sweetener he knew would change her mood.

"Celia, time to get Sara's bottom out of its icy bath. I think once you have dried her off she could do with some of my lovely cream being gently massaged into those poor, sore cheeks. Would you be so kind, please?"

Celia was quick to assent. She would know that she had been unwise to allow her thoughts to have been so transparent in front of the college mistress and there was relief as well as pleasure in her expression as she moved to prepare one of Stones' chaise longues ready for her task.

Dorothy left them to their own devices for the final act and Stones returned to his desk to start planning the next stage of Sara's full absolution. It would be nearly an hour later before the three became one. Sara, a lot happier now, having clearly enjoyed her appointment with Stones' luxurious body creams being massaged into her red buttocks as much as Celia had in applying it. Sara was then to spend a few minutes composing another document acknowledging her guilt and confirming her approval and thanks for the punishment received so far. She did not take any urging to scribe her permission for the disciplinary action to continue in any way, and for any length of time, that the college authorities saw fit, much to Stones' satisfaction. Her gait as she was escorted by Celia from the room suggested that her bottom would be causing her some discomfort for some time yet!

CHAPTER 10

JENNY REALISES THAT MAYBE SHE

HAS NOT PLAYED IT WELL!

Stones could hand-on-heart say that he witnessed the very moment that Jenny realised that her act of treachery, in exposing Sara to the wrath of the college, might not have been her brightest strategy. The second meeting with Jenny proceeded rather differently to the rather abrupt and hasty first. Stones had done his homework and was fully prepared. He was not best pleased with either Jenny or Sara, as he had needed to beg a few favours, but the old girl network had worked particularly well. He had put a resolution in place much quicker than expected and had contacted Jenny to return to discuss things further within days.

"So, Jenny, many thanks for coming in at short notice. I am delighted to say that I have been investigating solutions to our specific problems and think I have come up with a plan that will put an end to this little issue once and for all."

"Yes, well we will see about that. I have told you quite clearly what I expect. I want that woman on her knees begging for an apology from me before she is strapped down and given 500 strokes of your best cane by her new fucking boyfriend. I want her beaten until she fucking bleeds, I want her begging for forgiveness and mercy in front of me. Then I want you to fire her. Job done. Easy peasy."

Stones put his fingers together and smiled at the angry young former student sitting before him and making her demands so forcefully. His reply was very calmly delivered but perhaps not the response she was waiting for!

"Well, my dear, as I see it, you have attempted to blackmail the college into taking action against your former lover, Sara, on the threat of exposing the college's practices concerning its attitude and favour to the use of corporal punishment as a means of disciplining its members. Now, irrelevant to your wishes I have begun my own internal process to deal with Sara and she has in fact already undergone the first stage of most severe chastisement for her offences. You need to understand that I am in control and not you, young lady. I am the one who call the shots, you are the one that takes them. My question to you is, just how powerful do you actually feel you are in this scenario?"

Jenny pushed her chin out towards Professor Stones, her confidence perhaps not as it was when they talked on the telephone or over emails.

"Ah, you don't answer. Well, here's a thing, perfect and on time," said Stones as his laptop bleeped, signifying an incoming email. "Perhaps we could check our emails together?" A suggestion that perplexed Jenny but she went for her mobile automatically as Stones looked down to read his incoming mail.

Stones smiled and waited. Jenny looked at her emails, her face looked inquisitive, then froze in incomprehension, then looked aghast. There was a telling silence in the room before Jenny found her voice explosively.

"What! What! What the fucking hell! No! No! What the fuck is this? I've been fucking suspended from my job! Is this fucking you?

Oh you fucking cunt, you malicious old bastard, you've fucking well stitched me up, haven't you?"

Jenny worked for an investment bank in the city, as a trainee algorithm analyst researching development of programmes to remove elements of risk, personal emotions and bias from financial decision making. Her incoming email claimed that the bank had unearthed an error written into an algorithm she had approved that would have led to the bank losing millions if it had been integrated into their systems undiscovered. There were also rumours of an affair with a married senior female executive, but that was still unsubstantiated, although his contacts were still prying.

"Christine isn't a St. James' graduate! How did you do this? You can't, you can't, I am going to sort this out, you bloody well will not get away with this." Jenny's despair was not assisting her thought processes and Stones was happy to let her dig her hole deeper and deeper while she stood in the bottom of it.

"Your Christine is a junior manager, Jenny. I think you will find that her manager, Patricia Thornton, and her superior, Chantelle Braybrook-Turner, are both college-connected in one way or another, as are several of the female executives at your workplace. The world is sometimes a small place, young Jenny, small but very loyal, and that's where you have really let yourself down. Very disappointing to see a St James' girl disgrace herself in this way. The college has values, my lassie, and you have clearly failed to embrace them and have brought problems and disquiet to my door. You have also been most offensive and rude, but the price you will pay is a harsh one. You crossed me my girl, and that was a no-win scenario for you. You have tried to ruin Sara's career in a jealous fit of pique and she will pay the price in the college's traditional way, but she will only lose her pride and her dignity, not her job. So, how well has this gone for you then, Jenny?"

The young woman was openly sobbing now as she envisaged her future disintegrating. The reach of the college was legendary and only now could Stones see someone who was looking beyond today and not seeing a very hopeful tomorrow.

"As I suspect you can imagine, I have the power to make some of these work issues dissipate if I so desire. I suggest that you take your clothes off, and go and stand in the corner of the room, hands on your head. You know the drill. You have one minute exactly to come to your senses. You do not have time for questions. Accept the inevitable. You have been idiotic, malicious and disloyal. I am going to damn well thrash you, Jenny Goldman, hard and true. Undress now!"

Jenny jolted at his words, her face colouring up, her top lip trembling, eyes wild in her head looking ready to unleash another steam of invective words. Then, as Stones hoped it would, came the moment of enlightenment, the realisation of what was happening, the recognition of her own vulnerability and powerlessness. She nodded, muttered a profanity, then rose and unbuttoned her top. Within seconds she was naked and facing the wall as directed.

"All you now have to do now is to consider what you have done and whether through contrition, acceptance of your guilt, the search for improvement and withdrawal of your demands and claims can lead you down a path towards redemption. You may want to think about what you will write when I allow you the opportunity."

Jenny's response was immediate and definite.

"Of course, sir. Yes sir. Anything you say, sir." There was clear belligerence in her response and Stones replied swiftly.

"Oh Jenny, please don't start scheming any further. Understand this. I have no wish to ruin your career at Johnson-Redgrave but I will have no hesitation in doing so unless you fully comply with the process I will put in place to resolve our issue. I am fully intending to give Sara her just desserts and I think we should be looking at treating the two of you the same. Granted she is the older, more mature woman, a member of staff who has acted totally unethically and her relationship with a young student is intolerable, and I am thankful that you have brought it to my attention. However, the vindictiveness and spite in your appalling attempt to threaten and blackmail Sara, myself and this college, has left you requiring the highest level of chastisement to teach you right from wrong. I think that in the circumstances you do both owe each other an apology, so I hope that I can create the circumstances to allow you both the opportunity to make good the problems between you. I will be very much expecting that the two of you will be in a position to resume a tolerable, if not a platonic, friendship of sorts after we all work together on this. You now have the opportunity to attempt to make amends by volunteering a suitable punishment, so think on. One more word of warning: if you continue to use foul and abusive language in these rooms, particularly if directed at myself, then I will have no other choice than to consider further action that will be even more severe, and I promise you, effective. I am obviously considering giving you a short thrashing now to remind you of the way to behave in my office. I would advise you to not make things worse. On the plus side, it is most delightful to see your perky little breasts and bottom again, especially those gorgeous dark nipples, a real treat, thank you, Jenny. Now I will check if you are clean enough to be seen to now."

Jenny stiffened but held her tongue, finally seeming to remember the games the Professor liked to play to tease and provoke his victims with,

"I showered before I left this morning, sir, but I have been on a train for an hour so may be a mite sweaty." Jenny's shaky voice belied her attempt at calmness and assurance. Stones knew she was in turmoil and was determined to keep knocking the tottering confidence and fake cockiness out of her.

With one mighty hand sweeping under her stomach, Stones pulled her away from the wall and bent her over with his other arm. He manoeuvred her legs apart and used the fingers of one hand to spread her legs. He took a deep long sniff in between her cheeks, sighing with pleasure.

"Yes, you are correct, I can smell your sweet scent of sweat, mixed very sexily with the lemony scent of your shower gel, I assume. Yes, indeed, very attractive anal scent and a rather lovely aroma all round. I do remember that yours was a damn fine bottom to beat, these firm but quite fleshy cheeks being a pleasure to spank if memory serves me well, but of course the stars of the show were your little crinkle and little winnie, if I remember correctly."

With this, Stones burst out laughing, having recalled the stricken young girl and her reluctance for him to see her anus and vagina, and her outburst using her family names for the intimate parts. Jenny blushed at the memory, the less than confident, shy young student resurfacing now under Stones' tutelage and manipulative words.

"Apparently you soon lost that original shyness and innocence. Please don't blather on about Sara having used and abused you. I have it on pretty good authority that you are a bit of a player when it comes to the art of seduction with the ladies."

Alluding to that card now was taking a chance that he was exposing his hand too early but Jenny's jolt was enough to confirm that those rumours were most likely true. He could see her fighting with the conflict in her mind and reluctance to say anything in her own defence that might expose her more.

She wisely chose to remain silent.

"Good girl, I can see things are coming back to you. You see, you have missed us and let your standards slip. Here is something worthwhile you remembering young lady, for future reference. Cast your mind back to when you were last in this room, shall we? I recall that despite warnings you could not be trusted to treat electrical equipment with anything close to respect, let alone an esteemed colleague's papers that you had borrowed. So we had a fire brigade incident and a very upset fellow of this college, who, to be blunt, young lady, would have had you thrown out on your ear if he had been able to have his own way. You arrived late at my office, a very dangerous act when due for physical chastisement. Thankfully and quite luckily for you, our mutual friend Sara came to the rescue. Not only calming you down and escorting you to my rooms, but staying with you and helping to guide you through your flogging. A move that, to be fair, elevated Sara in my eyes and opened up a path for her to become more involved in the corporal punishment aspect of the college. This incident having come to light has made me realise that that might not have been the soundest judgment on my part as she clearly did take some advantage. That is for another day, and not really your concern. However, I will remind you that she did you a massive favour on that day in getting you to these rooms and helping you to take your rather just punishment. Am I correct?"

Jenny gulped and her self-assurance had left her completely as she answered:

"Well yes, I suppose so. She was lovely that day."

Stones fixed her with a steely gaze.

"You still want her career here to end in dishonour and disgrace then, do you?"

Jenny's jaw jutted out. Stones could see her stubbornness and

thirst for revenge fighting with her feelings for Sara.

"Ok. Maybe not have her sacked but I still want her thoroughly thrashed, Professor. She deserves that, doesn't she?"

"Oh indeed she does, Jenny, and indeed she will be, but how dare you presume to tell me how I should discipline members of this college! Do you really not understand how much trouble you have caused and how much trouble you are now in? You silly, silly woman. Have you any idea just how much I want to blister your backside until you understand exactly how bloody stupid you have been?"

Jenny blanched, now totally on the back foot and now fully appreciating the reach that the Dean and the college had.

"Oh shit! I've well and truly fucked up, haven't I?" The naked woman stood before Stones and as their eyes met, he saw the mixture of defeat and regret as her gaze faltered and he knew now was the time to push home his advantage.

"Go and sit your cute little bottom down over there, my dear, and write me a short note explaining how you followed an incorrect thought process in daring to try and blackmail this college. You can explain how you regret that you tried to undermine my authority, how you are very repentant and how you would appreciate being soundly thrashed to help you improve and correct your poor performance. You may request part of your punishment to be carried out now and the remainder to be inflicted when you return to view part of Sara's chastisement. Before you venture to speak, please realise that you do not have any power, that I can destroy your planned future with a click of my fingers and that I am very, very angry with you. You have disappointed me greatly and you have been a very naughty girl. Now, sit down and write."

Ten minutes later Jenny was draped over the Professor's knees as he delivered 200 hard smacks to her bouncing bottom and kicking legs. Stones was enjoying this. Jenny had a beautiful bottom and her open cheeks and flailing legs gave a most acceptable view of her pretty pussy and neat little arsehole. He pummelled her hard and fast, his hand slapping up and down, her cheeks flattening and springing back as they turned redder and redder. He could not help but be impressed by her resolve, as barely a yelp of pain or distress came from her lips. He pushed her from his lap.

"Fetch me a suitable paddle from my cabinet, come on, quickly,"

Jenny sprang up, and with her face wet with the tears streaming down, walked in some discomfort across to his display of punishment implements. With no hesitation whatsoever, she selected a thick wooden paddle and handed it to Stones.

"This should really sting, sir. Please give me your very best sir, you know I deserve it, beat me and make me a better person, please sir."

Professor Stones felt that he would never reach the point whereby one of his miscreants could not fail to surprise him with their supplication and acceptance of corporal punishment. Her eyes glistened and Stones could read the desire and pleasure of a true masochist in her demeanour.

"Would you like me over your knees again for the paddle, sir?"

Stones looked at the pretty naked woman before him, full breasts standing proud with pointy nipples, a full bush of pubic hair with her rather neat slit showing through, a flat stomach and a pretty face.

"It's not for my miscreants to determine their position for receiving improvement, young lady. I will very much decide the best and most painful way for you to take chastisement. Turn around and present your buttocks, first six on full fleshy cheeks, you can bend over for the second six. That'll be a good contrast, a slapping stinging followed by a bruising battering. Excellent, hands on head, hold tight and try and stand still, please."

Still seated, Stones was able to swing his arm back and bring it forward with great speed. The resounding smack caused Jenny to stumble forward two steps and she hollered and tears began to flow once more. She quickly moved back into position, highlighting her lack of discipline in stepping forward.

"Sir, I am so sorry that I failed to stay still, please reapply the stroke sir so that I can show you that I wish to take my punishment properly and without complaint." Her voice faltered but was clear and strong.

This certainly impressed the Professor, unused to such fortitude and compliance, and he did wonder what sort of complex sex life Jenny and Sara may have enjoyed. He decided to take advantage,

"Between strokes, young lady, you can fill me in with details of your sexual liaisons with my Chief Academic Administrator."

Stones ended up taking his time with this paddling as he discovered that Jenny very much did want to tell Stones all about her sexual adventures with Sara Morgan! They both had developed quite a penchant for the use of sex toys during their trysts, according to Jenny, and seemed to be in competition as to who could suggest the most outrageous devices to use and how. Stones was pleased to hear that their meetings had mainly been after Jenny had graduated and she did admit that she often failed to entice Sara into intimate episodes due to Sara's concern for her job and the rules of the college. Although from Jenny's perspective, this was apparently more about the fear of being found out that any ethical or moral code operating. Jenny told Stones that she had chosen the wooden paddle for her punishment implement today because Sara had bought her one very similar and that it was her favourite item to have her bottom slapped with. Jenny did ruefully admit that Sara's arm was not as powerful, or as full of intent, to be able to make the impact that the

Professor had and that she would have preferred to be lying face down on a comfortable bed to receive her strokes. However, as Stones informed her, one was a sexual act whilst the other was a punishment and therefore designed to sting and cause as much discomfort as possible! Jenny struggled to keep talking once bent over, though by then Stones had got to his feet and the paddle was hitting taut, already sore, buttocks. He paused with three strikes to go to allow her to take a breather and rub herself before continuing her discourse. Keeping her bent over, Stones took great pleasure from watching Jenny, with supposedly no self-awareness whatsoever, pull her bottom cheeks wide apart inches from his eyes, as she tried to squeeze and rub the ferocious stinging pain away. He watched, far too lustily he acknowledged, as she kept opening her perfect little crinkled anal slit and exposing her full labia in front of him and very much suspected that this was going on far too long for Jenny not to be conscious of the display she was giving. He was captivated but the moment he found himself fantasising about licking his tongue down both of her slits he managed to snap himself out of his reverie.

"Lovely though your anus and vagina are, my dear, and your mosaic of tiny wrinkles and crinkles are really pleasing to view, I think that you may be turning this little break into an opportunity to give yourself a bit of a thrill. If you could just return your hands to your ankles and off your bottom, we will continue the beating. You may finish your story about the strap-ons and this 'pegging' you were mentioning as I did find that of interest."

Jenny sighed, clearly disappointed that her tactics had been noted, but she was happy to continue her less than diplomatic retelling of her bedroom antics with Sara. Stones, of course, knew exactly what pegging involved but could see that his pretence at naivety was spurring Jenny on and very much enjoyed her regaling of the two women's sex lives. As Jenny took a breath to continue, Stones slammed the paddle down against the least fleshy part of the bent-over buttocks before him. In truth, he was not such a fan of the smaller, pert bottom, however sexy they were and however much they best accentuated and gave access to the view of a woman's twin cracks. He much preferred a fleshy bottom to a bonier one, both from a sexual intercourse viewpoint and from the flogging aspect. Stones recognised that his obsession with bottoms was beyond the norm, but felt that as long as he stuck to certain behavioural standards and didn't abuse his position overly, then he was just about on the right side of the line before any mention of perverted behaviour was voiced. One of the reasons that the college mistress had live access to his CCTV feeds whenever a student was in the room was to safeguard him and also to ensure that he didn't succumb to temptation.

He slammed the paddle against the centre of her red buttocks again, flattening them completely for an instance. She gave a small cry but retained her position.

"Carry on," instructed Stones.

Jenny continued with her rather treacherous retelling of the foibles of Sara's and her sexual peccadillos. "Oh sir, she is definitely a submissive, sir, however much she tried to fake being a dom. She loves to be fucked and dominated in bed and really likes taking a dildo, a double-headed vibrator or a butt plug. I would be the one with the strap-on. She is so much a receiver rather than a giver. She loves cunnilingus and gives really good head, sir. To be honest, she is fucking wonderful in bed and I am really sad that she ditched me unceremoniously for a bloody man, begging your pardon, sir."

Stones was far too wise and experienced in the ways and wiles of his students not to know when they thought they were being just a tad clever in taking opportunities to score points, settle old scores and add a bit of flowery fantasy to their stories when in vulnerable positions. He decided to help Jenny regain her focus and keep things honest and slammed the paddle down again, catching the still bent over student by surprise. Her buttocks fully relaxed and benefitted, in Stones' eyes anyway, from the full slapping impact effect. Jenny yelped as her cheeks again flattened and then sprang back into shape; even with a small bottom such as Jenny's it was a sight that however many times he saw it, he never tired of watching.

"Don't drift into storytelling please, young lady. Remember that there will be a fair chance that if you drift into fiction it will be exposed. I do not intend to take everything you say as fact but if you are found to have deliberately misled me then I will have you back here on a separate set of charges. My contacts at your employer will be perfectly happy to send you back to me for further correction of your wilful ways. In fact, I do believe that your colleagues, Chantelle and Patricia, did hint that they might quite like to come back and watch you perform for me. I have said no, as your punishment is not for entertainment purposes, however there are always elements that could be added for shaming purposes if I feel a recipient of my improvement technique is not getting the full benefit. It's amazing what the addition of a selective audience can lend to proceedings, young lady, particularly in raising the humiliation levels."

Jenny was twisting round, fighting to maintain her supplicant position, her face aghast, her total horror so plain to see as Stones once more floored another student with his cutting words.

"Oh no, sir. Please don't, sir. Sorry, sir. I was not lying, sir. Oh God. You wouldn't really do that, sir? Oh shit, they bloody know what's happening to me, don't they? Oh my God! Oh, please, sir. I am so sorry, please forgive me."

"Get back into position. How dare you." As she quickly adopted the pose, Stones unleashed a volley of blows with the paddle. "You have truly earned these, you scoundrel. A dozen extra will remind you for now and will give you fair warning of what else is heading your way when I get you and that wretch Sara in here together shortly." He was surprised at her resilience as she managed to hold the dominated pose until he landed a final huge stroke, which caused her to stumble forward. She dropped to her knees, finally breaking down and wailing hysterically from the sensation of the wooden paddle hitting the same spot over and over in quick succession. Stones allowed her to rub frantically at the bright red patch of her bottom before ordering her back to her feet to face him.

"Now, young lady, that wasn't such a good idea, was it? No more outbursts like that unless you want me to start making some calls to our mutual acquaintances at Johnson-Redgrave. You chose to play with fire, my girl, so you should not be surprised that you have got badly burned. Now you may continue to impart factual information about your unwise sexual shenanigans with our chief academic administrator and I may forgive you your little spat. However, let's have you over my knees again with the paddle to hand if you veer off the path that you should be following."

"Yes sir, indeed sir, sorry sir. Ow! Ow, ow, ow! Sorry again, sir, it really bloody stings, whoops sorry. Well, she really likes to be treated quite badly, sir, she pretends that she doesn't, sir, but I have tied her up lots of times, sir, and she is so meek and submissive, sir. But she also liked tying me up and I guess that she likes it when her partner is helpless and cannot fight back. The harshest beatings she gave me were when I was unable to move or resist, and that would be when she showed little mercy. I think she has some conflict over what she likes doing to others as, to be honest, I felt that she had a bit of a sadistic side wanting to come out more but she would fight giving in to it. She also seemed scared and apprehensive about any repercussions, which was odd given how much of a submissive she was. I am surprised that I have lost her to a man, sir, as she was such a good lover and really knew what a girl wanted!"

Stones raised his eyebrows and tapped the girl's cheeks.

"Expand."

Jenny was not fazed though.

"Oh my God, sir. She is soooooo good with her tongue and lips, sir. Just so gentle when you need gentle, and rough when that moment comes, and she instinctively knew when that moment arrived, sir. She just had a perfect sense of when to change momentum and pace when making love, so attentive and so loving. God, sorry sir, I really miss her. She was an exquisite lover, we had so much sex, sir, she really loved to be pampered and adored being suppliant. Sara gave me the greatest orgasms, sir, she made me come and come. Is this too crude and sluttish, sir?"

Stones was not going to tell her that she was quite an arousing speaker but just nodded at her to continue her sexual, and sexy, rhetoric.

"Sara loved sex toys, sir, she was always buying things for us to try out. The amount of dildos and vibrators I have had in my winnie and crinkle, sir. Oops, I need to start saying fanny and arse, really. It is hard to get out the habit and Sara used to love me calling them that."

Stones interrupted.

"Jenny, I am perfectly happy for you to use your own childish, but sweet, names for your vagina and anus. I infinitely prefer their use to the alternative crudities you suggest. Continue."

"She liked being pegged sir, especially a double header, you know, crinkle and winkle at the same time, sir. When she was at her most submissive, she would do the crudest things on command. I used to try to come up with more and more disgusting acts to make her carry out, sir. It turned me on to have a woman that much older than me, sir, grovelling to obey my commands and totally obedient and accepting of anything I asked her to do. You want me to be specific, sir, I can see. You are going to use what I tell you to really grind her into the dirt, aren't you sir?"

Jenny's head was turning up to look at him, her eyes were sparkling bright now, and Stones could see what a true sadistic side this young woman had to her. Her tongue darted in and out as she spoke and her gleaming eyes and blushing cheeks made her arousal plain to see. He decided to see how far she would go.

"No questions, Jenny. For me to know. Continue, please."

"Yes sir, of course, sir. Well what I used to do is shag her senseless with the double heads and when she had come, I would make her suck and lick the strap-on heads clean. Then I would sit on her face, sir, she'd often been tied down so wasn't much use for giving me any pleasure back so I'd just use what I could. I would sit on her face and push down really hard so she could hardly breathe, then I would make her stick her tongue up either my crinkle or winnie, sir, and I would tell her I'd only get off if she got her tongue in far enough. I nearly suffocated her once, sir! But she would never complain. I would sometimes tie the strap-on to her, sir, and ride her cowgirl style sir, that means me facing her, sir, sometimes with the double-double headed one, sir. That has two heads either way, sir, so all four holes filled but it takes some doing as the giver, sir, to keep them in your own holes. So, I would more often use one that just had one head for the giver, sir, and that one I would use in my winnie. It is easier to tighten up your vagina muscles to hold just one cock stem in, sir. It takes some practice to be able to hold one up the bum as well, sir, sorry, sir. I beat her a lot, sir. I tied her face down, beat her hard, then fucked her up either or both holes, sir. Sometimes I would work two different vibrators or dildos up her, sir, she always had to lick them clean afterwards, she'd never say no. She let me pee over her in the bath once, she didn't like it but she didn't stop me. She just gets off by being dominated and abused, she loves the degradation and humiliation. I think she'd be happy being a sex slave, sir."

Stones could see how excited Jenny was in her retelling: traces of wetness on the lower vaginal lips were visible and although he suspected that she might be starting to play to her audience a bit, he felt there was more to come.

He caught her unprepared by bringing the paddle down quickly to slam into her very relaxed cheeks. The scream was rewarding, although Stones appreciated the element of surprise was as key as the pain of the stroke.

"Thought you might be getting a bit too comfortable for a moment there, Jenny. Let's not forget that you are here to be punished, however entertaining your storytelling is. Do continue Jenny, this is all rather interesting and does add some context to this otherwise sordid relationship the two of you were having. Spill the beans, girl. There weren't any beans involved, I take it?" Stones was aware that he was probably only amusing himself, but he had inadvertently hit home and Jenny went right on to prove it!

"No, no beans sir, but there were a few vegetables, I can tell you!" Twisting to face him again, her face flushed as she realised that she was perhaps letting on as much about herself as she was Sara. The hesitation was far too little prudence, far too late. However, there was no way Stones was going to let her stop there.

"Right, up you get and stand beside me, my dear. I am still in mind of the words you directed at me earlier. I am a 'fucking cunt' and a 'malicious old bastard' if I remember correctly. That was it, wasn't it?"

Jenny gulped. Genuine fear flashed across her face.

"Oh shit! Oh sorry, I mean, er, er. Oh, Professor Stones, I am so sorry. That was dreadful. I am sorry, sir. I do really respect you, sir. That was appalling. Oh God, I had forgotten I had said that. I am so sorry. Should I fetch a cane for you, sir?"

"I do not normally cane without allowing my reprobates time to think about what is coming. I do think it adds to the sting of the cane when you naughty girls have a few days to sweat on the prospect of its cutting, savage sting. To be honest Jenny, much as I enjoy your company and find you at times quite a charming young lady, I do admire a bit of spunk."

Jenny's snigger interrupted his flow.

Stones let out a long slow breath, the pause just long enough for Jenny to reconsider her wisdom in allowing herself to see the humour in his remark.

"Oh, I see the use of the word 'spunk' amuses you. That is a perfect example of what I intended to say. You do actually let yourself down with your snidey little remarks, rather spiteful temper and clearly a toilet-based humour level. Further to your punishment today and the more severe beating to follow in a couple of days when you attend a further disciplinary meeting with your nemesis and former lover Sara, you will write me an essay explaining why you found the word 'spunk' so amusing and how the word should be used in its proper intention. For the time being, you may go back over my knees now, and since the paddle is still at hand, shall we see how many more blows of that you can take? You are a silly little girl but I will correct and improve you, and hopefully, send you back out into the world of work having learnt a few lessons and gained some benefit from my guidance. I will set this lovely little bottom back on fire with a quick-time twenty and then you can continue your food-based monologue on yours and Sara's interesting love life."

The beating was savage. Stones' arm was a whirl as he slammed the bat down hard in the same spot, the prominent arc of her bent-over buttocks turning almost purple by the finish. He balanced the bat on the writhing cheeks, the pressure being enough for her to understand that she was to be still.

"Do not let the paddle fall off your behind or I will reapply that little spell. Take a breath, control your blubbing and start talking. I suspect that by now you have realised exactly how furious I am with this situation you have caused. I could beat and berate you for the rest of the day and it still wouldn't be enough!"

Stones was determined to ensure that she realised that her scheme had created her far more harm than good so that there was little chance of any sort of repetition. It took her a few seconds to recover her composure and her sobbing was far more traumatic than earlier, but she definitely had become a more resilient person than she had been when he had beaten her as a student. Stones very much suspected that this was due to having indulged in disciplinary sexual play on many occasions and that her recovery from fierce beatings was a learned and mastered behaviour.

"Yes, sir, thank you, sir. Can I say again that I am so sorry that I was so rude to you sir. I did not mean it. I was just angry, so thank you for assisting me so that I can indeed improve my lot and my attitude and be a better person in the future, sir. Sara, sir, as I was saying, she was turned on by all sorts, sir. Sometimes I would challenge her to bring me over something to use on her when she visited. Sir, I have put a courgette up her bum, a cucumber in her winnie, whipped cream, yoghurt and cottage cheese smeared all over both holes and her breasts, sir, and this is a bit mucky, sir, but she got really turned on when I smeared wet mud from the garden all over her bottom sir. I made her wash my sheets in the bath, sir, and spanked her bottom with a hairbrush the whole time she was doing it. Sir, I once put a banana in each hole and then peeled them and ate them out of her. I put grapes in her winnie and maltesers up her bottom once, sir, then made her shoot them out and eat them, sir."

Jenny paused and Stones suspected that she was now wondering if she had said too much but in keeping her face inches from the carpet, he couldn't see her expression. It crossed his mind that it might be easier for her to fabricate and lie when she was not facing him but let her continue her tale.

"Time for another round with this lovely paddle," was his only verbal response. He picked up the weapon once more and this time began a slow, methodical beating up her legs to the top of her buttocks and then repeated the order over again. He needed to keep one arm wrapped firmly around her as she screamed, fought and struggled under the brutal assault to her beleaguered bottom and legs. Eighty times his arm raised and fell before he placed the implement once more to rest on top of her blazing red bottom cleft. He began to gently stroke the battered cheeks under the paddle as Jenny sobbed and sobbed in real agony and anguish.

"What do you say, Jenny?"

"Oh Lord, oh my, oh my, sir. Thank you for my beating, sir. Oh lord, it hurts, sir. Ow! Fuck! Ow! Ow! Bloody hell!"

Stones stroked the throbbing cheeks.

"They are certainly hot, young lady, I'll give you that. But do watch your language; any more of that and I may have to beat you really hard. Now, have you any more tales to tell out of class?"

Jenny, still twitching sporadically as the pain from her buttocks kept registering in waves, stuttered out one last thing.

"That was hard, sir! Sir, sir, sir, I have to tell you this one, sir, sir, sir, and this was quite funny really. I once pushed a cucumber all the way up her winnie, um, her vagina sir, and lost hold of the end, sir, and she sort of sucked it all in and I couldn't keep hold of it. It was so funny, sir, because Sara panicked as to how she would get it out and I had to put my fingers in to try and get hold of the end, but it just disintegrated, sir. Oh sir, I really shouldn't tell you this, but in the end I lubricated my hand up to my wrist and God, sir, I managed to get my whole hand in her winnie and pull the mushy crap out bit by bit sir. And sir, the dirty cow, sir, she kept having frigging orgasms while I was doing it. It's called fisting, sir, if you do it when you are, you know, shagging and that, and I loved doing it. I stretched her winnie open so bloody wide, sir, she was gaping open and I could see inside of her. Sir, it was so funny and it took ages to get it all out, my hand was in and out of her hole so many times, covered in gel and mush and all her creamy come, sir. And she kept doing fanny farts sir and shooting gunge out, sir, it was brilliant! Sorry, sir, that was a bit rude, wasn't it?"

Jenny was flushed and exhilarated as she recounted this, back to twisting around to face him in her excitement, and Stones did wonder at her capacity for enjoyment at other people's misfortune. He certainly thought that she was a young woman who deserved what she got, and he would be quite happy to fulfil his obligations as far as that went!

Not being one to judge normally as his hobbies were not what you would term mainstream, he was not particularly bothered by Sara's sexual desires and preferences, but Stones still could not quite see what Jenny thought was in it for her to keep outing Sara's sexual proclivities and almost perverted fantasies. Although, he contemplated, it appeared that these were hardly fantasies as she seemed to have fulfilled them all! However, it was all very interesting and certainly Sara would be devastated if she was to find out to what level Jenny had betrayed her confidence. Clearly Jenny was not a young woman to cross lightly, he thought, as he resolved to ensure that she would leave his company totally under his control. Unfortunately for Jenny, she had excited herself a bit too much with her recounting of his amorous adventures that she forgot about the paddle left precariously balanced on the small of her back and further twisting on his lap caused it to drop to the floor.

"Oh dear," said Stones ominously.

"Oh shit," said Jenny without thinking.

"Pick it up, potty-mouth."

Jenny leaned over to scrabble rather ungainly across his lap, handing the paddle back to him.

"Oh dear, so that will be some more then, won't it sir?"

"Of course," replied the Professor with a smile, his hands roaming over her sore bottom. "Now this fine bottom has not got an unblemished square centimetre left to work on and as you are going to be bruised as much as I feel is appropriate, I think we should find some fertile new soil."

His hands pushed Jenny's legs apart to their limits bringing a full display of her whole pussy into view. He heard Jenny gasp and suspected she was now fearing that her intimate areas were about to be paddled. He allowed her a moment of terror before reassuring her.

"No, you naughty little urchin, I am not going to paddle your vagina. My target area is the inside of your legs. Nice virgin territory and a definite punishment for deviants like yourself as I am very confident that you will not find any sexual solace from these six beauties."

He shoved a giant fist very indelicately underneath her and between the tops of her legs to prevent her from closing, before he slammed the paddle down six times in quick succession. This did the trick as far as Jenny vocalising her distress went, gratifying Stones no end as the banshee howls reverberated around the room.

"Oh my, oh my, oh my. Fuck! Fuck! Fuck!" Jenny screeched and writhed rather spectacularly around on his lap.

"Up you get, hands on head, facing me." Stones' voice sounded bored but internally he was delighted at having reduced this little madam to a bit of a wreck as she struggled into position, her legs buckling at the knees, her hands barely touching her head and her body askew.

"Effective then, Jenny?" Stones queried, raising one eyebrow at this young lady who had reverted back to something like the petrified and stressed student he had spanked for the first time a few years back.

"Aaaaarggghh! Ouch, ouch, ouch. Oh my, Professor. That stings so much, oh my."

"You'd better help yourself to my tissues, young lady, the snot and tears mingling around your mouth and chin is not an attractive sight."

The whimpering gratitude followed by unseemly blowing and sniffing was an unusual confirmation of a job well done, but Stones figured that it was perfectly acceptable in the circumstances.

"You will now stand in the corner, hands on your head, nose touching the wall. You will leave when I decide that you have had long enough to consider why you needed to be beaten so severely today. You are to return here in a few days to join your one-time friend and poorly-chosen lover and you will be beaten again, and this time, Jenny, it will be severe. You will be thrashed and caned as will Sara again. Now think on and please try and stop that pathetic blubbering."

Minutes later the doorbell sounded and Stones could see the tension in Jenny's shoulders, back and buttocks as she strived not to turn around and stiffened in obvious horror at the sight she would be presenting a visitor.

"Ah good, Emily Govan, thank you for coming. Just a little job for you. This is Jenny Goldman, a graduate of this college. As you can see, the reach of the college has extended from beyond these walls to allow me to issue some just chastisement to her lovely bottom and legs. So there is a lesson for you, young lady: you won't necessarily be out of my reach when you leave this institution."

Emily's face was as full of joy as it had ever been as she read between the lines of the Professor's words. He decided to improve her lot further.

"Now my dear, if you could take young Jenny over to the chaise longue there with a pot of my rather sumptuous soothing cream, I think she would appreciate a layer or two on her swollen parts. Jenny, you may turn around. You will answer to Emily as you would to me as far as her authority extends over you. Any nonsense and you will be here a lot longer and we can recommence your lesson. Full compliance, please, so wipe that sulky look off your face or I'll have Emily strapping you down over the caning table instead of caressing your bottom."

Jenny evidently knew better than to follow her first thoughts of rebellion against the young student being allowed to treat her so. It was apparent that she was soon glad she did as Emily, hands on her buttocks and between her legs, nudged against her labia to give a pleasurable distraction from her stinging legs. Stones watched intently as the two women settled into their roles and cast Emily a quick knowing wink to allow her to indulge herself for a few more minutes.

It was hardly unexpected to Stones to hear signs that Jenny was beginning to allow her arousal to grow and that Emily's fingers were working their magic between her legs. He brought the little aside to a halt and made Emily leave separately as he didn't want to give the two of them an opportunity to take things any further. The situation had got quite complicated enough already, he thought!

Jenny, of course, wrote him a perfect letter of contrition, remorse and gratitude, although he was glad to see that she chose to stand and write rather than placing any weight on her beaten cheeks. Once fully dressed, she gave him a charming curtsey as she thanked him for his attention and said that she looked forward to seeing him again soon. Clearly got her mojo back, he decided as she left, albeit he was pleased to note that her walking stance was decidedly askew!

CHAPTER 11

WHEN THE SEVEN SISTERS ARE

DEALT WITH

Professor Stones addressed his visitors and assembled colleagues. "You have all be invited here today because my investigation into the activities of the little bunch of toe-rags called the Seven Sisters, originally the Secret Seven, has been concluded. You are all employees or members of this college that have had some involvement in the activities of this rather tiresome and unruly little tribe. Sadly, their reign lasted a bit longer than I am comfortable with but they did manage to intimidate quite a few people into silence. That silence has been broken and very soon these wretched females will receive evidence of how very much the silence is broken. Five of the gang are in an adjoining room now awaiting the next instalment of the corporal punishment part of their sentence shortly; some of you will actively take part and the remainder will be allowed to witness their discomfort and shame. The sentence imposed is one of the most severe punishments we have ever had to deliver.

This morning Chloe Tang, Zoe Taylor, Charlotte Penfold, Helen Smythe and Saffron Booth, having stayed here overnight, were formally notified of the college council's decision about their punishment. With the agreement of their parents or guardians, they will be allowed to complete their final years remotely, being allowed back to college prior to the start of each term for a single day of supervision and tutorial mentoring on a one-to-one basis. This will be subject to review and allowances may be made for exemplary behaviour and clear evidence of remorse. They will also be allowed to return for their graduation, and all five, with the addition of Miranda Booth, who we will come to shortly, will also appear at Freshers' Week to give talks on the evils of bullying and the support network available for victims. Each of them will therefore be fortunate and privileged enough to leave this institution with their reputation intact and their career path unfettered with their disgrace. To this end, and again I reiterate with the total backing of their parents and guardians as well as at their own request, they have begun the process of full contrition through corporal punishment and verbal readdress. We will shortly sit down to watch a recording of this morning's beatings conducted using a mechanical thrashing machine which delivered 250 strokes of five different canes and paddles, intermixed, timed and distributed to ensure that the greatest area was targeted and the blows spread, to avoid breaking skin whilst applying the severest thrashing. The young ladies are soon to be strapped to moveable table-style platforms in the garden, placed and fastened in position for the next stage of the proceedings. They are unaware of the agenda and have no knowledge that we have planned a particularly apposite punishment that they will almost certainly find an unpleasant and thoroughly humiliating experience.

Their blushes are not to be spared for one instance. This is to be the most belittling and degrading time of their short lives so far. Long may they remember this. The punishment was determined by myself after due consultation with senior colleagues, by my trusted partner Jamie and, most notably, by Emily Govan here, who has suffered more mistreatment from these rapscallions than anyone. Each of the girls will then receive 20 strokes of five specifically differing punishment implements, each brandished by my accomplices in this endeavour. Namely myself, Jamie, my erstwhile assistant, Emily, Professor Martin Flanagan, Senior Fellow, and Ronald Beaumont, Head Porter. Everything will be overseen and monitored by Elizabeth Young, the Head of Health & Welfare and in the attendance of the aforementioned Emily Govan, representing current students, Shirley Barrow, Head of Housekeeping, Lady Annabelle Tyler-Smith, Senior Fellow, Sara Morgan, Chief Academic Administrator and Sonya Coombs, Pastoral Care Tutor. Professor Dorothy Winslow-Bellingham, our Mistress, will join us if she can get away, whilst the Dean of Chapel, Dr Reverend Alex Folsom, has declined to join us."

Stones took a moment to bring down his viewing screen and indicated the chairs for his audience to take.

"So I've had this morning's doings edited to capture the essential processes. For your information, Hilary Brooke-Taylor is suffering from Post-Traumatic Stress Disorder and as such will take an intermission for a year and then will be only considered for a remote final year if she agrees to the punishment determined. Miranda Booth, however has been deemed to have been a reluctant and generally non-active member of this little gaggle and as such will be allowed to return to complete her third year as any normal student. However, and this has been agreed and signed up to, she will be subjected to corporal punishment of a high severity, her crimes being by association and therefore still of major concern, when she returns a few days ahead of the rest of her year in October. But for now, please enjoy the sight of five very naughty naked girls, bottoms up high, legs apart, while my wonderful machine flayed the living daylights out of them!"

The film took the audience through the late morning's events, the five being led in by the Head Porter, the Pastoral Care Tutor and the Senior Tutor. All five had read out their previously approved statements accepting full responsibility for their actions during their time in the college. Each requested the maximum corporal punishment the college was able to give, apologised to a scripted list of the people who had suffered from their behaviour, and thanked the council and the Dean of Discipline in particular for allowing them to complete their degrees and so be able to graduate with a full qualification from St James'. Each stated that, as they had often illustrated a lack of empathy or mercy to the victims of their deeds, then it would only be fair and just for no mercy to be shown to them. They all stated that they wished their punishment to be delivered to their naked bodies as they wished for their shame to be total and complete. Whilst Chloe's face remained impassive and devoid of emotion throughout, the others, including Zoe, who had begun stoically, were sobbing and clearly in terror of what the day held in store for them. At a word from Stones, they had silently and quickly undressed and stood naked before Stones, Emily, Celia, Sara, Nurse Elizabeth and the Head Porter, Ronald.

Each girl had in turn been strapped down on his purpose-designed table, with their bottoms raised, legs spread and their cheeks naturally opened by their pose and the position of the raised mound on the desk edge.

Each girl had been made to wait deliberately by Stones as he positioned them one-by-one for their turn at the mercy of his device. He set the machine to deliver a blow every four seconds, 50 swipes at ten changing positions, and one minute's break between implements. Stones rotated thin canes, slim long leather paddles and wooden paddle bats whilst the college nurse, Elizabeth Young, checked over the lashed cheeks of the scolded reprobates during each break in the thrashing.

The audience watched in almost virtual silence as the screams, entreaties for mercy and desperate apologies were offered. Each girl broke at different stages but none held their silence beyond the first 50 lashes; even the imperturbable and impassive Chloe, whose spirit finally broke as the cane landed on an already bright red raised weal.

Stones watched his guests, an audience with particular and specific affinities with the culprits, some more connected and involved than others. Ronald Beaumont, the Head Porter, was eager and engaged the whole time; granted, these troublesome vixens had manipulated his staff over the last few terms, using feminine wiles to gain favours and a blind eye turned more often than he could feel happy with. Notwithstanding this, the licking of lips and enjoyment of the savage thrashings seemed slightly too enthusiastic in the Professor's eyes. Despite the fact that some of those present were seeing five attractive female students displaying rather a lot of their charms as a novel experience, a dispassionate poker face was the order of the day as far as Stones was concerned. When Ronald had volunteered to be one of the five castigators who would soon be delivering the awaited thrashings, Stones had thought that it would be highly appropriate and most suitable. His obvious and unbridled excitement at watching the recording of the earlier beatings was making Stones wonder. Today was principally about retribution and chastisement to aid improvement and supply justice appropriately. Due to the nature of the acts perpetrated and the punishment very much aimed at befitting the crimes committed, it was understandable that there would be a sexual element to the session for participants and overseers alike; the five were beautiful and naked after all, mused Stones. However, he hoped that the audience didn't view this solely in a voyeuristic or sadistic light, as he had no intention to titillate the gathering. Nevertheless, any added discomfort applied to this guilty five by means of their shame increased by a spot of lecherous behaviour by the watching group was not altogether to be disapproved of in his eyes.

Eventually the recordings came to an end and Stones addressed the group again.

"As you are aware, Celia, Elizabeth, Jamie and Emily are not with us, and I am sure you will have guessed that they are with our reprobates in the garden awaiting the next stage. To save young Emily any embarrassment, I will make you aware that the treatment that will be applied now is in response to the gang putting the poor girl through a similar process. So it is not a random act of sadistic pleasure for no reason, it is entirely justified and totally apt, if not perhaps to everyone's taste." The querulous and intrigued looks amongst the gathering was just reward for Stones' deliberate ambiguity. He did so enjoy a tease!

"Let the final chastisement begin, ladies and gentlemen. Please follow me through to the garden and take your first actual view of the little demons in all their glory. Certainly displaying all their glories anyway!" Stones chuckled as he led Martin, Annabelle, Shirley, Ronald, Sonya and Sara through to the garden at the back of his lavish set. The others, Emily, Elizabeth, Celia and Jamie, were standing chatting in the centre of the lawn but all eyes were immediately drawn to the tableau on the path in front of the plant-filled border at the side of the garden. On a series of wheeled tables with a variety of straps and attachments sprouting on all sides laid the five miscreants. Strapped down on their backs, legs akimbo, pulled back towards their shoulders, and attached to poles rising from the table corners, their buttocks lifted clear of the surface so to present their opened legs and cheeks to full view of their audiences. The students' heads were propped up so that they were looking down their bodies, through their own suspended legs, the crude display of their most private and intimate places as obvious to them as they were to any watchers. Alongside from them was a large container of creamy coloured liquid with various tubes and apparatus feeding off.

"Oh excellent, Edward, we're giving the rascals an enema, are we? Oh first class, Edward, first class!" Professor Martin Flanagan clearly voiced his approval as the understanding of what they were about to witness dawned on the rest of the group.

All five of the strapped down females automatically turned their heads towards the machinery and Stones was delighted to see the fear and apprehension etched on their features.

"Oh yes, my lovelies it's time for your flushing now." He walked along the line of the displayed students, letting his hand run along their buttocks as he did so.

"These malefactors, these villains, this bunch of bullies felt it would be a fun thing to do to young Emily. So today they are going to find out how much fun it is. Two litres of a warmed saline solution will be forcibly introduced into the rectums of these reprobates by insertion of a rubber tube into their anus. Sorry, Charlotte, I'm using you as my model, although I am sure my guests can see where your anus is, since you are presenting it so well."

The sob from Charlotte rewarded Stones perfectly as he deliberately increased the level of humiliation, moving along to push a fingertip into Saffron's anal opening.

"Each of our five will be lubricated with gel. Actually, Emily, would you like to don a pair of Nurse Elizabeth's surgical gloves and give them each a good dollop before we tube them?"

Emily beamed, clearly enjoying the retribution and vengeance being brought to bear against her serial tormentors.

"Oh sir, it would be my absolute pleasure. Are they all a bit tight at the moment, sir?"

Stones had moved along and was running a fingertip around a noisily weeping Helen's anal ring.

"Yes indeed, Emily. Young Helen here is definitely going to need a good portion of gel up her narrow tunnel here – goodness me, it feels like the drawbridge has been dropped! Never mind, I expect the nurse can get a tube up there. Zoe's anus feels quite challenging too. Relax my dear and it will all be do much more bearable." He laughed scornfully at the girls' discomfort at his actions as he scratched a fingernail over Chloe's cheeks before slipping a finger harshly into her anus.

"Oh dear, very dry and you being such a fan of penetration of other peoples' rear holes. But plenty of room up there for a tube and a lot of warm water. Emily, over to you for the preparation and then Isobel can slide in the tubes. It's a simple process, my friends, two litres of our saline solution injected into the colon via the rectum and then our performers will be spun around to face the garden fence and encouraged to unload and relieve themselves into the garden. They are all aware that this would be part of their punishment and advised to take the necessary steps to ensure they do not disgrace themselves any more than they already have done. So no breakfast or lunch for them today although they have been well hydrated so we may see number ones added to the fun!"

All five girls had closed their eyes during his inspection and breaching of their rear holes and each was now displaying rosy red face cheeks to go with their striped and lashed bottom cheeks. Unable to move much more than their heads and shoulders, and shuffle their lower backs, all five looked distraught and frightened witless but resigned to their fates. The time had well passed for any reprieve or curtailment of the decreed chastisement and Stones was pleased that none of the women had seen fit to begin pleading for forgiveness or mercy. In truth, they had all accepted the severity and nature of the sentence, although no word of the planned enema process had been shared in advance, that he had communicated a couple of weeks before but how much that had to do with parental involvement and influence he could only guess at. From the conversations he had participated in with the families of the errant group, there was much relief that they would not be sent down and very little sympathy shown for their little darlings once Stones had documented, or given visual supporting evidence of, the shenanigans the Seven Sisters had got up to. In fact, Stones had needed to make a firm point that as the trouble was caused in-house and the punishment was administered in-house, then the parents and guardians of the seven should resist further recriminations being applied. He strongly made the point that if the college was allowed to act as 'in loco parentis' as was its right under the terms signed up to, then the young ladies' punishment plus its full disclosure to them and other college members was sufficient reprimand. It had helped every single one of the seven that Emily had wanted the punishment to be a mirror of the group's behaviour in college and no outside interference was required. Stones and the college Mistress, Dorothy, had held long heart-to-hearts with Emily to ensure that she was not affected long term by the harrowing treatment she had received and she was absolutely thrilled to be included in the plans and implementation of the punishment to be meted out to the abusers. Stones was not in the least surprised but did have a quiet word in her ear as to toning down her enthusiasm for the chance to be involved in the disciplinary action to be taken. He understood her desire for vengeance very well but felt that the others who were attending the defrocking of the scoundrels might find her eagerness and zeal slightly unbecoming for the seriousness of the occasion. Emily had taken this on board and the young lady now preparing lubricant to smear around and up five spread bottoms looked angelic with her white gloves readily loaded for the first recipient of the enema tubing.

"OK, Emily, you may begin the process please, along the row beginning with Charlotte, then Saffron, then Helen and then Zoe and Chloe, our two alpha females at the end here. Nice and charitable with the lubricant, my dear, grease them tight up their dark tunnels. We have lube aplenty and more than enough water to wash out the bowels of these flighty young shameless floozies! Lube away, Emily, to your heart's content, slide that finger right up young Charlotte, there you go Charlotte, say thank you to Emily, then."

A wriggling sobbing student spluttered out her thanks as Emily moved on to Saffron, and Isobel followed behind with the first of the five tubes to insert. Stones kept his eyes on Emily and was much amused to see the relish and pleasure on his young accomplice's face, as her generously lubricated gloved finger slid up Saffron's back passage. Emily's face was beaming in joy. Stones could hardly criticise or fault her for her desire to exact revenge on the women who had subjected her to a fair amount of fear, pain and abuse, and he couldn't fail to approve of her enthusiastic approach to the proceedings. Whilst Stones thought that a like-for-like punishment was so apt in these particular circumstances, he was always careful to ensure that, to the best of his knowledge at least, any remedial action taken was without maliciousness, spite or intent to cause long-term stress or anxiety. To this end, the college's senior management team, which included Isobel as Head of Health and Welfare, were always kept informed of students due to be punished or having recently been subject to corporal punishment, so that due care and monitoring could be applied fairly discreetly. For all Stones bluff and bluster concerning modern day and first world problems, Mr Politically Correct he most definitely was not, but he was well versed and trained in mental health issues, causes and treatment, Hilary's absence from this day being a case in point. Stones had been quick to acquiesce to her doctor's report and had no problem in the college granting her leeway to put her chastisement on hold to prioritise her well-being with support and commitment that the institution was renowned for. As Stones and Dorothy had agreed, she might be a damn scoundrel but she was their damn scoundrel and as such would be looked after. However, Emily, he granted, had not signed up to the college staff's code of conduct and he was happy to allow her to indulge herself in creating as much discomfort to her pernicious tormentors as she wanted. He had developed faith and trust in this formidable young woman, albeit her impetuous nature and quick-fire temper were always as likely to have her on the end of his ire rather than just an accomplice in dispensing his particular brand of judgement.

The second of the connected tubes was now firmly embedded in Saffron's bottom causing her a fair deal of distress that everyone around was dispassionately noting and ignoring! Emily, meanwhile, was probing Helen's arsehole and from the grin on her face was enjoying teasing the tight entrance by moving a fingertip in and out before she suddenly jerked her arm and the finger went to its limit inside of a squealing recipient. The spluttering of a released air bubble combined with plentiful lube caused much merriment and a smatter of applause from those watching, increasing Helen's discomfort even more. As Elizabeth took over, Emily with a real look of intent showed Zoe her wet thumb and was greeted with a grimace of pain as it slid firmly into her arsehole. Stones was glad to see her give him a quick glance for approval and he nodded, but his raised eyebrows were intended to give her the message that she was not to take liberties. He suspected that her relish levels would increase even more so, as she gave way to Elizabeth and her long tube, and began to reapply more of the lubricant to her hand as she moved between Chloe's outstretched legs and leaned in to grin right into the impressively stoic-looking student's face, before very gently brushing her lips with her own. Chloe's expression barely changed as, with Emily still looking into her eyes, her anus was infiltrated. Stones moved in closer, causing all the others to follow so he could see around Emily's body, which he suspected was being deliberately positioned to shield what her hand was up to. He was tight-lipped as he saw that Emily had pushed four fingers up to her knuckle into Chloe's rather stretched rear entrance but his slight cough was enough to make her withdraw them slowly, though with a certain amount of reluctance, he could tell, allowing the gaping hole to snap shut. Elizabeth took over and her tube slid effortlessly inside Chloe's rectum and completed the tableau of the disgraced girls, hog-tied and prepared with multi-coloured tubes rudely displayed from their arseholes. All five were now bereft in their discomfort, humiliation and shame. Stones was confident that the spectacle presented had caused the ultimate in belittlement.

"Thank you, ladies, nicely done. Now we will just carefully turn each table around on their wheels so that our delightful little anuses are pointing at the garden fence and my shrub border here. Emily, Sara, Celia and I will be joined by Elizabeth at the side of each girl. I will take Chloe, Emily you will be Zoe's assistant, Sara take Helen, Saffron is yours Celia, and Charlotte on the end nearest Isobel who will be controlling flow and input. The rest of you please take a position to suit. some of you may prefer to enjoy watching our victims' faces as they evacuate and some of you may rather focus on the all-action end," Stones chuckled, apparently enjoying the moment to the full.

All eyes turned to Elizabeth as she switched on the elaborate machine, with a quick check for the signal from Stones to continue, and the hum from the machine indicated the pumping mechanism was beginning.

"Easier to cope with if you relax, ladies. People pay good money for this, I'll have you know. We do not, of course, forget or forgive that seven of you were going to force this procedure upon a most reluctant Emily. This then is justice and there is no reason why anyone present should care about your clear unhappiness of what is about to happen to you, thoroughly unpleasant though it is. Anyway, just so you know, we are using normal saline to cause least irritation to your expanding colons and a substance which can be most safely held inside your bodies. We will be leaving you to enjoy the sensation for a good ten minutes or so before we give you the opportunity to release the liquid and cleanse yourselves internally. Think on, ladies, how do you think Emily felt at being used and abused like this? I am delighted that she kicked out and smashed your device. I am afraid that my version is more substantial and you are better restrained so it does not look like there is anything to rescue you."

Stones walked along behind each of the presented bottoms with the tubes protruding and slapped each one hard in turn.

"Let's hear the five of you apologising to Emily before we unleash the torrent inside of your bowels. Come on, speak up. Show us all how remorseful and contrite you are."

All five began to babble at once, heartfelt pleas for mercy mixed with apologies, their distress at their state fully evidenced for all.

At the Professor's signal, all went silent. One by one, he turned the distraught, weeping women back around to face their audience.

"How are doing, Elizabeth, all set and ready to fill the wenches' bottoms up?

As ever, Stones was in his element as he turned the screw on the women's sense of embarrassment and shame, illustrated by all five now having shut their eyes to help endure this new, belittling experience.

"All set to deliver two litres to each of them, sir, as we discussed. It would be safe to increase this amount if we have any resistance to emptying. The more we put in, the more pressure they will be under to relax their bowels and unload," was Elizabeth's cheerful response.

Charlotte, Saffron and Zoe had all opened their eyes as she spoke and the look of sheer mortification on their faces brought pure pleasure to Stones' heart.

At that moment, the Mistress, Dorothy, entered through the rather disguised back entrance to Stones' garden, one of the few who could access his property this way.

"Ah, made it in time for the evacuations I see, excellent timing if I say so myself. Now, you girls, are you all well? Is everything going to your liking? I have read your sincere and heartfelt apologies and was most pleased that you all thought that this day of punishment was one that all of you subscribed to so willingly."

The five now all looking at Dorothy, originally with hope in their eyes, seemed lost for words as they took in the implicit meaning to them. It took them only seconds to realise that no hope, no mercy or any shortening of their disciplining was on offer, and the momentary expectation drained from their faces.

"Welcome indeed, Mistress. What joy that you are here to witness the moment when our little tribe here embarrass themselves totally by emptying their bloated bottoms all over my garden in front of our little gathering. Something we shall always remember, I expect. What do you think, girls?"

Another round of uncontrolled sobbing from all five was the only answer received and Stones decided that he had put the gang through enough.

"Well, ladies, I have news. There is to be no flushing, no enemas, no internal cleansing. I just wanted you all to have a taste of the ordeal that you thought it so entertaining to have planned yourselves. Not such an amusing activity when you are on the wrong end, is it ladies? Take the tubes out please, Elizabeth, and we will content ourselves with washing them down with some freezing water from the hosepipe."

With chuckles all round from the audience, the tubes were plucked out in a rather perfunctorily manner, and there was a fresh round of wailing and sobbing from most of the recalcitrant women. Their relief at being spared the ordeal of an enema tempered with the clear vision that Stones had instilled in them as to what had almost been their fate.

"Now we will have to clean our rascals up," he announced. Picking up a high pressure hose, Stones approached the tables before turning the tap on that released the water in a powerful sprayed deluge that was aimed at their bottoms. The force was substantial and soon all five were crying out, suffering in a new form of distress. Stones paused and, at his signal, Elizabeth and Emily quickly soaked each girls open holes, before once more they found their most intimate areas feeling the force of a high pressure water hose. As Stones finally threw down the hose, both he and Elizabeth donned gloves once more.

"Before we give these thoroughly rotten little schemers their final thrashings, we have a quick little application to make to ensure that they are nice and clean for their next lesson."

The two of them moved to Charlotte and Saffron and wiped an antiseptic liquid liberally on the women's exposed openings, before moving on to Helen and Zoe. Unfortunately for the errant students, the liquid contained a good percentage of alcohol and before they had begun their second application, Charlotte and Saffron had felt its bite, and the screaming and cursing, that was to continue for a few minutes, began. Receiving a handful of lotion from both Stones and Emily, even the phlegmatic Chloe succumbed and was howling in agony from the fearsome stinging. Stones let them suffer for a couple of minutes before instructing them to be wiped down with wet sponges.

"So, all your bits and pieces have been washed down and are scrupulously clean, good, good. It is now time for the main event and we will reposition these wretched girls to present their bottoms for a monumental thrashing."

With little resistance, the five females were removed from the tables before being strapped face down, their bottoms bent over in the classic punishment position with legs apart. Stones had distributed five bamboo canes to Jamie, Ronald, Martin and Emily, with one for himself.

Stones knew that the most resistance would likely come from Chloe and was deliberately rough in his handling of her. He was happy for her to be the last to crack as it would make her the centre of attention when she did and she would gain no benefit at all from her intransigence. He had slightly different plans for her anyway: clearly the ringleader and the brains behind most of the gang's activities, he had already talked through his feelings with her parents and they had instructed him to take whatever action he saw fit.

Daughter of an English graduate of the college, an industry leader, and a Chinese banker from Hong Kong, Chloe had been told in no uncertain terms that they supported whatever it took to ensure that she graduated from St James' and brought no shame to the door of the family. Her mother had never been anything but a model student at college and had wept copiously when Stones had regaled her with tales of her daughter's misdeeds. Chloe had stood beside her as her mother had turned crimson in embarrassment and anger but to her credit at least had agreed to all and any disciplinary action that the college felt inclined to impose. Stones well remembered her mother's parting shot, much to Chloe's chagrin, that whatever the decided punishment was, then the college could feel free to double it with her blessing, as neither her or her husband would have the resolve to punish her themselves.

"Twenty strokes of your finest to each of the reprobates' bottoms, and then move on to the next. On my word, Jamie will thrash Helen, Ronald will begin with Zoe, Martin takes Chloe, Emily has the pleasure of Charlotte, and I will pay homage to the beautiful bottom of Saffron. On my word, my friends. Cane!"

For many minutes the air was full of the sound of swishing canes, impact thwacks and the screaming of vanquished villains. Each moved on and begun their 20 again, with no letting up as each new bottom inspired the hitters to renewed efforts, most notably, thought Stones, when Emily reached Zoe and Chloe; no sign of the weaker sex here then, he reflected.

Elizabeth cast a professional eye over the angry redness of the five thoroughly thrashed bottoms before confirming to Stones that all was fine before he continued with what he had forewarned her of earlier.

"To finish off, I have saved a particularly nasty surprise for you ladies. A very unpleasant experience but one which I believe you deserve, will remember always, but will cause no lasting damage."

As the five tried to twist and turn to see what their tormentor had planned, for a moment at least their sore, stinging backsides forgotten, all that was visible was Stones donning gardening gloves and holding two hessian bags.

"One of my bags contains a plentiful supply of dock leaves. Can anyone guess what the other one contains? Oh, and please feel free to leave now, my friends, as this makes you feel a bit squeamish. But, and this is a big but, as opposed to the delightful array of not so big butts on display, ho ho, we have good reason for proceeding down this road. Our lovely ladies, five here presenting their naked bodies for our entertainment, threatened Emily with a thorny bramble in her vagina and anus. Think on that, my friends. Dominated and totally overwhelmed by their number, Emily was beaten, abused and subjected to rape threats with the added menace of the threat of prickly plants in her most intimate places! So, we have five double cracks and openings here awaiting five fresh and lively stinging nettles to torment and add anguish to their day. I say they deserve it. Emily I see is nodding, Celia too and, of course, Sara agrees."

Stones' barb caused Sara to shrivel visibly and in her discomfort clearly had no will to respond. There was decided disquiet and uneasiness around the use of the simple but effective irritant but Stones' power was all-consuming and not one voice raised an objection. The atmosphere became tense as the five students realised what was planned and began pleading and begging for all they were worth.

"Unless you wish to have these stems pushed inside of you, you will all desist that noise this instance!" Stones' voice boomed out and silence reigned once more.

"Right ladies, listen carefully, your new best friend here, Emily, has the nearest thing to a remedy for nettle sting." He handed a smirking Emily the bag of leaves. "Once I have tickled your fancies, so to speak, Emily will apply the dock leaves to relieve your agony. However, you will have to ask her nicely as there is only one of her and five of you, so her time will be limited. Just to add a fun element, you will be able to select which of your two delectable openings on offer should receive the nettle. To ensure that the nettles are applied to you all in the shortest period of time possible, you need to make this choice now. However, please note that I will take any hesitation as a request for both holes to be given a tickle. It's straightforward: your answer is either anus or vagina, please Professor. So let's start with Charlotte."

"Oh no. Anus, please Professor."

"Thank you, Charlotte. Saffron?"

"Please, no. Anus. On my anus. Anus, please Professor. Oh no. No. Please."

"That's quite enough, Saffron. Helen?"

"Anus, please professor."

"Perfect, thank you, Helen. Zoe?"

"I forbid this. I won't have it. No. No fucking way!"

"Thank you, Zoe, that will be enough of that, thank you. I think we may have all heard you ask for a double-hole dose! What about you, Chloe?"

"Anus please, Professor." Chloe's voice was calm and mellow and Stones could not fail to be impressed by the resilience and stoicism of the group's leader.

"Thank you, Chloe. Well, you all seem very anally obsessed, even young Zoe who has volunteered to receive a double dose. Ready with those leaves, Emily? Right oh, let's get on."

With no hesitation, Stones took the five nettle stems in his gloved hands and wiped one first down Charlotte's anal crack, then moved swiftly to Saffron. He followed with Helen before swishing a new set of leaves up and down Zoe's open legs from the top of her vagina slit to the very top of her anal crack and finished by spinning a nettle all around Chloe's anus before he discarded his crumpled load into a weed bucket. Charlotte's initial solo scream had now been joined by the others as they all howled and wept whilst calling out for Emily to help. Emily had dock leaves in both hands and frantically began rubbing both of Charlotte's and Saffron's stinging arseholes, before responding to the desperate begging of Helen and Chloe. She stretched around the writhing, yelling Zoe to wipe and scrunch the leaves roughly into the open anuses of the two students. Finally, she concentrated on Zoe, working two leaves into her open cracks and eventually the screams and moans receded as the leaves neutralised, to a large degree, the acidic burn of the nettles. At an indication from Stones, Nurse Elizabeth moved in with her own remedy of a baking soda paste, coating each of the red itching irritating areas liberally.

"What a sight. What a sight. OK, a couple of minutes and then we will have another spray down, then we can get these women inside for a final chat."

A couple of minutes later, with the hose back in his hand, the high pressure spray was directed between the five's open legs again. Within seconds, they were all cleaned up and Emily, Celia, Sara and Elizabeth assisted Stones in drying the subdued women before wiping them with mildly antiseptic cloths, once more reducing the five to wails of pain as they were introduced to yet another new stinging sensation. Eventually, as their sobs subsided, they were unfastened and marched, albeit with rather unsteady and wriggling gaits, inside. The audience all took their seats as five very much defeated and broken spirited young women were made to display their beaten buttocks and sore anuses, with Zoe being made to present on her knees on a table, bottom in the air and holding her cheeks apart to display her swollen red vaginal lips and bright red anal opening. Stones invited them all to inspect her intimate areas, then, with a final slap to her abused buttocks, he sent her back to join the others.

Stones addressed them using his most severe tone:

"You young women may stay in the quarters allocated for the next two days, isolated from others, and you will be released to return, shame-faced but hopefully repentant and wiser, to your families after that. As we have previously decided, all things being equal and assuming positive feedback from the tutors who will guide and assist you through your final year, you will be welcomed back to college to take your final examinations and, all being well, graduate at the end of your final year. An exemplary performance will see you given the opportunity to attend the Great May Ball. This will be a token from myself, my colleagues and the college to acknowledge that you have taken on board your punishment, accepted the errors of your ways and shown clear improvement in behaviour, demeanour and attitude. I suggest that you all accept this challenge in the grace and manner of its offering and work diligently towards this goal. We have no wish to prolong your punishment or take retribution any further; the road to redemption is available to you all and I suggest that you set out on the long road there as soon as possible. This should not blight your lives in any way but that is really in your own hands now. As far as the college is concerned, justice and retribution have been dispensed and accepted. You have expressed regret, remorse and contrition, you have admitted your guilt, apologised and accepted the punishment that you earned and brought upon yourselves by your behaviour.

Chastisement has been severe, the corporal punishment given has been unequalled in the history of this fine institution, and the restrictions placed upon you until the year end will give you a long and suitable time period to reflect. Your thrashed bottoms will heal, but hopefully the memory of your debasement, your humiliation and your shame will last far longer than the pain of your throbbing buttocks and legs!"

The young women stood silent and subdued, eyes still full of tears as the stinging of their throbbing bottoms burned and their bodies and minds struggled to cope with the residual and smouldering pain. However, some light was returning to their eyes at the Professor's words as he indicated the light at the end of the dark tunnel they had entered.

"Chloe, I have not finished with you yet. You will remain here and face further vindicatory punitive action. You are undoubtedly the force behind the evil activities and horrendous deeds of this gang of rapscallions and rogues. You will be made an example of and will be subject to further reprimand. You others may thank my friends here for giving up their time and all write a personal note to signify that you are happy that you have received suitable punishment for your behaviour at your request. Then, and only then, once I am satisfied with your words, you may dress and be escorted back to your rooms. For now though, young Chloe, in the corner, hands on your head. No one wants to see your naughty face."

As instructed, four naked young women, heads bowed, spirits broken, thanked Stones' guests before sitting down to write their words of shame, apology and thanks.

Martin, Ronald, Sara and Sonya were asked to see them back to their rooms once Stones had approved their scripts and they had dressed, Elizabeth, Annabelle and Shirley having already departed.

Stones, Celia, Emily, Jamie and Dorothy were then alone with the naked Chloe.

"Well, young Chloe, what has it come to, eh? Nothing to say for yourself, still feeling some sort of sense of being hard done by? I note the little rebellious and challenging streak that reappears in those huge eyes after every little session of punishment and, to a small degree, I acknowledge and respect your refusal to give in completely. However, I will break you, Chloe, one way or the other, not out of anger or spite, not because of your reluctance to bend to my will but because until you do submit in totality then the chastisement has not really worked and you will not have been put on the road to self-improvement and righteousness. You may well think that this is a pompous and outmoded process, my dear, but it is proven in my eyes and I will persist."

Chloe briefly flicked a moody glance at Stones but quickly lowered her eyes as she met a steely gaze that, by now, she surely knew in her heart should not be provoked unnecessarily.

"Well, Dean, I am probably going to leave you to it. I can always switch on my screen when I get back to my room to see if the task has been completed. I assume this is still on the live stream?"

"Of course, Mistress, every second streamed live and recorded for posterity. Let's hope I have not been hacked, Chloe, and thousands are not watching around the globe!" This cheery throwaway remark got the reaction he was looking for as a mortified Chloe searched out the cameras.

"Oh, what fun," laughed Dorothy. "That's put the wind up her. They are all hidden, you silly thing, but they are everywhere, no hiding place for scoundrels and their shame in these rooms, Chloe."

"Well fuck you, Mistress, and fuck you, Professor. Fuck you and your fucking college. I fucking hate you all, you and your bunch of arse-licking cunts!"

Dorothy shrilled with laughter. "I'll leave you to it, Dean. Give her one for me. Enjoy!"

Stones smiled and waved his farewell as the Mistress left them.

"Excellent riposte, Chloe, that's the spirit. Bring her here and bend her over, please Jamie. Emily, put her head between your thighs, Celia behind Emily and grab hold of Chloe's hands please."

They moved into position to hold Chloe bent over before the Professor. He saw Celia's grin as she knelt behind Emily and her pleasure as she positioned her face on a level with Emily's trouser clad bottom. As he knew she would, Celia planted a gentle kiss on one of Emily's cheeks, but her surreptitious little smile fooled Stones for not a second.

"Any more of that you two and you will join Chloe here with your bare bottoms in the air and I will ask Jamie to give you a taste of what Chloe's about to receive."

Jamie's face broke into a huge smirk as he twisted to look at his two blushing accomplices.

"That would be my absolute pleasure, Professor." Jamie was clearly enjoying that possibility, thought Stones.

"Sorry, Professor," both busted women said with faces illustrating their embarrassment.

Stones had armed himself.

"Now, Chloe, brace yourself. The 25 strokes of my heaviest cane are coming your way via Jamie's arm but your little outburst was so offensively directed at me personally, that I am angered enough to impose a further 25 that I will now deliver. Think on, young lady, this is a bruising cane that will give you long term discomfort. It's known as the Eton cane and was historically delivered on trousered buttocks to misbehaving young lads, but you will have yours on the bare, so good luck bearing up."

The cane landed with more of a thud than a slap but Chloe stayed silent. Stones took his time, spreading the strokes from the top of her bottom crack down to her upper thighs, working methodically and diligently until her already damaged cheeks glowed bright red once again. The fifteenth time the heavy cane flattened her cheeks, Chloe yelped in pain and the tears began to flow.

By the time the Professor handed the thick bamboo cane over to Jamie, Chloe was wailing loudly, her thighs and buttocks bright red once more.

"Give her a few moments, then pick your spot carefully, Jamie, this is a bitterly battered bottom and you will need accuracy to avoid breaking the skin. Ladies, please hold onto her."

Stones ran his hand over the ridges of the cane welts, causing Chloe to flinch, her sobbing beginning to subside.

"Still a way to go before I feel that you may see the word redemption appearing on the horizon. Jamie is going to explode the bamboo cane onto these poor little cheeks in a moment, then a trip to my little wheeled bed for a meeting with the braided whip and then to finish off there's a little treat planned before the thick strap sends you off, hopefully in absolute agony. Assuming of course that I am convinced that you are defeated, fully ashamed, totally conciliatory and deserving of redemption."

Chloe got her weeping under some type of control and made a heartfelt plea.

"Please sir, I am really, really sorry. I have been so bad and I am so, so sorry. Please sir, stop it now. It hurts so much."

Stones tutted patronisingly and then began stroking her bottom again.

"This is good news indeed, sweet cheeks. So progress is being made and you are starting to beg and show some regret. Sadly your regret is possibly more around how you regret being caught rather than for how you've acted, but it's a start, at least. Now thrash her hard, please Jamie." He withdrew his hand and stood aside as Jamie drew back his arm.

The strokes of the cane from Jamie came thick and fast, Chloe's body being jolted by the sheer force of the muscular and fit younger man. Celia and Emily rocked as they struggled to hold the frantically squirming student, who was now screeching out in her anguish. The blows landed methodically and accurately, Stones watching carefully as the buttocks before him flattened and then swelled when the thick bamboo landed. When Jamie stepped back, his count finished, Chloe continued to fight and writhe as though the cane blows were still landing on her severely striped bottom. Her face screwed up in anguish, her body juddering uncontrollably.

"Emily, ice her please. We need to get these weals down a bit before we take her to the next stage. I think that Celia and yourself will both recognise that, won't you? You will very much remember that, I am sure, since it is the point where you both decided to get to know each other a bit better. Hah!" The Professor was keeping them both on their toes with his references to Celia's previous indiscretion with Emily. Stones had pulled down his table, built into the wall cupboard, for the next stage of Chloe's punishment, exposing the site that had landed Celia in such hot water.

Whilst Emily and Celia got busy soothing Chloe's bottom with ice flannels and packs, Stones could see from their concerned expressions that their sympathy was rising for the stricken student and that he might need to remind them of the heinous acts committed by Chloe. He decided to take Jamie out of the equation.

"Thank you Jamie, but I'd like to finish this off myself. Thank you very much, my friend, and hopefully we will be able to resolve the Sara problem without too much awkwardness."

Jamie shook hands with Stones and assured him of his loyalty and that he had absolutely no problem with Sara having to face further chastisement and the full force of the college's ire for her behaviour.

"Right ladies, time to continue, if you please. Let us get Chloe over to my table of delights and get her strapped in!"

The table of delights, the rack, the torture table or weals in wheels. It did not matter what it was called – there was not a person who had been strapped into the contraption who had not been so relieved to get off of it! Chloe's face betrayed her fear and reluctance as they marched her over to the table. She suddenly stood stock still as it dawned on her how she was to be strapped down and exposed, and would have dropped to her knees if Emily and Celia hadn't held her firmly.

"No. No. I don't want this. No, please. No. I don't want it."

Stones guffawed and reached behind her and slapped her bottom hard with his big meaty hand.

"Of course you don't want it, my dear. If you wanted it, then the whole punishment thing would be pointless, now wouldn't it? You silly child, of course you do not want it, it is going to be hell on earth for you!"

With the aid of his two female assistants, he virtually lifted a limp and weeping Chloe onto the table and in seconds she was cuffed and strapped. With a quick flick of the wrist and a turned handle, Chloe found herself looking between her spread raised legs, her bottom in the air and her feet and knees up towards her shoulders.

Stones held a thin cane, the thick leather strap and his braided, knotted leather lash in his hands.

"Welcome to my form of hell, Chloe Tang. It's time to make you repent."

With those ominous words he began to whip her swollen and now oddly misshapen buttocks fast and furiously with the whippy thin cane. Chloe screamed from the moment the cane landed on the tops of her thighs and it continued as Stones worked those thighs and lower bottom cheeks furiously. The swipes were coming twice a second and hitting with relentless accuracy as the helpless Chloe could do nothing to avoid the vicious, stinging implement. With her legs spread so far apart it was easy for Stones to target the previously unblemished fleshy insides of her thighs, many of the strikes landing close to her unprotected pussy. With barely a moment's pause, Stones discarded the cane and picked up the knotted leather lash. In a flash, his arm had come down and the lash landed on her open crotch and bottom crack. It was a light stroke but it was all that was required. Emily moved to Chloe's head and wiped her brow as she writhed and screamed. Stones paused for several seconds, then took deliberate aim and whipped Chloe's open cracks again, causing her to thrash and pull violently against her bindings. Emily whispered into Chloe's ear.

"Oh God! I know, Chloe, I've had this and it does wear off, I promise. Try and breathe slowly and deeply, it won't last much longer. Please don't fight him, Chloe, he won't stop until you are broken. You'll just wind him up and he will give you more and more."

Chloe exhaled noisily, screeching once more as the knotted lash bit into her vaginal lips and anal slit for the third time.

"Dear God, please stop. No more, no more please. I am so sorry about everything. Please stop, Professor. I am so sorry, Professor Stones, so sorry."

Stones laid down the lash; three was plenty in his opinion anyway.

Chloe's vagina was bright red and her bottom cleft had visibly swollen.

"Emily, sooth her brow and wipe her eyes and snotty nose, she's a mess. I'll give her a moment to compose herself and then I'll apply my lovely thick strap to those blistered buttocks."

Chloe's sobbing was music to his ears. He had no real sympathy for most of his malefactors and taking bullies down gave him nothing but satisfaction. He could see that Emily's will to dismantle Chloe completely was wilting but Celia, he noted, still had a look of enthusiasm and exhilaration. As Emily whispered calming words to Chloe and tenderly wiped her eyes and nose, Stones murmured to Celia his plan to crown the punishment and crush Chloe's spirit completely to her amusement and approval.

"Oh Edward, yes, that should be fun. If she doesn't piss herself, I'll take my hat off to her!"

With Emily preoccupied, Stones moved forward and kissed Celia on the lips tenderly, his hands caressing her bottom.

"Perhaps when they go you might want to stay back for a moment?"

"A moment, Edward? Of course, my love. You want to fuck me doggy style over the desk I guess?"

Stones pinched her bottom.

"You know me too well, Celia, but yes you are right. I just want to use and abuse you for a few minutes."

Stones knew that Celia was just as happy to share these occasional moments and liaisons between their more adventurous and longer lasting lovemaking sessions as he was. This was why they suited each other so well: they understood each other perfectly and the trust and love was very real and meaningful to both of them.

"But time to return to the main purpose of our gathering, ladies.

Are we all ready for the application of the thick strap?" Stones merrily brought things back to the present, producing a grin from Celia, a sympathetic grimace from Emily, whose thirst for vengeance had been sated somewhat, and a squeal of absolute terror from Chloe, who began to babble.

"Oh no. Please, sir, I am really sorry sir and will never, ever behave in that way again. I am so sorry, Emily, I really am. Please, no more. I promise that I have learnt my lesson."

Once in a blue moon, Stones might decide that the designated full punishment need not be completed as the recipient was truly repentant, very unfortunate to be in the position they were in or had clearly been sufficiently disciplined. This was not to be one of those cases.

"There, there, my dear. That is all well and good, but needs must as the devil drives and I think we might not have reached the depths with you yet. So continue I must. Please do prepare yourself for the first of 20 with the favourite of my improvers, my lovely thick leather strap."

He was still speaking as he swung and landed the first blow so the reality was that Chloe had no time at all to prepare before the strap whipped across the centre of her reasonable relaxed buttocks. It would be several minutes before they were to relax fully again. Stones took his time, pausing with his arm raised, until her body ceased its writhing and Chloe's screech of agony had subsided to pitiful sobbing and deep spluttering breaths. After five strikes, her bottom had been covered with bright red bands on top of the previous damage and he passed the strap to Celia.

"Give her five yourself Celia, share the fun, why don't we? Then Emily can show us how much power is in that athletic body, and do remember what this wretch put you through my dear. I would not want to have to strap you in her place for not carrying out my instructions would I now?" Emily didn't answer the question she assumed was rhetorical, and as she watched Celia deliver five strokes that echoed precisely those of the Professor's, her face hardened and Stones knew that she would do her duty.

Celia passed the strap on.

"Do you think that you can go harder and get a louder scream? Be my guest, I challenge you, my dear."

Emily smiled, she knew the game by now and she was not going to break any rules. Choosing her own path, she landed her first heavy blow halfway up Chloe's ravaged cheeks but then went very low to the soft fleshy underside of the buttocks, then immediately followed up by striking at the thin flesh-covered top where Chloe's bottom crack came to a halt. As the screams ratcheted up a further notch, she repeated the last two with a real vengeance causing Chloe to buck so high and hard that it looked as though either the table or the cuffs would give. The scream was of banshee level and, with an intimate and discreet little wipe of her fingers down Chloe's pussy, she handed the strap to Stones,

"Your turn, I believe, sir. I hope I passed," she coyly whispered to the Professor.

"Any further quips like that young lady, or sneaky little fingers in Chloe's folds, and you'll be sitting buck and butt naked in the nettles patch." Stones' look carried a lot of threat and Emily immediately stammered an apology.

"Yes, please don't get ideas above your station, you little madam." Celia's face betrayed a high degree of jealous venom and Stones inwardly smiled as the two females allowed their green-eyed monsters to show.

"There's always room in the nettles for two naked bottoms, Celia, just as a reminder of when it is wise to speak and when it is best, maybe, to just hold your tongue. If you two wish to play silly beggars between yourselves, all well and good. I am quite happy to pause in my administrations to Chloe to put the two of you firmly back in your boxes!"

Stones' words had the effect of the two women colouring up in competition with Chloe's bottom and they both dropped their eyes, accepting the rebuke and the familiar besting of them, as always, by the Professor.

Stones moved towards Chloe who was oblivious to the slight tension in the room, her breathing heavy and laboured as she struggled to retain some sort of control of her emotions and remaining dignity. He swung the strap and made impact once again with the beleaguered bottom cheeks before him. As Chloe began her screeching once more, Stones dispassionately drew back his arm and unleashed onto her lower buttocks, and then again before readjusting his aim and striking her high up across her upper cheeks before finishing with a forceful slash vertically down her open bottom crack.

"Quiet now, sweetheart, it's done. We have just a little detail to finish off, do we not?"

Stones knew that Chloe was oblivious to his words but this was not something that mattered to him. His own script often ran contrary and lacking in relevance to what was actually occurring.

"Ladies, I will just uncouple my table here and then we can wheel her into the bathroom to have a little chat about whether or not she now has a full bladder."

Minutes later, Chloe, feet now released and her legs flat on the table, her hands still cuffed above her head, was looking in horror as Stones approached her with a metal contraption.

"You may look and wonder, young lady, you may look and wonder. But you have given me a problem and a challenge which I accept. Your reluctance to request to evacuate your bladder is noted, Chloe, and it is in some ways admirable that you have fought so hard to retain a shred of dignity. However, it has been a long, long day for you and many hours since you have had the opportunity to relieve yourself. I assume that would be the purpose of your defiance, one little battle won, one point scored, and one small victory to give you a tiny element of consolation and pride. But on the other hand, a poor decision as I really can't allow you to have even that shred of dignity and self-respect left at the end of a punishment. The only pride you are granted, on leaving my rooms after a punishment, is to do with the fulfilment of forbearance, the self-esteem and self-regard earned by you and afforded to you for completing your chastisement and receiving your just desserts and improvement. You leave here a better person, having learned a harsh lesson, been shown the error of your ways and having taken a big step to improving your worth as not only a member of this wonderful and renowned institution but also as a member of wider society. A wiser and more aware young lady will emerge."

Stones enjoyed these moments when he flourished rhetoric around and pontificated on his favourite theme of improvement. However, the words disguised his impatience and frustration over Chloe's stubbornness to yield. The fullness of her bladder was of no real concern in the sense that it was surely causing her discomfort and in theory was no skin off his nose, but to Stones it was a sign of an unvanquished foe, a recalcitrant refusing to submit and equivalent of an act of defiance towards him. Unbeknown to Chloe, his large figure-of-eight shaped potty had been waiting under the table while her punishment had continued and Stones had mistakenly assumed that her bladder would release once he slapped the vagina with the knotted lash.

"Now my petal, this little contraption can fit in your sore vagina or your foul mouth, which is it to be?"

Chloe's mouth immediately snapped open; she clearly had no idea what it was that he had planned but the thought of the metal implement, which he now had in his hand, being fitted into her pussy was obviously not one she wished to contemplate.

"Good girl, hold her head firmly, Celia. In it goes. Fell for my little bluff there, Chloe. It is a piece of dental equipment; basically, we clamp your mouth open and it is held in place by the rubber surround. It is a tad uncomfortable but not painful at all. I can see that you're wondering what the point is as clearly I do not intend to carry out dental treatment. You are correct in this belief, however, the more worrying aspect should surely be why did I wish to have you unable to close your mouth?"

Celia and Emily exchanged a smile, both knowing what was to come next, and at a nod from the Professor and, out of sight of Chloe's now terrified face with her mouth fixed wide open, Emily began quietly to remove her lower clothing until she stood naked from the waist down. A warning look from the Professor made Celia quickly avert her eyes that were visually feasting on Emily's exposed pubic area.

"Now, my little reprobate, earlier I asked young Emily here what she'd do to you if she got you alone and helpless and could do anything she wanted. You will never guess what the disgusting child said?"

Stones' words made Chloe twist her head frantically to try to see what Emily was doing behind her head but to no avail. Her frantic head shaking was accompanied by the only gurgling sounds she could make with the dental gag and clamp in place.

"No, you cannot guess? OK, Emily, tell us all what you said you'd do to her, please."

"Certainly Professor, not only will I tell you, I'll show you. I said I'd like to shit in your mouth, Chloe!"

Chloe bucked and roared as Celia held her down and Emily climbed on top of her from behind. Chloe eyes widened in absolute and unadulterated fear as Emily perched her split cheeks over Chloe face and then pushed down so her arsehole was directly over Chloe's mouth. At this point Chloe's bladder gave up its fight and a torrent exploded from her lower regions. As prepared as he was for this eventuality, Stones struggled to position the potty to enable him to direct the flow into the bowl and a fair amount went onto the floor or soaked the table beneath her. As Emily wriggled about on Chloe's face, Celia and Stones cheered her on until the Professor decided to put their victim out of her agony.

"Off you get, Emily. That would appear to have done the job. Just teasing, Chloe, just teasing! However, that must feel like a weight off! Ho ho!"

Emily slipped backwards off the table and retrieved her clothes whilst Stones moved to a very distressed Chloe and removed the gag from her mouth.

"It took us a while but we did find your cracking point in the end. There, there, don't fuss now it's all over. Your final disgrace, peeing yourself in front of us all. All that's left is for me to release you, open the cupboard door here so you can find the cleaning materials and then I want you on your hands and knees mopping up all this spilt piddle. Come on, girl, stop your blubbing and get on." A yelp from Chloe as Stones applied a large hand to her wet backside before stepping over the expanding puddle to the sink and washing his hands.

"We are going to have a celebratory glass to toast our success while you make sure everything is sparkling clean. Empty your potty down the loo and wash that out too, please. Then you can have a shower to clean yourself up and maybe, just maybe, after we have inspected you closely and checked you over, you will be able to take your leave and return to your room to lick your wounds."

Leaving the door ajar and a sobbing Chloe on her knees just balefully looking at the bowls and cleaning equipment, the three vacated the bathroom.

About half an hour later, a naked Chloe was bent over before the closely gathered group as they touched, prodded and poked her swollen bottom and legs. Stones applied the final indignity as he forced her hands to the floor and her legs wide apart to inspect her reddened arsehole and vulva to see where the braided knots had landed.

"Emily will have you right over her knees now, legs apart, to rub in some soothing cream. It's perfectly safe for those sensitive areas, Emily, so work those fingers right in, please."

It was the quietest both students had been for a while, albeit Chloe was still gently mewing, and clearly in a lot of pain. Stones discerned that Emily was well aware that he was keeping an eye on her activity and patently made sure that she did not linger too long in the most intimate areas, but he could see her pleasure in caressing the swollen and blistered cheeks.

Fifteen minutes of laying on the floor, face down with ice packs applied to her buttocks followed, while the three martinets sat around her animatedly discussing the day's events. After writing her script of apology for her misdemeanours and thanks for her punishment, Chloe was allowed to dress, although Stones still had a little tip of a knife to twist.

"Actually I was thinking that we would have Emily here escort you back to your room. However, just to make an example of you, I am thinking that you should remove your knickers and carry them in your hands and we will have your skirt pinned up at the back so that anyone around can see that I was true to my word and that you have the battered backside to prove it."

At his words, a distraught Chloe fell to her knees and threw herself towards the Professor, actually wrapping her hands around his legs.

"Oh no, sir. No, sir. Please, sir. I beg you, sir. I have learnt my lesson, sir. I am truly sorry, sir. Please sir, I beseech you."

"Well, I haven't been beseeched for a long time but when I ask something I expect compliance, I am hoping that you have learned that at least today, young lady. Now get up off the floor and do as you are damn well told!"

With tears again streaming down her face, Chloe rose, then stooped and removed her knickers before she turned towards Celia, who had produced a safety pin, to have her skirt lifted high and pinned.

"What a lovely sight to behold. Most proud we can be, ladies. Good job, good job. Emily, you can have the pleasure now of parading Chloe through the college and back to her room. The walk of total shame, the thrashed villain returns, head bowed, bottom bright red and stinging. Swollen and throbbing, clear cane strokes marking the fallen scoundrel's golden buttocks. The queen of nothing, the nasty strumpet and bully brought down to earth, disgraced, humiliated and bloody well flogged to within an inch of her life. On the plus side, you took it very well. Now get out of my room, worthless wretch."

Chloe took Emily's proffered hand and, head bowed, turned to

Stones and Celia, and prompted by Emily's squeeze on her hand, Stones was fairly sure, spoke quietly through her weeping.

"I would like you to please accept my apology for my behaviour and my thanks for you for taking the time and effort to correct me and show me the error of my ways, sir and madam."

"Good girl, well said. Let's hope that the next few months will evidence that and you will return here to take your examinations and graduate later. Now, turn around and present that lovely bottom for me once more. Put your knickers back on and Emily, take that pin out and make her presentable. That was just a little test at the end, Chloe, I was never going to make you do such a walk of shame. Straight back to her room, Emily, no hanging about please. Of course, if Chloe is stupid enough to issue a single word, a glance or a gesture that offends you in any way, Emily, please bring her straight back and I will strap her all over again. Otherwise, the rest of your evening is free, Emily. Thank you for your help today."

Emily handed Celia back her safety pin, curtsied to the Professor and retook Chloe's hand to lead her out.

As the door closed behind them, Celia walked straight to Stones' desk, lifted her skirt up and looked coyly over her shoulder.

"Take what you want, Edward. You can rip these knickers off if you want, just give me some nice hard cock please."

Stones did not waste any time; his trousers were unzipped and his erect cock out before he reached her. With one hand he ripped the tiny briefs off Celia's bottom, the other hand landing on her bent-over cheeks with tremendous force. Celia just moaned and parted her legs as Stones reached around in front of her and his fingers went straight to the already damp folds of her quim. Within seconds his fingers were slick with her juices and he pushed the tip of his cock up and down her slit as the other hand slid up her top to fondle a breast.

"Come on in, my dearest, up you go. Home to mama, my darling. Up to the hilt, don't spare the horses." Celia once more the rampant sex goddess rather than the stern and reverent senior tutor!

Celia pushed back to help his entry, the slurp of wet contact, suction and air being expelled as their bodies working together in that familiar unison that loving couples know so well. His fingers worked expertly on her clitoris, her slippery nub so used to the pinch and twitch of his finger and thumb as he works her towards her orgasm. Stones knew exactly how hard she wanted her nipples pinched and her breasts kneaded, and alternated his hands smoothly across her breasts. A master of maintaining a consistent pumping of his large cock without losing control, he thrust deep and hard into the wet, tight tunnel. As always, Celia's language deteriorated further and further down to gutter level when having sex.

"Go on, slam it up there. Get that big fat dick up my tight cunt. Yes, fuck me you big bastard, fuck me hard. Go on, ram it up there. Fuck me good, ream my fanny, you big bastard twat. Shit! Fuck! Fuck! Arseholes!"

Stones never ceased to find this filthy talk highly arousing and with a loud grunt he came copiously into her. His ability to orgasm had been little affected by his age, though maybe his recovery rate was longer, but the amount he released was still copious as always. Celia had not reached her pinnacle yet but Stones was a master of maintaining his commitment to his partner's pleasure. He kept pumping even as his manhood began to wilt, his hands working methodically as Celia's breathing became faster. Releasing her breast, he offered his fingers to her mouth and she automatically dribbled a mouthful of saliva into his grouped digits. One spit wetted finger slid to the bone straight up her welcoming arsehole and Celia pushed down and back hard to feel his cock and finger almost touching through the thin tissue walls. The effect of this was enough, as Stones had good reason to know from past experience, to send Celia over and she shrieked as her climax came, her body wracked with tremors.

Stones pulled out of her, and with his cock still hanging and dripping from their congress, moved to his cabinet, selected a switch and before she had drawn breath to recover from her violent orgasm, he unleashed a volley of swipes across her bent and vulnerable buttocks.

"This is for your lustful behaviour towards Emily. Take that, and that, and that! Now get out, I'm done with you, get out slag."

A squealing Celia flipped her skirt down to cover her red streaked bottom, scrabbled away from Stones and headed for the door. She stopped to blow him a kiss.

"Love you, Edward."

"Get out!"

He turned away, a huge smile across her face, his eyes alight. It had been a good day all round.

CHAPTER 12

REBECCA DISCOVERS THE MEANING

OF CONSEQUENCES

Stones fetched a whippy cane from his cabinet and handed it to her.

"What the fuck! What am I supposed to do with this?" was the snarled and impetuous response he received. "What? Is this supposed to be some kind of threat?"

"Rebecca Parsons, you will just stand there and you will hold the cane," he ordered.

The haughty student raised her chin and then dropped the cane to the floor.

"Pick it up now!" was Stones' thundered response.

There was a long pause as Rebecca tried vainly to hold the ferocious stare of the Professor. Fight it as she did, he could sense the pure fear that would have begun to course through her veins and could see the doubt begin to creep into her mind. Stones' rage was at its most ferocious when his authority was challenged, and Rebecca would know full well that his power was close to supreme in this college, and his personal aura of control was virtually undeniable. But, however unwisely, her nerve held.

"I will not, and I am leaving. You cannot stop me. This is

ridiculous and I am not partaking in any of your games. Good day to you, Professor Stones." Rebecca turned her back and took the steps to the door, her hand reaching out as Stones responded:

"That behaviour has just earned you a doubling of your punishment, young lady. Before you take another step, you might like to listen to the telephone conversation that I am now going to have with your mother." Stones' voice was suddenly quiet and mild, but his words stopped the confident young lady in her tracks.

"Why would you call my mother? What has anything got to do with her?" Rebecca's words weren't quite delivered with the authority she had intended.

"Because, Miss Parsons, your mother signed an agreement, as did you, that stated that, in the instance of unacceptable behaviour warranting punitive action, you were to be given corporal punishment to the appropriate level as befitting the misdemeanour. I have the agreement here and am happy to give your mother a quick call to see if she agrees with me that you are deserving of a bare-bottom thrashing. Of course, that is a bit of an inconvenience for me, and so will need to go on record in detail, let alone the fact that I would consider that you have displayed impudence in putting me to the trouble and therefore further additional strokes will be added to your punishment. In fact, I may actually call the Mistress and Senior Tutor first, to see if they are available so that we can discuss your behaviour in detail with your mother."

Apprehension was written all over Rebecca's face and Stones sensed the first tingling signs of fear in her widening eyes. Stones watched and waited as she took a deep breath to calm her beating heart which Stones imagined had certainly accelerated in the last few seconds. Stones played on his reputation as being a man who oozed power and authority, his words now delivered with a cold, chilling and controlled fury that she found almost impossible to oppose.

"Do I need to remind you what I asked you to do?"

He looked down at the cane lying on the carpet and then back into her eyes. As if transfixed, she walked meekly back to her earlier space, bent down and picked up the cane with trembling hands.

"Bring it to me," he snapped. Rebecca hesitated, her mind whirling as she realised that she was being drawn into a scenario of her own making that showed little signs of an escape route.

"Sir, surely you don't mean to use that on me. I don't believe that my mother would willingly allow such a thing. This is just a threat, isn't it? Surely this is something that can be resolved without resorting to such barbaric behaviour?"

Stones took the proffered cane from her shaking fingers.

"Thank you, Rebecca. Please refrain from offering your opinion until a direct question is asked. Now you will take a seat and you will write a short essay explaining what you have done to have caused this situation, how sorry you are and how you wish to receive an appropriate punishment. That punishment can be the one I have outlined which would bring a quick end to your predicament or you can choose to go before the college council to plead your case as to why you should be allowed to remain in this hallowed institution without feat of repercussion or punishment for unacceptable behaviour. You do, of course, run the rather high risk of then being suspended or sent down in disgrace but you are free to take that route if you so wish. Alternatively, you may propose the aforementioned corporal punishment as an option, in which case you need to request that you be beaten thoroughly on your bare flanks, whilst naked, and that you will accept the implements of use that I determine. We can telephone, Monica, your mother, now if you wish to discuss it with your wider family, however, I do refer you to the signed agreement your parents pledged, with your support, when you entered this fine institution. I hope that you do remember the conversation I had with your parents at the time? As I recall, your mother was perfectly clear in that she insisted that you be subject to the rules and laws that have made this college's students the force in the world they are today. Or maybe you do not recall? Please enlighten me."

Stones watched in amusement as the young student went through the predicament that many before her had struggled with. He was prepared to wait as the outcome was only likely to go one way. The threat of being sent down from your college was most students' nightmare scenario, particularly from such an august institution as St. James'. The shame and disgrace, the long-lasting reputational damage and the catastrophic effect this could have on your future post-university career meant that this was a course of action that very few students would ever opt to take. In reality the college council would often allow a student in this situation a final opportunity to change their mind and elect to take the thrashing originally proposed; however, a final indignity would then be added. At Professor Stones' behest, not only could the proposed punishment be doubled, the council members could all be invited to watch the miscreant's denouement. Occasionally Stones had had to outline this additional vision to a dithering student to aid them in coming to a decision but he so enjoyed watching them struggle internally that the usual outcome was that which he could see Rebecca was about to pronounce.

"Um, sir, if I was to accept the punishment could I be allowed to keep my um, er, you know, um my bottom, covered please sir?"

As she delivered the words in a shaky and quiet voice, Stones noted a single tear slide down her cheek.

"Don't be so ridiculous child, of course not," snapped the Professor haughtily. "You will be naked, your legs will be spread well apart and you will put your most private body parts fully on display. That is the protocol and you will follow that established path to the letter. Now, sit down here and start writing your acceptance of your crime, and allocated punishment, as I have outlined, and stop dithering before I start considering adding some extra elements to your correction. Be warned, Rebecca, my patience is wearing thin."

Rebecca's crime was to have stolen cutlery from the dining hall. Students had traditionally attempted this over the years as one of the so-called *'Golden five acts of lawlessness'*, the quintet of tasks considered to be the ultimate challenge during the students' time in the college. This act being considered so daring due to the fact that the cutlery was all 17th century, Georgian sterling silver. Making up the five were: streaking across the college bridge; scaling the chapel tower; temporary theft of the college flag (removed when flying); and disabling the Entrance Great Gate to any degree that results in a temporary closure of the main college entrance. Rebecca had attempted what many considered to be one of the easier tasks along with the streaking, however, increased installation of CCTV in the college had foiled most efforts to tick the acts off in recent years. Rebecca had been spotted on camera slipping a knife into her handbag and was now trying to pass it off as a trivial error.

"Sir, would anyone be told that I have been given a, um, er, oh dear, a beating on my bare bum?"

Stones kept his face impassive.

"Your punishment would be a matter of record, not a matter of gossip. It's not a general topic for discussion for the chattering classes or a subject for titillation. This is chastisement, Rebecca, it is serious and it is intended to inflict pain as well as shame on the recipient, and provoke remorse, contrition and an improvement in behaviour and attitude. For many, this is more an act of salvation rather than one of chastisement. There will be an element of humiliation, particularly if the crime committed is a heinous one. At this point I would remind you, young lady, that you were caught in the act of theft of college property. The value of the knife and fork that you purloined is £100, and all for a silly game that I am trying to have outlawed in college. So I am actually rather angry with you, Rebecca Parsons, and yes, I do think you deserve corporal punishment and I do believe that a taste of the cane following a damn good bare bottom spanking would be just and appropriate. However, as I said earlier, I would be open to discussing this with your mother if that is what you prefer."

Once again, a single tear ran down her face as Stones waited for her to work through her limited options, knowing of course that there was really only one outcome. When Stones rapped the desk, indicating the pen and paper, Rebecca walked towards him as though under a spell.

"The cane," she said in hushed, rather reverential tones. "But I have never been caned. You are really going to cane me, sir?" Stones smiled at her as though educating a child.

"Absolutely the cane. On your bare buttocks, applied with force but affection and due diligence, knowing that you are deserving of correction and improvement that will be of a real benefit to you in the future, my dear. Now you need to acknowledge your wrongdoing, apologise for your behaviour, suggest an apt punishment of the corporal variety, ask for forgiveness and thank me for offering to give you guidance and improvement. That should do it. In your own words, Miss Parsons, although not necessarily in your own time. You have fifteen minutes, my dear. If your work is not close to exemplary then I will feel obliged to assist your application to the task with an immediate sample of a bare bottomed spanking."

The cowed student sat down and picked up the pen.

"Actually, before you make yourself comfortable, please remove your clothing and let the dog see the bone. Come on. Off!"

Rebecca looked around as though seeking an escape route, her face flustered, panic rising.

"Rebecca Parsons, I am not used to being disobeyed. Do you want me to undress you because I certainly will have no problem doing so. Now, off with these rags, I want to see you naked within a minute."

Tears now streamed down her face, but he had broken her spirit and, with her shoulders slumped, she unzipped her dress and stepped out of it to stand in her underwear before him.

"Don't even think about asking, get the rest of your rags off and quickly. The clock is ticking down."

She reached back and unhooked her brassière, her full breasts and perky nipples now exposed. Her tiny knickers followed and she dropped her hands in front of her groin, her eyes to the floor.

Stones spun her round by her shoulders and with a sharp slap on her rather prominent buttocks he guided her to the desk.

"Jolly good, nice body and a fine looking bottom that looks most suitable for a good thrashing. Come on, get writing, your time is slipping away. In fact, as we have not that much time before the end of term, we should look to get this whole caboodle over with this afternoon. That will be a big plus, young lady, you won't have to sweat on it for days and I won't have the inconvenience of trying to fit you in just before the May Ball."

Rebecca did not look enchanted by that bit of news but made the decision to hold her tongue. It was nearly 20 minutes later when she rose and took her paper over to Stones. She had managed to bring her haughty nature back into play and stood before Stones with an expression that suggested she was perfectly comfortable standing in front of him naked, her groin and breasts inches from his face.

"Turn round, turn round, hands on your head, legs apart," snapped Stones.

Rebecca was not to know that Stones had been challenged, threatened, opposed and even assaulted by far worthier opponents than her. She did not even scratch the surface of difficult in Stones' eyes. He had no real problem with his miscreant having a bit of an attitude, not that he allowed them to know this, but there was a line that he did not let them cross without serious consequences. Rebecca's immediate obedience to his order rather indicated that she was not fully wedded to her display of confident petulance.

"Let's see if you have received and processed the message yet as to the position you are in. Let's have a closer look at this gorgeous derrière. Bend over, grasp your ankles, legs wider apart. Lovely, neat wispy anal crack hairs, cute little anus, vagina looks nice and tidy and..."

Rebecca suddenly realised he was sniffing her bottom and span round in anger.

"What the fuck are you doing, you dirty old git. Are you sniffing my arse? You dirty pervert!" Stones was impassive and waited her out.

"OK. OK. OK. That was perhaps over the top, but what on earth were you doing? I am sorry about my language. I was just taken by surprise. Sorry."

"Sorry sometimes doesn't quite cut it, young lady. I was testing you and you failed. You will be punished further for that offensive little outburst. Perhaps you might like take up that position you were in previously and we will resume where we left off."

Rebecca's coloured-up face rather gave away her inner turmoil. There was a long pause before she turned, bent over and displayed her buttocks to him.

"Actually, if you could just reach back and spread your cheeks wide for me, my dear. Come along now, don't be shy, it's a lovely bottom, show some pride in it."

Rebecca gave a loud sob but her hands came back and she parted her cheeks presenting Stones with a perfect view immediately in front of his face. He went through the motions of taking a loud long sniff, his nose very close to her crack.

"Yes, pleasant aroma, flowery and fresh. Is it lilies I scent?"

"Oh my God, this is hideous. Oh Lord. Yes, yes, yes. It is bloody Lily of the Vales moisturiser. What is this? This is so obscene and bloody weird, Professor Stones, sir."

Stones put one large hand on her backside and pushed hard causing Rebecca to stumble to her knees.

"I suggest you keep your rather ill-disciplined mouth shut before I shut it for you," Stones said menacingly. He picked up the paper she had written and began to hum to himself.

"Not bad. You seem to have hit the gist of what I wanted. You think a good spanking followed by a six-of-the-best caning would be a suitable chastisement. Charming that you believe six would be sufficient, but wishful thinking my dear, I am afraid. Now, how are your bowels and bladder, Rebecca? Are you empty, my dear? Yes? Super. That's all good. Shall we go for it then? Up you get. Now over here, that's right, you go across my lap and I give you the spanking you have requested."

With no resistance, the bewildered and completely outmanoeuvred student allowed herself to be dragged unceremoniously across his lap, her hands grasping the chair legs, her eyes and mouth wide open. His hand immediately started to bounce off her buttocks to the accompaniment of squeaks and yelps that soon turned to longer screams and sobs as he increased the pressure and speed of the blows.

He finished the 50 slaps with a rapid flourish on the backs of her legs, accompanied by high-pitched screaming.

"Two minutes to recover then I want you over the desk there for your caning, my dear. I do not actually apply a mere six-stroke punishment but you were not to know that, so you can be forgiven for your request. No, young lady, it will be a dozen of my full-on strokes with a medium thickness cane. I think that should do the trick for now as long as we have no more resistance or abusive language."

Rebecca's face showed exactly what she thought about that but she managed to contain herself to a rather muted, "Oh, sir." Stones let that pass as he directed her to her place in the corner. He was more interested in seeing if he had received a response to his text to Emily Govan, requesting her immediate availability for assistance. Just as he was about to order Rebecca to her position, his mobile buzzed with a message to say that she was on her way. Stones decided to wait for her and let Rebecca stew; he doubted that she would complain about his tardiness and the extra time might serve well, in his view anyway, in building her tension and apprehension.

The door buzzer went and Stones released the door to allow a breathless and apologetic Emily into the room. But her explanation of where she was and how she'd run here at the first chance she had was interrupted by Rebecca, who had spun around at the sound of Emily's entrance and shrieked in horror.

"What the fuck, Emily, what are you doing here? What the fuck is this?"

"Oh Rebecca, oh my. Um. Hello."

Stones' smile broadened at the realisation that the two were reasonably well acquainted. Anything that added to the discomfort levels of those being dealt with by corporal punishment was gist to his mill.

"Excellent, excellent. Right then ladies, first things first. Rebecca, return to the wall now. Put your hands on your head. How dare you move from your position? I also note your use of foul language despite your earlier warnings so I will impose additional punishment. I will be lenient, however, and only give you two additional strokes of the cane. I must be going somewhat soft, I seem to be acting so leniently towards you, Rebecca. Emily, please compose yourself, my dear. I am delighted you are able to join me, but now you must remember that you are here to assist me with disciplinary issues."

Emily was nodding and trying to pull herself together, clearly having run a fair distance to be there and having to cope with finding a student she knew fairly well standing naked with a bright red bottom.

Rebecca suddenly turned and addressed Stones.

"No, I will not have this. I will not be embarrassed like this in front of a friend. I refuse to allow this farce to go on any further."

Before Emily could intervene to try and stop her friend spiralling into a hole that she would not be able to get out of, Stones spoke in a totally disinterested manner.

"That's fine, get dressed and back to your room. I'll get everything sorted out. Quickly now, let us not waste any further time on this, you are clearly a lost cause. Come on, chop-chop. Emily, looks like you will not be required after all. Rebecca's punishment has just been increased to 18 strokes of the cane with two lashes of the strap due to this latest outburst but unfortunately she has chosen to renege on our agreement and opted to leave the college in disgrace."

As Rebecca froze with her knickers half way up her legs, Emily beseeched the Professor:

"Sir, sir. Please may I just speak to Rebecca for a moment?"

Stones looked away and waved his hand at her.

"Oh if you wish, but seriously, Emily, I do not have time to deal with prevarication like this, she can damn well get those knickers back off, ready for a bloody good caning or she gets out if my sight for good. You have five minutes to have her strapped and cuffed over the table ready to be flogged, Emily, and then she is out. The clock is ticking."

He turned away, hiding the grin on his face as Emily whispered sharply to Rebecca. He went to his laptop on his desk as though he had moved on, disregarding the students, although in truth he was watching from the corner of his eye as Emily led a clearly reluctant Rebecca over to his punishment table set-up.

"Emily, please can you tell him to stop this. I don't want it."

Emily was doing her best with soothing words and persuasively encouraging Rebecca to the table that Stones had specially designed with adjustable legs, wheels, attachments, cuffs, straps and a hard rubber movable mound that would both push the victim's bottom up and assist in spreading their legs to full expose them. Stones was at the point where he felt Rebecca had stretched his leniency, perhaps suffering from the renowned end of term frivolity and slackness that always pervaded.

"Rebecca, my patience is exhausted. Be silent please, your voice is becoming very annoying, the sort of annoying that normally earns extra stripes on a bottom!"

Emily virtually put her fist in Rebecca's mouth to stop a retort coming, her eyes wide and drilling into her friend's in warning. Stones went to his cabinet and pulled out his medium sized cane and the dreaded thick strap. He swished the cane close to Rebecca's bottom which was now ideally presented, her legs strapped to the table, her pubic mound resting on the assemblage fixed to the table edge that forced her bottom up. Rebecca's tremor was the reward he was looking for, as she twisted her head round to try and see what he was doing, Emily cuffing her wrists securely and finally restricting her movements. Her buttocks jutted out, her backside being what Stones termed as a long bottom in that there was no real obvious line between her bottom cheeks and her thighs, basically dimple free. Aesthetically and sexually, Stones' preference was for a full cheeked, dimpled bottom with a clear dividing crease between the cheeks and the top of the legs. That notwithstanding, he did have to admit that caning a long bottom had appeal due to the fact it was easier to line up cane strokes nice and evenly with no overlap or slightly awkward angles. Rebecca's buttocks, being quite fully fleshed, also added the element of satisfaction as the cane would visibly bite into the skin.

"I call this cane the stinger, my dear. It's not a bruiser like the heavy cane nor does it carry the cut of a smaller whippier cane, but boy, oh boy, does this beauty sting!" he voiced conversationally, knowing very well that he had her full attention and her fear was at its anticipatory high.

"Emily, please push the adjoining table apart from this one, the wheels are unlocked, then kneel in front of her and hold her head while I attend to this splendid target."

Emily put her hands to each side of the terrified student's face.

"Be strong," he heard her whisper. "It is only 20 so it won't take long. Trust me, my love, I've had so much worse. Just accept the pain rather than fight it and just think about enduring and accepting one stroke at a time rather than how many to come."

Stones was in position and waited until the moment Emily spoke her last word before applying a stroke to the tops of Rebecca's legs. There had been clear signs that she would be a screamer and she did not disappoint or fail to meet expectations. The screech was loud and long, her body shaking the table with her frenetic thrashing, and attempts to flail her arms and legs added to a reverberating response to her first ever stroke of the cane. He gave her a few seconds; he could see that she was really feeling the sting and was keen to allow her the full benefit. The second one was placed fractionally above the first as Stones dispassionately calculated that he could fit the full 18 strokes on the target zone that would lead him to a final stroke across the top of her bottom crack.

Stones was impressed that the second scream matched the first and could see that Emily was having her work cut out to stop Rebecca's head from smashing into the table top. Another stroke to the tops of her thighs followed quickly by the fourth, accurately placed just above the others produced a perfect quartet of tramlines at the very tops of her legs.

"Do try and keep your lovely bottom still, my dear, I am so wanting to create a thing of beauty, a work of perfection of vicious red lines over a background of stark white. Now, point your anus at me, please. I like to see it as the bullseye. No, no, no, now. Don't clench and hide your lovely puckered rosebud, open up for me now, let me see your sweet little crinkly slit and those lovely thick folds beneath."

He enjoyed these moments of using his access and view of his reprobates' exposed entrances to diminish and belittle them as much as he could. He could hear Emily's quiet, calm voice telling Rebecca to be suppliant and do as she was told, and as he met her vibrant eyes over Rebecca's head he could see the excitement that coursed through her.

"Here we go, ladies. Let's see how accurate I can be at a faster pace. Here they come, hold tight!"

Ten strokes landed, hard and true, Rebecca's buttocks bouncing, flattening and then springing back into shape. Stones paused to look at his handiwork whilst the banshee howls of Rebecca filled the room. "Very slight overlaps," said Stones. "Otherwise not at all bad. A good space left at the top here where the skin is thinnest and pulled tight, so should be the most painful blows. They will be landing just here, my dear." He ran his fingers lightly along the top of her bottom crack and gently stroked her above the savage red lines until she calmed down and he felt her attention was being taken by the feel of his fingers.

"Are you ready, my dear? The last four with my stinger and then just the two with the strap to go. You're doing very well so don't spoil things now with any foul language. Hold her tight, Emily, these four will be the ones she'll remember most. I'll do my best not to let you down, Rebecca, these should hopefully be some of my best work! Hold tight, here they come."

However disturbing Rebecca was finding his verbal torturing, it was soon forgotten when the first strike landed across the top of her beleaguered cheeks. The screech was ear-splitting, she wailed and bucked, her face shaking from side to side, tears and snot dripping down her face. Emily produced a tissue and cleaned her up after a nod from the professor. The three final cane strikes were severe and perfectly placed, with the last one running right across the very beginning of her bottom crack, resulting in a long bottom wracked from high to low with long red and angry-looking, evenly spaced strikes.

"Come and have a look, Emily, I think I have given her a beautiful job. What do you think?"

Emily was round like a shot, her eagerness to see the flogged buttocks undeniable, and Stones almost admonished her when she actually licked her lips in lust.

"Oh wow, it's really beautiful, Rebecca. Oh, Professor, it's brilliant, it's like you've painted them on. She almost looks like she's been branded. It's gorgeous, sir. Well done."

Stones knew that in these circumstances Emily was easily pleased but still felt a swell of pride to be appreciated thus.

"Watch now, Emily, as I put the two strap lines diagonally across these beautiful babies."

Arming himself with the thick strap, he ran his hands tenderly across the blistered globes before taking a step back, and with an almighty swing, exploded the strap onto her tightly rounded cheeks.

Rebecca still had more to offer in the level of the shrieks she could produce, it turned out, and, away from her view, Emily was able to drop any pretence, her open arousal was so evident.

With a finger to his lips, Stones offered her the strap and, eyes wide with wonder and desire, she breathlessly took the opportunity. Licking her lips, she took a hefty swing as befitting the athletic and sporty student she was, and walloped the strap down to form a clear cross of thick red lines to the parallel stripes already beaming in red from the battered buttocks of the truly chastised Rebecca. The writhing continued for quite some time as Rebecca sobbed and sobbed before Stones instructed Emily to release her and led her to the iced-filled bidet in his bathroom.

"Give her five minutes to freeze some of the pain away and start bringing those bruises out and then you can dry her down. Maybe I will have you back over my lap, my dear, and Emily can rub in some of my special soothing cream."

Later, as Stones bent her securely over his knees while Emily diligently massaged the thick luxurious cream into the sore swollen cheeks, a warning glance was required as he spotted the straying fingers of Emily dipping down to tease the labia below.

"It is not too late in the year to have you bent over, young lady," he warned, albeit the smiling response he received from Emily was not the usual reaction to those words!

After delivering the expected words of apology and thanks, a rather fragile and certainly much subdued Rebecca was helped out of the Professor's rooms by a rather frustrated Emily, once more invigorated but then strangely unfulfilled by being in Stones' company.

Another university year was coming to its conclusion and another stepping stone was skipped over in the entwining lives of young Emily Govan and the Dean of Discipline of St. James' College.

COMING EARLY IN 2022:
The further adventures at St. James' College.

THE DEAN OF DISCIPLINE 3:
CANED AND ABLE

SAMPLE OF CHAPTER 1
MELANIE IS TEASED, GETS EVEN, IS PUNISHED!

The overweight student stood before him with tears running down her cheeks.

"I am so sorry, I really am. I know I shouldn't have done it, I am so sorry. I have never done anything like that before, I just got so fed up and I lost my temper just for a moment. Please don't send me home, Professor, it would break my mother's heart, I am so very, very sorry."

Stones, ever the poker face, just stared at the blubbing girl as she blustered on. Not as hard-hearted as he always liked to appear, he had plenty of sympathy for this transgressor. Bated and teased over her weight, Melanie Thorpe had finally snapped in the dining hall a couple of evenings ago and had pushed another student's face into her dessert. Unfortunately, she had probably not realised the strength her surplus pounds gave her and aside from mashing a rather slight, fellow student's face into her meringue and cream, she had given her a nose bleed and a bruised cheek. Having heard the full story from staff and students present, Stones was well aware that the offending student, a Prascilla Guptil, had been quite cruel in her jibes and that a complaint from Melanie of bullying would probably stand its ground under investigation. However, Melanie had made it clear that she did not wish to pursue this path, albeit Stones had pressed the point. This would not release Prascilla from any comeback though, as the Professor had already had an initial chat with her and suggested that she might like to reconsider her earlier thought of filing a formal complaint against Melanie for assault.

"This is a violent act causing actual, bodily harm, Melanie. I do hope that you realise that I cannot let this incident pass without the strongest and most thorough punishment. Might I suggest that you take a moment to gather yourself and then apply a little bit of thought as to how I can consider an alternative punishment to dismissal from our fine ranks? You might also like to consider what exactly you propose that could possibly be severe enough to punish you sufficiently for carrying out such a heinous crime. Into the corner with you, hands on head. Quickly now."

The Professor ushered the confused and distraught young woman into the corner of the room, placing her close to his cabinet of punishment implements. Deftly, he unlocked the door, opened up the cabinet to the trembling form beside him, and smiled in delight as he heard the sharp intake of breath as Melanie espied the arrangement of whips, canes, straps and paddles hanging alongside of her.

"In five minutes time I will give you one opportunity to suggest a route that could lead to you remaining as a member of our esteemed institution rather than being drummed out in disgrace. This route will necessitate you undergoing an extreme punishment befitting your crime and one that you will request most convincingly so that I may consider my options. Are you understanding me, girl?" he snapped, knowing full well that he had his fish already about to nibble at the bait offered.

As Melanie's eyes filled with tears, Stones turned away to leave her to stew in her dilemma. In his experience, it took a moment or two for his subjects to run through a variety of emotions before usually realising that the opening he was steering them towards was actually the only escape route on offer, however unpalatable it may appear.

As it happened, it took almost an hour before a quivering, timid Melanie found her voice. To Stones' amusement she had half-turned and opened her mouth on several occasions before she finally found the backbone and spirit to request with the utmost politeness if she could have permission to speak!

"Ah, yes, I had almost forgotten you were still here, my little reprobate. Well, get on with it. I presume that you have come to your senses and wish to offer to undergo whatever punishment it takes to clear your slate. Before you speak, I would like you to consider very carefully what you propose. I am not in the habit of giving counsel to timewasters, young lady. I expect you to acknowledge your disgraceful violation of the rules of civilised society and put forward an appropriate request."

"Um. I think so, sir. But I will change it to whatever you want if it's not good enough."

"Melanie, you really do need to consider ways to improve your self-assertiveness and confidence in your own actions. I will send a note to your pastoral care tutor here and we will see if we can get you on one of the courses we send some of our shy, docile, timid little flowers on. Oh, but you slammed one of your fellow students faces into the dinner table didn't you now? So maybe not quite as shy and retiring as you are acting? Well, I will tell you what, before I peruse your request for an alternate form of punishment fitting for the crime committed, I will give you a further few minutes to rewrite your little script. I suspect that you have skirted around the issue, so this will be your final opportunity to volunteer yourself for a suitable solution to our problem with you. To help you focus, you will now remove your clothing…"

Stones got no further as the student burst into tears and crumpled to her knees before him, a strange primal howling sound coming from her mouth.

"Desist that awful racket this very instance, young lady!" With deft speed and strength for a man of his age and of considerable build, he often moved with pace and dexterity that caused surprise and, as in this case, shock and fear. A terrified Melanie found herself hauled upright, her flowing dress raised high up her back and within seconds she had felt the impact of the Professor's huge hand slamming into her substantial knicker-clad bottom.

"Clothes off, folded neatly and placed on the chair, now!" he thundered, correctly adopting the persona that he judged would cause the response he required.

"Oh my God, I don't believe it! I am so sorry, sir," and with quivering lips and tear-flooded eyes, she looked at the Professor's angry face. He could see the realisation of her situation finally hitting her. "Oh dear, oh no. Yes sir, of course, sir, I am so sorry, sir. Yes. Yes. Take my clothes off. Yes. Yes. Yes."

The naked student soon stood before him, one hand and the other arm across her large, pendulous breasts.

"Legs apart, hands on your head. Come on girl, move yourself. That's better, now let me have a proper look at what I have got to work on. There's no need to be embarrassed about your weight or shape with me, young lady. I do not do fat-shaming or body-form taunting. All I am really interested in is the application of the most suitable method of improvement." He prodded her buttocks, squeezing a handful, and moving his spread hands over both cheeks, while Melanie whimpered and shook at his touch. "Yes, these beauties, and they are beautiful, Melanie, don't doubt that, will withstand an awful lot, I suspect. Now, come with me and see if we can select the right tools for the job, before you rewrite your little piece suggesting the form of justice that specifically needs applying to the issue."

He took her hand and Melanie gripped it tightly, suddenly seemingly spellbound and submissive. In the tone of a true supplicant, she spoke the words that caused Stones to smile in approval, causing her own face to lighten and revive.

"Oh sir, yes sir. Of course, sir. I am so sorry, sir. Of course, of course."

"Now Melanie, if you had to select the two implements that you wanted to be used to thrash your backside, that would best suit the occasion and help ease your conscience, for the heinous crime of violence you committed, which two do you feel are most appropriate?" His voice was delivered in his most hypnotic tone and it gave him much self-satisfaction to see Melanie stand before the display of punishment weaponry giving due thought and consideration to words that she would probably have never thought she would hear, even in her worst nightmare!

"Can I touch them?" Melanie's query was of no great surprise to him; he had often found that once a student had accepted that the punishment was inevitable, then part of the fear left them. His intention was to give Melanie a severe thrashing; her instinctive act could be deemed understandable but that sort of violence was not acceptable in college life and regardless of her reasons, she had used the advantage of her weight and strength to cause facial damage to another student. It was certainly in the arena of gross misconduct wherein expulsion via sending down was an outcome that would fit the crime. Stones' challenge with a girl carrying excess weight such as Melanie was that by nature of her size she had considerable padding on most parts of her body, particularly her backside. As Stones gave her the go ahead to handle his wicked but beloved, by him at least, array of "improvers", he stood back to look at the fleshy buttocks that would face his application. The hand marks of his quick slapping were already fading, barely pink outlines still visible, and he knew that a lot of force would be required to ensure that she truly suffered the sting and lash of his tools. A call to Jamie loomed and he suspected that this could be another opportunity for Emily Govan to join them and experience another session as support student to a punishment victim. Emily, now in her third and final year, would be perfect for Melanie, he mused, and he knew that she would appreciate the chance to be a part of another's correction. He also felt that she deserved a treat after her performance and involvement in bringing to account the dreaded Seven Sisters gang.

To Stones' surprise, Melanie continued to handle and seemingly appraise each of his "improvers" piece by piece, methodically feeling the texture, weight and thickness of each item. Her face was a picture of concentration, with no obvious fear and trepidation apparent.

"Well, young lady, you seem rather enraptured with my collection. Do you approve of my assemblage and is anything taking your fancy?" Stones decided the teasing approach was called for. As Melanie removed a cane, she took an end in each hand, bending the rod and flexing it in its centre. His words snapped her out of whatever was playing though her mind and she immediately coloured, quickly replaced the cane, and dropped her eyes to the floor.

"Oh, don't be ashamed, Melanie. It's nice to have someone who seems to have an appreciation of the tools of my trade. It is a fine collection, although this is only a selection. I have many more that I would be happy to show you but perhaps on another day. I could probably do with a test and sample student if you would like to be considered for the position?"

Melanie's face was Stones' perfect reward. In almost comic fashion, her eyes blinked and her mouth started to open and close, but soundless, as the student clearly struggled to find words for this situation. Stones decided to enjoy himself at her expense further. He didn't consider this a malicious act but more an essential part of the humiliation process he put each errant student through. Before Melanie, whose red blush had now travelled down her neck to the tops of her monumental breasts, could bring forth the required ability to put words together into a sentence, Stones pursued his belittling rhetoric.

"Now, have you chosen the ideal implements that you feel would best serve the purpose of allowing you to return to civilised society feeling as though you have atoned for your sins and learnt a valuable lesson? I would be interested in your opinion on the best way to deliver the corporal punishment that your disgraceful, thuggish behaviour deserves. I think you will be a student who will truly appreciate your shame and mortification being somewhat relieved with the weight of your disgrace lifted from your substantial shoulders after our joint enterprise. I am very much looking forward to combining with you to aid your reintegration into normal college life. I am offering you redemption and salvation, you lucky woman. Rejoice!"

Melanie's face was a picture of perplexion as she processed his words. Stones allowed her to wallow in her own confusion and could see that she was desperately attempting to come up with an answer that she would be happy with, as well as satisfactorily answering his question.

He tapped her buttocks with the back of his hand.

"Come on, girl. I do not expect to be kept waiting when I ask you a question. I know there were a lot of words to consume there but you are supposedly one of our bright, elite young ladies on her path to a successful career. Try and keep up. Your buttocks. My weaponry. Remember, we were trying to marry the two together. Share your thoughts now, please."

Melanie's hands grabbed at a cane, knocking several implements to the floor. As she scrabbled to pick them, Stones' voice froze her body.

"Slightly unusual method of selection, Melanie, and I did say two not five. However, I am happy to bow to your wishes."

"No. No. No, sir. I didn't mean that I wanted all of them. It was an accident. I am sorry, sir. I am just so clumsy." Melanie's protestations dried up as she looked at the expression on his face and the hand reaching out for the fallen items.

"I think realisation is dawning. My methods and processes may seem irrational and unfair to you now, Melanie, but one day soon I believe that you will see the light and understand them fully. So, we have a thin whippy cane, a split-end tawse, a medium cane, a thick cane and a riding crop. They should do the trick; harsh but fair. If you are going to assault people and cause physical pain to others, then you can hardly complain if you receive treatment in kind. You may now go over to that desk, sit down and write me a one-page essay detailing your misdemeanour and appalling behaviour, specific but concise, please. You will then request a punishment of the severity that is in accordance with your own foul act, naming these implements which you can take over to the desk with you. You should nominate your own amount of strokes that you think you wish to receive to help ease your conscience and guide you down a more righteous path. To save you going through any more conflict and disquiet in your mind over whether or not you dare ask for my opinion on the number of strokes, I advise you to listen carefully now, as I will not repeat myself without a requirement for you to double the punishment to act as an aide-memoire. My thoughts are that to serve you best you require a thorough spanking to warm those mighty cheeks up and get them prepared for what would follow. Two hundred slaps is a good start, generally." He paused to take in the absolute look of horror and astonishment that had appeared on the clearly stricken student's face.

"Oh, do you not think that is enough? Did you want to add some more, per chance?" The challenge and scorn in his tone was evident, even to a newbie entrant into the corporal discipline environment such as she was.

"Oh no sir. Sorry. Sorry. Sorry. I just don't know anything about these matters. Did you really mean 200, sir? Sorry to ask, sir."

"Actually I think you're right, that is a bit lenient, well done, Melanie. Good girl. Let's raise that to 250."

Melanie finally learnt to retain her silence but a tear trickled from one eye and gently ran down the cheek of the student who now looked scared witless.

"One tear, I will allow, now wipe your eyes, you are not in pain. Yet." He passed her a tissue from his desk. "But if you are going to blubber at this point, then I will take it upon myself to give you something to really cry about. Save your tears for when it will be appropriate. When your backside is feeling like it has been flayed by barbed wire and then set on fire, just to give you a heads-up. Actually, young lady, just bend over, legs apart fully so I can gauge exactly what level of application we might need to employ to get the job done properly."

Taking a deep breath in, Melanie complied, stretching her legs as far apart as she could while keeping her balance as her hands grasped her shins. Stones moved behind and first ran his hands around her surprisingly taut cheeks before taking firm grasps and squeezing tight. To her credit, Melanie stayed still, although Stones could feel the tension in her buttocks as he worked the fat of the cheeks between his fingers. Abruptly he yanked her cheeks wide open, digging his thumbs in to expose the student's anus and lower vagina.

"Damn well stay still. You minx. The dog needs to see the bone. I hope you are nice and clean in your nether regions? I most definitely do not deal with unhygienic trollops."

Melanie tried to stand and twist away from his probing, and he used all his strength to force her down to her knees with her flanks raised high.

"Head down and smell the carpet, bottom up, legs apart. You are already in big trouble for not adhering to a simple instruction to stay still. Do not make it worse. Now, do I need to shower you down first or are you relatively clean down below?"

There was a large gulping sound of anguish as Melanie tried to pull herself together and out of the nightmare he had foisted upon her. His iron grip held her neck down to the floor as she felt the power and strength that he still possessed in his later years.

"Oh my Lord, sir. I cannot believe that you are saying such things, is this normal? It does not feel appropriate, sir, I have to say, sir, sorry, sir, sorry. But I showered not long before I came to you, sir, but could you please not look at me down there? It is not appropriate behaviour, sir. It is, in fact, disgusting, sir. I am sorry, sir, but I will not allow myself to be demeaned in this manner, it is just not appropriate."

Melanie's whimper before he had even begun his response suggested that she may have realised that she had not perhaps taken the right tone or chosen the right words in her reply.

"Well bravo to you, found some backbone, have you? However, I very much doubt your victim with her face smashed into her plate, in front of the rest of the guests at formal dining, thought that your actions were appropriate, did they? Since we are making speeches, let me give you a little bit of information to digest. Listen carefully, I may ask questions! It is called retribution or payback. It is called learning and improvement by education and the use of emotional intelligence and behavioural psychology. We look closely at the four main behavioural types; optimism, pessimism, trust and envy, and we use the emotional information to guide thinking and behaviour. We look at curbing and resolving behavioural anger of which there are basically three types that shape the way human beings react in a situation when their ire is roused. These are passive aggression, open aggression and assertive anger. We do not include, and fight to retain the right to use, corporal punishment to amuse ourselves. Although I do indeed find most aspects pleasing, we believe that it assists us in producing fully formed, emotionally adjusted, strong-willed and strategic thinking young women, ready to take on the wider world for the benefit of all. This is information that was freely available to you and your guardians, in your case, your mother and your aunt, who I remember very well, and to which they signed a contract, witnessed and counter-signed by yourself, accepting the methods of this revered and august institution. Do I really need to continue or would you like to quickly get dressed and leave my office while I make a telephone call to your lovely aunt? It was agreed with your mother's blessing that any issues were to be raised with her older sister prior to informing your mother herself, as she has always handled disciplinary matters in your upbringing, as I understand."

There was a rather forlorn-sounding groan now coming from Melanie, who had ceased her resistance to his force and was now supplicant, with her forehead touching the floor and her flanks raised as he had demanded, albeit, Stones noted, with tightly clamped together thighs.

"Please don't call Auntie Wendy, sir. I am sorry about what I said."

The Professor sighed dramatically, as though reluctant to carry out something that he felt a necessity. He was well practised at this, never wanting to appear eager to dispense punishment, always presenting it as a matter of regret, a necessary evil, so to speak. He suspected that it didn't fool that many of the wretches he dealt with.

"Oh, get up girl, you look quite ridiculous in that position!"

Melanie hauled herself to her feet to face him, her cheeks flushed with the effort and her eyes full of tears.

"I am so sorry, Professor Stones. I have just failed some sort of test, haven't I? I am so sorry, I do realise that my behaviour was unacceptable and I do accept that I have to take punishment. I just was not ready for the, you know, the other stuff. The showing you my intimate areas and the sniffing and touching. I had not realised that that would come into it. Oh God, I am just talking rubbish now, sorry, sir."

Stones took pity on her; he had read her the pastoral tutor's notes that assessed her on the more non-academic performance and demeanour in the university and knew that she was deemed an earnest, polite and honest member of the college. His expression softened and her face immediately brightened in response.

"Think on what I have told you, young lady. I rarely waste time dispensing wisdom if I feel the recipient does not warrant the effort, so take that on board as a positive. For the record, if I ever ask you a question, or to adopt a position or to perform a task, regardless of what it is and definitely regardless of what you think, then I expect instant acquiescence. No matter what. Do you understand?"

"Yes sir, I do, sir. Thank you. Thank you so much, Professor." Melanie was holding herself to her full height now, her confidence restored by his words.

"Good. So if I command you now to turn round, bend over, open your legs and pull your cheeks wide apart to open up your intergluteal cleft and show me the orifices hiding beneath, what would your response be?"

Back came the facial flush as the naked student found herself once more on the end of one of Stones' renowned curve balls and change of directions.

"I – I – I - I would do what you asked, sir?" Her voice was reduced to a mouse-like whisper as her eyes resumed their study of the carpet.

"Just to be clear that we are in accord, please tell me exactly what this would consist of, my dear?" he coaxed.

"Oh no. I mean yes, sir, sorry, sir. I would turn around to present my rear to you, sir, then I would bend over before you, sir, with my legs wide apart and then, then, then, oh no. I'm sorry, sir. Then I would put my hands on my buttocks and pull my cheeks apart so that you could inspect my privates, sir. Is that alright sir?"

"Good girl. Now proceed."

With that instruction, Stones dawdled over towards the desk

where the canes, tawse and crop were sitting on the paper, ready for Melanie to show her writing prowess. His back was to her deliberately, knowing full well that this would add confusion and discombobulation to Melanie's thinking. Out of the corner of his eye, he watched as she slowly turned to present her back view to where he had been standing. She quietly sighed and then wearily bent over, her legs apart while her large hands took substantial handfuls of her cheeks in each hand. With a sob, she pulled the crack of her bottom wide apart and then stayed motionless.

Keeping his back to her but a sly eye to the side, Stones flexed and swiped the implements through the air and was impressed that there was no visual or audible reaction that he could tell. He replaced the tools of his disciplinary trade, his beloved "improvers" as he liked to taunt his victims with, before wandering across his room. After several minutes virtually ignoring the lewd display from Melanie, he sauntered over behind her.

"So, what exactly do you think you are doing?"

"Beg your pardon, sir?" was the not altogether wise response.

"I do not like repeating myself. I asked you a simple question!" Stones snapped back. "Now explain to me exactly what you are doing at this very moment, in detail."

"Waaaaaah!" was not the response he expected as the student hit a new level of utter despair.

"Oh, my goodness, oh my, oh my, oh my. Sorry, sir. Of course. I am so sorry, sir. I am bending over, my legs wide apart and am proudly and obediently showing you my intimate places by pulling my bottom cheeks apart, sir. I am ready for you to inspect my private parts, sir, and please, sir, I hope you will be satisfied with my display. Oh dear. I don't know what else to say, sir, thank you, sir."

"Oh yes, good heavens, stand up, you look absolutely ridiculous holding your behind stretched wide open like that!"

A loud gulp was the response before Melanie released her cheeks which sprang back into place which such force they created a resounding splat. So unexpected was this that Stones burst out laughing.

"My apologies, my apologies. That is something that I have never heard before but, my dear, please don't look so ashamed and horrified, it was a thing of beauty, not one of shame. Now to the desk and your chosen punishment implements. Get writing, get writing, no excuses now. I will expect a perfect script, full of remorse and a clear proposal to enable your conscience to be cleaved clean of guilt and shame for the atrocity you committed. Move girl, out of my way now, you have made me late and I do have other business to attend to."

Melanie went to the desk and sat down to begin her task, a giant sigh escaping from her.

Minutes later, Stones was nodding his approval at her efforts. Melanie had made a few queries as she worked but Stones could see that the student had applied herself to the task as if she'd been set a piece of written work for a university supervision.

His complimentary words had brightened Melanie up considerably and she was looking very self-satisfied when the buzzer sounded at the Professor's door. Melanie froze in shock and moved towards her clothes.

"Stand where you are! What the devil do you think you are doing? Put that dress down now and stand in the corner, hands on head. In fact I think you need a little lesson now so that you are a little bit more aware of how you damn well behave in my rooms."

Stones pressed a button releasing the door lock before moving across to Melanie and slapping her unprotected buttocks with his open hand. As Prascilla Guptil entered the room, she was presented with the sight of a gyrating and naked Melanie Thorpe, her massive buttocks being pounded by the Dean of Discipline while she howled in distress.

"Ah Prascilla, welcome, do come in," said Stones as he pushed Melanie into the corner.

"Just giving young Melanie a little taster of what you get if you do not behave at St James. Now eyes front, my dear. We have things to discuss, don't we?"

Stones looked at the young Indian girl before him. Her face still showed signs of Melanie's act of violence and retribution, mild bruising in particular around her eyes and a small healing cut on her forehead. An unusual visitation as it was rare for any of the students from the Indian subcontinent to be called to his office for disciplinary reasons. In fact, Stones had often complained at the college's monthly council meeting, the council being the governing body of the college, that if they wanted the level of obedient, studious and respectful students to increase, then they needed to attract as many young ladies as possible from outside the British Isles. 'Familiarity breeds contempt' was a much-used refrain from the Dean of Discipline, dutifully supported by Celia Ford, the Senior Tutor, and he advocated annually for the college to increase its percentage of undergraduates from Asian countries. Respect for authority and their elders was paramount and Stones hated disrespect for authority more than anything, making him the ideal person to dispense justice, right wrongs and dispassionately and objectively dispense and deliver physical retribution to transgressors.

Stones always enjoyed the moment when a reprobate came to his room, misguided in her assumption of innocence. There was always a lightbulb moment when the person under investigation actually realised that they were possibly in trouble. Prascilla's confidence was visibly draining away as her eyes flicked between the naked figure of Melanie, and her bright red bottom, and the unblinking stare of the Dean of Discipline.

"Now, I just need Melanie here to finish off her duty and she can get her disgusting self out of my sight until her punishment day in a few days time."

Prascilla's smirk seemed to suggest that she thought that she was on safe ground. This was duly noted by Stones and he made a decision to give her the rope needed to hang herself!

"Right, Melanie, fetch your essay of contrition for your appalling act of violence towards young Prascilla here and the items you have chosen to be punished with. She'll be back here soon, Prascilla, for the serious business. Those rosy cheeks were just a gentle admonishment for some minor disobedience in front of me today." His smile embraced Prascilla totally and she reacted in kind, although her eyes conveyed a definite disturbance of her calm exterior as she espied the contents of Melissa's hands.

"Right, young lady, let us hear what you have to say. I very much hope I am not going to be disappointed in you further as that would mean further remedial work today and I really need to get on."

Melanie's face reddened a shade deeper as she contemplated the words of the Professor and tried to avoid Prascilla's eyes, who was not making any attempt to hide her fascination in her naked body.

"Have I got to read it out, sir?" Melanie looked between Stones and Prascilla frantically as though she expected to have a say in the decision. Stones just laughed and Melanie gulped and continued:

"Of course I have to, sorry, sir, to question you." She took a deep breath.

"I, Melanie Thorpe, would like to express my sincere apologies for my act of mindless violence towards a fellow student in the dinner hall. I behaved in a manner unbecoming to any member of this college, or indeed wider society, and can only ask for forgiveness and to be allowed to make amends. To this end, I propose that I undergo severe physical punishment at the hands of the Dean of Discipline to ensure that I have paid the debt I owe the college for my actions. I am truly sorry that I reacted to what was just childish taunting and insults in a disgraceful manner and hope that you accept that I am truly apologetic and full of remorse. I therefore propose that I be subjected to a spanking on my bare buttocks and that 250 spanks be applied. I also request that I receive ten strokes each from the canes, the tawse and the crop that I have selected for the purpose, therefore 300 blows in total. This will serve to teach me a lesson in controlling my temper and serve me well in my future time at the college and beyond."

The Professor gave her a subtle bow of approval.

"An excellent piece of work, my dear. Acknowledging guilt and acceptance of appalling behaviour, showing remorse and a willingness to make amends, a proposal to correct wrongdoing and a clear and voluntary offer to submit to and select the means to do so. Textbook, don't you think, Prascilla? Wouldn't you say that young Melanie has taken the appropriate steps to begin to clear this matter up and have it consigned in time, a mere blip on the landscape, a momentary lapse, serious though it was, in an otherwise exemplary student and rather gracious and pleasant human being. Don't you agree, Prascilla? As the person who suffered physical harm in this incident, are you satisfied that the intended flogging of her bare backside is the appropriate response?"

Stones raised questioning eyebrows at the rather perplexed and somewhat uncomfortable looking student. He could see that she had enough about her to sense a possible trap set in his words but was also showing that she possessed a level of arrogance in that she simply hadn't realised that her role in Melanie's situation was anything but as the innocent and injured party.

"Oh. Um. Yes, sir, I think it would be entirely appropriate, sir. I am happy with your decision and thank you for dealing with this, sir."

Stones spotted the sly grin that made Prascilla's lips twitch upwards as she stole a quick glance at the naked Melanie, who was staring, motionless, at the floor, her face a picture of pure misery.

"Excellent news, Prascilla. Melanie you can cover yourself up, yes, yes, get dressed and get out. Seems like your mother is going to be spared the upset of your disgrace. It some ways, a pity. I would have enjoyed the opportunity to catch up again with your Aunt Wendy. I have some pleasant memories of her time here. She was truly appreciative, I can promise you, of my methods to cure misconduct and delinquency and is a great advocate of the expression 'spare the rod, spoil the child'. Never mind, time to move on to the next little issue. Seems like I have some more work to do concerning young Prascilla here."

PREVIOUS BOOK IN THE SERIES,
AVAILABLE THROUGH AMAZON:

THE DEAN OF DISCIPLINE- DEGREES OF PUNISHMENT (2020)

ABOUT THE AUTHOR

Dee Vee Curzon was born in May 1976 and is a widow and the mother of two grown up young ladies. Working in academia for many years, she has an insight into the machinations, idiosyncrasies and vagaries of day-to-day University life but has never, ever delivered a spanking to a student!

Printed in Great Britain
by Amazon